DARK AGES

DARK AGES

Sturmen Krieg

NPI

Northwest Publishing, Inc.
Salt Lake City, Utah

NPI

Dark Ages

All rights reserved.
Copyright © 1996 Sturmen Krieg

Reproduction in any manner, in whole or in part,
in English or in other languages, or otherwise
without written permission of the publisher is prohibited.

This is a work of fiction.
All characters and events portrayed in this book are fictional,
and any resemblance to real people or incidents is purely coincidental.

For information address: Northwest Publishing, Inc.
6906 South 300 West, Salt Lake City, Utah 84047
WC 8.24.95 /CA

PRINTING HISTORY
First Printing 1996

ISBN: 1-56901-459-0

NPI books are published by Northwest Publishing, Incorporated,
6906 South 300 West, Salt Lake City, Utah 84047.
The name "NPI" and the "NPI" logo are trademarks belonging to
Northwest Publishing, Incorporated.

PRINTED IN THE UNITED STATES OF AMERICA.
10 9 8 7 6 5 4 3 2 1

One

The morning air hung heavy with the pungent scent of rotten vegetation, biting at Richter's nostrils. It was hot—plain and simple. So damned hot you could feel the sides of your head ache, not knowing if it was the onset of fever or the outside temperature broiling your gray matter inside a skull oven. The Team Bravo leader weighed the mission while drawing in another deep breath. He caught a whiff of the day-old sweat clinging to his uniform. The fabric was laden with his secreted body fluids and the residual stench. The temperature and humidity only made their operation briefs more tedious, especially when in the confining limits of an inadequate facility.

The general-purpose, medium tent was glaringly insufficient for their mission briefs, and even less suitable for the conduct of daily air and ground operations. It was the largest SOUTHCOM provided such alien teams, however. It did not consider the paramilitary endeavors within the parameters of its Caribbean strategy. Captain Richter glanced about the cluttered quarters while waiting for his restless men to settle. As he paused Richter considered how the support effort had changed when he ceased to be a regular.

The shelter's twenty-by-thirty-foot dimensions appeared vast when vacant. But once burdened with a fieldtable and two chairs for each of the three staff sections and coupled with a radio section, cots for shift workers, a water buffalo, the support commander's desk and chair, and an eight-by-four-foot sand table, there was little working space left to move freely. As he waited for his few willful team members to arrive Richter glanced over those who were punctual.

Most of his renegade men, those on time, assembled in what was the best of an orderly fashion they could manage. They were no longer in the same status as their allegedly better trained and disciplined military counterparts; as such, their attitudes underwent a slight but obvious modification. But they were as efficient as any he missioned with, even if not strikingly military looking.

The falcon-eyed staff sergeant, Stan Marcoli, stood opposite him. The soldier leaned into the rough cut table's edge. Marcoli was no longer a true staff sergeant, but he retained the regular army grade out of a sense of professionalism within the group. All of the Team Bravo members regarded each other in this way. This philosophy originated from the team's foundation, the sergeant major.

Marcoli, a veteran of three tours in Vietnam with the 1st Infantry Division, appeared on the surface as spunky and brash. But underneath he was a cautious man who had a reputation for being quick-triggered. That aside, Marcoli was an excellent pointman, able to silently slip through the bush while using his hawklike vision for key terrain analysis. Next to Marcoli stood Greg Levits. The two men shared a cigarette partially soaked with perspiration from their fingers.

Levits, born and raised in Brighton Beach, New York, near Manhattan Beach Park, epitomized soldiering. A veteran of eight years in Special Forces made him one of the team's most valued members. He was a seasoned veteran of Vietnam when he was eighteen. During his tours he won the Silver Star with V device and two Bronze Stars for valor in three separate events. His additional attribute of being fluent in two other languages, German and French, with a working knowledge in Spanish, placed him in high favor for selection to Team Bravo. When he put his military career on hold for a girl back home, the absence of it ate at him.

His affair with the lovely and well-bred Magda was a rejuvenating episode in his life. But it alone could not fill the void in his wandering character. Everything about Magdalene was wonderful. Too wonderful.

Educated at Cornell University, Magda received her bachelor's degree in biology, and she was quite willing to overlook Greg's GED certificate. Sometimes, when they cuddled after sex, Levits would stare at the bedroom ceiling and wonder why this intellectual woman would waste a promising future on a man who had thus far spent his entire adult life in the U.S. Army. But Levits would just as frequently dismiss the question by asking himself why anyone would want a degree in biology. Magda's father had money. Lots of money. For Levits it was a significant plus.

A few feet up from Levits stood Gable, the Happy Destructor. Arthur Gable was a strong-willed man, as revealed by the almost shoulder-length hair he refused to cut. He seldom grouped with the others. He was a steadfast loner for the most part, but at the same time Gable was a malicious fighter when the shit hit. He seconded as the team's medical specialist and principally functioned as such in the central highlands of Vietnam. His primary contribution to Team Bravo was his knowledge of electronics, serving as the contingent's radioman.

A native of Jasper, Florida, Gable looked for a way out of a dead-end life. A rudimentary cashier and stocker's job in a Seven-

Eleven did not provide for his much sought after American Dream. Gable returned to the one thing he knew he did well and could make a sound buck at. The men called this sometimes sullen but dependable soldier the Happy Destructor, because he never participated in a mission without the M-72A2 LAW at his side.

For Gable, the one shot, throwaway antiarmor device was like an insurance policy for survival. He lugged the extra weight, so claimed, because he liked to watch things blow up—a peculiarity that he picked up during childhood. At the head of the sand table, alongside the shorter captain, stood Team Bravo's granite foundation.

Sergeant Major Clifford Stewart Ramsy stood a half-foot taller than most of his fellow team members. At fifty-five he had seen almost forty years of regular army service, all of which was in the infantry. Better than half of Ramsy's Spartan lifestyle transpired outside the United States as an instructor in the combat arms. Occasionally, the War Department interrupted his routine duties by assigning him to act as a participant in the neutralization of international nuisances. Though sometimes called defensive in nature, the infrequent and clandestine engagements were phenomena the War Department, later the Defense Department, refused to acknowledge. As a young man Ramsy had an inexhaustible itch to move. The isolated and hazardous missions gave him the mobility he needed.

He joined the army in early 1937. Ramsy had to lie his way through the enlistment as he had not yet reached the minimum age of seventeen. Reasonably sure something in Europe was about to take place, Ramsy did not want to be left out. He read about the fighting in Spain, and how Hitler actively supported Franco's rise to power. He was sure the hostility would soon ignite throughout Europe. Seeing that the entire element had finally arrived, Ramsy set the tone for the mission review.

"All right! Shut it up…Cut out the grab ass, Assaf!"

Sergeant First Class Mike Assaf, talking to Ray Copeland about his illicit interlude with a young woman in a nearby village, instantly went silent. He knew the sergeant major would not ask twice.

Assaf, originally from Palmerton, Pennsylvania, was a twenty-eight-year-old army veteran of seven years. As Greg Levits, Assaf was also a former Green Beret and served one twelve-month tour with the 5th Special Forces Group in Vietnam. He spent two years thereafter in Saudi Arabia before he was reassigned to the Canal Zone in 1978. There, Assaf endured his last year and a half as an advisor to the Panamanian National Guard prior to civilian contracting.

Upon hearing Ramsy's coarse rebuttal of Assaf all submitted to silence. Seeing his men were in a receptive state Ramsy relinquished the floor to the captain.

"All right, sir!" he bellowed. "The floor's yours."

Richter looked about the table. He knew he had the attention of the reckless men. He extended his telescope pointer and directed their focus upon the terrain feature.

"Not a complex mission, but from what Reiner said it'll be lucrative. We'll approach the objective from the northeast flying knap of the earth. We'll use what protection we can gain from the existing coastal terrain. It'll give us at least a minimum safeguard from observers and cover from radar. Sergeant Gable, your cipher and authentication tables."

Richter reached over the table and handed the CEOI extracts to the radioman. Gable's eyes enlarged when given the two thin tablets.

"All right! Now we can communicate. Let's get 'em, boys."

Quickly spotting the overconfidence in Gable, Ramsy decided to temper the soldier with down-to-earth caution. He worked with such men in the past, three wars' worth. Ramsy witnessed how they were seldom injured while those around them were riddled with bullets. *Put a stop to this*, he promised himself.

"Make damned sure whoever you transmit to authenticates," he said. "I don't want another Canal Zone fiasco. And don't make up your own radio language. Stay with the brevity matrix and the nine-line aeromedevac. That's what you got 'em for. Got it?"

Gable's enthusiasm withdrew instantly. He came down to earth with both boots firmly planted. Although second in command, Ramsey exercised free will over the men based on his active service grade, experience, and the admiration of his team leader.

"Understood, Sergeant Major," Gable said.

While listening to every word said by his much-favored top NCO, Richter considered the events of that unfortunate mission.

He recalled that the west canal operation failed primarily because of their improper COMSEC practices. No one suspected the allegedly ill-equipped civilians to enter their radio net and fill the airways with bogus information. More so, no one expected government troops, the presumed in-country hosts, to be assisting the supposed bad guys. It culminated into a costly mission breakdown. They lost a fully teamed helicopter that day; two regular army pilots, one crewchief, and seven combat veterans were torched. He did not want to repeat history, if possible. As Richter pondered over the incident he could not help but comment under his breath.

"Yeah—no more fiascoes."

"What if it is another Canal Zone, Captain? What then?" Marcoli asked.

"You just make sure that doesn't happen!" Ramsey said. "If you got traffic, know who you're talking to. If you're not sure, break off transmission. Gable! That's your radio. Without it we can't talk. If we can't talk, they're going to forget we're alive. Do you understand what I'm saying?"

"Loud and clear, Sergeant Major."

"Yeah, and make sure you know your target before you pop 'em, Marcoli," Copeland added, recalling the embarrassing error Stan made when up north.

Marcoli gripped the table's edge with both hands, unconsciously repositioning himself for a hasty defense. He realized the incident was his fault. He also believed that if someone else had been pointman that afternoon, the likelihood of a similar outcome would have been just as probable.

"Hey," he snapped. "I didn't know they were contras. If you remember, that was just outside San Isidro. What the hell were they doing so far south in Costa Rica, anyway?"

"What the hell were we doing in Costa Rica?" James said.

The team, minus Richter and Ramsy, laughed over Will James' comment. They were all aware that had the Costa Rican government known they were in-country, a patrol would have been deployed to hunt them down. It was the way of the Central American game.

Like small people with narrow concerns, the governments shared the same lofty interests only when facing one another. No sooner did one nation look away than the other reached out with its poverty-stricken tentacle and grasped for wealth from wherever it was to be had. There was no misunderstanding by anyone—the Department of Defense, the Justice Department, the Drug Enforcement Agency or their respective teams. All knew where they precisely and dangerously stood; in the center with all sides aiming on them. Money talked loud and cocaine was big money. Ramsy was not amused by James' comical side.

William James came on board at the team's inception, four months before. He left the U.S. Army after a not-so-pleasant tour at Fort Jackson, South Carolina. As an infantry NCO he felt out of place in the quagmire of the largest military personnel and administrative school in the nation. Ironically, it was his personnel record that had been incorrectly reviewed by the Department of the Army, and that had subsequently channeled James to his mistaken assignment at the school of administration.

It was a damaging mismatch, as James incurred the prejudice of a lowly infantryman in the midst of soft-face technicians who had a deeper appreciation for computer software. The techniques needed to maintain a zeroed M-16 rifle or M-60 machine gun had less priority to the orderly-room-bound trainees. The school cadre held the infantryman in contempt as well, although not officially. The academia believed their pseudo-intellectual administrative skills afforded them status over the ditch digger. It was a degrading event in his life, and one that James could not put aside. Ramsy listened to the team's laughter a moment more, before deciding to put them in check.

"At ease!"

The group once more receded into silence. Not one man regarded the dominating sergeant major as someone to take lightly. After the men settled themselves, Richter resumed his plan of attack.

"Each of you have the coordinates in the OPORD. If we're hit, we'll disengage as quickly as possible, disperse, then reassemble at the rally point. We'll wait one hour for stragglers. After that we'll call for extraction—whether you're there or not. Mike, you have the honor of flying with our host this time."

Assaf glanced to the ceiling. His eyes rolled back while he raised his hands defensively. *Why me,* he thought. *They're nothing but a bunch of new meats.* He understood the team needed communication with the host nation's troops, but Levits had a language ability as well. Well, not that good, he concluded. Giving in to his instructions, Assaf replied in the affirmative, but only as congenially as his volatile personality permitted.

"Wonderful! My turn to baby-sit the *federales*, again."

"It's their country. Like it or not, we're here at their invitation," Richter explained. "Granted, their people are a bit inexperienced for this sort of thing, but in this business you're green until you take fire, and then it's only after it's over that you can say you've got the experience—if you're alive to say it."

"Besides, they can't give us their good troops," Marcoli cut in. "If they gave us the seasoned ones, who'd get the stuff through for 'em?"

"Right. The young ones are still idealists," Copeland said. "They're not greedy—yet."

Knowing Copeland's comment had a high degree of validity, Richter felt the need to say a few words to temper Assaf but not to mislead him.

"Think of it as a teacher to student gesture. It might be a little more palatable."

"Why isn't this a Colombian operation, Captain?" Sanford asked. "They got their own DEA teams. Why us?"

"Reiner said that they're having a resource problem," Richter explained. "SOUTHCOM's holding back the logistics. Command's cutting costs. They want to broaden our sphere of influence."

"Panamanian troops in Columbia?" Sanford persisted. "God help us if they see 'em."

"Yeah, well—it is the way it is," the captain said.

Recognizing that the operational review moved left of the subject line, the sergeant major decided to put the men back on track. He knew that if these men intended to function more effectively than they had in the past, they had to seriously listen to what they were told.

"Each of you will have a strip map of the objective and the immediate area of operation," he said. "All of you, I hope, maintain an operational compass. You've got ten minutes to memorize those coordinates. If any of us are captured, I don't want those numerical locations written down. Got it?"

Richter looked about the sand table and spotted a compliant acknowledgment on the face of every team member. They might buck him, he knew, but they'd never consider an outright confrontation with Ramsy. After seeing firm team control reestablished, Richter glanced at his watch while concluding that the brief's high points were covered.

"Well, that's it, gentlemen. Time check: 0515. Be on deck and loaded in ten minutes. Liftoff: 0530. Questions?"

No questions followed, and Richter did not expect any. They were competent men, each professional in conduct and attitude—most of the time. They knew their jobs, and there was little if any crap out of them when the shit hit. Other team leaders were not so fortunate.

Other officers sometimes found themselves commanding murderers, rapists, auto thieves, alcoholics, and harder drug abusers as well. The Justice Department frequently failed in its screening attempts when placing many of the wayward men. On occasion, the teams included one or two unreliables who merely provided themselves as warm bodies looking for a paycheck. Sometimes, it came back to haunt the leaders.

Richter recalled that Team Alpha lost their leader three weeks before. They were at the southern fringe of the Gulf of Panama, just west of the coastal town of Jaqué. The team failed to link up for extraction and was listed as missing a day later. Treadwell sent in Echo, Max Ballard's team, to search for them.

They located Team Alpha's leader face down in the water. His inflated body rested high in a stream, snagged among overhanging branches. Had Jake's body not caught onto the bank foliage, Max believed they would never have found him.

As they pulled the body from the water Max heard the escape of residual gas from Jake's throat. They felt the stiffness in his limbs. There was another sudden release of air when the body was laid out. It sounded like the even expulsion of air from an inner tube just before the last bit of vapor seeped out. Just a soft, methodical *hush*, until nothing. When they turned the remains over, Max immediately noticed the three bullet holes in Jake's back.

To the untrained eye the punctures might have been misinterpreted. The small frayed tears in the fabric looked more like tiny branch or twig pricks. The small projectiles passed through the uniform so swiftly, the fibers partially returning to their original condition, that little apparent damage was evident. To the experienced soldier there was no mistake as to the tiny perforations' mortal meaning.

Max saw that the area looked undisturbed. There was nothing in the immediate proximity of the body to suggest a firefight ensued. He ordered his men to search the jungle up to fifty meters from where they found Jake. They failed to disclose any evidence of hostile action. The foliage was not bent or broken. There was nothing on the ground to suggest a scuffle—no expended round casings, no discarded weapons, no other bodies. Suspecting that whatever had happened took place further upstream, Max directed three men to cross. The team followed both banks for roughly a kilometer. Again, they found nothing. At that point Max admitted he could do little else. Team Echo returned to where they left Jake stashed in the bank brush and requested extraction.

The autopsy showed that Jake died by drowning, his lungs filled with water. This meant Jake was not dead when he either fell into the stream or they dumped his body into it. The hasty postmortem also disclosed that Jake was shot with three 5.56mm rounds, standard M-16 ammunition. No one ever had contact with the other missing Team Alpha people. Eight of them vanished into the jungle.

But his men were different—he hoped. As Richter watched the last man, Copeland, step from the operations tent, he felt that unlike so many who were contract hire his men were of a higher caliber. His men cared about themselves and what they stood for. They also cared about the people they worked with and fought alongside of. Richter knew he was lucky to have them.

Two

The cool February night forced a shudder up between his flexed blades. He gripped hard onto the steering wheel and braced himself to supress the reflex. It was not that cold, he thought. The radio announcer said thirty-one degrees. But for New Orleans anything below forty was too much, or too little, for the locals to contend with. As he guided his 1974 Ford sedan slowly along the levee summit he wondered how the low temperature would impact the process.

He looked to Courtney and eyed the pretty thing as she lay unconscious. She was so innocent and fresh looking, like Aphrodite, a symbol of love, the rejuvenator of affectionate impulses.

Courtney's torn blouse lay open, her supple breasts filled her brassiere to capacity. He recalled tossing her overcoat in the back seat. The event had to look a good deal the way it was, and, therefore, he decided against the imposition of covering her. Not that he intended for it to be that way. It was just that he had no control over the variables. Like Courtney, they consumed him. He saw the pimple-like reaction of her flesh. He considered covering her again, but decided the titillating exhibition was too pleasurable to overlook, since it was the last time.

He reached to her and gently moved Courtney's left arm aside. As he critically, hungrily, eyed Courtney's taut breasts, he noticed that their unfortunate skirmish left her delicate bosom badly bruised.

He was sorry the savage impromptu beating took so long before she lost consciousness. Such ruthlessness was not at all a part of his character. He was sure of that. Besides, he reminded himself, he was as frightened as she was, if not more. While steering the vehicle onward, he saw how the mellow luminescence on the far side of the river seeped through the darkness.

Glancing to his left he saw the soft radiance of the distant lights on the west bank. Algiers was just beyond the levee's opposite side. Just offshore, a hundred yards out from the earthen embankment, he saw how the huge freighters moored in the deeper waters of the Mississippi. He noticed the vivid bow and stern lights on each vessel. He saw the white light emitted from their bridges, and how the exterior deck levels revealed their lines by the overhead ceiling lamps. Looking ahead, he easily spotted the city's grand signature.

The bridge broke out of the darkness like a quadruple stringing of festive Christmas lights. It was the Crescent City Connection, the great link spanning the turbulent river. The twin span was far in the distance—miles—but its distinctive, fourfold chains of incandescence showed like ornamental holiday luster. *The holidays,* he thought. *We had two good ones. One bad, though loving.* He glanced at the lovely Courtney once more and wished it did not have to come to this. But he knew it did. While slowing the vehicle, he began to have an increased awareness of the sounds coming from beyond the car.

As the car rolled to a stop he focused on the sound of pulverized oyster shell compressing under the tires. He lowered his fogged window halfway and heard the erratic clang of a distant buoy. Far ahead was the flat drone of a petroleum plant. An occasional blast of steam accented the low thrumming of its converters. *Just enough noise to cover theirs,* he decided, while stepping forcefully onto the emergency brake.

He opened the door and felt the chilling effect of the wet river air on his skin. As he began to rise from behind the steering wheel, he heard Courtney release another subdued moan. Looking to the lustful creature, he reaffirmed the inevitable to himself.

Again, he settled behind the steering wheel. He reached over and ran his fingers under her loose skirt. He felt the tight elastic hem of her undergarment against his finger tips. It sent a momentary rush of anticipation through him. His firm finger manipulations, his caresses, were his way of reassuring her.

"Don't you worry yourself, now, precious," he said. "In a few minutes you won't be cold anymore. I always took good care of you, even though you weren't mine—nothing's changed."

He stepped out of the vehicle and made his way around the front of the car. He took notice of the grinding oyster shells condensing under his weight. He looked about the dark levee a final time to insure no one was nearby to witness.

Courtney fell out as he unlatched the door. He reached in with his left hand, briefly snagging his eagle talon talisman on the door frame. Reacting to the unexpected obstruction he swiftly reached over with his right hand and grasped the almost dead weight before it plunged groundward. After resettling the load onto the seat he took hold of Courtney by her ankles.

He thought the whole process was enormously clumsy. He had to make one vigorous tug to get the weight in motion, and optimized on the momentum with a constant and even pressure. When her head cleared the vinyl rim gravity assumed control. Her skull dropped swiftly and abruptly smacked against the interior running board of the vehicle's doorframe. He watched her crown bounce twice on the metal runner before continuing down and thudding on the shell roadbed. Hearing the fragmented mollusks displaced by the sudden impact he grew frustrated and pleaded for her understanding.

"Oh, baby. I'm so sorry. I'm trying to make this as—as if we were playing a game," he said. "It's not like I have a lot of experience. I know I can do better. I just have to think on this."

He released Courtney's feet and heard her fleshy heels thud onto the displaced shell. He clasped his hands and tried to expel the excess energy racing through him. Upon regaining some composure he eyed Courtney once more. He shrugged his shoulders to accentuate his sincerity.

"I'll—I'll try and do better...Okay?"

Again, he latched onto Courtney's ankles. He scraped her over the razor-edged shell fragments. The light from the refinery provided just enough illumination for him to examine her.

As he dragged her he saw how Courtney's sky blue blouse crawled up her back then out from under her. Only one button, the second from the bottom, secured the garment. As he guided the body off the road he saw how the material caught on a clump of dead weeds. The final intact clasp surrendered to the overwhelming stress. He watched how the remaining fabric worked its way out from under her. She was exposed from her waist to her shaven underarms. *Hygiene,* he thought. *She was always good about that.*

Pulling Courtney down the grassy knoll took little effort. Her body seemed to glide over the tall grass. The stalks gave under her weight and created a fibrous bed for her to coast on. Near the levee base the body began to build momentum. The impelling force caused him to hasten his rearward stride. Upon reaching the levee bottom he found himself backing into a large backwash.

Backwater, he told himself, *caught in the bottom land when the river last rose beyond its banks.* He continued their journey through the shallow pool, only five or six inches deep. He saw, by the dull glow of the petroleum plant, how the nipping water further tormented Courtney's already tortured body.

Her semiconscious state offered little sedative protection against the stinging water. She felt the freezing pool wrap about her. Courtney's body reflexively contracted its muscles into tight cramping knots.

"Ahhhhhhh—ple—please—n...," she mumbled.

Courtney became overwhelmed by a dreadful shudder. Her body trembled as the first stage of hypothermia began to raise her blood temperature. Hearing her almost inaudible plea, he felt compelled to reassure her.

"I'm trying, baby," he said. "It won't be much longer."

Upon clearing the stagnated pool, the dead weight grew more cumbersome.

He knew the huge waterway was only fifty or sixty feet ahead. The sandbar saplings became numerous. Their tall slender trunks rose high from the flat. The undergrowth became thick. As he twisted and turned the nimble torso through the thickets Courtney began to regain consciousness.

Her eyes partially opened. She was only marginally aware of the wooded surroundings. She felt a searing pain throughout her brutalized body. Her eyes opened wider. She spotted the starry sky filtering through the naked overhanging branches. She looked down and saw her flesh bare to the waist, except for her bra. She felt herself dragged over the logs and gravel.

"No! No!" she yelled. "I—I didn't—I..."

Panic raced through him. He did not realize Courtney had come to until she began to speak. Stunned by the sudden high pitch of her voice cutting through the night, he released her ankles. He took two stumbling steps backward while nervously considering what to do next.

He watched his victim double up. Courtney tried to fight off both him and the subfreezing elements. Upon regaining his orientation, a matter of seconds, he quickly glanced about the thickets. A second more and he was on top of her. He anchored Courtney to the bar with his left hand while bludgeoning her with his right fist.

His first hasty blow glanced off her high left cheekbone. It had little effect. He clasped onto her left arm. He maneuvered the limb across her body and pinned Courtney's right arm under it. He reared back again. This time he had full control and momentum behind the blow. He struck Courtney on the left temple.

To be sure, he cocked once more and delivered another solid blow. He rammed his fist into the side of her mouth, and felt the sharp edges of her teeth slice deeply into the first two knuckles. He repositioned for a fourth strike. As he reared back, however, he saw by her stillness there was no further need.

He dropped from his knees onto his buttocks. His lungs heaved. He felt the cold air burn as it filtered into them. He felt the damp sand soak through his trousers. After six rejuvenating gasps he looked down at the still body.

"I tried," he said. "Don't you understand? I really tried."

He lay on the sand and supported his weight with his quivering right arm. This was so out of character, he thought. A week ago he would consider something like this unthinkable. It was all so far removed from his usual lifestyle. Feeling more at ease after his short rest he rose to his knees. As he once again took control of Courtney he reaffirmed to himself that there was no other way.

Her agile frame slid over the sandbar with less effort. Its ease of movement revealed that some of his strength had returned after the short break in the saplings. As he cleared the last barrier of brush the river environment invaded his senses.

The water's pungent industrial odor flushed into his nostrils. It was a cooler air. He could hear the prominent clang of the distant buoy, moored somewhere in the channel. Its hollow clang sliced through the darkness more profoundly than when he first heard it from his car.

He scanned the vast river twice before spotting the indicator some two hundred feet offshore. It was a red signal. As he closed with the waterway he felt the weight of the body grow more burdensome.

The compressing sand under his shoes quickly transformed into pebbles. Then, almost as swiftly, the pebbles changed into rocks about four to six inches in diameter. He steadfastly kept up the pace, however, until he felt the Mississippi spill over the top of his left shoe.

The river soaking his shoe was both a pain and a pleasure to him. It was aggravating for him to feel his foot submerge into the frigid water. But the water was also a delight, as it signaled the end of his journey. After releasing her legs he again took a moment to collect his scattered thoughts. To simply throw her into the wet blackness seemed inhumane.

He envisioned Courtney regaining consciousness. He pictured the child inhaling water through her mouth and nose while trying to understand what was happening to her. He imagined her eyes opening wide and her hands and feet clawing and kicking at the hostile surrounding.

He looked about his feet but was unable to spot a suitable implement. He glanced about the dark bank, able to see only a few yards beyond where he stood. *Nothing*, he thought. Nothing adequate to save Courtney from what he felt would be agony. He continued searching while believing he had to extend her this final courtesy.

He stepped from the body and moved downriver. He kicked a few of the larger stones. He sensed their suitability by the dense thud he listened for and the firmness he felt through the toe of his shoe. Unexpectedly, he found himself stumbling over the precise tool.

He rose on his wobbling knees while feeling the effects of the cold, wet night. His joints were painfully stiff. He massaged his right wrist. The burning in it resulted from hitting the rock bed with almost all of his weight favoring the arm.

It was awkward for him to lift the unevenly shaped stone. Its slippery surface made it difficult for him to cling to. He felt the river grit wedge deep underneath his fingernails. While making his way back to her he decided a manicure was in order. But in the meantime, later that night, they required a thorough scrubbing. He could never allow himself to be seen at work with such hands. What would his students think?

Upon reaching Courtney he fell to his knees. The heavy stone drove him hard onto the bank. He felt the cutting pain as his kneecaps connected with the jagged surface. He clamped his legs tightly together in order to prevent the muddy stone from forcing its way between them. He looked at Courtney and took one last moment to fill his eyes with her sensual radiance. Her moans revealed her semiconscious state. He saw that she was coming to.

Her body shivered as it fell victim to the nipping temperature. Courtney opened her eyes. She spotted stars directly above her and wondered where she was. She turned her head and looked to her right. She saw the dim light from the petroleum plant. She looked to her left and jolted out of fear from what she saw.

He dug his fingers between the rock and his thighs. He scooped up the heavy instrument in his palms. He felt the strain on his biceps as he lifted the stone above him. Once overhead, his arms extended and locked, the rock seemed lighter.

He saw Courtney's eyelids slowly open. He saw her look to the right. She searched for something in the distance, but for what he could not guess. He watched as she faced leftward. When Courtney's eyes met his he knew time had run out.

He plunged his hands downward. The weight of the rock rapidly built its crushing momentum. He felt the tension on his limbs release. The huge weight moved by its own will. His emotions raced.

The sound of stone on skull cracked out. He closed his eyes while hearing the abrupt cave-in of Courtney's face. It sounded like the gradual compression of a walnut between tongs of iron. For him the outcome was both regretful and rewarding.

He knelt next to the once beautiful creature and thought how the natural order of things would assume responsibility.

Nature's process would generate almost immediately and reduce Courtney to little more than dust. It suddenly occurred to him that if he intended to reap some return for this grotesque conclusion it had to be within the next few hours.

He pushed the rock off of her shattered face. He was unable to look upon the result of his brutal labor. He eyed beyond the remains, to the blouse tail extending out from under Courtney's head. He grasped the garment's edge and pulled it over her once lovely features. He saw how the oozing blood quickly soaked through the fabric. The striking display looked like a Rorschach Chart presenting itself for analysis. He felt an uncontrollable desire build within him.

He glided his left hand over her flat stomach. He sensed the soft body hairs protruding from her skin. He took hold of the skirt's hem and gradually raised it along her thighs. His fingers cautiously crawled under the elastic band of her panties and searched ever so gently for that which he lived and had killed for.

He felt the fine, delicate pubic hairs collect between his fingers. He sought deeper and encountered the collected warmth of Courtney's most voluptuous organ. His body trembled. It shook with excitement as he slowly tugged on the satin.

"My god," he whispered. "You are so heavenly."

He kissed her stomach and felt the tickling body hairs against his sensitive lips. He rolled his aggressive tongue over her lower abdomen. A hint of pubic grazed the left edge.

As he unfastened his belt a flash of pity came over him. He wondered if Courtney ever realized just how precious she was to him. He told her he had loved her in the past. Right then, however, it seemed like only a marginal appeasement. He always took good care of her. That was something, he rationalized, while unzipping his trousers. As he guided his left leg out of his pants he thought of the many evening pleasures she provided him, and how on this evening Courtney would freely give of herself a final time. He was not the least bit conscious of his twitching legs.

He pressed himself against her left thigh, and felt the exciting body heat against his rigidness. His eyes rolled about their sockets as he vigorously massaged himself. As he rolled onto her he felt compelled to say something that would reassure her, to let her know that it was all okay. He stuttered uncontrollably as he whispered to her.

"I—I'm yours…forev…"

Three

Richter stepped out of the operations tent. He briefly stood at the entrance. He looked at his watch. It showed 0527 hours. He looked up and saw how the early morning sun's ash gray cast revealed the Spartan character of the small encampment. As he eyed about he heard the pilots induce ignition.

As he listened to the ascending whine of the UH-1 helicopters he considered their signatures. The distinct shallow popping of the rotor was unmistakable. The sound of the blades snapping at the air was an identifiable mark that no field soldier could mistake. He listened to the familiar sound while giving the staging area an eye-over.

The camp was wholly inadequate. Much the same as the underspaced tent he had just stepped out of. Richter also realized the location of the site was unacceptable as well, but that was Treadwell's decision.

By the early A.M. light Richter studied the encircling terrain. The basecamp sat in the western foothills of the Serranía del Darién Arc. The site was vulnerable from all sides, especially from the east. The hills varied from four to seven hundred feet in elevation. The terrain was easily accessible to anyone who wished to establish an OP. "Always seize the high terrain," was the first lesson in tactics at the NCO Academy, and later reiterated during OCS. For some reason the colonel dismissed the basics.

Treadwell established the camp near the east bank of a north artery feeding into the Rio Chucunaque. The converging systems formed a junction just south of the installation. The encampment was little more than a small outpost, manned by seventy to one hundred men. It would take less than a company element, Richter believed, to force the inhabitants into an entrapping wedge with the swift current of the junctioning rivers at their backs. He recalled mentioning this slight oversight to the colonel, and how the senior thanked him for his astute input, discarding it completely.

The brass from SOUTHCOM visited the site one week after its establishment. They said that they had dropped in to conduct a facility inspection. But it quickly became apparent that their survey was a ruse for meeting required flight hours to obtain the additional pay status. The officers were more concerned with the associated flight pay complementing their monthly incomes. It was a lucrative perk that few of the field grades could let slip by their wallets. Handshakes from higher left Treadwell feeling comfortably secure with his fragile tactical decision. Richter looked ahead and eyed the rows of gabled tents the interdiction teams used for shelter.

The men did not refer to their tents as housing, quarters, or the like. It was entirely too dignified of a term to describe the sparse conditions. The army provided them a standard military cot. Between the stretched nylon and the stifling Arctic sleeping bag, one had to lie a half-inch foam mat to protect yourself from rising moisture. The supply section told the men the mat was provided for comfort. *But who'd know it?* Richter thought. He peered down the rows of enlisted tents and saw the mess hall tent was logically positioned at the opposite end. *Wasn't that smart*, he considered.

Its unintentional placement, he was sure, was the only pragmatic thing about the staging area. At least the men did not have to walk far to eat; that is, if some wild-ass cook didn't sell their food to a local villager. Richter looked to his right and spotted the morning haze hovering low over the airstrip.

Spotter planes were the primary users of the oil- and dirt-packed airfield. It was carved out of the topsoil and compacted after at least three-hundred-fifty-year-old hardwoods were torn from the forest. Except for Danny's O-2 Skymaster, one lost Cessna 152, and a few disoriented chopper pilots mistaking the strip for a helipad, Richter never saw the runway used. He looked to his left and saw the helicopters waiting at the pad.

He readjusted the mini M-16 slung to his shoulder. He looked at his watch. It showed 0529. He felt that things had gone as well as possible under the circumstances. The old aircraft were warmed up, and the men had their gear loaded. And, as always, Colonel Treadwell waited at the helipad to send him off with a handshake and a few redundant words of encouragement. Everything was in order. The only thing missing was the always expected last-minute hitch. Murphy's Law always insured that.

While approaching the helipad Richter saw that protocol was expected. Treadwell gave a hard glare. It was his silent way of begging for a salute. As he was no longer a regular, courtesy between the brass and himself seemed absurd.

Richter believed it was paramount between the team members, however. It was one small way of retaining team discipline when in the bush. Outside of the operation, protocol was fairly lax. Particularly during standdowns. As he closed with the colonel, Richter delivered the customary gesture.

"Good morning, sir," he yelled over the rotor noise.

"Everything ready, Captain?"

"Yes sir," Richter said. "Lifting off in less than a minute."

Treadwell abruptly looked up, over Richter's right shoulder. He spotted two NCOs who appeared to be in a heated disagreement. He glared down at Richter and revealed a look of doubt.

"What's up, Captain?" he asked.

Treadwell nodded toward the ruckus.

Richter turned and saw the sergeant major and Levits approaching the aircraft. It was apparent that something wrong had taken place between them. Richter decide that whatever it was, it had to be resolved, and damned quick. He knew that if anyone could make it that way, Cliff was the man.

Ramsy persistently shoved the soldier on. He clung to Levits' collar while guiding him toward the helicopter. Levits tried to fight him off, now and then throwing a wild punch for the back of Ramsy's head. But Levits' efforts to repel the sergeant major were only halfhearted. They almost reached the helipad when Ramsy released him.

They fiercely faced off. Levits stood in a partial crouch, his rifle held guardedly across his body. Ramsy stood straight. They sized each other up momentarily. The sergeant major then decided to dispense with the macho gunslinger scene.

"What the hell's the matter with you, Levits? Where's your dignity?"

"Screw dignity," Levits countered. "I don't want to die."

"It doesn't make sense," Ramsy said. "This isn't your first mission."

"No! And it ain't gonna be my last, either."

The two officers returned to their own discussion. It was customary to receive last-minute instructions from the senior officer, even if he was not familiar with mission particulars. It was, however, another courtesy that an officer of junior grade, even contract hire, could not forgo. As Treadwell provided his supposedly pertinent mission input, the two officers once again became distracted by the arguing NCOs.

The whirling rotors drowned out most of Ramsy and Levits' exchange. But it was evident to both the colonel and the captain that the standoff had to come to an end if the mission was to get off the ground. They watched as Ramsy continued with furor.

"You contracted for this mission and you'll be on it!"

"Fuck you!" Levits said.

Ramsy believed he knew the source of Levits' refusal. The symptoms were familiar to him. He encountered many combat veterans who distinguished themselves in battle, then one day decided that was it.

The percentages worked against most soldiers after a while. In Levits' case it was a long while. Between the tours in Vietnam and the five missions he had already seen in Panama, Ramsy realized that Levits seriously began to acknowledge his mortality. He understood Levits' problem and truly felt compassion for the frightened man. But like any other mission, this one took priority over the personal feelings or fears of an individual. The mission first; the mail second. All else when you could get to it.

"I don't understand you, Levits. You got no sense of loyalty. These men depend on you."

"These men are hired killers," Levits said. "Just like you and me."

Levits saw the men in the aircraft peer out. None of the patient soldiers yelled for him to join them. None of them showed looks of disapproval either. All knew, or suspected, that what Levits went through was the identical queer sensation most of them encountered once or twice in the past. That familiar gut feeling that tells you it might be your last mission. Levits took a second for self-analysis.

He knew an evident lack of confidence existed in him. The others knew it as well. It would impair his performance; that is, his fear might cause him to hesitate when an immediate response was paramount. Sometimes fear would sharpen one's edges. Sometimes the fear renders you useless. Who can know which until it happens? And even then he knew it could be different every time.

"Look—I'm worried about this one," he said. "Didn't you

ever have one of those feelings? I…keep me out of this. Next time I'll do EOD."

The two officers looked on and wondered when the face-off would end. Richter looked at his watch. It showed 0537. The mission was already behind schedule. But then, what else was new? Treadwell also acknowledged the delay with a quick glance at his watch.

"You got a problem, there, Captain?"

Richter again observed the angry NCOs and felt compelled to get involved. But he knew to do so would be a direct affront to Ramsy. It would suggest the sergeant major did not have sufficient authority or will to direct the efforts of his men. He was the team leader, but they were Ramsy's men. To have it any other way was to create a breach in the mutual loyalty and trust held between his top NCO and himself. Richter turned and faced the impatient colonel. He gave the only answer he knew he could.

"No problem, sir. Sergeant's business."

Treadwell understood the captain's message and spotted the firm reinforcement emitted by Richter's piercing blue eyes. As he and the captain watched they saw the dilemma go from bad to worse.

"You volunteered for this one," Ramsy said, "and you got money in the bank for it."

Ramsy reached for the Colt .45 pistol in his shoulder holster. He swiftly pulled the side arm out and chambered a round with one violent yank on the weapon's slide. With the hammer cocked he pointed the cannon point-blank at Levits.

"You can either die out there with us, or you can die now. So—what's it going to be?"

"Go ahead!" Levits yelled. "Die here, die out there—it's all the same."

Ramsy slowly lowered his weapon. He replaced the pistol into its holster. He did not expect such a reaction from the soldier. The man's willingness to die at the helipad instead of taking a calculated risk in the field moved him. He had to frighten the man, Ramsy told himself. He had to make Levits more afraid of staying behind than catching a bullet.

"You think so? You think it's all the same? Well, I got a little something that'll put the fear of Jesus Almighty in you."

"I don't believe in Jesus."

"And I can accept that!" Ramsy blared. "But what I won't accept is you staying behind while the others move out. I got something that'll put more than the fear of death in you."

"Oh—and what's that?"

"Life!" Ramsy said.

"What the hell are you talking about?"

"Your life. That's what I'm talking about. Your shitty little life. What the hell are you here for, anyway?"

"It's a job!"

"Exactly!" Ramsy said. "It's your job. It's what you are. You found out what it was like back in the world, so you went looking for people like yourself."

"Yeah, okay. So you're some kind of limp-dick psychologist. What of it?"

"You want to stay behind?" Ramsy warned. "Fine. But after I'm through putting the word out on you, you'll be operationally sanitized worldwide. You won't be allowed to pack grease in tracks, much less get a job like this. We're all here for a reason. Mine is that it's better than playing pinochle with a bunch of old farts. You don't get in that chopper within a month, you'll be back in some New York shithole cooking *kishke* for the rest of your life. It's about life. Your life. It's not so much how you lose it. It's how you live what you got of it."

Holy shit! Levits thought. *What egg did this philosophical bastard hatch out of?* Seized by the sergeant major's threat, Levits took a moment to consider what the bold NCO had claimed.

He had no skills in the States. Soldiering was what he knew. It was what he did better than anything else. The likelihood of someone wanting to employ a proficient killer seemed dismal at best. But then there was always Magda.

Although he left her somewhat scorned, it happened only four months before. Levits believed that, if nothing else, he could return to her loving arms and harvest the benefits of Magda's well-off father. She would forgive him. He was sure of that. It then occurred to him why he left in the first place.

He was caught between facing hostile bullets and leaping into a marriage he knew would turn into an emotional plague. A split second later Levits made the only choice he knew he could live with.

"Oh, man!" he yelled. "You scare me, Sergeant Major. All right…but I know I'm gonna die!"

The sergeant major watched the soldier proceed to the chopper. He was not sure how Levits felt about his life back home. But the tactic had worked in the past to force other men to come to grips with who and what they were. Regardless of how much their stomachs rolled with the thought of catching a bullet, Ramsy knew they had to face their fears and continue on. He was familiar with the fear in Levits. He knew about it from personal experience. Richter was pleased with what he saw.

The captain watched the yielding staff sergeant step by the sergeant major. He saw Ramsy give a nod of approval accompanied by a smile. Richter concluded that whatever it was it was over. He looked at his watch. It showed 0548. They were late, but they were going. He turned and faced Treadwell a final time.

"That's about it, sir."

Treadwell looked at his watch. He felt troubled by the idea that Bravo could not depart on schedule. But instead of badgering the captain with criticism, Treadwell decided Richter deserved words of encouragement, no matter how futile the mission.

"Okay, Captain! Bring back a prisoner if you can, but don't put anyone in jeopardy—most of all, yourself. Don't forget Jake. We can't afford to lose team leaders."

"Roger, Colonel."

The captain delivered the salute he knew Treadwell lived for.

Prior to liftoff Richter had to verify that all of his people were in place, and that the sometimes contrary pilots were ready to assume flight. While standing next to the aircraft Richter stashed his jungle hat under the right strap of his LBE. He replaced the headgear with an air crewman's helmet after brushing back his light brown hair. The helmet allowed him to communicate with the pilots and the senior member of the team in the second bird. No crewchiefs accompanied the ships on this mission to optimize on aircraft space.

He pulled the bulky skullbucket over his head, briefly crimping his ears before they popped into the earphone slots.

Damned gooney bird hats, he thought while adjusting the mouth piece. He stepped out from the aircraft and looked forward while speaking.

"Eagle. This is Leopard. Prepared for liftoff?"

He barely understood the pilot's partially audible reply.

"Affirma—Leopard—prepared or li—ff…," the pilot said.

Using the short barrel of his M-16, the captain delivered a swift bang onto the side of his helmet. The static scratched at his eardrums for the split second it took for the wiring to settle. He reset the volume control, again hearing the rushing sound of poor terminal contact.

"Tiger. This is Leopard. You ready?"

Assaf's distinctive voice instantly replied in a loud and clear signal.

"Affirmative, Leopard."

Assaf stooped between the pilot and copilot, slightly rearward of the cockpit chairs. He looked over his right shoulder, back to the inexperienced Panamanian *federales*. *Aren't they precious*, he thought.

He saw the young soldiers attempt to settle themselves into some kind of military semblance. Some had their weapons dangerously slung with the muzzle up while others forgot to snap the securing strap on their helmet. Every one of them were taught how to enter, store gear in, and exit a helicopter under combat conditions. But to look at them now, there was little evidence of any training recall. A grip of fear dominated the cabin. Assaf sensed it before physically spotting it. He knew these boys were nothing but a token effort by a government that was not truly interested in curbing the drug network.

They were young soldiers who followed their orders out of a loyalty to each other and to Torrijos—and to a president who had to be told twice before recalling that such boys were assigned to the interdiction effort. With a deep conflicting sense of comedy coupled with tragedy, Assaf commented further.

"All my babies are secured, Leopard. I stored some pabulum for their midmorning feeding."

The captain shook his head in agreement over the veteran's comical remark. *Virgins or not*, he thought while turning and climbing into the ship, *they go with us. The cards will fall for them like anyone else in this business of sometimes limited career progression.*

As the helicopters ascended from the pad Treadwell's eyes fixed on them. He watched the birds with uneasy interest. They looked like huge dragonflies rising from their nests. Their unmarked bodies showed flat and dull against the hills surrounding the encampment. At roughly ten feet off the iron pad the pilots of each aircraft glanced at one another. Each wanted to be sure he did not maneuver his rotor into the path of the other's. Treadwell imagined the radio traffic between them, each pilot demanding to know the other's intent.

Observing the aircraft bellies coming into view, Treadwell noticed their uniformity with one moderate exception. For the most part their undercarriages looked like the rest of their drab skin. One was completely devoid of any color variation. But the other bird had one minute deviation from subdued criteria.

The aircraft Sergeant Assaf commanded showed a thin white line down the center of its belly. Normally, the helicopters lacked any contrasting marks. Only subdued decals were mounted to reveal the placement of engine and weapons components secured under the skin. The telltale line did not look out of place. As it should be, Treadwell thought.

The helicopters were approximately fifty feet over the ground. They pivoted in unison and faced into the eastern morning sun. Treadwell saw how the ships' blunt noses gently dipped, before beginning their slow ascent into the glow of daybreak. He watched as the dragonflies' dimensions began to diminish. Their imposing images lost their threatening potency as they gained distance.

The sun was just behind the eastern ridge. Like the rolling terrain, the helicopters fell victim to the yellow-red fireball hiding just beyond the crest. The ships melted into the gradually intensifying daylight. The whine of their turbines and the percussion of the rotors dwindled like their images.

Hardly able to hear or see them, Treadwell considered their potential for mission success. In the final analysis, he decided that the foe these men were about to encounter would look upon them as weak and without fortitude.

Four

His trembling body floundered off Courtney. He lay back and settled close to her warmth. He felt the shore's blunt stones dig into his back. But even as the uncomfortable bed seemed to gouge at him, the orgasmic interlude left him tranquil and serene. It left him sapless.

He peered skyward and saw the constellation Orion through the low river mist. He recalled how the son of Poseidon, according to some accounts, was blind by an enraged father for wooing his daughter. He thought of Alex, but repressed the notion upon eyeing the big dipper, and followed straight up from the ladle's brim to the north star. He reflected on the infamous Grecian gods. He recalled how they indulged in the lewd pleasures of mortal life while they were exalted as deities. Lewd, the way Courtney made him feel.

He looked to his right, to the partially denuded remains of Courtney. Her cotton skirt rested high on her stomach. The blood-saturated blouse still concealed her collapsed face. He reminisced how although Courtney was not congenial at first, time, wisdom, and tolerance evolved a little girl into a mindful, erotic woman.

She was a creature of such untinged carnal intensity, he thought. He recalled the surging transference of her energy when they made love. He remembered how her undulating body moved like low wavelets in unison with his own, then increased in velocity like a heavy swell before ending in a climatic peek that matched the full force of a tidal surge. But that was when she was still alive. This time it was no less fulfilling—only a temperate divergence from the traditional. It was an unexpected morbid encounter and one worth particular noting.

He eyed about the bank. His vision had improved since earlier. Able to see perhaps thirty feet from where he stood, he began to search for a means to eliminate the evidence.

He glanced at the saplings and eyed the shoreline thickets with much interest. He considered whether to carry the body to his car and dispose of it somewhere in Algiers. Or, along the isolated river road leading to the Coast Guard Station across the river from Poydras. He looked at his watch. The timepiece showed 9:24 P.M. He knew Julia would soon phone the office. She was very protective of him.

He looked upriver to the refinery. Its brightly illuminated stacks dominated the northwest skyline. He wondered if there was somewhere within the plant the body could be disposed of. A moment later he dismissed the idea for what it was—hasty and irrational. He turned to the river and saw the intermittent lights on the Algiers bank and began to smile.

He laughed at himself for having to reconfirm the evident. The only reasonable solution had been decided prior to leaving the car. He made a mental note demanding that only staid, unimpassioned reasoning guide his actions from that moment on. He glanced about the bank for a suitable load while zipping up his coat.

He saw a multitude of weights to pick from. The shoreline was a rich and diversified field of loads. He lifted the bloodstained rock off the bank. It lay precisely where it settled after rolling off Courtney. As before, he fought with the heavy weight while awkwardly making the few steps to the water's edge. He lunged the stone through the air with one giant heave of his right arm. He heard the loud clunking splash. Upon returning his focus on Courtney, he pondered for a way to weight the body.

He raised the bloodied blouse tail from her face and grimaced over the sight of what was left. There was nothing but a shattered face. He lowered the skirt and rested the hem just above her knees, as the fashion dictated. He thought a moment more before deciding there was only one adequate item. Unorthodox, but acceptable.

He unbuttoned the blouse cuffs and slipped her arms though the sleeves. He turned the body on its side and unfastened Courtney's bra strap. He slipped the garment under the battered head and rested the halter at her neck.

He found two rocks, as great as her voluminous D cups could accommodate. Each weighed from six to eight pounds, he guessed. He forced the slippery stones into the pouches and tied the elastic strap securely around Courtney's throat. He redressed her clumsily. The uneven weights made it difficult for him to work with the body. After fastening the buttons there was nothing else to do but send the cadaver on its way.

He took Courtney by the heels and dragged her into the river. He felt the cold water ascend along his legs. When her head cleared the shoreline he saw how Courtney quietly slipped beneath the surface.

He stood motionless in the river. He looked downstream and envisioned the corpse taken by the current. In his mind's eye he saw the cadaver hovering over the mud bottom. It was an exasperating moment for him.

He believed that death was a clue to some kind of life; that is, it was at least an acknowledgment of one's past being. But at this moment there was no such realization, as Courtney's state of existence had reduced to a mere myth.

He recalled that the gods had lost their earthly attachments, but there still existed a record of their deeds. Their images were carved in stone and sky as a testament to their passing vitality. For Courtney, however, there would be no funeral to commemorate her passing. No grave site or urn would symbolize the affection they had for her. Just another soul, trite and insignificant, lost in time and space for eternity.

She would leave behind grieving parents with hopeful but beguiling premonitions of her well-being…helpless parents who would burden themselves with the best of hopes while battered with brutal uncertainty stored in the recesses of their tormented minds.

He eyed the water swirling about his waist. He waded through it with his right hand in an arcing fashion. He felt the current's persistent force push against his open palm. He knew the water would take her some distance. But eventually she would settle or snag and leave only a vague memory of her once perky personality.

He waded to the bank. He felt the frigid water drain from his pants. He felt the biting night air on his skin. It caused another chill to surge through him. He placed his hands deep into his coat pockets. He fisted his fingers while stiffening his arms to generate body heat. As his left hand closed he felt sheer material crumple within its grasp.

He pulled his quivering hand from the pocket and saw her panties clutched within it. He gazed upon the undergarment while tenderly kneading the fabric. He observed and felt the flowered embroidery stitched upon the cloth.

As he stepped among the thickets, the memory of her again occupied him. Images of Courtney in her school uniform flashed before him. He recalled how the boys followed after her, much the same as he had. While ascending the levee knoll, he remembered his first intimate encounter with her. He envisioned how at first she was not responsive to him, but that later she submitted on at least an acceptable level. Although she never fully gave of herself, there were moments when

Courtney's body assumed an automatic mode.

He would miss Courtney—her innocence, her gullible ways, her fears, her responsive body...even her death. He would miss all the good and bad they had brought to one another. But even he realized their nesting could not have gone on forever. As he steered onto the asphalt road, heading back to St. Bernard Highway, a sense of relief began to dominate within him. She was gone. This time completely and forever. The thought of her certain absence was an exhilarating release for him.

Five

Upon cresting the Serranía del Darién Arc, the aircraft began its descent. It slipped along the east face of the volcanic chain to the Caribbean Sea. As he observed the blue-green water ahead, Richter listened to the pilot's voice through his headphones.

"Leopard. Checkpoint two in view."

"Verified?" Richter asked.

"Affirmative. Approximately eight kilometers ahead; ETA nine minutes."

"At checkpoint two change heading to one-one-niner degrees," Richter instructed.

"One-one-niner degrees. Roger," the pilot confirmed.

Richter peered ahead and eyed through the forward windscreen to the distant coastline. Beyond the continental margin was the island cluster of Islas Sasardi, checkpoint two. There, the pilot would make the necessary course change to put the team on its avenue of approach. As he watched the tiny islet cluster grow closer and larger, Richter was distracted.

Although unable to hear the captain's voice, Ramsy observed Richter's lips move as he spoke into the mouthpiece. He worked his way forward in the cabin. As he placed his hand on Alex's shoulder, the sergeant major asked for details.

"What's going on, Captain?"

Richter eyed over his left shoulder.

"Islas Sasardi is just ahead. The pilot wanted confirmation of the new heading."

Ramsy nodded. He glanced starboard, south-southwest, and looked upon the mountain chain they had just flown through. The pilots gave the team a thrill when negotiating the wedge of a narrow gorge, narrowly missing a jagged outcropping.

Ramsy maneuvered through the men and equipment to the port side. He removed his jungle hat and revealed a short crop of brown hair salted with gray at the temples. He stashed the cover under the right strap of his LBE and leaned out the door. He faced north-northwest, further up the coast.

The seventy-knot wind on his face felt refreshing. Ramsy felt the collar of his uniform repeatedly slap at his neck and lower jaw. The wind rejuvenated his senses and caused a rush of excess energy to flash through him. As the sergeant major fixed his eyes on the horizon, he thought to when it all began.

Growing up in Hayward, Wisconsin was a small boy's delight. It was a tiny, close-knit community where everyone knew each other and kept their business to themselves; that is, as much as they could. The town was so complacent, orderly, and clean, it looked like a Norman Rockwell print. Ramsy loved his community, but the tragically tranquil surrounding was entirely too much for his boiling personality.

Ramsy's father, a carpenter by trade, was a good man and a reasonably sound provider. His mother was the typical homemaker of the time. She was a loving mother, affectionate and nurturing for both Ramsy and his two older sisters. They were not well-off. The children had always contributed what little money they made at part-time jobs or errands. Between his father's earnings and their small contributions, he and his sisters seldom wanted for anything practical.

He recalled pleading with his father to simply remain silent. He would never think of asking his dad to lie for him. Ramsy altered his birth certificate to meet the army's minimum age requirement of seventeen. By the time his reenlistment came due in 1942, he was already committed for the duration of World War II. When the army caught up with his fraudulent entry in 1949, the juvenile offense appeared insignificant to the investigating officer. Especially after all the much decorated NCO went through during the previous twelve years.

After a few dull occupation years, Ramsy was again asked to do what he did best during and after the landing at Inchon on the Korean peninsula. The deadlock on the 38th parallel knotted his guts. But it was what Truman wanted, he rationalized. After more arduous training assignments at Fort Benning, Fort Leonardwood, and the Presidio in Monterey, Ramsy returned to combat duty in Vietnam.

Like Marcoli, he served with the 1st Infantry Division and remained in the country for three consecutive tours. He enjoyed the inexpensive and exotic R&Rs in Thailand. Ramsy met Alex in 1971 at the Air Assault School at Fort Campbell, Kentucky. The close camaraderie that evolved out of this encounter resulted in a friendship that had lasted for over nine years.

Ramsy retired from the U.S. Army in 1979. Two months after his discharge Alex contacted him. Up to that time Ramsy had resided peacefully, too peacefully, in Sterling, Colorado. Alex's motivation for their reunion was twofold. First, he would reestablish their old military kinship and, second, he would address a mutual employment dilemma.

Ramsy felt the cool nontoxic oxygen bite on his lungs. Not a painful bite. More like a nibble to enjoy. He inhaled large purging breaths.

He faced forward, into the wind. Through squinting eyes Ramsy watched Islas Sasardi quickly advance on them. He observed the black beach of the southernmost island's southeast tip moving under the aircraft. He saw how the slender strip between jungle and water showed little sand. The demarcation consisted of jagged boulders and eroded stone shelves. The coastal water crashed against the deteriorating strand and its debris in albescent frothing surges. The verdant vegitation grew down the sharp hillsides. It extended its dominance to almost the water's edge.

He grasped onto a bulkhead as the pilot aimed the chopper southeasterly. They were on their new course, a 119-degree heading. They flew knap of the earth with Panama on their starboard and the Caribbean Sea on their port. Ramsy saw how the aircraft swiftly traversed Isla de Oro. Richter also took time to view the sea and landscape.

The crisp morning air revealed the jewel character of the South Caribbean waters. It reflected its polished points like a gem exhibit. The blue-green water showed like a turquoise slate. It stretched into the eastern horizon. Richter saw how it embraced the almost cloudless sapphire sky. At first, the sea's eight-foot swells, from a eight-hundred-foot altitude, appeared as a smooth glasslike texture. When the aircraft descended to fifty feet, however, its agitated features grew prominent. He studied the white cap's tempestuous details. Richter saw how the white-crested swells reach skyward, as if they tried to lap at the aircraft's belly. He also saw how just as suddenly the churning caps receded into the surrounding deluge. For every one that sacrificed itself there were a thousand more to take its place.

As the unrestricted sea below them, the cocaine traffic into the United States was like a giant swell. Like the withdrawing caps, the trafficking into the country showcased a contradicting impression of withdrawal. Then again, it boldly disclosed itself with the tenfold persistence of the dealers. He looked out the starboard side, upon the flaunting coastline.

He saw how the emerald sea aggressively lapped at the receptive coast. The sunlight reflected off the rugged demarcating ribbon in a variant of gray shades. The waves' silver crests were a clue to the constant pounding the petite zone between sea and earth succumbed to.

The water ate away at the less formidable coastline. It devoured the outer protective rim of a land, of a culture—of a people. Gradually, the dealer eroded the stamina of the user. He persistently, enticingly broke the users down until only grains of what they once were sifted between his fingers. *A fragment from here*, Richter thought. *A particle from there*. Like the rocks of the surrendering beach beneath him, scattered forever, the lives of people were fragmented and lost. He looked up and into the lush green interior.

Beyond the coast lay the fertile lowlands. It hid beneath the constricting jungle. The forest pretentiously displayed its tints of green. It clustered with palm, banana, and mango, mingled among the taller *cativo* and the tougher *orey* hardwoods. Foliage so lush, so jade in intensity, it seized the eyes.

Beyond the climbing lowlands, four to five kilometers in, the terrain graduated. It rose in the form of jutting tree-covered peaks. Beyond the forest was the Serranía del Darién chain, the range they had just maneuvered through. Beyond the peaks, their micro staging area lay wedged in a foothill system that could spell disaster. The country was undoubtedly picturesque, but it was also as deadly as it was breathtaking.

Richter watched the passing landscape as his ship swiftly traversed another and smaller coastline islet. It was one of the many offshore island sanctuaries of the Cuna Indians. Clansmen and their families occupied the tiny island to capacity. From shore to shore, covering the entire land mass, calves stood cluttered with grass hamlets and the narrow worn pathways between them. Extending from its banks stood hand-constructed piers of bamboo and palm timber, bound together by dried reed stalks and leather strappings. Adjacent to the landings moored the Indians' finely crafted, dug-out canoes. Richter recalled the time he visited one of the Cuna domains.

They were on a weekend joyride, looking for something different. Danny commandeered the 0-6 Skymaster, and the three of them—Danny, Cliff, and himself—flew to the Caribbean Coast for lobster. Although Danny was an army pilot, the aircraft he operated was on loan from the U.S. Air Force.

Southern Command's influence in support of the DEA effort proved marginal. The in-country army aviation unit declined an offer to hand over one of its De Havilland U-64 Beavers. The unit commander claimed that a critical shortfall in his semiannual combat readiness report would result from the equipment loss. As unit readiness was a key factor in sustaining a commander's career, the objection was not challenged. Instead, Howard Air Force Base ultimately obliged Reiner with a Cessna 0-2 Skymaster.

Though the aircraft was originally designed as a high-elevation platform for observation, liaison, forward air control, and psychological warfare, it was seldom used as such. The craft more frequently than not was employed as a cargo vehicle for the staging area's much needed beer, steak, and lobster runs.

The Cuna Indians were excellent fishermen. Their livelihood depended on their ability to take from the sea. There was always a ready supply of lobster, crab, oyster, redfish, swordfish, octopus, or squid available at wholesale, or for whatever you could barter with.

A few of the island fortresses possessed small, ill-kept airstrips. If a pilot had the courage to negotiate the narrow, undulated, and pothole-infested runway, he could buy just about any seafood delicacy...exotic specimens so fresh that they'd crawl up his arm. He remembered the high esteem the village official held them in upon their landing.

Richter smiled while envisioning the clan chief, who had stepped out from the hamlet cluster and onto the runway. He moved up to the aircraft with his hand held out, demanding payment for the use of the tribe's air facility. The captain remembered how the gentleman made no bones over their American status. The chief told them up front that Americans paid five dollars for use of the runway while all others incurred a mere two-dollar fee. As they were the only three palefaces on an island in excess of two hundred inhabitants, the price seemed fair enough.

Through the starboard door Richter watched as the ship advanced on Cabo Tiburón. Upon reaching the cape, the aircraft veered from the coast. The helicopters maintained their heading over the Golfo de Urabá. They would reach their entry point in less than twenty minutes. Richter knew the effluxing mouth of the Rio Caimán Viejo would shortly come into view and guide them into Colombia. As he watched the coastline recede, Richter resumed his analysis.

The countryside was alluring and seductive but it was also volatile. It harbored the marauding bands of outlaws, civilian and military alike, who roamed like soldier ants through the underbrush. The undergrowth cloaked the network of paths, trails, and roads created by the Zorrilla Cartel. Richter decided the day he arrived in the country that to presume death did not lurk behind every rock, every tree, every blade of grass, was to live your life in a perilous way. He weighed the prospects of success against the well-resourced organization.

What they attempted to do was comparable to a clawless mole boring its way through the Rocky Mountains. Scraping, biting, and pawing inch by inch while trying to gain some kind of foothold on a plague that beset the American people. In particular, those who did not see themselves as victims.

As long as there would be a demand there would always be a willing supplier. As long as people were willing to sacrifice the foundation of their existence there was little anyone could actually do. Athletes, movie stars, politicians, CEOs—all sacrifice their families, their wealth, and in some cases their lives to be a part of the chic scene. They are the examples by which other people guide their lives. When the wealthy and powerful enter drug rehabilitation it suggests a state of mind that runs through the jet-setter sphere. It looks enticing to the less affluent, and the street-level pushers are always there to offer those of lesser means a taste of the stylish fast lane. What slips the minds of the less fortunate is that there are no financial nets to catch them. There are no expensive rehabilitation centers to accommodate them, no countryside groves to walk through while returning to their dormitory for treatment. No round-the-clock staff to cater to and praise them for their courage to clease themselves, as aides make the daily change of their soiled linen. All that is available to them is a wet corner in a back alley, a dirty needle, and ultimately an untimely death.

Until the people back in the world were willing to treat the drug war like the war it is, then what they did in the field was just another part of the downhill spiral the interdiction program and country appeared to move in.

Other than that, Richter thought, *it's a nice day*. The captain heard the pilot's voice through the internal system.

"Leopard. Twelve minutes to objective."

"Roger," Richter said. He immediately sought conformation of message receipt from Sergeant Assaf. "Tiger. Did you copy? Over."

Like the captain, Assaf stooped between the pilots and slightly near the cockpit chairs. As commander of the second aircraft, it was Assaf's responsibility to insure mission compliance for his portion of the team, but baby-sitting didn't get it. He heard the transmission between Eagle and Leopard.

"Roger, Leopard."

Assaf looked over his right shoulder to the new meats aft the cabin. Their expressionless faces glowed with perspiration. *Their dead looks could contort goat guts*, he thought. As Assaf looked forward, he facetiously commented into his mouthpiece.

"We're good to go, here, Leopard. I got 'em tightened up. Every one of 'em a born killer."

He smiled over the sergeant's remark. As there was still time before reaching their entry point, Richter began to eye about the cabin.

Like Ramsy, Levits also kept his hair short. The dark uneven stubble protruded from his head like porcupine quills.

He was slim and stood five foot, nine inches in a tightly compacted 155-pound frame. He seldom wore a fatigue jacket. Normally, he donned a simple green T-shirt with a flak vest over it. But today Levits opted for full battle dress plus the light body armor. Richter looked to Gable.

Gable sat in the aircraft doorway, his feet dangling out. He carried the M-72A2 LAW as an additional piece. Richter believed he did this more out of a need to feel safe than to fragment animate or inanimate objects out of pleasure. His trademarc, the Happy Destructor, was little more than a cover for the deep-rooted fear Gable felt when in the field. But it was all right. One additional LAW per mission was an expense Uncle Sam could incur without much complaint, especially if it set a good soldier's mind at ease.

Gable's long locks swept over his left shoulder. The air racing by the port side whipped the entangling strands. He secured his shoulder-length hair using a field dressing tied about his head. Behind Gable sat Marcoli, who observed out the starboard side.

Marcoli sat cross-legged in the center of the cabin. He wrongly pointed his weapon muzzle upward after securing it between his legs. Perspiration rolled down the sides of his shaven face. The droplets crawled out from under his blond sideburns. They followed on a glide path parallel his jawline. Richter knew he was nervous, but Marcoli had a way of covering his edginess better than most men. After focusing on Copeland, Richter's attention was drawn back to Marcoli. He watched as Stan disclosed his nervousness by covering for it with another predictable prank.

Reaching over with his left hand Marcoli took hold of Gable's flak vest at the right shoulder. He thrust his companion forward, almost off the edge of the door frame. Before Gable could respond to the joke, Marcoli reversed his thrust and pulled the terrified soldier into the bird.

Gable bent forward at the waist. He briefly buried his face between his knees. He gasped to take in the vital air to replenish his constricted chest. He heaved three large breaths and released each slowly while trying to regain a normal breathing rhythm. He slowly raised while tightly flexing his muscles. After a few more deep oxygen intakes Gable regained the semi-composure he felt prior to Marcoli's prank. He looked over his shoulder and responded to the man's tasteless humor.

"Eat shit and die young, fool."

"Just testing the reflexes," Marcoli said.

"Yeah, sure. We'll test yours when I frag your ass."

"Hey man! Relax!" Marcoli said. "It's just another mission."

Richter was grateful for Gable's passive retaliation. Had it been him, the captain thought, he would have buttstroked Marcoli, damned near sending his head out the starboard side. But they were all good men, shortcomings included. However, some were obviously more childproof than others. Richter paused to take a critical look at James.

James was less talkative this time out. He sat against the back firewall. He pulled his legs up and into him and rested his chin on his knees. He stashed his jungle hat inside the sling assembly of his rifle. He jammed the headgear between the strap and the underside of the rifle's handguard. This time James also wore a flak vest. Apparently, Richter thought, the man was making a sincere attempt to avoid any inadvertent flying scrap iron. Their uniforms evolved from their personalities.

Each man donned the basic tropical BDUs, sometimes trousers only. Beyond that they stylized their garb to fit their individual temperament. Gable never wore a hat. Copeland favored a baseball cap. It was a memento from a Cincinnati Reds game the summer before. Bard never wore his fatigue jacket or body armor. He wanted everyone to have full view of his dynamic muscular frame. He adorned himself with a bold earring. Bard defiantly displayed the large gold ball on his right earlobe, especially when in the presence of seniors. He knew it offended them. It was his way of getting back. Marcoli preferred a tiny diamond in his left ear. He never made a big deal of it, however. Except for Ramsy and himself, who had to set some kind of dress code, the men of Team Bravo were as contrasting in make-up as they were similar in combat expertise.

But their dress was not an issue. What mattered was their desire to win. That they all possessed. In varying degrees, Richter admitted, but the desire was there. He glanced out the port side as the ship bypassed Punta Arenas del Norte. They were nearing the Rio Caimán Viejo. He looked to Ramsy and motioned for the sergeant major to move up. Ramsy crouched next to the captain.

"We'll reach the entry point in about seven minutes," Richter said. "Get 'em ready, Sergeant Major."

"Roger," Ramsy replied. He faced aft the aircraft. "All right, gentlemen! Lock and load—combat checks! Seven minutes to the shit."

Instantly, the men snapped out of their far-reaching thoughts. They began to prepare themselves and their weaponry for the short patrol that lay ahead, and the subsequent ambush and capture that they hoped to realize.

Gable, legs still out the door, shoved a thirty-round banana magazine into his M-16, but did so only after he struck the butt of the clip onto the aircraft door frame. The extra measure settled the spring-fed ammunition to prevent first round jamming. Richter looked to Levits and saw the soldier was preoccupied with his combat checks.

Levits also snapped a thirty-round magazine into his weapon. But before doing so he used electrical tape to fasten another inverted clip to the one inserted. He checked his grenade pins to insure there was no chance for a mishap. He preferred grenades as a modifier for aggression. However, he saw on occasion how men were disintegrated because brush or low tree branches snagged onto the safety pin ring. He did not intend to ignite because of a personal oversight. In the meantime, Marcoli gave himself a last once-over.

Marcoli pulled up his left pant leg. He never bloused his trousers in his boots. He claimed he had a deep appreciation for the sense of freedom it gave him. Attached to his calf was a twin barrel Derringer. He pulled the piece from its holster and inspected the two chambered .22 magnum rounds. He replaced the weapon after making sure its safety was on. After locking a round in his M-16, Marcoli pulled his peace medal from under his T-shirt. He kissed the tarnished medallion once for luck. Everyone tried to prepare for the best or the worst that could happen.

Bard slipped his bayonet inside his right boot. Copeland checked his first aid pouch to insure the field dressing was sealed in a dry and untorn wrapper. Colfield spent most of the trip sharpening his already razor-edged bayonet. He replaced the shank into its sheath after dropping the small grinding stone into his top left pocket. Sanford was ready, having checked and rechecked his gear during the entire trip.

Although the rotor above them canceled out most of the cabin noise, the aircraft was still filled with reminiscent sound spurts.

For a moment, only a flash, it was 1972 all over again. The clattering of rifles, the popping of bolts; all this, coupled with the radio traffic coming through his headphones, deluged the captain with flashes of Vietnam. All these nostalgic, nerve-tickling sensitizers prompted the suppressed memories within him. This was what he was, Richter admitted to himself. It was what all of them were, like it or not, for what good or bad it all meant. As the men prepared, Ramsy oversaw them.

Ramsy remained close to the captain. Twice he had to tell James to get himself ready. Ramsy yelled at Gable once. He told the radioman to be sure they had good communications before they hit the ground. Richter heard the radiocheck made by Gable with the pilot and was satisfied their PRC-77 would meet their communicative needs. Richter caught the gleam in Ramsy's eyes. He knew the sergeant major felt right at home.

On the threshold of combat and in it was when Ramsy was at his best. Richter believed that Ramsy was one of the finest NCOs he had ever known. No. He was the finest. Suddenly, the brash sergeant major surprised him.

"I'll tell you what, Captain!" he yelled out. "I don't know

when I've worked with such a good-looking group of men. Did you ever see a more handsome gathering of killers?"

Most of the men smiled over the top NCO's remark. Levits almost broke into laughter. It was a last-minute lightening of what had the potential to turn bad. Once on the ground it was no joke. They would make their way to the objective, set up for the ambush, and await the exchange.

The captain turned his head slowly. He faced the men and took in their images. He surveyed the group momentarily, then faced forward and observed the oncoming mouth of the Rio Caimán Viejo. As he looked ahead Richter could not help but comment under his breath.

"Oh, yeah—good-looking crew." Richter saw the entry point was on them. "Entry point just ahead. Get hot!"

Ramsy's voice blared throughout the cabin. He was easily heard above the rotor noise.

"Stay sharp!"

Six

    Henry raised the collar of his denim work coat. He folded his arms and pressed them hard against his once great chest. He felt how time reduced his mass to only a remnant of what it once was. The bony protrusions reminded him that he had lost another seven pounds.

    He limited his daily intake to a mere can of Campbell's Pork-n-Beans and what he could snatch from the river. Retirement meant lean times. As he looked along the east bank, Henry tightened his arms in an attempt to fight off the shiver.

    The abrupt chill caused him to lose his balance. He quickly moved his left foot out from under him to keep from heeling over. Once resettled onto the levee stones Henry reached for Ben. He ran his drawn left hand between the old dog's ears. In Henry's words, "Scratchin' dem spots where da dog likes it da bess." As he massaged Ben, Henry considered the shiver's intensity.

"Dat chill came all da way from ma toes, Benny."

Ben guardedly sat next to Henry. He raised his head and looked up into his master's warm gray eyes. He moved his head slightly leftward and allowed Henry's clawing hand to itch at one aggravating flea nibbling on his right ear. He opened his mouth wide and made a great canine yawn. Henry saw every tooth and the gaps where a few fell out. Once through the involuntary reflex, Ben lowered his graying face once more. He rested his white whiskered muzzle upon Henry's left thigh.

"Ya gittin' ol', too?" Henry said. "Dat's okay. We gittin' ol' togedder."

Henry eyed the river. He spotted the navigation markers almost directly across the channel. They delineated the entrance to the Intercoastal Waterway. The manmade throughway was an alternate river route. Tugs and barges used it as a shortcut to their docks down river, rather than follow the undulating Mississippi. He looked upstream and spotted the Chalmette Ferry landing on the west bank.

"Dem ferries bin goin' back an fort fo-ever," he told Ben.

Henry saw that one of the two rivercraft, either the St. John or Captain John Levy, had tied off at the far dock on the west side. He also caught a faint glimpse of the Thomas Jefferson, normally used as an alternate vessel, just within the cast of the nearby docklights.

He saw the intensity of the halogen light, and how its radiance shot skyward on yellow-white streaks of fluorescentlike mist. The luminous display silhouetted the features of the moored vessel. It revealed every window, every rail, every stack and line it could filter over, around and beyond.

Henry reached into the left pocket of his khaki trousers. From it he pulled his old but precious timepiece. He snapped open the goldplated cover. Marietta surprised him with it on his birthday nine years before. It showed 11:50 P.M.

"Dem boats oughta still be runnin'. Guess dem boys juss took an early night."

Henry eyed Marietta's gift. She was his third wife, "and da bess," he always claimed. But his first tangle with matrimony almost convinced him it should be his last.

He spent ten years with Marcie Joy. They married after he returned from the war in early 1946. He struggled with Marcie until late 1956. She had a dominating personality as well as a voracious appetite for other men.

They lived in Biloxi, Mississippi the entire beleaguering ten years. He worked on a shrimp boat to earn their livelihood. The money was not great but there was always enough for them to live on. There was, however, never enough for Marcie Joy. It was important for her to be on the go and to spend wherever she went.

After their ninth year together he was reasonably sure of what he wanted to do. It took Henry one more year to make up his mind. He got up one morning and dressed himself in his Sunday best before stepping out the front door. Marcie Joy never saw him again. That was a wise decision, he often told himself. Stella wasn't much different, though; but then again—she was.

He recalled meeting Stella Bodine in a bar on Dauphine Street. The bar was no longer there. It burned down after a love-wounded husband found his wife in one of the building's darker recesses. It wasn't so much that she was with another man, Henry heard later, as it was what she did for him under a table in a public facility. A fight ensued between them while the third-party recipient left through a side exit. During the conflict a gas burner fell over and ignited a curtain. The woodframe building turned to flames within minutes. The confusion of the rushing mob allowed the two love combatants to get away. No one ever heard from the angry mates again. Some claimed the woman was as striking as Stella, but Henry never saw the seductive feline.

Stella had a body like a serpent, and such smooth copper skin it made his mouth water. She was lean and hard. No excess except where it counted. The muscle in her arms and thighs rippled under her taut but soft flesh. The undersized dresses Stella wore left little to the imagination.

"Oh, she was da tastiess. Dat's fo-sho."

He married Stella two months later, in late 1958. For the next three years life was good for his hot-blooded mate and himself. He remembered coming home from a short haul. The shrimp weren't running much. He found his Stella waiting at the front door. She had on a flimsy see-through brassiere and a towel wrapped about her classic tight bottom. That afternoon was the most eventful of his life, vivid to this day. He could not recall when, before or since, he had underwent such a traumatic carnal escapade.

"Dat woman was on fire," he said to Benny. "She threw me dis way an dat. By da time Stella got done, she had ma little ass wrapped about da bedposs. Nothin' like it...nothin."

Stella was a religious woman, so to speak. She liked the bars but never missed church on Sunday. Henry could not always accompany her to services. He would try to make it back in time, but no self-respecting captain would turn his boat homeward with bins half full. Eventually, it became apparent that her church interests were not exclusively confined to prayer.

A close friend told him the reason for Stella's gospel orientations was the young preacher. A handsome, smart-looking man of about thirty. The man had a hold on his wife he never thought possible. When she filed for a divorce in 1963, Stella tried to enjoin his savings, along with alimony. But during the proceeding it came out that Marcie Joy and he were still married, thus voiding his reckless union with Stella. That was one pissed-off woman, he remembered. The judge was not impressed either. He spent eighteen months of a three-year sentence in Angola prison for that slight indiscretion. Two weeks after reporting to his parole officer he landed a job offshore with Texico.

He caught Marietta Chenier's eye at church services. The forward woman boldly walked up and introduced herself. The word among the congregation was that he was a freewheeling bachelor with a good-paying job at Texico. Money in the bank was how they saw him, he figured. Before he realized it Marietta moved in. But he had no regrets.

Looking back on it, he reminisced, Marietta had her own way of making a man feel like a man. But there was always Stella and her bedtime creativeness that he could not get out of his mind.

That woman's love-making was wild, Henry recollected, and remembered, and thought of again. *You never finished until Stella did*, he thought, *and if you considered otherwise, old Stella would crack you upside the head*. She was fire, burning coals through and through, but Marietta was grace.

She was a kind woman, willing to love and respect him as long as he reciprocated the same. It was not a problem for him as he never fooled around on any of his wives or girlfriends. Marietta was always there for him. She never messed around, and she never got angry. When she passed away in 1978, it became apparent to Henry just how much she meant to him.

Her bout with pneumonia lasted three weeks. She went down slowly, sometimes appearing to improve before suddenly relapsing deeper into the fatal condition. Although together for eleven years Marietta and he never married. For some reason they just never got around to it. But during the last few days of Marietta's life he could no longer accept that she would leave the earth without taking a part of him with her.

He phoned their minister. The one who scolded them years on end for not marrying. The pious man came to the hospital that night. They were married on June 18th, 1978. Marietta died the following evening. She was truly the finest woman he had ever known—and she would be the last. As Henry snapped the beloved timepiece closed, he looked upriver, past Algiers, to the giant structure spanning the Mississippi.

He could see only part of the Connection from where he sat at the end of Pine Street. The decorative structure showed against the dark horizon while jutting out from the deeper blackness of the foreground. It looked like a roller coaster, he thought. Strings of light rose along its superstructure to the first buttress, then descended on a lazy glide until again curving upward, reaching for the summit of the next buttress. He glanced at his fishing pole.

He raised slowly and used his hands to help his descent along the steep grade. Large rocks, put there by the Orleans Parish Levee Board, covered the lower bank. Upon reaching the pole, Henry gripped the thick shaft with both hands. He felt it tightly wedged between the rocks and believed it would take one damned big fish to yank the pole from its anchor. He slowly turned and began his ascent. Again, he used his hands to insure that he did not slip between stones. *A man of sixty-seven years could get hurt*, he told himself. He reached just short of where Ben poised.

Henry looked up. He saw the thick brown fur on Ben's back stand like wire bristles. Like his ruffled withers, the retriever poised stiff, frozen upon the rock. His rump raised high. His forelegs drew in, head dipped low. His grayed muzzle rose. His yellow, plaque-covered fangs showed in the dim light. A whine emerged from him then gradually transformed into a lingering growl.

"Boy, whatchu doin'?" Henry asked. "Ya actin like ya gotta gris-gris or somethin'."

He reached out with his left hand. He kept his eyes on Ben's, maintaining critical contact. Henry believed animals were much the same as people; their intent was revealed in their eyes. The light from over the levee caused the dog's features to silhouette. The enlarged whites about Ben's pupils glaringly revealed themselves. *Like the eyes of a demon*, Henry thought. But he could not help himself.

"Com-on, now, Benny. Ya know I'm da one dat loves ya. Ya know dat."

Henry lowered his hand as he spoke and gently touched the short hairs just behind Ben's snout.

"We bin togedder too long fo-dis. Now, com-on. Gives us ah little suga."

As soon as Ben felt Henry's touch his fears diminished. He dipped his head slightly then raised it to lick his master's caring fingers. Henry's scent was all the dog needed to verify that his premonition of death did not come from his master. He began to scamper.

"What da hell's got ya spooked?" Henry said. "Only time I ever seen ya act like dis was when dat coon nipped your tail. Had ya jumpin' Bayou Ducros."

Henry sat next to Ben. He rested his left arm over the dog's back while scratching Ben on his loins. The dog would not settle, however. He continued to try and soothe the animal. He massaged Ben's brisket.

He glanced about the rocks and searched for another dog. *Or maybe another coon*, he jokingly thought. Henry looked behind him and searched for strangers stepping along the road at the levee's summit. People had to be careful when on the levee at night. When he faced the river Henry saw the nudge on his pole.

The end of the cane rod bowed then sprang back to its usual rigid form. He saw it dip again.

"Think maybe we got somethin here, boy."

Henry retraced his steps to the pole. Upon reaching the wedged reed he yanked it from the narrow gap between the stones. He felt an unusual heavy resistance.

"What da hell we got here?"

The strain on his biceps and forearms suggested that it was a large catch. Much larger than he hoped for. Some gar were known to grow up to four feet long in the Mississippi. Catfish even larger, but they were as uncommon as fleas on a bald dog.

"Man! We got somethin, here. I don't know what."

Ben's barking intensified. He nervously moved back and forth on the rocks.

"Oh, it's big, Benny," Henry said, his voice filled with excitement. "We gonna eat for ah week on dis…I'm tellin' ya."

Ben raced to the water's edge. He excitedly skipped from side to side and agitated the shallow water at the shore.

The river was another ten feet down the bank. The light coming from over the levee caused a shadow at the water's edge. Henry heard Ben prancing in the water while growling but was unable to observe what the old dog snarled at. Whatever it was, he thought, it didn't fight like a fish. It didn't fight at all.

Henry reanchored his pole. With his left hand he followed along the reed until he felt the tied-off filament at the tip. He continued along the line, letting it glide between his fingers as he descended the bank. Upon reaching the water's edge Henry peered into the river. He wondered what it was that had such a strong grip on his line and his dog's nerves.

He took hold of the filament with both hands. He wrapped the thin cord once around his right hand to prevent it from slipping.

He tugged, heaving generously but not enough to break it. When the catch popped to the surface Henry lost his balance.

He carefully rose to his feet while feeling a sharp pain race through his left wrist. He cautiously moved to the water's edge. He took a close and wide-eyed look at what had attached itself to his line.

As Ben snarled Henry observed the white foot protruding from the water. He saw the line coiled about the leg. He eyed along the limb until it disappeared into the dark water, just above the knee.

"Oh, ma Lord. Who are ya, ya poor thing. Oh, ma Lord, Benny. Ma God."

Seven

Raphael slowly raised his head upon hearing the helicopter rotors. He peeped over the sandbag bulwark. In the distance, over the gulf, he spotted two airborne dots advancing. They scurried just above the splashing surf.

He had marauded for the previous three years as a freelancer. He accepted a soldier-for-hire condition when it became apparent his wife and child might starve. Like himself, his village was dirt poor.

He quickly found out that politics provided for the selected. It elevated the status and wealth of a precious few while leaving the majority of his fellow villagers condemned to eternal hunger. He angrily watched as the politically and drug connected families made their marks. He bitterly promised his wife he would provide for them no matter what he had to do, or who he had to do it to. He pulled on the bolt of his Soviet AKSU-74 assault rifle. He listened to the thrumming of the approaching assault ships. He waited a few seconds more before warning the others.

"Get ready!"

The men rushed about the makeshift fortification after grabbing their weapons. Three men abruptly put their card game aside. They inadvertently spilled the deck onto the sandy bottom while not one permitted a peso to slip from his fingers. They leaned into the front wall of the rampart. They kept their heads low and waited.

Next to Raphael crouched Ramos. Ramos was another starving villager programmed for a soldier's life. The comrade gripped the unit's only RPG-7V antitank weapon. The 85mm missile was a crude application for air defense, but it was all their headquarters would supply them. As Private Ramos was the most proficient with the rocket launcher, he was to do the honors. Ramos armed the device and patiently waited. The order to fire would come from Lieutenant Pinto.

Pinto took his position at the end of the earthwork. He stood next to their almost new Soviet PKM machine gun. He warned his undisciplined soldiers to wait for his command. He threatened that anyone who fired prior to his order would be shot by him, personally. The freelancers were not impressed with the young Colombian *federales'* threat.

Pinto searched the seascape through his binoculars. They were a gift from his father, the consulate general to the Colombian Diplomatic Mission in Mexico. He watched the aircraft make an abrupt turn port. The unexpected maneuver caused him to wonder. He studied the birds as they headed north, up the coast. He watched as they made another sudden course change and dropped from view upon paralleling the shoreline.

He believed, as his seniors had briefed, the birds would leisurely approach and land on the presumed cold LZ. *Do they know we are here?* he asked himself. He felt conspicuously stupid for losing sight of the helicopters. The men patiently waited while looking to him for swift and decisive action. Ramos heard the ships approach but could not as yet see them. As their engines grew dominant, Ramos grew edgy. He needed at least five seconds to insure accuracy.

"Lieutenant!" Ramos said. "They—are—coming."

"I said wait!" Pinto commanded. He looked up the coast, trying to spot the advancing aircraft. "Remember your orders, Ramos!"

"Yes sir!"

Richter leaned forward and rested against the back of the copilot's chair. His eyes strained to study the terrain's finer points. As he put it, trying to see the tree from the forest. Their helicopters drew within five hundred meters of the Rio Caimán Viejo. As he looked through the forward windscreen it became clear to Richter that the mission would become another bloodletting. Sergeant Assaf looked on as well.

Assaf volunteered for service in 1972. After basic training and AIT, he attended the John F. Kennedy School for Special Forces at Fort Bragg. After a year in the North Carolina pines, Assaf transferred to the Defense Linguistic Institute at the Presidio in Monterey. There, he participated in an accelerated Arabic program. Eight months later Assaf finished the course, graduating second in his class. He anxiously looked forward to putting his training to good use. The Department of the Army showed Assaf its appreciation by assigning him to the 5th Special Forces Group, Vietnam. *What the hell was the army thinking?* he wondered. Nixon reduced their involvement to nothing. President Ford, just sworn in the month before, had nothing up his sleeve—he hoped. The defense of Vietnam was left to the South Vietnamese. At least, that's what he was told. Upon his arrival in-country, Assaf found the language and culture unagreeable. It was his attitude, he later admitted.

Assaf finally got his tour in Saudi Arabia after a ten-month exploit with the Montagnard, or, by then, what was left of them. While completing his enlistment in Panama, however, it became apparent that the high opinion he held of himself was not shared by prospective employers.

He found out that linguists were a tarnished dime a dozen. He envisioned a six-figure paycheck as an interpreter, but found out that the old boy circuit in the State Department had a nepotistic design. It effectively eliminated this audacious unknown from Palmerton, Pennsylvania. Arabia had its own linguists. So did Mobile Oil, Texico, and Shell. Having such a vivid lesson in life smeared into his face Assaf chose to apply his alternate expertise.

As an explosives and weapons specialist in American and Soviet armament, Assaf served as both weapons training cadre and EOD for the team. He linked with Team Bravo three months after deciding not to undergo reenlistment. From Assaf's pissed standpoint, his military attributes far exceeded what the U.S. Army paid him. Contract soldiering paid the most for what he knew—for the meantime, anyway. Assaf watched as the string of vapor rose from the jungle.

Richter watched the telltale vapor trail of a rocket appear. He could not judge if the explosive was guided toward his aircraft or Assaf's. The ships flew close together and the rocket was still some distance from them. A few seconds later it became evident that the missile headed for the other aircraft. All Richter could do was hope for a miss. As the rocket surged toward them, Richter heard their copilot provide the delinquent news.

"Leopard. We got in-coming."

Richter wondered where the man's head had been for the last five seconds.

"I can see that," he said. "Keep going. Beyond the beach we'll have cover. Tiger. Did you copy?"

"Roger. Sta—"

Assaf watched as the nose of his aircraft burst into flames. A horrendous fireball shot past the dead pilots and into his face. He felt the hot pieces of plexi penetrate his eyes. The flames licked at his face and hands. The front of his uniform reduced to ash. He sensed that he still lived, but little else. Assaf shrieked into the helmet mouthpiece. Richter listened to the shrills and almost vomited.

Richter leaned back and peered out the port door. He saw how the flames engulfed the nose section of Assaf's ship. As they passed over the mouth of the Rio Caimán Viejo he watched the destroyed helicopter fall from sight. Richter swallowed twice to repel the nauseous sensation.

Upon witnessing Ramos' precision the soldiers lost their focus. Lieutenant Pinto was ecstatic. He raised to his feet and yelled out his approval for the soldier's aim. Raphael was also pleased, until glancing skyward.

The fireball headed for the beach on a lethal line. Raphael's peripheral vision first warned him. He glanced up to their kill and watched as the burning wreckage rushed toward their vulnerable position.

Raphael yelled for the men to disperse. He jumped from the rampart and ran past the lieutenant while yelling his warning to the others. His jubilant friends noticed his peculiar manner. When they turned to search for the cause of Raphael's unusual conduct the helicopter slammed into them.

Richter's chopper flew over the fortification while taking minimal damage from small arms. Once the aircraft cleared the beach Richter ordered the pilot to turnabout. Masterson made a hard bank to the right. The ship came about almost onto the exact path in the opposite direction. The men and gear inside tossed about the cabin. Gable hung onto the door frame after almost slipping off the edge. Upon returning to the crash site Ramsy and Richter made a quick damage assessment.

They saw the helicopter's forward section in flames. The aircraft separated just behind the cockpit. The tail section severed as well. Large fragments of the primary rotor snapped from its shaft after slicing into the semisolid wet sand. The skids flattened, both spreading straight out from the underbelly on impact. Richter watched as one of the surviving mercenaries darted from the destroyed bunker. He wildly dashed toward the flames.

Diago felt the heat of the burning JP-4 singe his black headlocks and whiskers. The acrid odor of flashing turbine fuel filled his nostrils. He wiped the bloody sand from the right side of his face. He looked about the devastated gun emplacement.

Half of the unit was dead, Lieutenant Pinto as well. Most were torn to bits or charred beyond recognition on impact. Two men lay on the trench bottom screaming for help. Diago cleared his eyes again. He looked at the bloody granules clinging to his palms and fingers.

He climbed from the wrecked bulwark and charged toward the downed helicopter. He roared at the top of his lungs while clawing his way over the berm. He pulled his 9mm Llama from its hip holster as he made his way to the burning wreckage. At the flaming cockpit he looked for survivors. There were none. He glanced skyward and yelled out his rage. He rushed to the cabin section and searched through the mangled and burnt bodies. He hoped for just one live Panamanian when spotting their uniforms. Upon shoving a fourth body aside, Diago found a suitable victim.

The unconscious boy came to when he felt Diago yank on him. The mercenary dragged the delirious soldier from the cabin and onto the beach. So weakened by the crash the soldier was unable to raise to his feet. While dragged across the wet sand he felt the butt of Diago's pistol repeatedly strike on his head and neck. Reaching a safe distance from the aircraft, Diago ordered the soldier to kneel in the sand. The boy did so. He gripped onto the soldier's hair and pulled straight up on the brown strands. The soldier's neck stretched as his head yanked upward. Diago aimed his pistol point-blank on the boy's right temple and squeezed the trigger. He watched fluid pour from the entry point as the head snapped sideways. As he felt the traitor's blood spray upon his face Diago let out with another screeching wail. He fired two more rounds into the air.

Marcoli passionately yelled a profound "mother fucker" from over Gable's right shoulder. Both men took aim on Diago and fired their weapons on automatic. A deluge of rounds descended around and into the killer. The sand about the executioner splashed as his stomach, chest, and face tore open.

Richter looked to Ramsy.

"They look torn up down there. We can get to the survivors, if any are left."

The sergeant major cared about his men, but he could not put the individual ahead of the mission. As if with an automatic reflex, Ramsy responded the only way he knew how.

"Captain! We got a mission. What about it?"

"The mission's changed," Richter said. "We got all the time we need, now." The captain looked forward while commenting to himself aloud. "They knew we were coming." He depressed the squelch button on his microphone. "Land about three hundred meters down beach."

"Captain—we go down there, we might lose our only way back," the pilot said.

"There might be survivors. We can't leave 'em."

Ramsy quietly observed his friend and the pilot. He could not understand the entire conversation. From what he could grasp, it appeared that Masterson did not want to follow his instructions. Ramsy was not surprised by Masterson's conduct. It had been his experience that when some pilots are in command of an aircraft they interpret the distinction as being in control of the mission. Ramsy listened as the pilot countered.

"I know, Captain. I can't let you do that. We'll place the ship in jeopardy."

Richter glared at the obstinate man. He never left a soldier behind before—unless he and the solder in question agreed upon it. He didn't intend to acquire poor mission habits at this stage of his dubious career.

Richter secured his M-16 between his legs. He pulled his .45 pistol from its hip holster. He yanked on the slide and chambered one of the low-velocity slugs. Richter laid the muzzle against the pilot's helmet and nudged the skullbucket.

"Do what I tell ya!"

Masterson looked up upon feeling the nudge on his helmet. He found the almost half-inch pistol bore bearing down on his right eyeball. His eyes widened, but his surprise lasted for only a short time.

"Oh, that's great!" Masterson yelled. "You kill me, who flies this?"

Richter glanced to his right, upon the younger copilot. He easily recognized the shavetail's innocent expression. He looked to the pilot, replying confidently.

"He will." Richter swiftly faced the copilot and showed hard eyes. "Won't you?"

Masterson eyed right. He saw the horror on his flight assistant's face. He looked down at the copilot's hands, which were shaking. He knew the oscillating fingers did not result from aircraft vibration. He watched his copilot glance to him then up at the rock features of the bullheaded captain, then again at him. It was obvious to Masterson the man would not hold his ground. If the crazy captain chose to shoot him the frightened copilot would comply with Richter's orders. Masterson grudgingly submitted.

"All right, Captain. You win. Make it fast while you're down there, though."

Richter uncocked the .45. He returned the weapon to its holster.

"Thank you. You're a good man, Lieutenant."

Richter turned, coming face to face with Ramsy's grinning features.

"Asshole pilots," the sergeant major said. "Put 'em in charge of an aircraft they think it's their mission."

"Not this one," Richter said.

The aircraft settled approximately two hundred meters from the destroyed enemy emplacement. As it was about to land Team Bravo began to disembark. Richter leaped from the chopper first. The team quickly followed and rapidly made its way to the treeline for cover and concealment. Ramsy was the second to leave the ship. He remained at the door to insure the men complied with the captain's orders. When James exited Ramsy stopped him and gave the soldier contrary instructions.

"Stay with the ship!" Ramsy shouted "I don't want our pilots becoming overly protective of their toy."

"Got it, sergeant major."

James climbed into the aircraft. He quickly scooted forward in the cabin and positioned himself between the pilots. He pulled on the bolt of his M-16, letting the mechanism slam forward for effect. As he had already chambered a round the one previously locked ejected. The discharged cartridge struck the copilot on his helmet.

"The sergeant major thinks you guys have a mind of your own," he said. "I'm here to change that."

The men converged beyond the beach. Richter dispersed the team for a movement to contact. He remained on line to establish the speed he expected his men to maintain. The sergeant major followed behind the line to insure that the men maintained their proper pace and distance. As they advanced on the enemy position, each man took measures to prepare himself.

Levits removed two hand grenades from their pouches. He stored them in his opened shirt under his flak vest. Marcoli pulled his bayonet and mounted the knife over the flash suppresser of his rifle. He tightly held to his weapon by its pistol grip. The veins in his forearms bulged. Gable was no less prepared, but no one would know it, Ramsy thought. Between lugging his normal issue of LBE coupled with the PRC-77 on his back, complemented by the LAW that he refused to discard, accompanied by an additional satchel of 5.56mm magazines, not to mention his standard weapon with magazines, Gable looked like a walking military surplus store.

Ramsy watched the soldier adjust the rocket launcher one second then readjust the ammunition satchel the next, then flex his back muscles to reposition the radio. *Too much shit*, Ramsy thought. *Got to talk to that boy.*

Richter stooped behind a fallen tree. He signaled the men to hold their position. They were approximately thirty meters from the enemy emplacement. From that distance Richter could see the destruction that befell the mercenaries.

Chaos besieged the parapet. Men screamed from their bodies torn open, flesh charred, or both. Some staggered along the trench with draining wounds. Others rambled on with insane ravings. Dead lay within the rampart and beyond it. A few were not injured physically. Richter watched as they stumbled about the earthwork, dazed. He saw that seven or eight of them still looked battleworthy.

Richter lifted two smoke canisters from his pistol belt. He aimed for just in front of the position. He watched the canisters strike the ground after hearing their detonation fuses crack while still in flight. He saw the yellow smoke pour from them. It hovered along the rampart's front. The wind was with them. Richter gave the order.

"Fire! Let's go!"

Team Bravo charged into the devastated position while spraying masses of automatic weapons fire. Richter saw that some of his men lost themselves in the excitement. They charged ahead of him and disappeared into the yellow cloud.

Ramsy wildly yelled obscenities while racing forward. He emptied his weapon twice before reaching the emplacement. Levits was also overwrought by the stimulating thrill of aggression.

He dashed through the blinding smoke and came face to face with a horrified enemy. He saw how the man's eyes went wide. They bulged from fear as Levits descended upon him. He watched the soldier's eyes roll upward, back into their sockets, after lunging the seven-inch bayonet into his chest. To be sure, Levits fired twice into the man. For expedience's sake, he jabbed his right boot into the dead man's face, lively kicking while pulling the blade free. Like a conditioned response Levits resumed his hostile labor.

Gable wobbled to the smokescreen. But upon breaching the cloud he found himself blown to the ground by the concussion of an exploding grenade. In his dazed condition Gable struggled to his feet. He searched for his rifle. It tore from his hands when he encountered the block-busting wall of compressed air. He dropped onto his knees and scrambled about the rampart floor. Gable heard the snap of a round penetrate the sand near him. He felt the particles spray upon his face.

He looked up from the bunker floor and saw his potential murderer step toward him. The soldier's weapon was apparently on semiautomatic, as the man popped off a single round at a time. Gable roared out an, "Oh shit!" while dropping backward. As he felt his radio connect with the sandy bottom, Gable reached up and behind him. He pulled a butcher knife from between the radio and his shoulder blades. In one graceful movement Gable lunged it over his head. The double-edged piece shot through the air and into the soldier. Once beyond immediate danger, Gable returned his attention to the misplaced weapon. He quickly found his rifle after a few desperate finger jabs into the sand. As Gable continued the fight, the sergeant major yelled on.

Before reaching the smoke, Ramsy had already expended two of his four magazines. At the rampart he quickly used his last two. He swiftly unholstered his .45. He thumbed back on the hammer and sent one of the slow-moving projectiles into the right shoulder of a man in the trench. He watched how the soldier spun around before slamming his face into the back wall of the fortification. Ramsy glanced to his right and pitied the poor creature coming at him.

The sergeant major reaimed his pistol. He popped off two slugs into the advancing soldier. The rounds struck the man center mass. He watched as the man lifted off the ground. Upon observing the dead soldier reconnect with the earth, Ramsy considered his dwindling ammo. He knew he had only four or five rounds remaining. Ramsy heard his name yelled out. He looked behind him.

Richter yelled at Ramsy while tossing a full magazine of ammunition. The sergeant major caught the clip on the fly. After replacing the .45 into its holster Ramsy picked up his discarded M-16 and quickly inserted the magazine.

"Thanks, Alex!"

Richter made his way to the machine gun. Reaching the

weapon, he found the gunner assigned to it and an officer dead. The captain pulled on the gun's bolt, trying to chamber a fresh round. The bolt jammed. He yanked on it three times before angrily admitting the gun was useless. But he did not consider it for long, as two soldiers rushed him from out of the bush.

They came from nowhere, he thought. Richter reached for his rifle while wondering if there were more hostiles concealed within the trees. He took aim on one, easily placing two rounds in him. He popped off three rounds at the other, but for some reason the man did not drop. Before he could get off a fourth shot, the blood-covered soldier descended on him.

The mindless man plunged himself on top of Richter. The captain watched as his bayonet buried all the way up to its grip. Richter fired a shot directly into his stomach, but it had little effect on the soldier's adrenaline-pumping frenzy.

The heavy man tried to stab him with a sheath knife. Richter gripped both of his wrists, trying to keep the blade from lacerating his neck and face. The soldier made three attempts to slash him before the captain felt the dying man's strength drain. After another two near misses Richter watched the man lapse into death. The captain rolled the heavy body off of him after a second, more substantial shove. When he lunged the cadaver to one side Richter noticed the abrupt absence of gunfire.

He picked himself off of the rampart floor and rose to the gun emplacement's edge. Richter looked over the top and saw that the firefight was over. But even in the semitranquillity of the firefight's aftermath, an all-encompassing image imprinted in his mind.

The black smoke from the burning JP-4 mingled with the yellow mist emerging from the smoke canisters. When the clouds converged it created a dirty yellow-gold vapor that hovered close to the ground. The offshore breeze rolled in and caused the repugnant-looking mist to rise up then curl over and back into itself. The wispy eddies appeared like some kind of mystical disturbance. Through the death cloud Richter spotted the intermittent images of his warriors.

It looked like something out of a book of legends. As the men stood on the battlefield the golden mist whirled about them and at their feet. They were visible one moment then gone the next, only to reappear even more sinister looking. The dead and wounded lay at their feet. The wail of the still living sounded, rising from out of the vapor. It rose through the mist like the agonizing voices of those condemned to the Styx. Whatever doubts he had of them were gone. These men were the epitome of professional soldiering. They were Satan's Centurions.

Eight

"Sergeant Major!" Richter yelled.

"Sir!" Ramsy replied.

Another burst of ocean wind swept across the beach. It agitated the golden cloud hovering over the battle site. Richter watched Ramsy step through the mist and felt better in knowing Cliff was all right. He looked like one of the Four Horsemen of the Apocalypse. Richter decided that it didn't matter which one. Anyone of them got the job done. When he spotted Alex in the trench Ramsy also felt easier.

"What's up, Captain?" he indifferently asked.

"Check the ship," Richter ordered. "There may still be survivors. And have the men search their kills." He gestured to Pinto's body. "Maybe we can find out who's trying to kill us—from our side."

"Sir," Ramsy said. He turned and faced the men. "All right, lads. Check your kills. See if there's anything we can use. Stan, get back to the chopper. Wait!" Ramsy faced Richter. "Captain, you want a dustoff?"

"Yeah. We're not done yet."

Upon hearing his reply Ramsy held a long analyzing stare on Alex. There was no plausible reason, that he knew of, for moving to the exchange site. Their cover was obviously blown since before leaving the staging area. The idea of going forward with a gutted mission and reaping some success from it seemed far-fetched at best.

Alex was not an illogical officer. He frequently knew precisely what to do given a tactical condition. But this time it seemed to Ramsy that Alex was somewhat lacking in his judgment. Either that or his longtime comrade was not telling everything. The sergeant major opted for the latter. Ramsy turned to Marcoli.

"Tell the pilot to radio in a dustoff." Ramsy looked about the field of dead and wounded. "We'll need two medevacs."

"Got it, Sergeant Major," Stan said.

Marcoli wheeled about and darted for the chopper. He made five steps.

"Wait!"

Stan tried to stop midstep and almost tripped over his feet. He froze while looking over his right shoulder.

"And tell that highfalutin chopper jock to use the Nineline aeromedevac," Ramsy said. "No point in telling the neighborhood any more than we have to."

"Roger, Sergeant Major."

Stan headed down the beach while Team Bravo began its intelligence survey.

Each man tended to the bodies nearest him. He searched through the uniform and personal effects of each casualty. He hunted for scrap-paper strip maps, identification documents, written evidence that might establish a link between the government and Zorrilla. Anything to help them know more about their present circumstance and to improve their chances for future success. While Ramsy gave Marcoli his instructions, Gable happened to overhear.

"Hey, Sergeant Major!" he yelled. "What do we need a dustoff for? We can take the live ones back with us. There's only a couple. We could cram 'em in."

Ramsy spotted Gable through the thinning smoke. He thought about what Alex had said. He wanted to tell Gable the truth. Being honest with your men was always the best policy. Always keep them informed, so they know what they're doing and why they're doing it. It was misinformation that broke down morale. It caused the men to focus more on rumor instead of concentrating on the moment. Ramsy did not like this precarious situation. The sergeant major gave the best answer he could.

"'Cause if I know the captain, we're not going back."

Ramsy returned to the intelligence survey. Up to this point, however, neither the DEA nor or their contract teams could uncover a paper or person trail leading to governmental influence. Most of their prisoners proved fruitless as well.

No matter how afraid of incarceration, or even of death, the captured seldom bargained for less. Like organized crime anywhere, there always existed a well-informed network from the prisoner to those he betrayed—a network of men who could make his loved ones the victims of his treachery. Ramsy glanced up from one of his kills and saw a peculiar image break from the brush.

First Lieutenant Masterson stepped beyond the treeline. He had removed his flight helmet and replaced it with a steel pot. A flak vest loosely hung over his meshed flight vest. He tightly held to his Smith & Wesson .38 revolver as he made his way through the bodies. His face showed a look of awe as he forced himself to step through the carnage. Sanford was the second to notice the gun-toting flyboy.

He looked up from his third body, a live one named Raphael. He eyed Masterson coming from out of the trees. He saw the look of astonishment on the officer's face.

"Hey Lieutenant! You can put that piece away, now."

Sanford eyed upon the nearly dead man at his feet. "You're about ten minutes too late."

Masterson glanced in Sanford's direction but quickly brushed off the derogatory remark. He did not need this shit, he thought. He was aviation and had no affinity for the blood that infantrymen lived and died by. When he reached the gun emplacement Masterson blared out his words. The officer unconsciously tried to cover the fear that consumed him.

"Captain!" he loudly began. "One of your men said you wanted a dustoff."

Richter slowly unfolded one of the three documents he lifted from Pinto's body. He pondered over the paper. Richter could not speak or read Spanish but he pondered anyway. He took another ten seconds then looked up from the blood-stained script.

"Huh? Yeah, Lieutenant. What was it you wanted to know?"

Richter immediately returned his attention to the document. Masterson gritted his teeth under his tightened lips. He believed that his regular army status, as opposed to Richter's renegade station, afforded him greater respect.

"What for?"

"What for—what, Lieutenant?"

"Why do we need a dustoff? We can bring the wounded back in my ship."

Like Sanford, Gable could not contain himself.

"Way ahead of you, Lieutenant!" he said.

Richter looked to Gable and saw the soldier kneeling over a kill. He did not believe Gable's comment was called for. He did not want to correct the man, however. That was Cliff's job. He looked up at the pilot.

"Leave the team behind? We still have a mission."

Richter reached down and took hold of another kill. He lifted the body from the rampart floor rather than kneel over it. He supported the dead weight against the wall with his left arm. As Richter resumed his survey, Masterson tried to comprehend the captain's intent.

"Mission!" he yelled. "Look around you, Captain. Half

your team is gone. You're missioned out!"

Richter clung to his usual calm demeanor. He decided to provide the officer a lukewarm explanation. Not that he warranted it, but for the sake of intercommand compatibility he decided to indulge the gentleman. He continued searching the cadaver.

"First off, Lieutenant, we didn't lose half the team. The only team member in that ship was Sergeant Assaf. Secondly, we have an alternate objective."

"Alternate objective!" Masterson blared. "No one told me anything about an alternate objective."

"You didn't have a need to know."

Masterson bit his lip. He tried to maintain at least a small measure of military courtesy. It was bad enough that he had to take orders from someone who was no longer in the chain of command, but to be treated as if he possessed no worth by a freelancer was unacceptable.

"I'm calling higher, Captain. I don't know anything about this, and when I plotted headings it was for one mission, only."

The boy is going to fight me, Richter thought. *He is honestly going to stand there and argue with me.* The captain took a moment and considered the pilot's words. As the seconds passed, his anger intensified at an exponential rate. He did not have time for this. There were too many mission essentials to think about, and this lieutenant was not one of them.

Using both hands, Richter abruptly thrust the corpse down into the trench. He disposed of the body as if it was an empty trash can. He glared up at the officer with eyes that revealed a deadly intolerance.

"Lieutenant!" he lashed. "I refuse to get into an intercommand pissing contest. It may be your ship, but it is my mission. Now, you will go back to that bird, and you will call in a dustoff. Then, you will wait for the next mission brief. Are we clear on that concept, Lieutenant?"

Masterson went rigid. He saw there was no compromise in

Richter. It was Richter's mission and he was a part of it. Richter was combat. He was combat support, and that distinction made the command structure all too clear.

"Roger!" he defiantly yelled.

"Out!" Richter retaliated.

Richter turned from the pilot. He reached into the trench and took hold of the body he discarded only seconds before. He yanked the cadaver off the pit bottom and slammed the lifeless flesh against the wall. Masterson saw there was no point in continuing.

The captain's eyes told him everything. They left him cold—drained. The frigid, icy blue eyes bore down from tightly flexed lids. *Eyes*, Masterson thought, *that could look upon your dead body just as easily as your live one*. He stepped down the beach. The sergeant major quickly followed after him.

"Sir! Can I have a word?"

Masterson stopped to see who called for him. Upon seeing Ramsy he turned away and resumed his trek to the chopper. "Yeah—what?" Masterson slowed his pace, but made it obvious to the top NCO that he expected Ramsy to follow after him. To Masterson's surprise, however, the sergeant major rested his large right arm upon his shoulder. Before Masterson had time to react he found himself guided to the treeline.

"Ya know, sir," Ramsy began. "The captain's a man with extensive combat experience. True enough, he's not a regular like you anymore. He still deserves your cooperation. You could show a little more military respect. In front of the men, if nothing else."

Masterson prudently removed the sergeant major's limb from his shoulder. The officer turned and faced off with the man.

"That I call you sergeant major and him captain is merely out of courtesy for what you both once were. What? You think I'm going to start calling him sir?"

The pilot wheeled about. He stepped down the beach, leaving the sergeant major to himself. Ramsy simply remained silent and watched the arrogant young man walk off. As he stood there he reminded himself how there were ways to fix little boys with attitude problems.

An unforeseen M-67 fragmentation grenade, an inconspicuous trip wire connected to a M-18 Claymore mine or a 5.56mm round coming from who knows where—all techniques to not necessarily kill but to maim. *Techniques to remove the belligerent man from the mission site until his attitude is realigned. And that's what its all about*, Ramsy told himself. As he watched the stiff-ass lieutenant move further down the beach, one word kept flashing through Ramsy's military mind.

"Attitude," he said aloud.

Team Bravo provided the wounded what expedient aid it could. But no one expected a man to give up his own field dressing to aid another. The decontamination kit in the M-17 protective mask carrier, and the one field dressing toted as part of the LBE, were the only self-administering aids. They were designed for the bearing soldier and to be used by the individual for himself, only. After giving what assistance it could, Team Bravo returned to the chopper.

The men gathered in a half-circle at the helicopter. Some stood while others stooped or sat in the sand. Richter stood opposite the men. Masterson sat in the aircraft's port doorway. His copilot leaned against the fuselage immediate to his left. Ramsy stood to the right of the group. He noticeably separated himself from them. He eyed each of his men to insure no one underwent a wandering mental drift.

In the sand between himself and the men Richter constructed a terrain display. It provided the team a sketchy reconstruction of the ground he expected the men to traverse. As none of them were aware of a second or alternate objective Richter realized an explanation was in order. He was about to begin the brief when distracted by two medevac helicopters. They came from out of the northwest sky.

The aircraft landed about fifty meters from where the men stood. The dry sand swept off the shore. The rotors sucked the granules into and through the flushing downwash, wildly scattering the particles. The men covered their eyes while turning away from the flying grit. They protected their eyes and exposed skin until hearing the whinedown of the turbines. When they faced the birds the team watched as a medical aid team from each helicopter disembarked. Ramsy watched the young men and women leap from the ships.

They dashed up the beach, some carrying stretchers. They headed to where Team Bravo waited. One soldier, a buck sergeant, rushed up to the sergeant major. She wanted to know where the reported wounded were. She didn't know Ramsy. She didn't know anyone on the team. She chose the sergeant major because he was obviously the oldest in the group.

"Where's the wounded?"

"Just over that berm, Sergeant," Ramsy said. "You got just under an hour to get our dead and their wounded out of here. If not, you'll be looking down the barrel of an El Totumo policeman's gun."

He pointed with the muzzle of his rifle. The buck sergeant immediately headed inland. As the junior NCO raced off she yelled for the medical teams to follow. Both teams instantly complied and ran to where the dead and wounded lay. Richter looked to his men.

"This is the alternate objective—in the southern Rio Balsas region," he said.

Richter pointed to a terrain reference roughed out in the wet sand.

"That's near the southern border, ain't it, Captain?" James asked.

"Roger," he replied. "I can give you an idea of the terrain with this. Jungle. Some hills. Some steep, but it's nothing we haven't overcome in the past."

"What's there, Captain?" Marcoli asked.

"Same thing as the original objective. But by now it's no surprise to any of you that they knew we were coming."

"Yeah, no shit!" Gable broke in. "What the hell's going on, Captain? What happened to security?"

Before he could answer Gable, Richter was again distracted. It was the medic buck sergeant. The aidewoman stood at the berm's summit.

"Hey!" she yelled. "These are Colombian wounded."

"That's because all of our people are dead," Ramsy said. "Any other questions?"

"Ah—no—sir."

"Then put our dead in one bird and the wounded in the other. Make sure at least one of those wounded stay alive." Ramsy commented to himself aloud. "Until after interrogation, anyway." He noticed Richter waiting to resume the brief. "Oh! Sorry sir. Please, continue."

Richter considered his words. He wanted to be forthright without committing himself to an ass-kicking by Cliff. They were honest men, for the most part. He did not like withholding crucial information, but it was the only way Reiner and he could limit the suspects.

"There's a breach," he began. "We have a leak. I wasn't going to say anything, but after what happened out here I think all of you need to know what you're dealing with."

"Great! A traitor," Levits blared out. "Not only do we have to fight what's in front of us, we have to watch our backs, too?"

"So what else is new?" Richter said under his breath.

"You, ah...You don't think it's any of us—do you?" Marcoli cautiously asked.

"No," Richter said. "Not at all. There were only four men who knew of this mission prior to the briefing this morning: myself, the sergeant major, Reiner and Colonel Treadwell."

"Why would DEA backstab us?" Marcoli asked.

"I don't think they did, Stan."

"Well, what are you saying, Captain?" Levits persisted.

"I know it wasn't the sergeant major or myself," Richter went on. "I don't believe it was DEA. Reiner and I planned for the second objective in the event of this. His sources reported two major buys within twelve hours, some seventy miles apart. Reiner and I were the only two who knew of the secondary mission. Four knew of the primary. If we're hit in the second zone, Reiner's our man."

"Or you," Sanford said.

"Yeah, okay, Sanford, or me." He decided to keep talking. "If not, that puts us back at the primary, and that leaves only one name in question."

"It's a loose theory, Captain," Ramsy said. "Why don't they just have the exchanges at the same time seventy miles apart? Why don't we send out two teams to hit both locations?"

"The pilots knew where we were going," Marcoli said. "They had the headings."

"Flight operations didn't give them to us until 0430 this morning," the copilot said.

"Who had 'em before that?" Levis asked.

"Treadwell," the copilot hesitantly answered.

"To your first question, Sergeant Major," Richter cut in. "I don't know. The word Reiner got was that the second exchange would take place at approximately 2100 hours tonight, and that it would be here." Richter jabbed his bayonet into sand. "The reason behind using one team is simple enough. The fewer people who knew what Reiner and I were up to, the more likelihood of mission success, or at least of pinpointing the breach in our security. It's all we have right now."

"The colonel? Treadwell?" Gable asked. "Oh, man! I'm gonna waste that fucker."

"You and me both," Bard added.

"That's enough out of you, Gable," Masterson broke in. He swiftly turned to the captain. "You mean the colonel? Is that what you're saying?"

"Oh, I humbly apologize, sir," Gable cut back.

The team, except for Ramsy and Richter, began to laugh.

"Can it!" Ramsy countered, reducing the belligerent NCOs to silence.

"I'm not saying anything, now, Lieutenant," Richter resumed. "Right now it's all conjecture."

"Colonel Treadwell is one of the finest officers I've ever served under. He's a hero, for christsake."

Richter saw the officer was hostile to any notion that his

senior should be a suspect. It was understandable that Masterson would feel that way. Loyalty to a senior in the military, or anywhere else, was always seen as an admirable trait—one that normally rewarded you with advancement.

In time and grade, one came to expect similar loyalty from those of lesser rank. It was a self-perpetuating system of loyalties nurtured by promotions, while those who advanced commanded unbending faithfulness. Knowing Masterson's West Point background, and understanding his dedication to the corps, Richter chose to give a marginal explanation.

"We were all regulars once, Lieutenant. We understand your sense of loyalty. But we're trying to survive under different conditions, now. This isn't Vietnam. We can't just call in artillery and saturate a grid square. We have to think beyond the operation order if we intend to stay alive. Out here we're isolated teams with minimal support, from an army that doesn't care a whole hell of a lot about us. We suspect everyone if we're going to stay alive."

"Roger," Levits added.

"It can't be the colonel. He—"

"Money changes people, Lieutenant," Richter said. "Greed has a way of grinding at your gut."

"Do you speak from experience, Captain?" Masterson countered.

Everyone froze upon hearing the pilot's reckless question. Even his copilot looked on in awe. Ramsy went numb. The men of Team Bravo did not know Richter well, but they did know of his dedication to what they did and his protectiveness of them. He was loyal to them; therefore, they reciprocated in kind. It was the one principal human mechanism that allowed a group of men to coexist and survive under hostile conditions.

Training and discipline were, of course, pertinent factors in mission success, but loyalty to one another was the cement that bound a group. The lieutenant attempted to chip away at the mortar in suggesting less than honorable motives by the second principle binding force of the team.

Ramsy glanced toward the group. He saw that every man

gazed upon the lieutenant. Some stood with their mouths hung open. Some showed hatred for the outsider's arrogance. Worst yet, the sergeant major saw that Alex was at a point of eliminating the annoying roach altogether.

Richter also found himself stiffened by the lieutenant's comment. But his rigidness was not so much out of shock as it was by repressed hostility. He incurred the man's insubordination. He endured Masterson's arrogance, but he would not withstand the officer's declaration that his motives might not have been honorable. Richter unflapped the holster at his hip.

Ramsy watched the captain undo the flap on his holster. He saw Alex slowly lower his hand onto the pistol's grip. Richter's tight slitted eyes showed a hard bitterness. Like Ramsy, the rest of the team looked on in horror.

"Oh, my god," Bard said just above a whisper.

Ramsy nervously looked on. He tried to think of a way to defuse the situation. When Richter's weapon was halfway out of its holster Masterson realized what was about to take place. A look of terror shaded over his face. Ramsy looked to the men then back at the captain. He thought a split second more.

"Sir!" Ramsy yelled. He saw Alex's arm freeze. The weapon's barrel partially remained within the leather pouch. Alex massaged the grip with his fingers. "You said something about terrain. We flying in?"

Richter held his glare on the officer. As the lieutenant eyed back he realized just how far the situation had evolved. It was the closest, that he knew of, he had ever come to losing his life. For the first time in his life, he found out what it was like to be held gutturally accountable for his mouth. As the captain lowered the .45 into its holster Masterson gave an obvious sigh of relief. Richter saw the man's reaction and decided it was enough.

Richter was grateful to Cliff for distracting him from blowing the smart ass away, although he concealed it. He reached into his top right pocket and pulled a folded piece of paper from it. Richter shoved the document into the pilot's chest.

"Here's your new coordinates and heading. That's where

you drop us," Richter said. The captain turned and focused on Ramsy. "Yeah, Sergeant Major."

He looked to his top NCO and spotted the look of doubt in Cliff's eyes. A silent acknowledgment transpired between them.

Both realized how infuriated Alex had become and what he almost did. Each was grateful to the other that the incident did not progress further. It was close, and they both knew it.

"We'll fly in but not up to their front door," he went on.

"Oh, man! This sounds like grunt talk to me," Levits said.

"You love it," Ramsy countered.

The team laughed over the sergeant major's remark. The forbidding atmosphere dissipated quickly. No one held a grudge for long under such conditions. They needed each other too much. Masterson looked up from the document.

"This 197-degree heading'll put us back over Panama."

"You need directions, Lieutenant?" Copeland said.

"Enough!" Ramsy counter, again suppressing the group.

"We'll drop about ten clicks out," Richter resumed, "then recon our way to the objective. Terrain's not that hilly, and we've got plenty of time. Remember—until we reach the objective, we're reconnaissance. Whatever we encounter, we'll stop, look, listen, then bypass, Sergeant Major." Richter pulled another paper from his top right pocket. "Here are the new rally point coordinates. Make sure the men know them. Sergeant Gable." Richter reached into the bottom left pocket of his jungle fatigues. From it he lifted a thin tablet. "Your new CEOI extract...Oh, and Reiner's the only one we can communicate with."

"That narrows it down," Marcoli said.

"Yeah," Richter said softly.

Richter abruptly eyed the pilot. He glared at Masterson momentarily and saw that no response was forthcoming—just a cautious look back that suggested the pilot's attitude had undergone a sufficient realignment.

"Okay, Lieutenant," he said, while gesturing toward the aircraft. "Fire it up!"

Nine

Masterson induced ignition while contemplating his near-death experience. He listened to the rotor gradually begin its sweeping pattern. Team Bravo managed inside the helicopter as best as it could.

The men hastily reboarded the ship. They crammed themselves and their gear into its restricted confines. Although no additional mission paraphernalia was brought on board, the less organized stacking of men and equipment proved problematical. So much more restraining that Marcoli grew aggravated by the sweaty backs and shoulders rubbing against him.

He joined the team two months prior to the Rio Caimán Viejo mission. He connected with the team after answering a dubious ad in a survivalists' magazine. After his separation from the regulars, Marcoli had a distasteful four-year episode in the States. He labored to keep his chemical operator's job at Monsanto in St. Louis. But after three tours in the jungle there was nothing else he knew of that gave him the psyche surge of full living.

He normally requested the unwanted point position. Marcoli felt more confident in knowing it was his eyes doing the searching and not some brain-dead troop that might relax when awareness was paramount. There was one other reason. The idea of him being alone, immersed within a chance environment, thrilled him, or so he claimed. He flexed his shoulders and arms, trying to maneuver for more space.

"Where the shit did all the room go, man? Push it over!"

Gable placed Colfield between Marcoli and himself. He remained in the port doorway, his feet dangling outside. To increase his chance for survival, knowing Marcoli was only an arm's reach away, Gable cut off a piece of rappelling line. He tied the cord around his waist and secured the ends to one of the aircraft bulkheads. As Gable settled himself onto the floor, the sergeant major climbed in next to him. His glaring eyes revealed the deep concentration that preoccupied him.

Although tempered for the time being, Masterson was obviously more dedicated to Treadwell than to the team. If it was as Alex suspected, it would only take a thirty-minute flight back to the staging area. The lieutenant could report to Treadwell of what took place at the Rio Caimán Viejo. If Treadwell was their critical shortfall, he could radio the coordinates Alex provided the pilot to those who needed them most. They could be cut to pieces walking into another ambush or waste the team's effort by setting up for nothing at all. Ramsy decided that Alex and he had to talk. As Richter stepped to the door, the sergeant major blocked his path.

"Captain!" he yelled. "We need to talk!"

"About what!"

"Let's take a walk!"

The sergeant major jumped from the aircraft as Richter turned about. The captain headed down the beach. Ramsy caught up and stepped alongside. When they were out of downwash range, Richter turned to Ramsy.

"What's on your mind, Cliff?"

"Alex, we can't let that chopper jock out of our sight. Once he drops us he'll have time to tell Treadwell of the second mission. If your suspicions are right they'll be waiting for us or not show up at all."

Richter looked to the helicopter and saw the lieutenant sitting at the controls. As he held his glare on Masterson, a smile emerged on Richter's face.

"That occurred to me," he said. "He's got a lot of spunk. He could use a little trigger time."

A broad smile emitted from Ramsy's face. He straightened his back. He stood erect and looked at Alex with a tucked-in chin. The sergeant major smacked the captain on his back as a reinforcement for Alex's sound decision. Ramsy let out with a loud laugh. The idea of Masterson's forthcoming and potentially hazardous adventure tickled him. What pleased him the most was that Masterson had no idea of what he was about to embark on. *Fitting*, he thought.

"Couldn't have said it better, Captain," he replied. "But that is going to be one pissed-off young man. Ain't nothing more humiliating for a hotshot flyboy than to be reduced to a grunt."

"I doubt if he'd appreciate the alternative."

The two men returned to the aircraft. Richter took his spot just behind the pilots. Ramsy knelt close to the door. The bird began to rise. The men watched how the beach receded.

The helicopter climbed to ninety feet above the shore. The surf took on a rolling effect instead of the hammering assault the men witnessed while standing on the beach. The white crests fluttered in the breeze. Mist feathered from their tips as the crowns edged forward their fluid bodies.

Ramsy watched how the powerful waves altered in character as the aircraft rose higher. They transformed into playful little wavelets, appearing to massage the sand. Like this mission, he thought, the waves looked as if though they coexisted with the beach, but instead ate away at it with a gorging vengeance.

Like the deceiving tidal thrusts, the generals and politicians in Bogotá and Panama City zealously claimed their willingness to put drug trafficking into remission. They demanded reform on the pretext of a greater good for their people, while cohortly incorporating their own militia as part of the substance distribution mechanism. *Their selected cadre fraudulently ate away at us*, Ramsy thought. *Like the rushing surf on the sand, they are winning*. The aircraft made a fifty-degree pivot starboard. Ramsy watched as the battlefield debris came into view.

Below, he saw what was left of Sergeant Assaf's aircraft. The gutted ship lay on the beach like a dead insect. The torn body lay open in two places, head and tail dismembered. The fiery internal organs spewed flames and smoke. It rose from out of the stumps of the dead bird's severed limbs. The flames lapped to just above the fuselage and charred the olive drab skin to a cindered ash black.

The offshore wind lessened. The smoke ascended on a gentle incline in the form of a collected canting column. It looked to Ramsy like a snake emerging from out of the sand. He saw it arc through the air, seeming to turn its head down to bore back into the earth. Ramsy looked inland from the crash site and spotted the medics attending to the wounded.

The two medevac helicopters rested just up the beach from where the team lifted off. The pilots stood nearby, prepared for a quick departure. Further inland, the medics tended to the wounded. From above, Ramsy saw two medical personnel kneeling next to battle-torn bodies. Each held a bottle of plasma above the wounded as they administered the blood substitute. A few, those who the team believed survived, had obviously died since the battle. Ramsy saw that three men left breathing on the beach had underwent stowage in body bags. The sergeant major looked down the beach from the battle site, to a spot adjacent the fire zone. He eyed the dead.

He counted eleven. All were uniformly lined parallel to

the water. Their feet pointed toward the sea, heads to the trees. The gentle breeze lifted the ponchos off some of the cadavers. Their bullet-riddled bodies lay exposed in the sun.

Bag 'em up fast, boys, he thought. They started to break down almost immediately. It was always the same, Ramsy then consider. He felt the helicopter's nose dip, followed by its acceleration toward their new destination. Always the same merciless carnage, but some how it was different every time.

He had seen blood in the Big War, Korea, Vietnam, and as part of almost every clandestine operation between the more historical events. Each time he witnessed good men die on both sides. The battlefields were different only in terrain. Although the men were frequently dissimilar in name and feature, their ages, their innocence, and their optimistic beliefs in the future were much the same; they had a common desire to leave the fighting behind and to live. Young men who wished they were somewhere else, but for their own reasons unselfishly relinquished their lives. They were so young, he thought. Like himself—like he had been.

How he had survived all these years was anyone's guess. There was no explanation for surviving a battle. Often, he found himself crawling out of a hole or regaining consciousness after the action was over. Or he fought men who were better trained and adapted and, still, after the last bullet, he unexplainably remained standing. A soldier looks around himself and sees the dead and wounded on both sides, and all he can do is ask himself why.

Ramsy viewed straight out from the port door. He gazed upon the elevating terrain and the horizon beyond. He took in the scenery's full intensity while pushing his thoughts of the dead into the far recesses of his mind. He could not allow himself to dwell on it, he commanded. At times it was too much to endure.

Ten

Treadwell stood immediately behind Tommy. He hovered over the specialist's right shoulder. The tacky sweat trickled down the sides of his face. He felt the droplets originate from his temples. He shoved his left hand into his rear pants pocket and pulled a handkerchief from it. He vigorously wiped his face and the top of his short cropped head. It was hot, but the air was also noticeably dead.

For the previous three days no substantial breeze had flushed through the valley. The collected afternoon heat in the canyon made for furnacelike conditions. He felt more drops emerge from his swollen pours. Again, they crept along his face. *This ungodly heat and a goddamned mission. What a combination*, he told himself.

Treadwell looked at the radio. He peered at the mechanism

while soaking up the recurring beads into his rag. He gazed upon the set as if waiting for it to respond to his thoughts. Flustered over his inability to know what took place beyond the perimeter, Treadwell turned away.

He stepped to the tent entrance. He remained within the protection of the overhead canvas. He looked over the encampment and saw the men from the other interdiction teams relaxing in the midday heat. It was customary to allow the men plenty of lax time between their missions. Some played volleyball while others lost themselves in costly games of poker. Some remained to themselves, looking to be in deep contemplation. *Or perhaps not thinking at all*, he speculated.

Treadwell looked beyond the camp proper to the airstrip some two hundred meters away. Initially, the short runway was suppose to be grass covered. It only took one dry season, the one they were then in, to turn the strip into a choking dust bowl. The previous monsoon season gagged it with runoff from the surrounding hills. The seasonal deluge transformed the eight inch thick, oil- and dirt-packed crust into a muddy quagmire. It was not until Captain Richter urged him to request engineer support that the tiny air facility began to measure up. *Richter*, he thought while observing the oscillating heat waves rise from the sunbaked runway supports.

He turned and faced Tommy. He saw the radioman intently listening for a word from Team Bravo. Treadwell felt he already knew the answer, but for the lack of something better he asked anyway.

"Tommy, anything from Richter?"

Treadwell stepped to just behind the radioman.

"Negative, sir. Not since they verified link-up with the medevac."

Treadwell watched the radioman tenderly rotate the frequency selector knob. Tommy slipped it a few megahertz beyond the primary frequency then reversed it a few increments below, before returning it to the spectrum established by the mission CEOI. He saw Tommy perform the sensitive probing four times. As he watched the conscientious technician explore the waveband twice more, Treadwell saw that Tommy was in no better shape than he.

The specialist wearily sat hunched over the fieldtable. His extended right arm dripped with sweat. The droplets fell from his right elbow and splattered upon the radiolog. His soaked hair strands clumped from the adhesive action of his body fluids. They formed thick, stringlike locks curling up behind his ears and at the back of his neck. The afternoon heat caused the young specialist to go drowsy. His eyelids uncontrollably lowered then suddenly raised while he tried to refocus on the waveband indicator. The boy was tired. *Eighteen years old and tired*, Treadwell thought. *How could that be*? He decided not to make anything out of it.

"Well, try to…"

Before able to complete his instruction the colonel stopped and looked down. A soldier charged into the operations tent. It was one of the personnel clerks assigned to the staging area's S1 section. He did not recall the frail-looking boy's name. There was a fearful look on his face. Treadwell glared at him from a half-foot advantage. He realized the clerk was somewhat shaken by almost colliding with a senior officer. The colonel gazed at the young man and waited for him to say something, until it became evident that nothing was forthcoming.

"What!" he said.

The clerk became rattled by the commander's terse manner.

"Si-sir, the S1 just received this message from SOUTHCOM Red Cross." He unbuttoned his shirt and pulled an envelope from inside his jacket. "It's for Captain Richter. It has a flash priority, sir."

Treadwell took the brown envelope and saw that it was sealed. He studied the package while flipping it between his fingers. He looked at the clerk and saw the boy studying him. Coming from the Red Cross meant some kind of an emergency. It usually indicated a serious illness in the family, but more likely a death.

Treadwell jammed his index finger under the glued flap and tore open the envelope. As he quickly skimmed through the message the colonel grew hesitant by its contents.

"Damn," he said under his breath. He turned to the clerk. "How many people know about this?"

"Just the S1 and yourself, sir," the clerk said. "Captain Laury made sure none of us found out what it was."

Treadwell returned his focus onto the document. Again, he studied every wrenching word. As he dwelled on the message's brutal truth he noticed the clerk shrewdly leaning into him. The colonel swiftly withdrew the paper while abruptly facing the soldier once more.

"Good! I don't want anybody to—"

Again, the colonel was sharply cut off. This time, however, it came from where Tommy sat. It was a voice on the radio. Tommy immediately alerted Treadwell.

"Sir, we got traffic!"

Treadwell stared at the wire-mesh speaker cover. He anxiously wanted to know why his medical support people were not on their way back. Even more, he wanted to know the captain's status. He listened intently as the medevac team leader's voice pierced the speaker cover.

"Lion. This is Panther. We are departing evac site. Returning your location. Over."

Treadwell, too anxious to wait for his radio technician to do his job, yanked the microphone from Tommy's hand. He pressed the squelch button while raising the phone to his lips.

"Panther. This is Lion. Have Leopard contact me ASAP. Over."

"Negative, Lion," the medic said. "Leopard departed area five minutes ago."

Treadwell pondered momentarily. He wondered why Richter did not notify Tommy of Team Bravo's return flight. *If not Richter, at least Masterson*, he thought. He envisioned a multitude of possibilities the persistent captain might embark on.

"Then he's en route to this location? Over," Treadwell

asked.

"Unknown," the medic answered. "Also, Leopard has radio trouble—unable to communicate. Over."

Unknown? It made little sense to him that his medical team leader would not know. If Richter had radio trouble he could simply let the medevac team know he was en route to the camp. Was there a bigger problem? Treadwell wondered. Was there a problem at all?

He pressed the squelch button while searching for the right question.

"We—well, what direction did he go off in? Over."

"Southwest. Over," she said.

Conscious of what just took place, Tommy quickly broke in. He wanted to point out the predisposed colonel's indeliberate but possibly menacing error. He swiftly turned in his chair to face the commander.

"Sir, communications breach," he said. Tommy quickly followed through with an explanation. The technician knew that being right was not enough to get away with putting Treadwell in his place. "If monitoring, sir, they now know which way the captain's heading from the beach action."

Treadwell bore down on Tommy with hard eyes. For a split second he became infuriated by the daring boy's curt manner. *He just wanted to know*, Treadwell thought. The colonel glanced to the personnel clerk and spotted a look of doubt on the soldier's face. He eyed the conscientious but bold radio technician. He knew Tommy was right in his COMSEC measure, but he still needed to know what the self-minded Richter was up to. And Ramsy was no damned better.

Their records showed that the two men recruited out of the Cleveland office. From there, Richter and Ramsy spent a week at DEA headquarters in Arlington, Virginia. There, the men underwent induction and orientation on the region of operation and mission parameters. After their speedy initiation the two were inconspicuously removed from Arlington. They showed up one month before the establishment of the staging area.

He met the two men at Headquarters SOUTHCOM, and quickly found out the sergeant major and the captain were inseparable. He did not think much of Richter, knowing his background. He believed highly in the nobly decorated NCO, however. If there was any drawback to Ramsy, Treadwell concluded early on, it was the aging soldier's years. Richter was another story.

Treadwell admitted that although far from the finest junior officer that ever served under him, Richter did have a quality. Most men of Richter's years and background were by then majors or lieutenant colonels like himself. Because of an untimely incident during his last month in Vietnam, the captain had to forego his next higher grade and ultimately an orthodox military career. It was Richter's tenacious quality that suited him for this work.

Whatever it was that motivated Richter it had a dramatic effect on the officer. In some cases to the extreme. Unlike the other team leaders, Richter was not inclined to terminate an operation when pursuing it appeared fruitless. The other team leaders were more Hessian inclined and often claimed that to move deeper into the bush without adequate combat support was too risky. In the mountains the small teams were vulnerable to bandits, hostile villagers, government soldiers, as well as the profiteering cartel henchmen. Even the forbidding rain forest proved a challenge for survival. But Richter was more mission than survival oriented. And that goddamned Ramsy.

Like his team leader, Ramsy was a soldier unto himself. He moved more by his own will than by the limits of mission parameters. Their close relationship was obvious to those who came in close contact with them. Apparently, a bonding out of blood and steel, Treadwell determined. It made the two inseparable and at times highly troublesome. But it was more than that, some claimed.

There were those who felt that Richter and Ramsy had surpassed mere camaraderie, bound by something more than the customary loyalty or fidelity that evolves out of a combat experience. Ramsy never married. He had left behind all connection to his previous life except for an occasional letter to his sister. Richter came up through the ranks from private E1. He had a strong NCO background before attending OCS and looked strikingly younger than he actually was. It made for a set of variables that germinated a kindred seed.

Ramsy was twenty years older than Richter. Coupled with his many years of in-the-trench experience, enhanced by a strong self-image as a tutor of organized hostility, he subconsciously took on a protective and nurturing course when first meeting the junior officer. Most saw a not-so-unusual camaraderie between the two. But to those more acute, able to catch the look between them from across a bar room or a bunker, there was no question that a tribal kinship evolved.

Richter was keenly sensitive to the sergeant major's subconscious paternal needs and grateful for the reassuring wisdom and loyalty that came from this bond. He readily relinquished any alleged military status to retain the strong bond between them. They were trouble, Treadwell thought.

He squeezed the squelch button and spoke rapidly into the microphone.

"Panther. Lion. Break communication. Head for home. Over."

"Roger. Out," she replied.

Treadwell angrily tossed the microphone onto the fieldtable. He watched as the young technician jolted back from the table's edge. Treadwell felt foolish for frightening the boy. At the same time, however, a rage raced through him. He needed to know what the derelict captain was up to. He lowered his head, positioning his face only inches from the technician's. His eyes bulged.

"First off, Specialist, it is acceptable to transmit in the clear if immediacy is required. Secondly, as your commander you do not interrupt me when I am communicating with my people in the field." For a flash of a second Treadwell considered what he just said. *The boy doesn't need this shit*, he decided. "Thirdly..." Treadwell's eyes went soft, his voice lowered. "Thanks, Tommy. Keep me on my toes."

He gave Tommy a reassuring pat on the shoulder before turning away. He stepped to the entrance of the operations tent. As before, Treadwell remained just within the rolled back tent flaps. He looked over the encampment. *That crazy captain's off to somewhere*, he told himself. Off to somewhere to make trouble for someone. Submerged in deep thought, Treadwell forgot the radioman and personnel clerk were still within hearing distance.

"What the hell's going on out there?"

Eleven

The 197-degree heading aligned the aircraft on a south-southwest path. From the Rio Caimán Viejo, the ship flew over the Golfo de Urabá. It brushed just above the access to the Brazo Matuntugo upon closing with the delta. Richter gazed upon the depositing system. He saw the leaner sediment-rich vein branching from the Rio Atrato. The muddier hinterland waters spewed from the great artery. Its heavier brown silted water invaded the crystal fluid of the gulf in the form of tumbling dirt clouds.

The ship resumed over the delta and traversed the Brazo León. It skimmed the Bahía Marirrio before reentering the north Colombian mainland just west of the Rio Suriquillo. The ship increased its altitude to escape the peaks of the Serranía del Darién chain. After a tight negotiation of the tree-covered range the helicopter slipped down the west face of the arc, into the lowlands of Darién Provincia in Panama. Their aircraft grazed the treetops, flying knap of the earth. Richter viewed the lush vegetation and an occasional rock formation.

He guessed they were about eighty kilometers southeast of the staging area, well into Darién Province. The region was known as the lowlands. The rolling jungle-covered hills, however, were intermittently broken by rock outcroppings. The fertile rain forest was rich with *cativo*, *orey,* and *mango*. He watched as the ship popped over the crest of a moderate ridge then slid down between two perpendicular spines. Richter envisioned the many acres of coca the jungle hid from view. Morality made little difference. Beside soldiering, it was the best poor man's game in the country.

Beneath the jungle canopy was a multicultured people made up of a mosaic of racial origins. The Cuna Indians, the small bands who migrated over the Cordillera de San Blas, sporadically populated the region along with the Chocoe Indians, who were indigenous to the locale. Africans brought to Panama during the colonial times filtered into the forests to merge with the natives. The Spanish two hundred years earlier, who explored and exploited the land, united with and into the tribes and villages they came upon. Except for the Cuna Indians of the *San Blas Comarca* there were few who possessed an intact cultural line. There was no telling who was a part of your family down there, he thought. Just like America. If there was a common denominator among the people of the region, it was poverty. Zorrilla insured it.

The cartel aristocracy was a network of mostly patrilineal-linked families in diminishing orders of importance and control. The regional controllers recruited help from the local villages—men, and some women, who sought more for themselves than a mere scratching out existence from the forest. The laborers were seldom permitted upward mobility within the controlling circle. Marriage was a political, financial, power and trust issue more than a union out of human regard. The workers labored as harvesters, processors, or as trailblazers to haul the semirefined cocaine through the mountains. There was no tolerance for a rising star unless he was a part of the principle dynasty.

Villages decimated by economic ruin were sometimes duped into incorporation. The human resources culminated into small production units comprised of twenty to thirty villagers. Although baited with the notion they could achieve financial surety, it never materialized. They remained the same as they were looked upon—as peasants. Ultimately, the enticed workers slipped into a condition of slavery, controlled by both Zorrilla's enforcers and the regional officials. Whole villages were degraded to a labor-camp mentality. Once brought into line they were helpless to fight off the hold of the regional drug lord and the supporting political framework. Richter became distracted upon hearing Masterson's voice.

"Leopard. Will arrive DZ in nine minutes. Ready your drop rigging."

"Negative," Richter said. "DZ is now LZ. I repeat, LZ. You will land aircraft."

"What?" Masterson excitedly countered. "You crazy? If you're right they may be waiting for us down there."

"They think the mission's scrubbed. Put us down in a clearing close to the coordinates."

"Your team is suppose to rappel in," Masterson said. "I can't risk the ship."

Oh, this boy is trying me. Of all the bullshit issues to come up with, the safety of the bird is the least on his mind. Richter pressed the mouthpiece to his lips, shouting into the circuit.

"Panther! Wait one. Out!"

Richter angrily disconnected the communications jack from his helmet. The cord flung to the opposite side of the cabin. He pulled off the flight helmet, dropping it onto the cabin floor. He replaced his jungle hat before leaning forward for one more intercommand confrontation. He stuck his head well into the cockpit section.

"Lieutenant!" he yelled. "How many times do you have to have a .45 in your face until you get the message?"

Masterson looked up at the captain and saw that peculiar look in the officer's eyes. He glanced to his copilot and searched for a sign from the FNG that would suggest an inkling of support. Like before, all Masterson found was a glare of uncertainty on the wide-eyed assistant's face. *Nothing*, he thought. *Absolutely nothing.*
"All right, Captain!" he yelled. "Whatever you say."
"Well, thank you, Lieutenant."
The captain returned his focus forward. Like Masterson, he scanned the jungle for a break in the trees. The aircraft maneuvered at treetop level, skimming just above the younger growth. Occasionally, the ship's skids came in contact with the seedlinglike limbs, brushing them aside. As Richter preoccupied himself with finding an LZ he became conscious of the copilot's glare. He noticed the second lieutenant in his peripheral vision.

He was a new pilot out of Fort Rucker, in-country for only seven weeks and more affectionately known as the Rucker Rookie. He attended the University of Oklahoma. He graduated with a B.S. in psychology and commissioned a second lieutenant through the school's ROTC program. From college he was Fort Benning-bound for infantry officer basic. He headed for Rucker for the rotary pilot's course immediately thereafter. When the army handed him his dream sheet, he selected Panama as his choice of duty. He thought highly of the military for being so considerate. Upon arriving at Tocumen Airfield, however, it became apparent he would not enjoy the highlights of the country.

He heard about the cushy canal zone reconnaissance flights. They were suppose to entail routine daily junkets over the wide security zone paralleling the waterway. Simple security flights sporadically interrupted by shuttles of colonels, generals, or admirals from the city to the beach. Or maybe a quick shot into the interior and back, so the brass could maintain their flight pay status. That's what it was suppose to be.

Three days after arriving in-country, he found himself on

a truck, bouncing over forbidding roads and fording streams that seemed impassable. "I'm a pilot, for christsake," he remembered saying, "and they wouldn't even fly me in." By the time he arrived at the isolated encampment, a five-hour truck ride that could be flown in less than forty minutes, his high expectation of a choice tour reduced to a grumbling, no-alternative situation. Upon observing the inhabitants of the camp he acknowledged his doom.

This wasn't an army installation, he told himself. It was an outpost for Attila the Hun. In the first two weeks of his new assignment he witnessed two broken arms and a compound fracture of a left collar bone, three shootings, and one stabbing—all in separate incidents and all resulting from arguments between their own men. He was horrified upon seeing a scalp. The long black locks dangled from the pistol belt of a proud Team Golf member. He recalled how the clumped strands extended almost to the man's knee. They brushed against his left thigh as he walked.

One ill-minded man nicknamed Lizard, now dead, acquired the distinction because he liked to crawl through the brush looking for someone to pounce on. Lizard always claimed to taste the blood of his kills, but no one ever witnessed the barbaric act. He was not a large man, but no one caused him aggravation. Everyone was aware of the metal plate in his head that protected what was left of his brain. He was quiet but efficient, willing to shoot anything you pointed him toward. He never spoke to Lizard. That would be too risky. If by chance he said the wrong thing Lizard could go off his head. As the time the half-minded soldier climbed a four-hundred-foot hill to bay at the moon.

He could be heard throughout the valley and likely the next one as well. The men in the camp heard Lizard's eerie howl echoing between the hills. They thought of it as a unique change from the usual between mission boredom. Some of them barked up the hill while laughing, drinking, dancing, or vomiting on themselves, each soundly taking advantage of his quality time. All he could do was stand by and watch. No one had the courage to quell the maniacs with weapons. *And now,* he thought, *I got this demented grunt officer standing over me. The same one who stood by and smiled while the crazy men roared back up at Lizard. What the hell is my life coming to? What do you do when nobody gives a shit about anything?*

He looked over his left shoulder, up to Richter. He did not want to stare but could not pull his eyes from the image. He felt damned threatened by the mad officer's willingness to kill them. He simply glared at the man, in awe over the grunt's audacious and deadly demands.

Richter caught the copilot peering at him. The captain swiftly lowered his head until his face was only a few inches from the copilot's.

"What are you looking at?"

Richter watched as the nervous copilot quickly looked forward. He turned his head so fast it appeared as if he might twist it off. The captain briefly held his glare on the young man then faced forward to the jungle ahead. As he eagerly sought for a place to land, Richter could not help but feel some guilt.

The copilot couldn't have been over twenty-two years old. Richter recalled that at that age the army promoted him to corporal. It was not the copilot's intent to upset anyone. He was too new. The man was still trying to find himself amidst all the ridiculous crap that went on around him. He did not expect a combat tour in Panama, much less Colombia. The idea of losing his life over a drug lord, or by a freelancer contracted by his own government, was the furthest thing from his fresh military mind.

The captain glanced to the fledgling copilot. He watched as the man resumed his vigilance of the aircraft instruments. He saw how the man skimmed over the air chart neatly folded and attached to a clipboard. *Busy work,* Richter thought. The coldness melted from his eyes.

Somewhere within him a sense of compassion began to emerge. His hard features transformed. A hint of a smile evolved. His amusement over the second lieutenant's show of fear, and the copilot's indisputable willingness to cooperate, consumed him. His amusement did not last for long, however, as Masterson spotted an opening in the forest.

"Over there, Captain," he said. "About two o'clock. Near the stream."

Richter eyed in the direction Masterson pointed and saw the clearing. As if by reflex action, he gave the pilot a nudge on the right shoulder while commanding instant action.

"Get it!"

Masterson gave a hard yank on the control stick. The aircraft banked starboard in a tight lunge. Richter almost lost his footing. Gable's excess equipment proved too much weight for him to fight against. He watched as his feet flew almost straight up. He helplessly fell back onto the unsuspecting Colfield. When the aircraft leveled off, the men readjusted themselves. The captain was not impressed.

"You could have injured someone, Lieutenant."

"Just hang on, Captain," the pilot said with a smile. "It'll all be over in a minute."

The aircraft began a straight descent. Team Bravo watched as the giant *orey* began to rise high above them. When the aircraft reached three feet off the stream bank the men began to disembark. They leaped into the knee-deep grass covering the shoreline. As their feet touched the earth each man assumed a fighting posture. Almost instantly they followed through with a dispersal. Each man rushed in a different direction to establish the hasty defense. By the time Ramsy exited the ship the skids rested upon the grass. After the team secured the zone Richter decided it was time to enlighten the pilot.

"All right. Shut it down."

"Shut what down?"

"The helicopter, Lieutenant. Turn—it—off."

"But we've got to get out of here!" the pilot said.

"Do what I tell ya!"

Masterson angrily switched off the circuits. While hearing the turbine mellow to silence Richter forwarded his invitation.

"Gentlemen. Would you join us outside, please?"

Masterson and his assistant glanced to one another. An

expression of resistance emitted from the pilot while his copilot blankly looked on. Richter watched the two unbuckle themselves from their chairs. He backed into the main cabin and dropped out the starboard side after watching the pilots exit through their doors. As the three stepped to the trees the captain snapped his directive.

"Greg! Pull the cowling on that engine. Rip a few wires out." A second thought flashed through Richter. "But hang on to 'em."

"Yo, Captain," Levits said.

He moved to the bird.

The pilots watched as Levits returned to the helicopter. They stood muted, numbed by the captain's order. Neither could understand Richter's intent. Nor could either justify a reason for becoming stranded in the middle of northwest Colombia. In particular, with a group of killers whose leader was not especially fond of them.

"What is this?" Masterson asked.

Richter turned slowly. He purposely took his time to face the two inquisitive men. When they came face to face the captain spoke in a mild, unaffected manner.

"You and your shavetail are coming with us, Lieutenant. Right now there's only one man besides us who knows where we are and what we're doing. I'm not going to sacrifice that kind of an edge."

In the short distance the sound of uncoupling metal rang out. The three men focused on the noise and saw Levits pull the cowling off the engine. He tossed the detached aircraft skin onto the ground. They quietly stood by while watching the soldier yank three wires from out of the engine compartment. After hopping down from the ship Levits coiled the wires around his right hand. He kicked the discarded fuselage section under the ship's tail. The reckless dismantling of their only way out horrified Masterson. It sent the lieutenant into an uncontrolled rage.

"Oh great!" the pilot yelled. He wildly stomped on the ground. He waved his arms about, overcome by frustration and fear. "Now what do we do? How do we get back?"

The captain was shocked by the pilot's total loss of control. It surprised Richter that with all of Masterson's training and background he could not contain himself. Emotion was for the others, not officers. To allow a display of inner feeling was to leave yourself vulnerable.

The team watched in silence while maintaining its frail defense. Richter looked about the encircling men and saw that they witnessed the lieutenant's irrational outburst. The pilot's conduct in the helicopter was tolerable. Most of the men could neither hear nor see what took place. But in the open where all could see, his actions were unacceptable. Masterson realized it as well.

The pilot caught himself, but it was too late. He had already made a spectacle of himself, and he knew it. He knew that such a display only planted the seed of doubt in his character. Under controlled conditions it was easy to contain your emotion. The flight into the beach action, the unexpected alternate objective, forcing him to land his craft then watch it be disabled was too much to silently stand by and let go unquestioned. Masterson looked to the encircling men and saw their glares of astonishment and doubt. He glanced at his novice pilot, also spotting an inquiring expression. That hurt the most. When he looked back to Richter, the captain spoke softly, but showed eyes that suggested a possible alternate course of action.

"Settle down, Lieutenant," Richter softly cautioned. "Not in front of the men."

Masterson took a deep breath. He let the air out slowly, making a sincere attempt to subdue his anguish. He knew Richter was right about his impetuous display. He also recognized the contrary signal given to him by the captain's gnawing pupils. Richter contemplated an alternative. One that was not compatible with his existence. There was more death in that captain's eyes than in the eyes of all the bodies left back on that beach. The two men were abruptly dislodged by Levits' timely interruption.

Levits stepped away from the chopper. As he moved past the three officers, he gave the captain a confirmation of the aircraft's status.

"It's not gonna fly, Captain," he said.

Levits crammed the coiled wire into his top left pocket.

"Okay. Thanks, Greg," Richter said. The captain refocused on the lieutenant. No sooner did their eyes connect than Richter experienced a slight sense of insecurity. He turned to Levits. "And don't lose them wires."

"I'll keep 'em close to my heart, Captain."

Richter coldly eyed off with the lieutenant once more.

"I want you and your copilot, here, to pull your camouflage nets and have that bird covered by the time we move out."

"Captain," Masterson countered. "When we get back to camp I'm going to have you up on a half-dozen court-martial charges."

Richter evaluated the pilot's sincerity by an intense analysis of his eyes. He could see that Masterson meant what he said. That was all right. It was when a person didn't mean what he said that a problem evolved. *It's when a man's word is reduced to nothing more than defecation spewing from between his lips that he loses the respect of his people. Most of all, he loses himself*, Richter thought. A smile emerged on his face—whether out of amusement for the flier's boldness or admiration for the man's forthrightness, he could not be sure. Perhaps a bit of both.

"What makes you think we'll get back, Lieutenant? Get that ship covered."

Twelve

A liberal interpretation of what they called securing the perimeter was agreed upon. Ramsy deployed Bard downstream, about one hundred meters. From the grassy shore Bard maintained a vigilance of both banks. Although tactically sound in its intent, Bard was not comfortable in his exposed location. One of those combat paradox where the security of the team took priority over one's highly vulnerable ass.

He stooped close to the shoal to keep his line of sight just above the fluttering stalks. The water rose through the sand and soaked into his canvas jungle boots. He sensed the warm liquid rising along his Achilles' heels, as his weight forced porous sand to condense under him. It was not the getting wet that bothered him. It was the idea of not being able to move off the shelf fast enough if caught in a crossfire. *And all for what?*

he asked himself. Men who cared little for him, if at all.

Again, the image of the court martial flashed through his mind. He recalled the quick judgment laid down by a board of five officers and one noncommissioned officer. It was a sudden and remarkable transition; within a matter of days, he regressed from a line company NCO to unwanted military surplus.

He was new to the post and still unfamiliar with most of the men in his unit. He spent many of his off-duty hours at the base gym, toning. At first he simply preoccupied himself, but gradually his time-filling workouts grew to a passion for excellence. His focus intensified, and the muscular gain he made over the short haul was profound. But when he immersed himself into the narrow sphere of lifting he unconsciously began to lose the world around him. It was an isolated lifestyle for him, but one that Bard knew was by his own design. To compensate for the loneliness, he committed himself to the one thing he knew he could achieve on his own. But his dedication to physical prowess marked him for suspicion. Although unjustified the stigma was there, and it was a much greater label than that of a mere body builder.

He heard about Master Sergeant Edwin Casidy and his favorites. He frequently encountered them at the gym as well. Until that night behind the NCO club, the unofficial word was just that—heresay.

Occasionally, Casidy would converse with him during his workouts. The sergeant, himself, was an avid weightlifter who also possessed a striking physique for a man of forty-nine. As much as he tried to regain his youth, however, Casidy appeared as only a token effort when standing next to him before the weightroom mirrors. It was always professional talk or a discussion about their physical routines. He had no real clue.

After six focused months his efforts paid off. He cinched the first runner-up spot in a local ironman contest in Leesville. Talk among the contestants suggested that he gave the winner a strong run for the trophy. It was a proud night for him, Bard remembered, and the most devastating.

He took the military shuttle bus back to the post. Bard

recalled how he set the second-place prize next to him, on the vacant seat closest to the isle. He got off the bus in front of the NCO club. From there, it was a three-block walk to the company area. Instead of returning to the barracks he decided it was one night he could afford to ease up.

He proudly strolled into the club and stepped to an empty stool at the far end of the bar. He set his two-foot trophy conspicuously upon the counter. He ordered a Seagrams and 7-Up and settled back. A few minutes went by, as well as a couple of congratulations from passersby, when he felt a solid slap on his back. He swiveled on the stool and came face to face with Casidy.

The tall man was obviously in a stupor state. Casidy's condition did not impress him. Not that it never happened to him, Bard recalled thinking. It was just one of those occasions when you wanted to take in all the pleasurable purity of the event without your senses deadened.

As his eyes fixed on the undulating crowns of the river grass, Bard remembered how the big man kept pawing him. Casidy constantly grabbed at his right arm while rubbing on his back, as they drank and spoke of future tournaments. An hour and a half and five Seven & 7s later, he succumbed to the effects of the alcohol. He began to slur his words almost as much as Casidy. Frequently, he had to take a few well thought-out seconds before responding to some of the man's awkward questions. Damnedest questions, Bard remembered thinking, but inquiries that made perfect sense after coming to grips with Casidy's true motive—questions about sex and sensuality, what kind of women he liked, what size, what shape, what color. Had he ever had an inkling to test strange waters when a youth, or thereafter? Questions that he felt were peculiar between grown men. But the lighthearted way in which Casidy asked them suggested nothing more than adolescent bull between the boys. He saw no reason to rebuff the senior NCO, especially since Casidy was a close friend of his company first sergeant.

One more Seven & 7 and he was ready for bed. He grabbed

his trophy and moved along the counter to the club's main entrance. He stepped outside, into the refreshing cool October air. He took in two large lung-filling breaths, trying to negate the dulling effects of the liquor. He reached the end of the walkway and began stepping along the street. Casidy rushed up from behind. The senior NCO offered him a ride to the company area.

Bard recalled how he told Casidy that his barrack was only three blocks away, how he was rational enough to make it there on his own, and that the fresh air would help to clear his head. The master sergeant fervently insisted, however. Casidy urged that he be permitted to insure his return to the unit without incident. He told him that his car was in the parking lot behind the club. Feeling slightly pressured by the association between Casidy and Leffler, he relinquished his will.

They used the sidewalk at the building's east end. For some reason, Bard remembered thinking, Casidy stayed a half-step behind him. When they rounded the corner, moving between two parked cars, Casidy suddenly stopped him.

"Hey, wait a minute."

Bard saw himself stopping. He turned to face the man after pausing between the vehicles.

"What?"

Casidy's voice altered. It was no longer loud and rowdy. His mannerisms underwent an abrupt change as well. His eyes looked weird, Bard remembered. They revealed what appeared to be a searching inquisitiveness of some kind. He could not clearly interpret it.

"I, ah—I've been watching you," Casidy said.

The NCO gently grasped his left wrist while ticklishly stroking him up and down his right forearm.

"Hey, man!" he said. "What the hell is this?"

He pushed Casidy's hand away while feeling his body go rigid. Casidy immediately withdrew. He raised his hands before him as a gesture of showing no ill intent. He crucially reevaluated his method of approach.

"That's okay, Bard," he began again. "It's all right. We're

all in this together. You take care of me, I'll see to it that First Sergeant Leffler makes your career go in the right direction. Understand?" Casidy stepped up to him. The master sergeant delicately rested his hands on both of his shoulders. "You know what I mean?"

Bard saw himself take two steps back while pushing aside Casidy's large hands. He was about to counterattack when he heard the sound of agitated gravel from behind. He swiftly turned and saw two of Casidy's favorites.

They moved to the rear of the cars and blocked his way out from between them. He turned and faced Casidy. The man's huge frame blocked his path to the sidewalk. He heard the sound of grinding gravel coming from his right. He glanced over the car roof and saw Casidy's third favorite approaching. The man moved to the car and leaned on the hood of the vehicle's engine compartment. *It was a stupid attempt, looking back on it*, Bard thought. But at the time desperation dictated his tactic.

"Look, I got a few bucks," he said. He reached into his back pocket and tossed his wallet onto the car hood. "I don't want any trouble. Just take the money. I won't tell First Sergeant Leffler nothing."

The men began to laugh. Casidy's smile was the broadest. His teeth profoundly showed against the contrasting darkness. Apparently, his money was not an adequate substitute, Bard remembered thinking. At that point he pretty well knew what they wanted, but the idea of it was so outrageous he naively asked anyway.

"What?...Take the money. What did I do?"

"You can't guess?" The man leaning on the car said.

Casidy eyed over the car hood to his companion. His wide grin started to diminish. He looked at him, Bard remembered. The smile was gone. A glassy gaze of power or anger, or both, appeared to emanate from his eyes.

"Oh, I've been looking at you for a long time, Bard," he said. "We all have." Casidy looked beyond him to the two men blocking his retreat. He looked to the man across the vehicle before returning his focus on him. "You're considered prime beef around here. Don't you know that? Haven't you heard?"

"What the hell are you talking about?" he nervously asked.

"I think it's time we induct you into our little society, Sergeant Bard," Casidy said. "You never know. You might like it."

With a flip of his hand Casidy signaled his men. Bard recalled how the two behind him approached and took him by his arms. They were strong, but he was stronger. He was on the verge of breaking their grips when Casidy uppercut him into the solar plexus. The punch sent him down onto his knees while he heaved up the Seagrams & 7-Up. Casidy watched, entertained by the show.

"This boy's a real lifer puke," he said. "He's a real slob. A big, soft, meaty slob. What do we do with slobs, boys? Get 'im ready!"

The two who held to his arms lifted him to his feet. Casidy hit him again. It was a right cross to his left eye. As the blood spewed forth it mingled with the vomit oozing out of the left side of his mouth. He felt himself slammed bellydown upon the car hood. When he connected with the metal, the man across the hood from him reached over. He took him by both of his wrists and pulled, rendering him defenseless.

Bard envisioned how they spread-eagled him upon the car hood. He recalled the duct tape pressed over his lips. He saw how the rubberized strip wrapped twice about his head. He tried to kick at them with his free legs, but surrendered to two agonizing blows to his kidney. He was on the threshold of unconsciousness, but his state of semiawareness was insufficient to lessen the trauma that followed.

Casidy undid his belt buckle. He pulled the strap free of his trousers in one vigorous yank. Bard remembered how the master sergeant whipped at his bear shoulders after tearing his shirt from his back. He felt them yank on his trousers. Their first attempt to separate the material was unsuccessful. A second, more volatile thrust detached his pants at the seam. He felt the material pulled aside, exposing his shorts. The three men enthusiastically responded to the sight of his skivvies. Their faces showed delight while complementing their expressions with lewd and pleasureful sounds of expectation.

He felt his shorts dropped along his hips. Not all at once, however. The cloth lowered in sporadic little measures as the men teasingly tugged while delivering words of praise for his anatomy. Gradually, ever so meticulously slow, they lowered his underwear to his ankles.

Casidy maneuvered close in, up to his back. The look on the master sergeant's face appeared to undergo a continual change. He did not know whether the man hated or desired him. He heard the zipper on Casidy's trousers go undone. He vividly remembered the zipping sound of the metal teeth separating in one rapid thrust. Casidy's words kept flashing through his mind. They sounded repeatedly like a rifle on automatic.

"Oh, I'm gonna fuck you, boy. I'm gonna fuck you so good." As if switching off a light, his psyche altered. Casidy grabbed him by his hair, yanking his head back. The master sergeant whispered in his ear. "I'm gonna make you my barracks bitch, Bard. From here on out you're gonna tighten up that beef for me."

Bard recalled how he vomited once more, as he felt Casidy's organ enlarge. He spat upon the car hood ahead of and below him. He was helpless, forced to submit to something he never believed could happen to him. They had their way with him, all four. The military got the rest.

He envisioned how he tried to keep himself covered. How he grappled at the back of his halved trousers with his left hand while clinging to his trophy in his right. He tried to fight back his tears. At one peaking point he lost all control, unable to cap the rage that burned within him. He reminisced how the MPs were unsympathetic to him, but still expected the police to follow through on his charges. What he did not count on was Casidy's survival instincts.

His charges against the longtime veteran fell on deaf ears. Everything neatly turned around. Two of the four assailants claimed that at the time of the alleged crime they played pinball in a greasy spoon on the north side of Leesville. A hamburger dive, Bard later found out, that both men had part ownership in. The third man claimed to be with a lady when the questionable rape took place. They were married two weeks later. When brought into the provost marshal's office, Casidy performed well. The convincing sergeant appeared as if he had just left his bed, groggy-looking enough to convince the duty officer.

The only claim in question was that Bard suffered an assault. That was later substantiated by a physical examination, performed that night at the post hospital. All the attending physician could state on the standard form 600 was that Bard had undergone anal penetration. This was insufficient evidence to sustain his charge against Casidy, but it was enough to place his own career in jeopardy.

It was a lynch-mob mentality. His general court martial was swift. The one military judge, board of four officers and one noncommissioned officer spent less than thirty minutes in deliberation. It became apparent during the pretrial investigation that the army was more interested in finding out who his presumed lover was, and if the man also wore a uniform. It was a unanimous judgment by the court that he be found guilty of sodomy under article 125 of the UCMJ, and that he be released from active service. But prior to his dishonorable discharge, that he be reduced in grade from sergeant E5 to private E1, forfeit all pay and allowances and sentenced to one year of confinement at hard labor. And now he was here, Bard thought. On a sandbar protecting the backs of men who hardly gave him the time of day.

It surprised him when Captain Richter specifically asked for him as a replacement for a Team Bravo casualty. Richter knew of his background, of course. The captain always made it a point to review the record of a potential team member. But he knew the costly attrition rate among the elite teams forced management to settle for experienced manpower from whatever background. Richter never spoke of his incident with

Casidy, except perhaps with Ramsy.

That was understandable, Bard thought. As the team NCOIC, Ramsy had a legitimate right to know about his men. But up to that point, the sergeant major never spoke of the matter. Not with him, anyway. Ramsy got into the middle of a scrap he had with Marcoli two weeks ago. He put them both in their place, and that was about that. The word of his court-martial did filter through the camp. Probably by that squirrely little personnel specialist in the S1 section, he presumed. That boy could be taken care of. Bard broke from his thoughts upon hearing Sanford.

"Bard?" Sanford whispered from the bank.

Bard sluggishly backed off the soft bed. He stayed low as he lifted one boot after another out of the sucking sediment. Sanford saw the soldier retreat through the brush. He waited for Bard to reach where he crouched next to a tree.

"Yeah," Bard said.

"Richter wants us back for a move-out brief."

"What?" Bard replied. "Another one?"

"You know how our luck's been running lately. He just wants as few mistakes as possible."

"Yeah," Bard said. "We've had plenty of those."

The two men maneuvered through the bank foliage. As they advanced on the team, Bard saw that Colfield had already returned from his upriver security post. While stepping up to the group they heard Ramsy announce their arrival.

"All right, Captain. Team's assembled."

The captain knelt on one knee. He oriented his grid map with the compass that he laid on top of the chart. After turning the map another inch counterclockwise, aligning the magnetic declination in the chart's legend to the compass needle, Richter began the final orientation.

"We'll move south-southwest on a 225 azimuth. It looks like some of our route will parallel a trail Stan located during his quick recon. We won't use the trail, but it'll make a good reference if we get turned around in this mess. That's it. It isn't much, but with what you were told back at the beach it does gives you a picture. Questions?"

"Yeah. Just a thought, Captain...," Bard wondered, "ah...does in-country DEA know we're here?"

Richter's subtle pause was all that it took for the men to realize what they were truly up against. Although he obliged the soldier with an answer, it was not necessary.

"Reiner felt that security was paramount," he began. "If we would have shared our intent with Colombian DEA, our suspect list would have grown by another twenty people, at least. The coordination effort alone would have gone through a minimum of another four separate offices. It would be almost impossible to narrow down the leak. This way we can keep our focus on just three or four people instead of four or five office levels."

"Double trouble," Sanford added, under his breath.

The team's deliberate isolation and the vulnerability that derived form its lack of official support angered Masterson. He saw the entire operation as a reckless, haphazard escapade without sufficient sanctioning from higher. He did not feel obligated to render his copilot or himself as guinea pigs for Richter's dubious experiment.

"You don't expect us to help you, do you, Captain?" Masterson asked.

The junior officer's query stunned Richter. For a moment he could not find words. *Does this man have so little regard for the team that he would not help*? Richter wondered. *Is he so embittered that the idea of helping these men is foreign to him*?

The captain glanced at Ramsy. Their eyes connected like magnets. Ramsy showed another one of his jaw-jolting expressions. He gave a slight cock of his chin while showing a clear look of disbelief. Richter glanced over the team, also seeing surprise and confusion on the faces of his men. He looked to the copilot and recognized the shock on his face. When Richter spoke, his tone reflected his incomprehension of what the man suggested.

"I'm sure they didn't teach you this at West Point," he

thoughtfully began. "I expect you to follow your orders, Lieutenant. I expect you to care more about the welfare and safety of these men than how you intend to rebuild your shattered flyboy ego. Although you are a regular, as opposed to us, in a hostile zone we expect your full cooperation. Is that a problem, Lieutenant?"

Unknown to everyone was that Colfield had heard much of the consternation between the officers, even in the ship. He grew weary of the pilot's continual verbal barrage of them, as well as his unwillingness to cooperate. While the group anxiously paused to catch the officer's answer, the distinct click of a rifle selector switch sounded. As the men glanced to one another, attempting to identify the source of the deadly snap, a shiver clawed its way up Masterson's spine. The pilot knew that the metal-on-metal rap was in his behalf.

"No—no problem, Captain."

"They could stay with the bird, Captain," Ramsy said. "They're not going anywhere."

Richter glanced at Ramsy. He considered his NCO's suggestion. It was not like the sergeant major to leave people behind. The two men alone in the jungle would become vulnerable to any armed group that came upon them. Although the helicopter was to be left in a semioperative state, there was a strong possibility the team would not return. He had planned for an alternate route of evasion as well. Cliff had had it, Richter knew. He was willing to suggest almost anything to get the two out of their hair. Richter halfheartedly went along with the recommendation.

"If we let you stay with the ship, will you try to repair it and fly out of here?" he asked.

Richter believed he already knew the answer.

"Of course," Masterson said.

Upon hearing the officer's answer Colfield silently raised his rifle to his shoulder. He pointed the weapon's muzzle only inches from the back of Masterson's head, while sounding out with a "bussssssh." Levits quickly reached up with his right hand and pulled downward on the rifle's flash suppresser.

Richter saw Colfield's antic at Masterson's back and considered the worth of the soldier's idea. He dismissed the impetuous notion, however. Too many witnesses.

"Well, Lieutenant," he resumed, "I have a deep regard for your honesty. That's why you and your copilot, here, are accompanying us. About time you get your feet wet, anyway."

"Whattaya mean?" the pilot asked.

"Judging by that pale green color on your face back at the beach, you could use some trigger time."

"Captain, I have seen—"

"Lieutenant!" Richter lashed. "Enough! Now, you do whatever else you want to render that chopper and its armaments useless. But keep in mind—whatever you do, you will have to undo later to get us out of here. In the meantime, Sergeant Gable will ri—"

Richter cut from his instructions. The captain whirled about, as did the entire team. They faced the dense foliage and the general direction of their intended path. In the distance was the sound of automatic weapons fire. The multiple firings sounded as if they came from an element of at least squad size. The constant rat-tat-tat echoed throughout the countryside. It was difficult for them to pinpoint the exact direction from which it came.

"Could anyone get a fix on that?" Ramsy asked.

"That way, Sergeant Major," Sanford said.

He pointed across the stream.

"No, man!" Marcoli countered. "It came from over there."

"It's hard to tell," Ramsy said. "Captain, you get a fix?"

Richter picked up his compass and map. He replaced the instrument into its pouch. He eyed in the distance while folding the chart. As he stashed the map inside his fatigue shirt he held his gaze in the general direction of the gunfire.

"Yeah, I got a fix," he said. "Right in our way."

"You think they know we're here?" Marcoli asked.

"I doubt it," Richter answered. "It's about four or five clicks off—but it's in the direction we're going."

"Is there another team out here?" Levits asked.

"Treadwell and Reiner didn't say."

"Would they?" Gable cautiously inquired.

Richter ignored the question. He believed that anything was possible at this stage. He did not want to give the men any more reason for doubt—not in Treadwell, Reiner, the mission, or himself. He looked at his watch.

"It's 1340 hours. We'll be there by 1800, 1900 at the latest. We're not in a rush. Take it slow and cautious. Sergeant Major, select the point. We move out as soon as Gable sets his charges."

Thirteen

One soldier buttstroked an unruly woman some fifteen feet from where he stood. He incapacitated the middle-aged wench with one swift swing of his rifle stock. Mendez heard her skull give from the impact. He saw how the left side of her face tore open. She yelped a sharp shrill before striking the earth. The screech sounded like the fatal cry of a puppy he once heard, when the canine succumbed to the weight of an automobile. A helpless puppy, he considered, who thought she was a wolf. Mendez looked to the crude but effective pacification process.

The village of San Delbaro was little more than a scattering of grass and log hamlets. It rested deep within the forest highlands of northwest Colombia. The tiny community situated at the southern rim of the Sierra de Jungurudó arc. The spur extended southward from Darién Provincia in Panama and harbored the source tributaries to the Rio Balsas. Only a few kilometers from Panama's southwest border, forty kilometers from the Pacific coastline, there was little difference in the surrounding typography and only a minute idiosyncratic variance in culture between the people of San Delbaro and their nearby Panamanian neighbors.

The inhabitants of the isolated community were known as Mestizo, a people deriving from a mix of European and Amerindian origins. They subsisted on agriculture and limited pasturing of sheep, goats, and a few head of cattle—this, in conjunction with the vast variety of plant and wildlife the surrounding forest afforded them. During the harvest season the men and infantless women migrated south and east to the higher elevations. They labored for meager earnings from the powerful coffee plantation barons. After harvest they would return to San Delbaro with the few pesos that helped to make their lives less burdensome. It was not an advantageous existence, but it allowed them to meet their basic needs without surrendering their dignity.

The village poised along one of the less traveled routes through the northwest forest. It was a marginal economic and social artery. The route was little more than a dirt pathway through the dense jungle. It accommodated perhaps one motorized vehicle, weekly. It was often impassable. Frequently, it washed out in the low areas during the monsoon, from May to November. The road bisected San Delbaro on an east-west line.

At the village center the road broadened. The log and grass huts set further back to create a wide community square. The villagers converged on the township central for social and commercial interaction. Adjacent to the square stood a corral, fabricated to accommodate sheep, goats, and pigs for sale and barter. Similar pens stationed at the rear of the hamlets, where individual families maintained their personal livestock. Beyond the private coops, farther back, were the family gardens. Each household provided for its own needs from one growing season to the next. For the young, San Delbaro was little more than a stopover.

Like the vulnerable route bisecting the community, it fell victim to the lack of use. Like in many villages, San Delbaro's youth chased after rumors of prosperity in Bogotá, Manizales, and Medellín. They left behind the toiling land and inhospitable forest to seek their riches in the cities. But most encountered the indifference of a subtle cast system within the great towns. It reduced them to little more than backstreet dwellers in servitude to a well-defined political and commercial aristocracy. Those who remained in San Delbaro realized that the village was on the threshold of withering away. What they could not foresee was that a genocidal variable would hasten San Delbaro's evolution.

First they destroyed the livestock. Initially, the people thought that the soldiers wanted only to replenish their food stores. They believed that if they complied with Mendez's command, the soldiers would take some of the food and go. Upon witnessing the execution of their livestock, the people were hard-pressed to grasp the purpose behind the colonel's deed.

The soldiers separated the men from the women, and the children from them. Children appearing between nine and sixteen years old, those who could withstand the march, were herded into the corral at the town's central. The infants sat or lay where left. Some of the older children tried to console the younger. They took the toddlers in their arms, holding on to the infants while begging for mercy. A few of the older boys tried to break for the jungle. None could outrun the spitting muzzles of the soldiers' AK-47s. The children cried for their mothers and father, but their powerless parents stood impotent.

Three soldiers contained the children within the pen. Another four threatened the women to the edge of the village square. Unlike the two dead boys, the women knew they could not survive a rush for the forest. They looked upon their men, who also huddled tightly.

The grandfathers, fathers, and sons stood by silently. They looked as defenseless as their slaughtered animals, the colonel thought. Some of the faces reflected a tinge of defiance, from arrogant men and boys with a deep desire to fight back. Most showed a more humble side. Their eyes revealed their sense of futility.

Sergeant Gorgas demanded swift compliance to Mendez's orders. The soldiers suppressed the villagers into silence. Everyone went mute except for one child weeping at the stable. When he saw that they were at last reduced to dumb onlookers, the colonel stepped out of the hamlet.

He looked to the men of San Delbaro first and gazed upon the human debility. He turned and faced the women. He critically eyed each of them. He spotted only one woman, hiding in the back, that might suit him. He deliberately waited a few seconds more.

"We came to you as friends—partners," he told the women. "We offered your men wealth. Power! All we asked for in return was for your labor…"

Mendez stopped speaking, interrupted by a child's cry. He paused, believing the irritating voice would subside. As he anxiously waited for the child to cease its yelping, the colonel grew annoyed.

"Sergeant Gorgas!"

"Sir!" the noncom replied.

"Shut that kid up!"

Gorgas gazed upon the colonel's face. The deep weatherworn lines in the commander's features, coupled with his glare of intolerance, clarified the NCO's directive. If he did not silence the child, Mendez would silence him. He knew the officer had the authority of the government and of the cartel to make it happen. Gorgas turned to the soldier's positioned at the pen. He ordered them to stop the child's whimpering.

One soldier swiftly moved under the wooden enclosure's top bar. He misinterpreted Gorgas' meaning, however. He stooped next to the little girl and gently took her by one arm. He tried to soothe her. Her whining persisted.

"Gorgas!" Mendez yelled again.

Gorgas instantly raised his rifle. He pointed it at the soldier attempting to console the child. He yelled out the order again. The soldier realized that if the girl was not silenced, Gorgas would make him a victim. He looked to the other men at the corral. He searched their faces for a sign of sympathy. All he saw were reflections of the unfeeling souls that dwelled within them. He had no choice. It was either become like them or be killed by them.

He released the child's arm. As he rose to a stance he pulled back the rifle's bolt. He glared upon the infant while lowering the weapon's muzzle to her head. He looked at Gorgas. He searched for some kind of reassuring sign but found only the sergeant's weapon zeroed on him. Mendez grew furious over his NCO's lack of action. He decided to give one last command while pulling his own weapon.

"Gorgas!"

"Colombo!" Gorgas yelled.

Colombo closed his eyes. He did not have the stomach to witness his own deed. He was too ashamed that the child's life had to be sacrificed for the sake of his own.

BANG!

Upon hearing the rifle shot, the soldiers quickly returned their focus onto the villagers. They did not want to become overwhelmed by an impetuous citizens' revolt. To the soldiers' dismay, no one lunged for them. Not one even spoke.

The villagers went numb. Every life-giving sense within them momentarily evaporated. Mendez was acutely aware of the psychological empowerment that his men and he briefly had. He also knew that this momentary mental entrapment could quickly dissipate. Instead of taking the time to explain the reason for the cartel's measure, the colonel chose to follow through on his orders.

Mendez yelled out his command. The soldiers responded to the colonel's directive without hesitation. They sent a wall of jacketed lead into the men of San Delbaro.

The village was to be a showcase for empowerment. It

would send a message, showing the surrounding villages the futility in declining a cartel offer. As their rifles spit forth Mendez watched the defenseless men drop.

He saw how the hapless men raised their hands before them. He took particular notice of one man's worthless attempt. A hot round bore its way through his raised palm. It continued out the back and into his left temple. The villager's effort was only one inept measure among many. All of the ill-fated men fell back and upon one another. Their perforated bodies heaped at a central point within the human glob. When the last man dropped, the overheated rifles went silent.

For a few seconds a deadening silence engulfed the village. Not a sound emerged from the women behind him or from the children cloistered in the corral. As before, the killing left those still living paralyzed. Only the sounds of the surrounding jungle were present. The wind brushed through the higher tree branches. Birds screeched out their alarms, signaling to those like themselves to take flight. Mendez looked about.

The sergeant redirected his men onto the women. He ordered them to herd the women to just beyond the edge of San Delbaro, into the jungle. As his men threatened the screaming villagers with potential bayonet jabs, Mendez again took notice of the woman he saw earlier. He watched as she tried to remain inconspicuous.

"Sergeant Gorgas!"

The loyal NCO turned from his duties. He quickly stepped to his colonel's side. He did not speak. Instead, he silently waited for Mendez to explain his wants.

"Bring her here," Mendez order.

Gorgas looked at the women but saw only the entire group. He eyed Mendez, showing an inquisitive expression. Mendez caught the NCO's look of indecision.

"There!" he said. Mendez pointed with his pistol. "That one. Bring her here."

Gorgas pushed the undesirables aside while grabbing for the petite young woman. He took her by both arms and guided her to the colonel. From a distance her soft features tickled his interest. When she stood before him, he became captivated by her.

She was perhaps sixteen or seventeen, he guessed. Maybe 160, 162 centimeters tall. No more. About 220 kilograms. Maybe less. The delicate outline of her body suggested no excess. He judged this by her thin smooth arms protruding from the cut-off sleeves.

He peered at the revealing cut down the front of her dress. He saw how her breasts pushed hard against the cross lacing. He keenly inspected their youthful firmness while following their contour along the uplifted material. Her nipples heaved hard on the cloth. Their impressions on the fabric showed like the blunt heads of bullets. They briefly seized his eyes.

He eyed her smooth calves extending out from under the peasant garb. Like her arms, there was no excess. Only firm sun-brown flesh enveloped her small frame. Her feet were cradled in hemp sandals. Although signs of toughening were present Mendez thought of them as satisfying extensions to a greater reward.

He maneuvered the short barrel of his Makarov PM, placing it between her legs. He ran the steel up and along the inside of her left thigh. He saw there was no undergarment. The raw, primitive idea of it stimulated him.

Her midnight black strands framed her narrow face like a shimmering veil. So intense was this blackness that the sunlight reflected off of it in radiating blue-black casts. Her lips were thin and soft. Somehow she prevented the parching heat from blistering them. Her nose was narrow, extending along a straight bridge. It revealed the dominant European genes in her blood. *And the eyes...*, he thought.

Eyes that appeared as deep in blackness as the hair that highlighted her face. They were almost almond shaped and complemented by long thin eyebrows. They were beautiful eyes; they revealed the hate and fury the woman was hard-pressed to cap. Although she did not fight off his antic with the pistol, her eyes delivered a warning. She had to be tempered.

"What is your name?"

The woman did not answer. Instead, she defiantly paused while looking into the soldier's eyes. She saw a desire in them that she had often witnessed in the eyes of the men from the village, young and old alike. She had only become aware of her pleasing affect on men within the last few years. Her parents knew of it as well. They kept a strong hold on her as a result. As all good parents of the village, they demanded strict accountability of her activities. But her father was dead, now. She looked to her left and watched her mother driven into the jungle with the rest.

"I am Alicia," she sternly said.

Mendez ignored Alicia's resisting tone.

"Turn around."

Again, Alicia hesitated. Her pause was not out of defiance, however. She simply did not understand why the soldier asked her to perform the simple move. The colonel saw the look of doubt in her eyes.

"I said turn around!"

Mendez grabbed the woman at her shoulders. He whirled her about. With her back to him he took hold of Alicia's dress at the neckline. He yanked at the fabric. The back of her dress gave under the force. The material divided down the center of Alicia's back, to just above her pelvis. He swiftly pulled down on the cloth and exposed her from the waist up. Mendez saw how Gorgas' eyes went wide upon viewing the woman's attributes.

Almost as quickly as the material collected at her waist, Alicia raised her arms. She folded them across her, uselessly trying to deny her admirers. She cradled her large supple breasts behind her thin arms. She lowered her head and looked to her feet. She glanced up once, however, to take notice of the hungry expression on Gorgas' face. As she returned her glare to the ground, Alicia felt herself whirled about once more. Upon facing Mendez, Alicia waited while the colonel filled himself with the sight of her.

"Alicia, you are a lucky woman," Mendez began. He saw

how her frail arms insufficiently concealed her fullness. He tried to maintain eye contact, but Alicia's attributes seized him. "Nature has done for you what it could not do for the others. And it is because of that, and only that, that you get to live. Are we in complete understanding?"

Alicia slowly raised her head. Her eyes met Mendez's. The hardness seemed to drain from them. It was like a blank or neutral gaze. They gave the wanting colonel no assurance, but at the same time they suggested no denial of her womanly favors.

"I will be whatever you want," she said. Her arms slowly lowered from her breasts. "But please, don't kill anymore."

Mendez stood in awe by the woman's maneuver. Her limbs fell aside like curtains. He watched as she inhaled a large breath. Her taut firmness elevated on her small frame. She watched his eyes. His gaze persisted until distracted by a rifle shot.

Alicia looked to the treeline as well. When she again turned and faced the colonel, Mendez saw that her hardened features had returned.

"That is up to you," Mendez answered. He gestured to the sergeant. "She's coming with us. Put her in one of the huts for now."

The sergeant yelled for one of his recruits. A man double-timed up to the NCO. A moment later Alicia felt the soldier's grip on her arm. As he guided her to the nearest hamlet, Alicia looked back at Mendez. She watched the colonel step in the direction of the herded village women. Mendez made ten paces before Gorgas stopped him.

"Colonel. What do you want done with the women?"

The colonel considered his options while watching Alicia guided away. He knew the village's fate before entering San Delbaro. But he made an indirect promise to his new prize, suggesting to her that no more killing would take place. At this juncture she would give of herself without much resistance. If the killing began again, he would have to destroy her as a means to control her. He waited until Alicia was inside the hamlet.

"Morale for the men. But then they must also be made an example of. No more shooting, though…quietly."

Gorgas acknowledged his orders. He turned from the colonel and stepped off. Mendez watched his loyal NCO. He was grateful to have someone obedient enough to respond without question, while strong enough to maintain proper discipline within the ranks, unlike those idiotic mercenaries his government paid for. The ones up north were even worse, he thought. It took uniformed men with proper military training to instill good order.

He slowly turned. His eyes took in the remnants of San Delbaro. He observed the dead livestock strewn about the village. He paused upon eyeing the corralled village children. He heard the cries of the little ones and the pleas from the older. They would bring a good price across the border in Ecuador. They just had to get them there in one piece.

Mendez looked at his watch. It showed 1355 hours. There was more than enough time. It was only six or seven kilometers to the rendezvous. The truck was under adequate security. At 1400 hours he would have his radioman make a radiocheck to verify an audible link with the buyers. A clear and open line of communication was essential for good business, he knew. Mendez looked upon the heap of dead next to the penned children.

He blocked out the whines of the traumatized infants. He looked skyward while using his right hand as a visor. It was the hottest part of the day. It would only be minutes before the dead began to decompose. Within a few hours the stench of rotten meat would permeate everything within fifty meters. The flies had already begun to converge upon the new food source. The insects descended upon the small pools of coagulating blood. Mendez held his gaze on the stack of human residue until distracted by the high-pitched sound of a screaming woman. Her voice sounded out the horror that still remained for San Delbaro. *It was their choice,* he told himself. *This was their doing. Quietly, Gorgas—quietly.*

Fourteen

    Gable double-timed to the helicopter after obtaining a mine, each, from Levits, Copeland, and Sanford. Not all of the men carried the extra explosive baggage. Normally, four men loaded one mine a piece in the event a supplemental persuasion capability was necessary. As Gable made his way to the ship, the sergeant major took notice of the abundant cargo dangling from him.
    Gable's rifle was in his right hand. The three slings of the M-18 satchels were in his left. The PRC-77 radio was, of course, mounted on his back. The M-72A2 LAW slung over his left shoulder along with the ammo satchel he refused to let go of. Three grenades haphazardly clung to his LBE, not to mention the bayonet, canteen, two ammo pouches, first aid and compass pouches, along with a flashlight and an old-style

army butt pack that reverberated off Gable's ass every time he took a step. No telling what was in that, Ramsy thought.

The soldier reached midway to the helicopter when something fell from one of his pockets. Ramsy could not tell what the item was. He saw how the dangling paraphernalia swung out and about Gable's body when the soldier made the abrupt course change. The sergeant major shook his head.

"Too much shit," he said aloud.

Ramsy turned from the romping Gable. He considered the events that led up to Team Bravo's predicament. One kept flashing through his mind. He glanced at the soldier in question and wondered if mentioning it was necessary.

He made a quick survey of his men and saw them preparing for the move-out. He looked at Alex and saw his friend eyeing about. Again, the captain checked and rechecked the team's location by terrain analysis. It was probably nothing, but Alex needed to know. The sergeant major looked at his men a final time before moving to the captain's side.

"Captain. A minute."

Ramsy took his friend by the arm and guided the captain farther into the trees. He wanted them out of the men's line of sight.

"I overlooked something, Alex," he began. "It's been eating at me, but I doubt if it means much."

"What?"

"James," Ramsy said.

"James?"

"Well hell, Alex," he resumed, an obvious tone of annoyance. "You didn't tell me what you were up to. After you wrote the operation order, I gave it to James to hand carry to Treadwell—so we could get his blessing on it."

Richter's eyes focused on the ground before him. He contemplated the possible implications of another man knowing about the original objective prior to the brief. Richter did not know James well; that is, not beyond the man's personnel record. He made it a point not to become too familiar with the team members. It had nothing to do with the men. In many ways he knew he was no better off than they. The distance did afford him a command edge over the other team leaders who became too close to their men. At times the others found it difficult to ask what was necessary of their people, especially when the outcome could be devastating. Richter glanced in James' direction.

"What do you think, Cliff? You have more contact with 'im than I do."

"Can't tell. Probably means nothing, but I thought you should know."

"Ah, hell," Richter replied while shaking his head. "That's not your fault. I should have kept you informed. Reiner and I were so damned security-conscious on this thing. I should have let you in on it."

Ramsy jumped at the opportunity to scold the prefect. He saw Alex's admission as an occasion to provide some fatherly coaching. He leaned into the smaller captain, but not so close that it appeared he attempted to intimidate him. Above all else, Alex was his friend—his heir.

"Well, in the future, Captain," he sternly began, "I'd appreciate it if you'd have a little more faith in your senior NCO corps."

"Yeah, you're right," Alex submitted. "Understood, Sergeant Major."

Ramsy cocked his head back. He was delighted by the officer's ability to admit a mistake. He taught the man well. Although Alex had a few good years of NCO time behind him, the captain still had a bad habit of wanting to do everything himself. He would eventually break him of that as well. For the meantime, the sergeant major was satisfied with what he heard. He gave the captain a hard smack on the back. Before Richter could react to his mentor's assault, Ramsy wheeled about and stepped off.

"Alex! I'm going to make a damned fine officer out of you, yet."

Richter stiffened. He tried to regain his balance while clamping onto his rifle. The one thing he could never do before his men was to drop his weapon. It was tantamount to a mortal sin. It showed a profound lack of respect for the one instrument that had a direct impact on a soldier's longevity. Weapons were looked upon with as much regard, if not more, as the men one teamed with. Catching himself before tumbling forward, Richter froze in a bent-over posture. He looked at Ramsy and watched the sergeant major move off.

A mix of emotions charged through him. It was a little embarrassing. He hoped the men did not see the Godzilla love tap Ramsy planted on him. He understood his close friend well, however. He knew Cliff's slap was nothing more than a reflex of fondness; that is, fondness coming from a man whose concept of compassion coincided with that of a black widow devouring her mate after a carnal episode. Richter eyed James and wondered the relevance of what he had learned.

Granted, James had access to all the details that encompassed the first objective. Like the rest, he had no knowledge of the alternate objective. As long as James continued the way he had, there did not appear to be a cause for suspicion. But the idea of the soldier being privy to the first operation had an affect on him. Richter held his glare on James while trying to put aside a gnawing persistence of doubt. There was little justification for it, but the crawl at the back of his neck would not go away.

Richter redirected his attention upon the helicopter. He wondered how far along Gable, Masterson, and the shavetail were to completion.

Gable planted the three charges within the helicopter's interior. He entertained himself with the notion of providing instant hemorrhoid surgery to anyone who sat in the pilot's seat. He situated one of the antipersonnel mines in the cockpit section. He positioned the explosive under the pilot's chair. After insuring an adequate flow of current, using the M-40 test set, Gable worked the M-57 firing device under the seat. He positioned the detonator with the bail pulled back and the plunger elevated. The top of the plunger was an eighth of an inch from the underside of the chair. Gable knew that anyone plopping themselves onto the seat would inadvertently depress the lever and forever be without hemorrhoids, or anything else. As Gable completed arming the final charge, Masterson put the finishing touches on their concealment effort.

They draped two woodland-green camouflage screens over the fuselage. Masterson hacked three branches off a nearby wild fig tree and utilized them as support poles with which to raise the screen from underneath. It created a distorted image from both a side and an above view. It was not so important to hide such an enormous piece of equipment from sight, he knew, though it would be advantageous. As it stood, the best they could hope for was to break up the bird's distinct and unnatural lines. Under the conditions it was the best they could hope for. Richter knew this as well and sent Marcoli twenty-five meters ahead.

As pointman, Marcoli was both the eyes and the ears for the team. He cautiously moved ahead and utilized all of his senses as alert systems. His eyes looked for anything that did not appear as part of the natural setting. His ears differentiated the sounds of the jungle from the minute noises coming from under his boots. He applied his acute sense of smell by easing the air into his nostrils, to pick up odors that were not indigenous to the setting. He felt the ground through the rubber soles of his jungle boots. The tender tissue probed for vibrations that might suggest an approaching vehicle. The only sense he did not apply was that of taste. He knew it was better to keep your mouth shut and hoped the men following him felt the same way. Team Bravo progressed slowly but steadily. They moved into the higher country using a patrol formation.

Each man tactically positioned himself five to six meters behind the soldier in front of him. The placement was necessary for minimizing casualties should they stroll into an ambush. Ambushes were peculiar animals, they knew. Most had a similar fundamental design and, of course, all had the identical aim.

The men of Team Bravo realized that although the basics of ambushing were similar, the human element always allowed for a variability in tactic. Your ambush was as functional or devastating as your creative mind could conceive. The concept applied equally to both sides.

They knew that any soldier could go from military genius to utter incompetent in the time it takes to trek from one ridgeline to the next. In either case the leader tried to do what was best for his people while pursuing the mission. The men of Team Bravo were fully aware of their risky endeavors. They knew that whenever human elements collided, even in a proposed civil atmosphere, the end result frequently degraded to little more than reason exchanged for chaos. For them, however, the work simply paid too well. Marcoli maintained his aggressive lead. At times he moved entirely too far ahead.

As he approached the clearing Marcoli signaled the men behind him to remain in place. Richter spotted the pointman's raised fist. He turned quickly and motioned for the men to disperse. The team responded swiftly and scattered into the foliage in alternating opposite directions. The tactic created a mini defense perimeter, with half the team directing its weapons to the left and the balance to its right.

To gain a better view Marcoli pushed aside the greenery. From where he stooped there was little for him to see. He saw chicken coops, small enclosures for other animals, and the tiny hamlets beyond. It was a conventional Colombian mountain village. Small. No more than twelve or thirteen hooches. He saw that they had approached the settlement from the side. The main entrance would be either east or west from where he observed. As Marcoli studied the village he wondered for the lack of activity.

There was no noise except for the sounds of the forest. There were the breeze, birds, and an occasional screeching monkey, but nothing human or even the byproducts that supported a village. He did not see any livestock. There were no sounds of children. Simply nothing. The absence of life forced an eerie feeling to crawl through him. He quietly backed away.

Marcoli swiftly retraced his trail but still stepped lightly over the brush and twigs. Upon reaching the captain he dropped to his knees. Richter waited to hear his pointman's report.

"We ran into one of those villages you mentioned."

"Activity?"

"That's just it," Marcoli said. "There isn't any."

"Whattaya mean?"

"I mean, Captain, there is no activity. There's nothing. Just empty."

"You went in?"

"You said to bypass. I looked from the edge. There's nothing. No people. No livestock. It looks as if it's been deserted."

Richter considered the soldier's claim. Nothing Reiner or he saw suggested an abandoned village along their route. *If a village is there*, he told himself, *it's suppose to be inhabited*.

"No. Reiner showed me the aeroreconnaissance photos, and they show these villages as active. The photos are only two days old."

"I'm telling ya what I saw, Captain," Marcoli said.

Richter pondered a moment more. Marcoli convinced him his assessment was accurate. He looked at his watch.

"We're way ahead of schedule. I didn't figure on any contact this early. Circle around. Have a look from the other side. Don't take chances."

"Don't worry, Captain," Marcoli replied. "My middle name is stealth."

Marcoli quickly rose while pivoting on his heels. He moved ahead two steps and tripped over a ground vine, landing flat upon his face. As the pointman picked himself up he looked over his shoulder. He saw Richter's look of disbelief. Marcoli shrugged his shoulders then headed for the village rim. Richter scooted back to his radioman.

"We'll hold up until Stan can recon the village ahead. Pass it on."

Gable wheeled about and moved to the next man. The chain reaction proceeded without delay. By the time the data flow reached Levits, however, a slight modification in the team's status manifested. Levits darted to the sergeant major and reported precisely what Colfield had told him.

"Sergeant Major. We're holding right now. The captain sent Marcoli ahead to check out a village. Possible cartel stronghold. Maybe twenty, thirty heavily armed men."

Twenty or thirty, Ramsy thought. Usually, the team tangled with ten, maybe twelve, but more than that was truly an auspicious occasion. Ramsy looked ahead. He checked the placement of his men. Their positioning looked good.

"Okay. The team looks dispersed well enough. I'll cover our rear. Let me know when the captain's ready."

Ramsy began to step down the trail the team had just blazed. He intended to move another thirty meters down to cover Bravo's backdoor.

"Wait," Levits said in a loud whisper. "I want to ask you something."

"What's that, lad?"

"We got a few minutes. I want to ask you about the captain."

"What about him?"

"You think pretty highly of 'im, don't you?"

Ramsy closed on Levits. He almost stepped into the man.

"Any reason why I shouldn't?" he asked defensively. "One of the best Mustangs you'll ever work with."

"Well now, wait, Sergeant Major," Levits replied. He raised his hands before him. "I'm not looking to shit on the man. I admit, he knows his job. It's just that it's hard to talk to 'im. With him it's business or nothing. None of us know much about him."

"It's the only way to be in this business."

The two men settled onto the ground. Ramsy leaned against a tree and remained vigilant of the team's rear area. Levits sat close by. He casually held to his weapon while trying to find out more about the mysterious officer. He forgot himself somewhat. His mind drifted from the mission and the lethality of the team's location. Ramsy noticed the man's momentary loss of mission consciousness but decided not to say anything. Levits pushed to know more.

"You say he's a Mustang?"

"That's right. Good one, too." Ramsy held his hands body width apart. "Got an NCO streak in 'im this long."

"What's a Mustang?"

The sergeant major turned from downtrail. He looked to Levits from over his shoulder. The look on his face revealed his astonishment. Levits stared at the man. He shrugged his shoulders.

"You don't know what a Mustang is?" Ramsy asked. "How long you been in service?"

"Long enough," Levits answered. "I've heard the expression before, but I never knew what it meant."

"That's an officer that works his way up through the ranks. Private, corporal, sergeant—then goes to shake n' bake school. Starts all over again as a butter bar."

"He's got some enlisted time?"

"About six, seven years, I guess," Ramsy said.

Ramsy watched as Levits' eyes widened. He knew the soldier considered the lowly background the captain originated from.

"Why do they call 'em Mustangs?"

"'Cause the regular brass can't stand 'em," Ramsy answered. "Too much NCO in 'em."

"How do you mean?"

"Ah, Mustangs tend to know more because of their mileage. They're more incline to question the brass. They also know how to use the system. Higher ups don't like a junior officer who knows how to manipulate the regulations. Reason they call 'em Mustangs is because they see men like the captain as a wild horse. He's always trying to break from his corral. Move up. He doesn't know his place."

"Sounds like a class thing."

"Now you got it," Ramsy snapped. "I think it's one of the

reasons he left the regulars...among others."

"How long you known 'im?"

"Well, let's see. About eight years. Late '71, early '72. About that."

"Yeah? How'd you guys meet?"

"Oh, that's a story in itself."

The sergeant major resettled himself against the tree's rough bark. He beamed a large smile. He thought back and allowed his mind to drift to that day eight years before. He envisioned the columns of soldiers double-timing. He heard them sound out the cadence, their loud rhythmic intonations bellowing in unison. He pictured the trainees dropping from out of the UH-1s.

"I was a master sergeant back then," he began. "Assigned as chief of training cadre for the Air Assault School."

"Fort Campbell, huh? Air Assault!" Levits said.

"Yeah. That was a good tour. I enjoy motivated troopers. Anyway, we had just bloodwinged a class. Had a whole company of new meats starting the next day. I looked out the orderly room window and saw this young officer. Sized 'im up. Decided I'd keep 'im in mind for zero day."

Ramsy thought back. He envisioned Alex as the boy looked the first time he saw him. Ramsy recalled watching the new meat from the orderly room of building 6738. He remembered having a cup of coffee in his hand. He sipped the steaming liquid while eyeing the would-be air assault soldier standing near the corner of 21st Street and Colorado Avenue. Alex looked lost, but Ramsy knew all of that would change the next morning.

Zero day came early, 0600 hours. Every training quota was filled, Ramsy was proud to realize. One hundred and fifty nervous men stood at attention in four ranks. He stepped out of the orderly room and walked the center of the training area.

"The captain, he was just a shavetail, then," he said to Levits. "He was in the second rank. I found 'im right off, but made like he didn't exist."

"What? One of them officers who stand out above the

rest?" Levits facetiously said.

"Hmmmm. Well he stood out, but I wouldn't put it quite that way."

Ramsy recalled that there was not one trainee standing in the formation under six feet tall; that is, except for Richter. Although the junior officer was not truly that short, compared to the men around him, he appeared dwarfed.

Ramsy silently stepped along the ranks. He eyed every man. He searched deep into their eyes for signs of weakness. He glared intently, beyond the iris, and probed for the character of the man. He stopped before some and cut into their eyes with his own. He would then abruptly turn away and move to the next soldier. He continued his character analysis until reaching Richter.

Upon making a right-face maneuver, Ramsy stood directly before the rigid officer. The master sergeant took a half-step forward. His chin almost touched the officer's cap. As the other trainees were larger than the lieutenant, Ramsy chose to capitalize on the circumstance.

The master sergeant leaned slightly forward. He placed his chin just above the smaller man's head. He looked to the tall soldier on Richter's right. He glanced at the larger trainee on the officer's left. Without a word Ramsy abruptly turned away. He stepped to the front of the formation. Upon centering himself on the first rank, Ramsy began the training process.

"I thought you were told to fall-in!" he roared. "When told to fall-in you are supposed to form into four equal ranks, at which time you shall perform an automatic dress-right-dress to establish your proper interval. After achieving a proper interval you will automatically assume a position of attention. I assume you were taught this technique during your basic training phase...Is someone going to recognize my existence?"

"Yes, Air Assault Sergeant!" the men shouted in unison.

Ramsy quickly returned to where Richter stood. Upon reaching the officer he placed his right hand above Richter's head. He moved his flat palm back and forth. He grazed the shoulders of the men standing left and right of the officer. After a couple of fruitless swipes, Ramsy snapped his hand down to his side.

"Then!" he began again. "If you understand this segment of drill and ceremony, why is there still an inordinate amount of space between these men?" Ramsy pivoted away from Richter and moved along the second rank. "You will try again. You are soldiers. You will never quit. You will get it right or die before you quit. I will insure this. Now! Let's begin again. Company…dismissed!"

At Ramsy's command of execution, all 150 men broke from their rigged stances. They began to move off in random directions. He purposely allowed them to scatter for ten full seconds before delivering the preparatory command.

"Company…fall in!"

The air assault wannabe's darted to their previous positions within the ranks. They bumped into and stumbled over each other as they hurriedly reformed the formation. Upon obtaining their required spacing, the men relaxed their arms and assumed a position of attention. The master sergeant briefly studied them, then stepped to the second rank.

Richter was precisely where he stood before. The same much larger men were there as well. When Ramsy reached the officer, he rose onto his toes, while placing his chin above the lieutenant's head. His Adam's apple grazed the bill of Richter's soft cap. He turned his head from side to side and inspected the dead space.

"Naw. Naw, you still didn't get it," Ramsy said. He looked down. "Oh! What's this? Is this a soldier who wants to wear air assault wings? My goodness, sir. We have coils of rappelling line stacked higher than you."

Entertained by the condescending remark, a soldier in the first rank started to laugh. He realized he was wrong for doing so and quelled his impetuous snorting almost as quickly as it surfaced. But it was not quick enough.

"Who laughed!" Ramsy blared.

The master sergeant charged for the first rank. He stepped back and forth along the string of men like a bull elephant.

"Tell me who laughed, or I'll have this entire company force marching for the next three days in full combat load."

Ramsy waited. A constricting pause ran through the formation. Silence hung over the men like a terminal epidemic. No one would say who released the snort, but everyone, especially the culprit, knew that if the company succumbed to a three-day march, the impulsive soldier would not survive it. Reluctantly, the guilty man took one step forward. He said nothing. He simply stood at attention while waiting for the consequences.

"You! Was it you who laughed?"

"Yes, Air Assault Sergeant!" the nervous man said.

"What's your name, soldier?"

"O'Connor—Gregory, Air Assault Sergeant."

"Well, O'Connor, Gregory," Ramsy pressed. "You sound to be a bit of the Irish."

"Yes, Air Assault Sergeant!"

"But you don't look it, O'Connor, Gregory. It appears your mamma had a spic in the woodpile. Do you think she got confused between spic and mick—or are you just a slimy tick?"

"No!" O'Connor yelled back.

"No, what? O'Connor, Gregory."

"No, Air Assault Sergeant!"

"Well, thank you very much for using my title, O'Connor, Gregory. It gives me a sense of security. You're a decent man."

"Yes, Air Assault Sergeant!"

"And where do you hail from O'Connor, Gregory?" Ramsy persisted.

"New York, Air Assault Sergeant!"

"New York? Where abouts in New York, O'Connor, Gregory?"

"The city, Air Assault Sergeant!"

"The city!" Ramsy shouted. "Would that be Albany by any chance, O'Connor, Gregory?"

"No, Air Assault Sergeant!"

"I see. Well, could it be Riverhead, New York? A lot of nice people out there on Long Island."

"No, Air Assault Sergeant!"

"No again? Well, pardon me, O'Connor, Gregory. You must be talking about Yonkers, New York. Right?"

"No, Air Assault Sergeant!"

Ramsy reared back to gain full momentum.

"Then what the hell city are you talking about? Don't you know the name of the place you came from?"

"Yes, Air Assault Sergeant!" O'Connor said. "New...New York City."

"New York City! As if I couldn't have guessed."

Ramsy eyed the man up and down. He detected a subtle quiver in O'Connor's lower lip. He liked it.

"We don't laugh at anyone at this training facility. Is that clear O'Connor, Gregory?"

"Understood, Air Assault Sergeant!"

"Are you sure, O'Connor, Gregory?"

"I'm—I'm sure, Air Assault Sergeant!"

"Yes, I know you're sure," Ramsy vindictively piled it on, "but are you *really* sure, O'Connor, Gregory?"

"Re-re-really sure, Air Assault Sergeant!"

"Oh, I am so pleased! Now, get back into that rank."

"Ye-yes, Air Assault Sergeant!"

O'Connor withdrew. He was grateful to blend into the mass of green clad men. At that moment his only desire was to forego any association with himself. He knew Ramsy would remember him throughout the training cycle.

As before, Ramsy pivoted at the end of the line. He moved along the second rank at a moderate pace. He stopped at the point directly behind O'Connor. He glared at the back of the man's neck. Although he could not look behind him, the invasion of his personal territory signaled O'Connor that something had closed in. On that morning there was only one man who could do that. Ramsy leaned into the trainee. He maneuvered his chin to just above the man's left shoulder.

"The closest you'll ever come to wearing wings," Ramsy said, "will be on the edges of your maxi pad."

The sergeant major broke from his memories and rearranged himself against the tree. He worked a jabbing piece of bark into the small of his back. He removed his jungle hat and wiped the perspiration from his brow. He rubbed the top of his head after clearing his eyes with a dry portion of the field dressing. As he retied the scarf about his neck Ramsy resumed his memoirs.

"After O'Connor, I thought I had put a halt to all the smart asses…I was wrong."

His mind drifted. He saw himself stepping along the second rank. He had not quite reached Lieutenant Richter when coming upon a soldier showing a grin. The man did not laugh, and so could not be disciplined. He wanted to laugh, Ramsy knew. On account of what happened to O'Connor. So did a lot of the men, but unlike the others this one was hard-pressed to contain his emotion.

"Are you amused by something?" Ramsy asked.

"No, Air Assault Sergeant!" the soldier answered.

His smile appeared to broaden.

"Are you sure?"

"Yes, Air Assault Sergeant!"

Ramsy lowered. He maneuvered his face close the soldier's. The tips of their noses almost grazed.

"Then alter that grimy lower lip of yours before I pull it up over your face and suffocate you with it."

The man's grin instantly disappeared. Ramsy eyed him a few seconds more then resumed his inspection until he reached the lieutenant. He looked straight ahead, over the man.

"I thought I sa…" Ramsy looked down. His face showed a mild look of surprise. "Oh, you again! I beg your pardon, sir. I forgot you were down there." Ramsy eyed the officer's name tape. "Lieutenant Richter. Tell me, sir. Do you believe I showed preferential treatment by coming to your defense?"

"No, Air Assault Sergeant!" the junior officer said.

"And why do you presume that, sir?"

The lieutenant glared up at the much larger man.

"I don't need a defense, Air Assault Sergeant."

Ramsy looked deep into the officer's crystal blue, angry eyes. Richter peered up into the master sergeant's knifelike, cutting stare. There was no relenting from either. No grace. No forgiving. Ramsy liked what he saw. The master sergeant returned to the front of the formation.

"I concur! None of you need a defense. All of you are either animal waste with no direction or you have direction. Here, all are treated equally. Enlisted do not laugh at officers or vice-versa. Yesterday, some of you were privates. Yesterday, some of you were majors or colonels. But today, you are all beaver residue on an equal standing and shall remain as such until your bloodwings are seated into your chest...or you are asked to leave. I am a fair man. I am a just man. I am an angry man but a fair one just the same. I have no greater enjoyment than to watch a motivated soldier perfect his craft. Don't disappoint me!"

Fifteen

Marcoli maneuvered east. Upon reaching the narrow trail he peered west and into the village proper. He had a partially unobstructed view into the settlement. From this point he believed he spotted the reason for the lack of activity. He decided to reconfirm the unimaginable from a better position.

He dropped onto his belly and low-crawled from out of the jungle's protection. He squirmed to the mud edge of the forest throughway. The early afternoon thunderburst had already come and gone. It left behind deep, turbid puddles where ox cart wheels furrowed into the surface. The afternoon sun hung high after the downpour. It rapidly evaporated the runoff from the higher margins of the road. Within minutes of the rain, the water-saturated surface transformed into a thin crust. Once repositioned closer to the trail Marcoli took a longer look.

He gazed along the route. He saw the bodies piled in the town central. He observed the older village women, who foraged while the killing took place, kneeling at the base of the human heap.

Some prayed as they clung tightly to the limbs of their dead. Others wailed out their agony. Their bodies pulled into fetus positions while screaming. Others walked about as if unaware of their surroundings. They stepped clumsily— silently. All, in their own suffering ways had lamented over the wrath that befallen their community. Stan judged the women to be from midlife to old.

For this part of the world these women were well past their prime, old by Colombian outback standards. He noticed the absence of young children, except for toddlers. There were no women of child-bearing age that he could see. What further baffled him were the animal carcasses strewed about the grounds.

Everywhere he looked, dead farm stock rotted in the afternoon heat. The sun accelerated their decomposing. Some of the goats, dogs, and lamb bloated. As he winced from the repugnant sight Marcoli accepted what he believed was the totality of the devastated settlement. Then, it came over him.

He could not pinpoint it. Marcoli felt the goose bumps rise on his limbs, even his thighs. The sensitivity of his hair rising through the pox seemed tenfold to the touch. *A sound*, he thought. *Something*.

He snapped his head back and glanced over his shoulder. He hoped that it was Richter or Ramsy, or one of the other teammates. There was no one. As if by reflex, he rolled onto his back. He searched the foliage beyond his feet. His eyes darted side to side. His mind raced with anticipation, but for what he had no clear idea. He made a darting glance across the road.

When he spotted her Marcoli became visually paralyzed. He glared up and upon a young woman hanging in a tree. She hung stripped from the waist up and impaled onto a broken tree branch. The limb on which she was suspended oscillated from the breeze passing through the higher branches.

Marcoli peered down the trail and saw the village women engrossed by their own agony. They were not yet aware of what was only a hundred meters from them. He rose to his feet and stayed low while darting across the narrow roadway. When again concealed within the undergrowth, he took in the magnitude of the holocaust.

He cautiously moved toward the body but not out of any sense of fear. His steps felt controlled, as if he moved in slow motion. He stood before her. His legs seemed locked. He saw how the blood oozed from around the three-inch-thick branch protruding from her chest. It ran over her flat stomach and collected at the bunched material about her waist. Some of the blood soaked into her skirt. Some of it seeped under the waistband and resumed its run along her legs. He saw where it dripped into a semi-coagulated puddle a meter beneath her feet. He stepped out of alignment with the body to see beyond.

Farther into the forest Marcoli saw one body after another snagged in or bound to the trees. All of them young, perhaps twenty to forty years old. All of them women. "Jesus," he whispered to himself, while stepping along the slaughter.

Most of the dead were bare from the waist up. Four were completely disrobed. Like most of the others, the naked suspended from the branches in various modes. Two had their wrists bound, their tied arms slipped over a tree limb. One stood against a trunk, her body lashed to the trees with rope. Her head hung limp, and her legs spread wide.

Marcoli waved his rifle muzzle to dissipate the gorging flies gathering on the food. As he moved the rifle barrel back and forth he noticed the small pile of soft hands and callused feet at the center of the hysteria.

Two young women, he guessed to be in their late teens, hung in the trees by their necks. The waist band of their dresses acted as the suffocating line. He had sufficient stamina to withstand everything up to that point; that is, until eyeing one he simply could not stomach.

As he approached, Marcoli felt his guts unsettle. The sight

of the woman caused a rolling effect of his gastric juices. That coupled with the undigested MRE he had for lunch, was too much for his system to take. He dropped onto one knee and heaved his noon meal. He saw the chunks of BBQ beef splatter onto the toe of his boot. After a second, less substantial upchuck, he cleared his throat using his finger. He wiped his puke-covered digit onto his pant leg. He then looked to the village and was grateful that his momentary loss of control did not compromise the team. He returned his attention upon the once pretty villager.

They had split her open like a gutted steer, severed from under her sternum down to her crotch. Marcoli flushed his mouth with a gulp from his canteen while observing her midsection that lay open. Her entrails spilled onto the ground beneath her feet. He looked down at the drying, fly-infested pile of intestines. As he backed away he collided with another dangling corpse.

Upon striking the cadaver Marcoli instantly went on guard. He whirled about, his trigger finger poised, and sounded a gritted growl. Every muscle in his body went tight. Every nerve ending intensified to their height of sensitivity. After what he witnessed, Marcoli wanted to kill, kill, and kill again. But instead he found only a swaying corpse and heard the knotting fibers as the hemp threads strained under the weight of the gyrating load.

He lowered his weapon, letting the hand guard slap upon his thighs. He took in a large breath and tried to clear his mind on the exhale. With his composure somewhat rallied Marcoli returned to the team. Ramsy continued to entertain Levits.

Day seven of the cycle, Ramsy recalled. Many of the men, about forty, had already withdrawn from the program. *Washouts*, he thought. *No time for 'em*. He pictured the class in the rappelling phase. The trainees stood at the top of the platform. All of them satisfactorily made their first four descents after taught how to configure and apply the Swiss seat hookup. Ramsy recalled the four men at the platform's base. He pictured himself leaning beyond the edge to observe the soldiers below, acting as belaymen. He visualized the soldiers in the distance, their jackets and gear grounded. They double-timed along Colorado Avenue, their voices echoing in unison.

He imagined the UH-1s flying low overhead. The percussioning sound of their rotors rhythmically drummed in his mind. He remembered hearing of a new machine coming to Fort Campbell and speculated its true worth.

At the time it was only a rumor but spoken of highly. The brass talked of the novel chopper as if it were the new phoenix of air assault mobility. Its was the UH-60 Alpha. An assault ship that had twice the manpower and equipment tolerance of the UH-1. It had a cruising speed of up to 153 knots. Sixty-three knots faster than the tactical speed of the UH-1. It was bewildering for him, Ramsy recalled thinking. After all the years he trained, worked, lived, and almost died on the old dependable Southeast Asian workhorse, it was to be put to pasture within eight years. It would make room for something stronger—younger. It would retire. From the top of the rappelling platform the master sergeant provided his guidance.

"You are now in your seventh day of training. You're almost home but not quite. Most of you are performing to standards. That is good. By reveille tomorrow all of you will meet criteria, because those who cannot will not be here. As your rappel master, I will insure it. Today, you were taught how to configure and utilize both the Swiss and Australian seats. This morning, all of you adequately negotiated the tower using the Swiss seat hookup. The Australian technique is a different matter. This afternoon, one of you will be gracious enough to give a demonstration in the configuring and application of the Australian hookup. Do I have a volunteer?"

Ramsy recalled looking from one face to the next. The eyes of every man, including Alex, showed a striking lack of energy. They knew how to do it, he knew. They just needed a little coaxing. Ramsy eyed the group three times before commanding the shortest soldier on the platform to step forward.

"Thank you, sir!" he sounded loudly. He pointed to Richter at the rear of the group. He then returned his attention to the class. "Now, this is a motivated junior officer. He is eager to lead. Watch him and learn. Sir! Prepare your Australian seat and hookup."

"Yes, Air Assault Sergeant!" Richter helplessly submitted.

The lieutenant wrapped the line about his waist and slid the carabiner along it to the small of his back. Meanwhile, the rappel master descended the platform by way of the stairs. Once grounded, Ramsy stepped out from the structure, about seventy feet, to gain full view.

He watched as the officer eased his upper body beyond the platform's edge. Richter remained rigid as he allowed his frame to slowly descend like the hand of a clock. His grip was firm, permitting only an incremental sliding of the line through his gloves and the snaplink at his back. His body lowered from a twelve o'clock position at the platform's rim. He stopped at the three o'clock position. When stationed and anchored he waited for the master sergeant's signal. The lieutenant patiently waited while facing the ground with his body perpendicular to the platform's vertical face. As he waited the muscles in his hands and arms began to knot from the strain. Richter waited and waited—and waited. When Ramsy felt sure Richter's hands could not withstand much more he made his query.

"Sir! Are you prepared to make your descent?"

"Yes, Air Assault Sergeant!"

"Go!"

"On belay!" Richter yelled to the man at the platform's base.

"On rappel!" the belayman responded.

The lieutenant began to quick-step down the platform's face. He allowed just enough line to slip through his hands to give himself an even and steady descent. The farther he dropped along the vertical front, however, the more gravity took control. The momentum built all the way to the base. When a few feet above the ground he stepped from the platform in one giant step. He continued his pace off the wall and onto the ground. He maintained the steady gait straight out from the platform until his line cleared the carabiner. Ramsy loved it.

"Outstanding, Lieutenant!" he yelled throughout the training area. "Now! Get back up on that tower and do it again. Who will be next?"

"I will, Air Assault Sergeant!"

Ramsy looked to the platform's summit and saw O'Connor standing at the edge, his hand raised high.

"Oh, my goodness!" he blared. "It's New York City. Prepare your Australian seat and hookup."

O'Connor quickly wrapped the line about him. He also positioned the snaplink at the small of his back. As had the lieutenant, he lowered himself from the platform's edge and stopped when perpendicular to its face. O'Connor held in place until Ramsy asked for his status.

"New York City! Are you prepared to make your descent?"

"Yes, Air Assault Sergeant!"

"Go!"

"On bally—"

"Wait!" Ramsy shouted. "New York...did you say on belay or on bally?"

"'On bally,' Air Assault Sergeant!"

O'Connor's hands grew weaker by the second. He could feel the hot sting on his over-gripping fingers through the gloves.

"'On bally'...New York, are you aware of how difficult you make it for me to earn my pay?"

As if cued the men on the platform began to laugh. Ramsy listened to the laughter but only for a moment.

"The next man who laughs will give a demonstration of the dying cockroach—and he will maintain that position for the remainder of this training cycle."

Every man instantly regressed into silence. They remained emotionally gagged while the rappel master clarified his intent.

"This is not about humiliation," Ramsy resumed. "It is about training. Giving a point, getting a point, and keeping it. Have I made my point?"

"Yes, Air Assault Sergeant!" the men yelled in unison.

"Did you get my point?"

"Yes, Air Assault Sergeant!"

"Will you keep my point?"

"Yes, Air Assault Sergeant!"

"I'm so happy." He looked to O'Connor at the platform summit. "New York! Do you recall my question?"

"Yes, Air Assault Sergeant!"

"Then, what is your answer?"

"No, Air Assault Sergeant!"

"No what, O'Connor, Gregory?"

"No, I didn't know about your pay, Air Assault Sergeant!"

"Well, you should!" Ramsy fired back. "It is belay. On belay! When delivering this phrase, you are signaling the belayman that you are ready to make your descent. It is a safety measure used in all rappelling operations except under tactical conditions, when speed is essential. If you are unable to give a proper notification of your intent, how can your belayman respond effectively?"

"I—I don't know, Air Assault Sergeant," O'Connor said.

"You don't know!" Ramsy countered. "Merciful Mary. O'Connor, are you a turnip? On belay! On belay! Say it, New York."

"O-On—belay. On belay, Air Assault Sergeant!"

O'Connor felt the line inching through his grip.

"Then, we begin again," Ramsy resumed. "Are you prepared to make your descent?"

O'Connor watched as the line slid through his hand. Only a few inches, but compounded by the five or six that had already inched through, his upper body was by then dipped well below floor level. Gravity pulled at his head while his feet remained at the platform's edge. He gripped the line as hard as he could but felt and saw the inch-by-inch slippage continue.

"Ye-Yes, Air Assault Sergeant!"

"Go!"

Gravity seized O'Connor before he had time to signal his belayman. His weakened hands allowed the line to slide freely. His upper body defiantly began to descend. Realizing his hands were useless O'Connor attempted to realign himself by stepping faster along the wall. He was almost at a dead run, hoping his feet could overtake his shoulders. But the soldier became so preoccupied with regaining a perpendicular form that he forgot his rate of descent. He haplessly resumed his pace into the dirt, face first. As the dust clouded around O'Connor's flattened frame Ramsy deliberately took a doubletake.

"Oh, my god!" Ramsy bellowed. "New York—are you dead?"

"Nnnnnn-nooo, Air—Assault Sergeant," O'Connor said into the half-inch-thick dust.

"You mean," Ramsy went on, "after putting this training facility through such an embarrassment, you can't even extend us the courtesy as to be dead? Where is your loyalty! Lieutenant Richter! Descend the tower by means of the stairway and take a position next to New York City."

The lieutenant acknowledged his instructions while moving to the stairs. Richter descended quickly, skipping every other step. He double-timed to O'Connor's side and stood at attention next to the man. O'Connor remained face down in the dust. Ramsy stepped to the two and critically eyed them.

"No sir! I did not say stand next to him. I will repeat. You will take a position next to New York City."

Richter took a second to consider the man's intent. He then realized that he did not follow the rappel master's instructions, explicitly. He dropped to his knees and stretched himself onto the ground next to O'Connor. When both men were in their face-down, dirt-eating postures, Ramsy roared at Richter.

"Sir! Although your demonstration was an outstanding one, a lack of communication is evident. You must insure that all of your men know their instructions to the letter. Your noncommissioned officer will teach your men what they need to know. That is sergeant's business. But you must insure they know it. If they do not they will fail their mission objectives. If they fail, you fail. Therefore, you will provide Corporal O'Connor, Gregory with all the personalized instruction called for, until he can adequately negotiate this tower using the Australian rappelling technique. He will not eat until he does. He will not sleep until he does—and being the kind of junior officer I know that you are, you would never think of eating or sleeping until your men have. Is that understood, sir?"

"Yes, Air Assault Sergeant!" Richter answered.

A tiny cloud of dust rose out from under Richter's practically buried face.

"Then detach New York City's face from my dirt, escort him to a secluded corner where humanity will not have to look at him, and enlighten this twinkle toes, sir!"

"How long did it take 'im to show the guy?" Levits asked. Levits jammed the butt of his rifle into the ground and used the weapon to support his left arm.

"About thirty minutes," Ramsy said.

"That's not bad."

"Well, the captain had an added incentive."

"What?"

"It was getting close to chow."

A lull took place. Ramsy and Levits quietly observed the forest around them. Each was in his own mental place. Ramsy resumed his reminiscing, entertaining himself with the special events that encompassed his life. Levits pondered the cause for the sergeant major's apparent dislike for those from New York.

"Sergeant Major...you got something against New York?"

The question yanked Ramsy from his thoughts. For him, there did not appear to be a reason for asking.

"Why do you ask that?"

"O'Connor. Then me this morning," Levits explained.

"Lad!" he began warmly, a fatherly air about him. "It wouldn't have made any difference where you or O'Connor came from. If you came from St. Louis, I would have said you'd end up shining shoes at the back door of the Busch Brewery. If it had been New Orleans, I'd have said you'd end up licking the lint out of the astroturf in the dome. None of it's personal. It's motivation."

"Yeah, I guess so," Levits said.

Ramsy focused ahead and checked the placement of his men. He saw the pointman break from the trees. He watched Marcoli rushed up to Richter and drop next to the officer. Eager to know more about what was ahead, Ramsy decided to move forward.

"Stan's back," he said. "I'm going forward. Stay put."

"Roger."

Levits lifted his weapon and wiped the mud from it. He took Ramsy's position against the tree. As Levits' eyes darted back and forth, searching the undergrowth, Marcoli reported in.

He broke from the trees unexpectedly, putting the captain on alert. Not realizing it was Marcoli, Richter swiftly raised his weapon while poising his trigger finger. When he saw who it was the captain went rigid. He realized that he almost blew away his own pointman. Stan knew better, he thought. Richter decided to inform the man of how close he came to becoming a statistic. But when face to face with the sergeant, Richter saw that the issue would be pointless.

Marcoli dropped to his knees. His rifle slapped down and across his thighs. The veins in his arms and neck bulged from the heavy pumping of blood. He was out of breath and appeared to be on the verge of hyperventilation. His face flushed. It looked as if the top of his head might blow off. Richter waited a half-minute, allowing the pointman time to settle. He caught the look in Marcoli's eyes.

It appeared as if the man tried to understand something. Marcoli's eyes were wide and held a steadfast glare on the ground before him. Richter reached out and gently took the rattled man by his left arm.

"What did you see up there?"

"Captain," he began after two additional breaths, "I can hardly believe this shit."

"What?"

"I ain't seen anything like this since Cambodia."

"What?" Richter asked.

"It's completely wiped out."

"What?"

"All I know is that village is wasted," Stan answered.

Marcoli looked up from the captain. He peered over Richter's shoulder. Richter glanced over his shoulder and eyed to where Marcoli focused. They watched as the sergeant major advanced on them. Ramsy dropped to their side, his question forthcoming during his descent.

"What's up?"

"The whole village was wiped out, Sergeant Major," Marcoli resumed. "There's nothing left but a few old women. At the other end it looks like they killed all the men and stacked the bodies. You won't believe the women."

"Did you notice any government troops—mercs, bandits, anything?" Richter asked.

"Naw," Stan answered. "Whoever did it moved on. No soldiers. Nothing."

"Why would anyone want to kill off a village in the middle of nowhere?" Ramsy asked. "What harm are they to anybody?"

"They're not," Richter said. "There's more to this."

"There's something else, Captain," Marcoli resumed. "It looks like they took all the younger women just east of the village. Beat 'em to death then strung 'em up. Some they even opened up."

"Strung? You mean hanged?" Ramsy asked.

"You got to see it to believe it," he went on. "There's about a dozen women secured to the trees. I mean, up in 'em. Some tied, some hung—you wouldn't believe the others. What are we going to do, Captain?"

"Think we ought to have a look, Captain?" Ramsy snapped.

Richter considered their options. He did not want to reveal the team's presence, but at the same time he wanted to verify what Marcoli had told them.

"If we go in there we're compromised," he explained. "All it'll take is one observer from the hills. I think we need to know why this happened, though...Stan, move out front. Keep to the east. I want as much of a kill assessment before they know we're here."

"Roger."

Marcoli quickly rose to his feet and moved ahead into the brush.

"Would they really wipe out an entire village?" Ramsy asked.

"Well," Richter replied, businesslike, "we'll soon find out."

Sixteen

Marcoli marked twenty meters ahead of the main body. He led Team Bravo to the trail's margin at the east end of the village. One by one, the men darted across the open strip and converged on the carnage at the opposite side. As the bewildered men moved among the dead, most said nothing.

Richter stepped around Marcoli, who waited at the edge of the torture site. The captain took the lead. Ramsy stayed a few feet behind Richter. As they made their way among the dangling corpses Masterson could not contain himself.

"Damn! Who would do something like this?"

"I don't know," the copilot replied, "but I'm glad we didn't stay with the ship."

Gable followed closely behind the sergeant major. Behind Gable, Levits bunched up. He switched from the tail position after clearing the road. While advancing among the human debris Gable suddenly grew conscious of his religious upbringing. As a precaution he made the sign of the cross. He motioned through the symbol while adding an enhancing remark.

"Jesus-Mary-Joseph," he whispered.

Levits heard Gable's request to his savior. He believed it was a little too late for the soldier to petition for mercy. *It's too late for all of us*, he thought.

"That's not gonna help us, now," Levits said.

"Yeah, screw you," Gable said over his shoulder. "I ain't taking no chances…this is some crazy shit."

The team moved beyond the array of mutilated dead. The men quietly stepped to the jungle's edge and peered beyond the foliage, into the village of San Delbaro. Richter signaled his men to disperse on a wide margin. The men extended at five meter intervals along the front. As Marcoli had earlier, each man gazed upon the agony that the villagers succumbed to. While Team Bravo observed the human wreckage a burst of wind scooted across the square.

The slender whirlpool skipped across the open area. It momentarily blocked their view of the heaped bodies and wailing women. The spinning air column pulled the poorly worked thatch from a few of the hamlets before continuing on, dissipating at the trees. Richter looked behind him, upon the slaughter nearest them.

He gazed upon the women suspended from the trees. This was not the work of soldiers, he thought. The men who did this may or may not have worn uniforms, but in any event they were not soldiers.

He recalled the warning given to him by his company commander upon returning to Vietnam as an officer. He was already well aware of such precarious situations from his first tour a year and eleven months earlier. "Beware of the civilians," his commander kept repeating. It was the civilian who lashed out irrationally when under stress. If capture appeared imminent and you had a choice, you were better off a prisoner of soldiers. As soldiers, themselves, the enemy normally had a code they lived, fought, and died by—for the most part. A written instrument outlining acceptable standards of conduct when closing with an enemy. Their discipline enabled them to cap much of their fear when taking a captive. The captor was aware, in most instances, that the prisoner was no different than he—just another man in a different cut of cloth. He may have been cautious, but a captor feeling gripped by fear because of an enemy, once that enemy was surrounded and subdued, was not likely. Unlike the trained regular, it was the civilian, country peasant, or city dweller that heightened a soldier's anxiety.

It was his lack of exposure to military conditions that caused the civilian's irrational tendencies. His limited depth triggered him to over react, especially when seized by a mob mentality. These were the peace lovers—people who alienated themselves from the actual event until confronted with no tidier option.

People, Richter believed, who silently praised themselves for their ability to remain at a distance. People who sound out loudly when committing other men and women, someone else's son or daughter, into the havoc of fire and steel. Too good to dirty their hands but too dirty to abstain from a process that puts someone else's child on the firing line. Whether committed to sudden unthinking overkill with a garden hoe or guiding the efforts of others by way of their eloquent halved tongues, it was nothing but a hack job. Richter gazed upon the barbaric display.

"My god, Cliff. Look at this…it's medieval."

Ramsy looked to his left and saw Richter staring back at the human devastation. The sergeant major glanced back as well.

"Yeah. It's the Dark Ages, Captain—and we're right in the middle of it."

Richter shook his head in agreement then faced Marcoli.

"Pick a man and cut 'em down," he said. Richter looked to Ramsy. "Okay, Sergeant Major. Let's go in. See what they've got to say."

Team Bravo broke from the foliage on line. As the soldiers stepped from the brush, the preoccupied villagers did not notice them. The team moved cautiously, weary of snipers, as they closed on the township square. Richter was perhaps thirty meters from a lamenting woman when she looked up and in his direction. She apparently believed they were the killers returning to finish off those they missed.

She screamed out, signaling to the others the potential for slaughter. The other women responded to her warning and turned quickly. They hastily rose to their feet while discarding their dead and scurried into the jungle. There was nothing they could do, Richter knew.

"I guess they don't feel like talking," he said.

"We'd spend all day just trying to find one of 'em," Ramsy replied.

The team resumed its encroachment until closing with the fly-ridden pile of dead. The men watched as thousands of flies crawled over the plentiful food source. As the bodies were in direct sunlight, bloating had already began. Richter motioned his left hand before his face to dissipate the rising stench. He brushed aside the hungry insects seeking nourishment from him as well. He eyed the pile for a quiet moment.

"Looks like they've outdone themselves," he said to himself.

"What's that, Captain?" Ramsy asked.

"What? Nothing. Have the men sweep the village. See if we can come up with anything that'll shed some light on this."

Gable, Colfield, Sanford, and Bard began a hut-to-hut search. Each took particular care when entering a hamlet. Proven cautious habits were not easily discarded by the men. They knew that although this was not Vietnam, all it took was one careless assumption to get them blown away—in particular, when there were three times as many dead around as there were living.

From one hamlet to the next, two men alternated along each row. Each man grudgingly took his turn charging through the doorway and into the unknown. On his third hut, fifth along the row he and Colfield searched, Gable found what he did not want to.

Upon bursting open the door Gable caught a glimpse of a man from the corner of his eye. He zeroed his weapon on the unexpected occupant. He studied the apparent noncombatant while the villager attempted to hide himself in the corner. The fearful man stooped behind a large reed basket. He yelped his desire to live as he buried his face in his arms. Gable stepped to the man and observed him for a moment.

"All right! Let's go, friend."

"No. No, please. Don't shoot. Please," the villager said.

He had an obvious Spanish accent, but there was no doubt that whoever the man was he spoke English well. A flavoring of the old country, but not so much it hampered his articulate pronunciation of the foreign words. Gable was impressed but not for long.

"I ain't got time for this," he said. "Get up. Move!"

The villager slowly lowered his arms. His eyes looked as if they emerged from behind a shield. They were a piercing black and readily emanated the terror that consumed him.

"You're not them," the villager said. "Who are you?"

"Elton John," Gable answered. "Now, get your ass up and move."

The man slowly rose. He used the grass walls for support as he stood up in the corner. As the villager straightened, Gable took two careful steps back.

"I thought they came back, to kill the rest of us," the man explained.

Gable grew impatient and stepped forward. He took the man by his arm. He yanked the villager toward the door, forcing him out of the hooch and into the open.

"Don't press your luck," he said, while pushing the villager through the doorway. "When I tell you to move, that's just what the fuck I mean, Gomez."

Gable guided the man along the throughway to the village square. Colfield continued his search of the last three huts with Levits. As they approached Richter and Ramsy, Gable allowed for a few meters of distance between his weapon and the man's back.

"Hey, Captain!" he said. "Look what I found."

"Where'd you find him?" Richter asked.

"In that hooch over there."

"Anything else in there?" Ramsy asked.

"Nothing we can use." He looked to the prisoner. "Let's see what you got."

Gable grabbed the villager at the back of his shirt collar. Using both hands he vigorously ripped the material in two. After discarding the cloth he kicked outward on the inside of the man's ankles. He stuck his hands between the prisoner's arms and body, forcing the villager's arms upward. He ordered the villager to hold his arms straight out from his body. As Gable searched along the baggy pant legs Richter and Ramsy began their questioning.

"What's your name?" Richter asked.

"I am José Murillo."

"What place is—or was—this?" Ramsy asked.

"It is the village of San Delbaro, or it was."

"Why were you hiding in there?" Ramsy went on.

"I thought they came back, to kill the rest of us."

"Who did this to you?" Richter asked.

"I don't know—only that they were soldiers."

"Then they were soldiers? Government troops?" Richter asked.

"Yes."

Gable completed the body search. He slapped Murillo's hands down to his sides.

"He's clean, Captain."

"Everyone else hides in the jungle," Richter began again. "You hide in a hooch. If we can find you, they can."

"I was afraid. I didn't think."

"How long ago did this happen?" Ramsy asked.

"Three—almost four hours."

"That was the shooting we heard in the distance," Ramsy said.

"Seems so," Richter replied.

The suspicious tone in Richter's voice was equal to his gaze of disbelief.

"How many soldiers were there?" Ramsy asked.

"Five, six."

"What was their armament?" Richter asked.

Murillo paused. He looked at the captain with questioning eyes. He spoke English well, Richter thought, but he was apparently not familiar with all the jargon.

"Weapons," the captain added.

"Pistols, rifles. One truck."

"Truck! What was in it?" Ramsy asked.

"I do not know, sir."

From Richter's viewpoint there was no acceptable reason for Murillo to be alive. Every man Murillo's age, give or take twenty years, lay in a pile not more than twenty feet from where they stood. But for some reason this man miraculously evaded the penalty for being a part of San Delbaro.

"Okay," Richter resumed. He rested his rifle in his folded arms. "I've got a very important question for you, now. It will have a direct impact on your life…How come you're still alive?"

"It is because of me all this happened—or they try to make it that way," Murillo explained.

"How do you mean?" Ramsy asked.

"A week ago," he began, "soldiers came to our village. They said if we cooked the leaves for them that we would have wealth. More than we could imagine."

"Leaves? Cocaine?" Richter asked.

"Yes."

Richter looked about the human tragedy.

"And you refused—obviously."

"Yes."

"You could have made a lot of money," Ramsy jabbed.

"No," Murillo countered. "There is no money for the worker. We heard about the villages that agreed. It only brought them misery. My people picked me to speak because

I was in the army. I told the soldiers we didn't want it. They said they would return in case we changed our minds. They came back but not to talk."

"That doesn't explain why you're still alive," Richter drew down.

"Because I spoke for the village, they punish me by letting me live. Making sure that I know my—their refusal caused all this. Look around you. There's nothing left. When the old women are gone there will be nothing to remember…This village is dead."

Again, Richter eyed about the village. He visually took in the nearby dead. He considered the young women in the trees. He gazed upon the dead livestock strewed about the village grounds. *Peculiar punishment for a spokesman*, he thought.

"Very profound," he said. "You speak English well. Where'd you learn?"

"The army," Murillo explained. "I was a translator."

"An educated man, leaving a soft military job for this?" Ramsy dug.

"They are—were—my people. I wanted to give something back."

"Where are the children?" Ramsy asked. "I don't see any. They weren't with the women."

"They took the women, some children. The old women hid the infants in the jungle."

"Labor?" Richter asked.

"The women are for the soldiers. The children are taken across the border. There, they're sold."

"Sold? Slavery?" Ramsy asked. "That's a new one."

"They didn't take your women," Richter said.

"What do you mean?"

"You'll find 'em about seventy meters back in the bush. My men are cutting 'em down now."

"Cutting them down?"

Another questioning expression beamed from Murillo's eyes. The two men simply looked at him, Ramsy with blank brown eyes that suggested indifference, Richter with cutting blue pupils that disclosed his neutral point of view.

Murillo slowly backed away from them. He accelerated his pace while turning in the direction Richter nodded. The villager made only six paces when the captain stopped him.

"Wait!"

Murillo immediately stopped. He did not want to test the man. He turned and faced Richter.

"Slowly," the captain warned.

Murillo turned about and guardedly resumed to where Richter motioned. The closer he came to the jungle's edge the more his steps quickened. As they watched Murillo disappear beyond the treeline Richter and Ramsy evaluated the awkward variables.

The captain pulled out his chart, again making a terrain analysis. Richter had a deep appreciation for always knowing where he was. He oriented his grid map to the north and compared it to the surrounding terrain. He easily located San Delbaro once pinpointing three prominent terrain features. There was no name shown adjacent the lighter colored depression on the chart.

"We got another four hours to H-hour. My guess is two more in the saddle, judging by this."

"We don't want to get there too early," Ramsy warned.

"Hm. No sense in making ourselves a target."

Richter eyed about and judged the amount of dead. He made a quick estimate of time in relation to labor.

"We don't have enough time to sort and bury. I guess this is one time the typographers showed some insight."

"How's that?" Ramsy asked.

"The village," Richter replied. "They left San Delbaro off the map. It just shows a slight depression along the trail—and that's just about all that's left."

"Nothing like vision," Ramsy said. "Just a minute, Alex. Levits!"

The sergeant major made a quick scan of the village. He spotted Levits stepping from behind a hamlet, zipping up his fly.

"Yeah, Sergeant Major!"

"Put a man at each end of the village, fifty meters up the trail. I don't like surprises."

"Roger!"

Levits looked about while rearranging his belt. He saw Bard and Sanford searching through a makeshift corral at the rear of a hooch.

"Hey! You two come with me," he ordered. He turned his attention to Ray Copeland, who scavenged through one of the huts. "Copeland! Get somebody to help you take down that pile. Lay 'em out."

Richter observed Levits as the soldier provided thorough and confident guidance. Whatever it was, the captain thought, Levits appeared to be over it.

"Levits' problem seems to be behind him," he said.

"Premission jitters. That's all," Ramsy said. "On the move, you can't keep 'im down."

"That surprised me," Richter added. "In the past, solid as a rock."

"Still is, Alex," Ramsy defended. "That's what they call fair wear and tear."

"We all got a little bit of that."

"More than our share," Ramsy said.

He spotted Murillo step from the jungle. The villager moved straight for them. Only Ramsy saw him coming.

"Well, here comes Mr. Anguish, himself."

Richter faced Murillo and made a snap judgment.

"What do you think, Cliff?" he asked. "Seem real enough?"

"Who knows? Story seems to have a touch of truth."

"The reason he's alive?"

"You want 'im dead, don't you?" Ramsy said. "Ah, we've seen some squirrely shit in our time, Alex. Some of it making no sense at all."

"We better keep an eye on him. There's something about that man that aggravates me."

By the time he reached the two soldiers Murillo had undergone a change in psyche. He concentrated on his new, self-imposed mission. He knew Mendez would permit his men latitude, but Murillo did not believe their actions would go so far. Upon closing with the two soldiers he confidently spoke up.

"If you're not here to kill us, what is it you want?"

"Well!" Ramsy countered. "That's a striking change in attitude."

"I can help," Murillo said.

"You know why we're in-country," Richter said. "You're not that isolated out here. If the Colombian *federales* can find you way out here then you probably know our mission."

"Drugs?"

"Hm," Ramsy responded.

"Let me help you."

"Why do we need your help?" Richter asked.

"I can take you through the forest twice as fast," Murillo explained. "You show me where you want to go, I'll get you there, safe. No soldiers."

"Speed's not an issue," Richter said. "Now, if you know of any other patrols in the area, that would help."

"The soldiers went that way," Murillo answered.

He pointed to the trail leading out of the village.

"Southwest," Ramsy said.

"West-southwest," Murillo countered. "Their truck could not leave the road."

"Why that way?" Richter asked.

"I don't know," Murillo said. He took a few seconds to look over the team. "I count eleven men. Is that your strength?"

"Why?" Richter asked suspiciously.

"Please, let me help. If you don't, I'll follow," he demanded.

"Oh, I don't recommend that," Ramsy said.

"Why?"

"Because if you do," Richter countered, "we'll kill ya."

"Please! Understand…"

"What?" Richter lashed.

"I don't believe they killed all the women."

"Some are missing?" Ramsy asked.

"One," he said. "My sister. She—"

"Well, now!" Richter cut in. "Why would they let you and your sister live?"

"Oh, now you want 'em both dead," Ramsy added.

"I told you why they left me. My sister is a young and beautiful woman. She will bring a good price in Ecuador."

"How young?" Ramsy asked.

"Seventeen."

It was all up in the air, Richter thought. Could they trust him or couldn't they? He felt that Ramsy was reasonably satisfied with Murillo. He knew the sergeant major would never allow the man to venture into the jungle by himself, if not. Ramsy believed the man was nothing more than a spared messenger to spread the word. It was Murillo's questions that troubled Richter.

Asking for their strength, wanting to know the location of the alternate objective, demanding to accompany Team Bravo on the pretext that he could shorten their travel time. They were questions and demands that caused Richter to throw up an immediate defense.

"Right now you can help my men sort your dead," Richter said. "After that, I'll let you know."

"Thank you. Thank you, sir."

"Don't thank 'im," Ramsy snapped. "He hasn't given you anything, yet."

Murillo quickly backed away. He turned about and moved to assist the soldiers with the collection and sorting of San Delbaro's dead. While Murillo helped Copeland and two others dismantle the stack, Ramsy and Richter stepped aside. They moved next to a hooch about twenty meters from the villager.

"He makes my skin crawl, Cliff."

"Same as our illustrious pilots," Ramsy said. "The only way you can be sure of 'im is if you never take your eyes off 'im."

"Yeah, well—like our pilots, he wouldn't much care for

the alternative. Where the hell are they, anyway?"

Richter scanned the village, spotting Masterson and the copilot sitting at the settlement's edge. The two men rested some fifty meters from where Marcoli and two others tended to the remains in the trees. They settled themselves in the shade. Masterson rested his elbows on his knees while the copilot munched on what appeared to be a cookie. What gall, the captain thought.

"Hey, Lieutenant!" Richter blared. He pointed to the stack of dead. "Why don't you two give my people a hand, here?"

"We're pilots," Masterson shouted. "Not graves registration."

"Attitude," Ramsy said just above a whisper.

"Right now, Lieutenant," Richter commanded, "you're whatever the hell I say you are. Do it!"

Richter turned to Ramsy. He wanted to satisfy his curiosity over something the sergeant major had asked. Cliff never showed much interest in women. At one time he suspected Ramsy of being a homosexual. Not that it would make any difference to him. The old war-horse showed him so much over the years that Cliff could screw a knot hole for all he cared—as long as it wasn't his. The homosexual thing turned out to be a dead issue, however, when he pulled the then first sergeant out of a back ally hooch in Saigon. He saved Cliff from three boom-boom girls trying to screw the life out of him. As Richter recalled, they damned near succeeded.

"Why did you ask how old the girl was?" Richter asked.

"Hm," Ramsy replied.

He shrugged his shoulders while glancing down at the captain.

"Why, Cliff. You dirty old man."

"Alex," the sergeant major answered. "I might be twenty years your senior, but that doesn't mean the plumbing's gone rusty."

Seventeen

The deads' relocation was tedious at best. The team dismantled the heap of male remains and lined the bodies adjacent the stable in the square. Marcoli and two others carried the butchered women to the town's central. They placed the bodies in a separate line parallel to their dead men. The men of Team Bravo were not unaccustomed to dealing with the dead, but this grotesque task left them emotionally rattled. The dead had already surrendered to biological aggression.

The men had to cover their faces with bandannas and don their leather gloves before handling the remains. At the women's execution site, one man removed his shirt. He waved the material about, trying to scatter the assailing flies and dissipate the fetid odor of rotting meat. When they completed the placement and covering of the bodies Marcoli raised his right arm to his face. He caught the scent of rancid flesh. It permeated the fabric.

As he took in the stinking fragrance a chill rose through him. Marcoli shook off the spasm then brushed his hands over his sleeves and down his front. Dead was one thing, he thought, but this was on the level of garbage disposal.

Given the team's time constraints and their limited resources, the men provided only a nominal measure of courtesy to the dead.

They shrouded each body with what loose paraphernalia was at hand. They used bamboo mats from the hamlet floors and beds, and blankets or other fabrics that were readily available. As they negotiated the west trail the men of Team Bravo suppressed their visions of San Delbaro, returning their focus to the mission at hand.

At approximately two hundred meters outside the village the team varied from the road. They moved southwest into the jungle. As they advanced to the alternate objective, Richter kept thinking of what Murillo had told him.

The captain considered the *federal* troops as a possible link to the team's destination. Murillo described the small contingent as basically infantry with one motorized vehicle. Had the vehicle been a jeep it would obviously be for the officer to ride in. The villager spoke of a small cargo truck, however. He described the characteristics of what was possibly an old three-quarter ton removed from the U.S. inventory a decade before. The team continued its southwest trek. The men returned to their routine of sharp lookout, but there was always a degree of lightness.

Levits positioned himself behind Masterson. He broke dispersal criteria by moving up, close behind the pilot. Upon reaching the lieutenant, Levits removed the aircraft wiring from his top pocket.

"Hey, Lieutenant."

When Masterson turned he saw the wires practically pushed into his face. The pilot glared at Levits for a bitter moment, then reached up and yanked the useless cords from the sergeant. Levits saw how his jovial disposition got the better of the officer. He decided to capitalize on his edge.

"You might need 'em later," he said.

Ramsy watched the born-again sergeant reduce the pilot to the level of a numb-nut. It amused the sergeant major, knowing that Levits' sense of humor derived from his new-found confidence. *And besides*, Ramsy thought, *the piss-ant pilot deserves it*. Levits' ploy conjured visions of his own playful personality. Ramsy recalled that when he first met Alex the man was a second lieutenant. Perhaps one with good enlisted time behind him, but Alex was a butter bar all the same.

Day ten of the cycle. *Wing day*. Graduation if the men could traverse the final hurdle. Eighty-seven men reported for inspection at 0600 hours. Their shivering bodies stood as rigidly as they could before their downed combat load. The cadre stepped from one equipment display to the next. They were to assure that every man had an equal weight bearing load. Ramsy stood off to the side and quietly observed as his fellow cadre verified each cadet's readiness. When told to load their gear, the cadre permitted each man to pack his equipment in whatever fashion he chose. Lieutenant Richter was not afforded the same courtesy.

Ramsy deliberately hovered over the man. His knee pressed into the officer's shoulder as the lieutenant stored his equipment. When Alex finished packing and strapping, Ramsy grabbed the ruck before he could take hold of it. As the rappel master simulated testing for appropriate weight, he slipped an eight-pound lead piece under the rucksack's flap. The lieutenant had no idea he was about to embark on the air assault stroll with an equipment load eight pounds heavier than any other soldier. The rappel master thought it was a cute little prank, and Alex did not suspect any difference until about mile six.

The march began at the corner of Colorado and 25th Street and encircled the Clarksville base. All of the cadre, including Ramsy, accompanied the trainees. The tutors made the march suited in lightweight physical fitness or sweat clothes. The cadets hustled to the sound of the badgering groomers clad in full battle fatigues, steel pot, combat boots, LBE, rifle, and what seemed like an added ton brimming from their rucksacks. What began as a simulated stroll through the park quickly transformed into a menacing, man-by-man elimination.

The December day was a chilling thirty-three degrees with heavy overcast. A five-inch snow fell two days before. A nominal surface amount melted away a day earlier. Most of the paved roads were clear, but all of the forest routes rapidly turned thick with mud. The heavy, half-frozen paste gripped at their boots.

The farther along the route the more sluggish their pace became. It was a twelve-mile force march. The men were originally told they had three hours in which to complete it. Four miles into the trek, however, the cadre informed them that if they did not complete the march within two and a half hours they should turn in their weapons and head out the front gate. Ramsy was there to make sure that did not happen.

At mile six the men began to scatter. The younger, more agile troops, who ran cross-country in high school and college, happily made their way through the course. The older, less flexible soldiers, who tried to relive their youth, pulled up the rear. Most hung in the middle and steadily trudged through the weighted mud that helped to enhance their training. Alex was forward the mass. Just ahead of the middle but well behind the cross-country buffs.

It was at mile ten that the lieutenant had his insightful experience. He did not know from where the notion came. Nothing external triggered it, that he knew of. All Alex knew was that something from within him said to face forward. To whom or about what, he could not say. When Alex looked up he realized that he had not lost his combat intuitiveness since returning to the States.

He eyed ahead and upon a Green Beret. The proud soldier donned his prized headgear as a show of *esprit de corps*. He could not eliminate his steel pot's weight, however. He affixed the helmet to the back of his rucksack. The man was perhaps ten feet ahead of him and stepped adjacent to the right margin of the trail. Alex stayed at the trail's center. It was just as he looked up that it happened.

The Green Beret suddenly turned about. He faced Alex with eyes that revealed the anguish he had succumbed to. His face glowed, showing an almost purple cast. Alex watched the soldier take two staggering steps backward and tumble off the trail, down the snow-covered embankment. As he watched the body drop from sight, the lieutenant stepped to the trail's edge.

He peered over the rim and watched the Green Beret tumble down the fifty-foot incline. Alex saw how the man lay on his back in the snow. There was no movement except for the rapid expansion and contraction of his chest. Alex could hear the accompanying loud, air-sucking gasps the soldier made on every intake. The lieutenant saw how a heavy cloud of steam rose from the green-clad body. He watched as the hot vapor blasted from between the man's lips. His first impulse was to help. If not descend the hill at least comment to one of the cadre. Before he could remark on the disappearing soldier, however, Alex found himself under siege.

"Don't you stop!" Ramsy yelled. He charged to behind the lieutenant, yelling at the back of Alex's neck. "We'll send someone back for the body after the thaw."

Alex glanced up at the rappel master. He knew the man's statement was insincere. Ramsy's words were a training ploy more than anything. They kept the men believing they possessed little or no worth until awarded their wings. It had been awhile since he heard such cold indifference to life. The remark struck him funny. Alex revealed a slight grin before turning about and resuming the last two miles.

Alex rounded the last corner and ran into the training facility proper. Ramsy noticed the officer fall back to mid-class. He watched the lieutenant double-time to the pull-up bars. Every cadet had to sling his rifle and perform ten pull-ups with the weight of his combat load dangling from him. Just as Alex squeezed out his tenth pull, Ramsy stepped to the bar and commanded one more pull for the school. Alex strained out one more as commanded.

He dropped to the ground and double-timed to the push-up area. He lowered himself into the partially coagulated, freezing mud. Alex laid his rifle over the back of his hands to keep the weapon from touching the gumbo-pasty ground. He heaved out the required twenty push-ups, seriously believing the last two might not happen for him. As before, Ramsy was there to provide training enhancement. He demanded that Alex deliver one more push-up for the school or make the short but final trek out the post front gate.

Alex lowered himself for the twentieth time. His knotting arms failed to stop his descent. His nose plunged into the chilling mud. He squeezed out the additional push, but from where the strength came from Alex never knew. With the final trial behind him the lieutenant rose from the freezing paste and staggered along with the others.

It was nothing like Alex or the others expected. Instead of a ceremony in a warm auditorium, the emotionally distraught, physically drained, sweat-soaked, mud-covered, shivering-cold soldiers found themselves directed into a gutted World War II barrack.

There was nothing in it, Alex saw—no chairs, no desks, no tables. The interior walls were the backs of the boards making up the exterior walls. The electricity was off. The only light seeped through the dirty windows from the dull overcast day outside. And of all things, no heat. The building felt as cold, if not colder, than the falling degrees outside. As the men filed in, both Ramsy and Richter overheard one soldier's spontaneous comment.

"Hell!" he said. "These guys don't give ya nothin'. We finish the course, they still treat us like rhinoceros shit."

Two men fell to the concrete floor. The muscle spasms in their depleted legs rendered them useless. O'Connor passed out. He inadvertently struck his head onto the granitelike pavement. The cadre called for a medic after having New York removed from the formation. Two other graduates dragged him aside and anchored the unconscious graduate against a wall. As the weary men maintained their limp attempts at a position of attention, one of Ramsy's assistants entered the building. In his hand was a box containing the prize that culminated the last ten days of training. Before they opened the container, however, Ramsy felt compelled to say a few words of praise.

"Today is the most memorable day in your life," he began. "Today you men become Air-Assault qualified. Now, what does that mean? It means that when you're sent home in your box, your mother will be proud to recall that your Bloodwings came from the 101st Airborne, Air Assault. And now, the tagging."

Ramsy and three of his cadre moved from one man to the next. They adhered the coveted wings upon the chest of each graduate—literally. After removing each award from its carton they discarded the clasps. Instead of piercing just the fabric of the graduate's uniform, a profoundly Air Assault ritual manifested. The proud cadre pressed the sharp prongs against the soldier's breast just above the U.S. Army tape. They anchored the wings against the graduate with their left hand. They then followed through with a solid blow onto the badge with a clenched right fist. It drove the half inch prongs into the soldier's breast. These were the Bloodwings, Ramsy thought. Wings seated in flesh, baptized in the fluid of life. When his assistant reached Lieutenant Richter, Ramsy could no longer hold himself in reserve.

"Wait!" Ramsy cut. "This one's mine."

Ramsy looked into Alex's tired eyes. He saw that the fatigued junior officer could barely keep them open. Alex was on the edge, Ramsy knew. Almost on the verge of collapse. That was good.

The rappel master slowly lifted the wings from the box. He took an unusual amount of time to turn the badge over and remove the clasps from the needles. He wanted the full psychological impact of having the sharp prongs sunk into his flesh work on Alex. He pressed the needles against the man's breast and gradually worked the tips through the material. He lingered for a short time, letting the points slowly lance into the skin.

"Lieutenant," he said. "I'm so proud."

Ramsy delivered a horrendous blow onto the wings. The half-inch needles drove into the lieutenant's chest. Ramsy watched as Alex's eyes rolled back in their sockets. The officer's upper body gave from the driving impact. Alex took one step backward to maintain his balance. He quickly regained a semisolid stance. Ramsy looked down at the much younger man. His eyes showed the joy that he felt for the tough little son of a bitch that took everything he imposed. The lieutenant raised his tired eyelids and eyed the rappel master. He revealed a mutual look of satisfaction.

Spellbinding! the sergeant major thought. Ramsy realized that he had drifted from the operation. He was not sure for how long, but he felt that it was for no more than a few seconds. He felt a little self-conscious for permitting himself a luxury he scolded others for. While he maintained his distance behind Levits, Ramsy wondered what took place ahead.

Richter positioned Murillo behind him. He knew his radioman would cover his back if the villager attempted something stupid.

Ray Copeland switched with Marcoli for the point position. Marcoli located himself farther back, behind Ramsy. Like the others, he kept his distance and a sharp eye and ear out for anything looking or sounding out of the ordinary. Of course, what ordinary was under such conditions, Marcoli did not have a clue. Ahead, Murillo grew impatient over his ineffectiveness on the team. He hurried his pace to catch up with the team leader.

"Captain, I could do more ahead with your pointman."

"Why?" Richter asked.

The captain maintained his forward gaze, acting as if the man were not there.

"Because I know this place. I can lead you anywhere you want to go. We could be there in maybe half the time," Murillo persisted.

"We could also be dead."

Murillo immediately stopped and refused to advance any further. His defiance caused Richter some momentary aggravation. The captain raised his right hand and made a fist to signal the team to halt. Whether intending to or not, the stubborn villager forced Richter into a confrontation. Richter decided to listen but purposely glanced at his watch.

The villager surprised himself. He was caught off guard by his own impulse and equally surprised to see how the tactic worked.

"Captain," Murillo continued. "I came along for my sister, and I'll do whatever I have to do to save her—if she's still alive. I'm not interested in your mission or whatever you call it. All I want is for my sister to be safe…and to kill the man that took her."

"How do you know they're where we're going?"

"I don't, but there may be a chance."

It was the first thing that Richter heard from the villager that made him feel Murillo was forthright. If there was one thing he could readily relate to it was vengeance. Self-styled retribution was always a good motivation for keeping demoralized men going.

"Now, that's an emotion I can understand," Richter said. "All right. Move ahead. Tell Ray why you're there, but you stay in the lead."

"Yes, Captain."

The villager quickly started off. Richter grabbed him by the arm.

"As I told you," he warned. "We've got time. We take it slow and safe. You know our heading. That's enough. We'll let you know when we get there…No mistakes."

Richter watched Murillo move ahead. If they were in fact looking for the same man, he knew, the villager would not like the outcome.

If the Colombian officer was the commander of the exchange he had to be categorized as mission essential. It was imperative the butcher soldier be captured, brought back for interrogation, and conscripted into their service, if possible. As Team Bravo closed to within a grid square of the alternate objective, Captain Velázquez directed his men to encircle the phantom helicopter.

His pointman raced back to the column, describing what he had found. Ahead, some eighty meters, an unmarked helicopter sat on a small stream bank. Velázquez, a Colombian regular temporarily detailed to a small detachment out of the battalion headquarters in Quibdó, ordered his pointman to move ahead. Upon reaching the site Velázquez cautiously surveyed the area.

From the brush he saw the helicopter draped in camouflage screening. It suggested that whoever had attempted to conceal the aircraft did so with the intent of returning to reclaim it. It did not seem a prudent measure to leave an operational aircraft in the middle of a forest without adequate protection. After his returning scouts informed him there were no sentries or other troops spotted within the sector, Velázquez radioed his headquarters. He informed them of what he had found and of his intent to investigate.

Two soldiers moved forward utilizing a tight bounding overwatch technique. One man advanced while the other covered his movement. They alternated the maneuver until both men reached the aircraft. As he observed his men step under the camouflage netting, Velázquez considered the relationship between what had happened that morning and the helicopter sitting in the clearing.

He had known Lieutenant Pinto for only a short time. But in that time Captain Velázquez had come to realize that Pinto was a young military man of promise. Like himself, Pinto graduated from the *Universidad Nacional de Colombia* in Bogotá and majored in civil engineering. He heard of Pinto's demise over the radio earlier that day, and how the murderers flew from the battle site in a southwesterly direction. Finding the helicopter in such a secluded area compounded his suspicions. It convinced Velázquez, from his retributive standpoint, that a link between the infiltrators who abandoned the ship and the murder of his friend existed. *Providence*, Velázquez told himself. *Pinto killed this morning at the Golfo de Urabá, and now his killers are delivered to him only five kilometers from Salaquí.* Velázquez pondered a course of action while his men completed their inspection.

One man remained outside the helicopter while the other boarded. The one who entered searched aft of the aircraft first. As he rummaged through the cabin section he was conscious of possible booby traps and felt safer after not finding any. When he entered the cockpit he looked about the control panel and the copilot's seat before settling himself into the pilot's chair. When he attempted to entertain himself with visions of being a gunship pilot a whole new concept of expendable soldier flashed before him. Velázquez watched his men ignited.

The Claymore cracked loudly. The windscreen, along with the piecemealed soldier, blew forward. The blast created a chain reaction and set off the two concealed mines aft. The two succeeding explosions cut through the fuselage and into the fuel tank, igniting the remaining thirty-four gallons of JP-4. The roof of the aircraft shot upward. Flaming chopper fragments and spraying fuel spread over the clearing. The man thrown onto his stomach, outside the helicopter, became dazed and disoriented, just before his clothing ignited. The captain looked on, mesmerized.

Velázquez stood stupefied by the sudden devastation. For a moment he was unable to think, numbed by the incident. As the last piece of aircraft fell to the clearing, Velázquez released a wild, incoherent yell that echoed throughout the valley.

Within seconds he capped his overwrought emotions. The captain ordered his men to sweep the area. He demanded they go over the ground until locating the trail he knew the murderers would leave. It took his men twelve minutes to spot the worn path leading southwest. He ordered his pointman forward.

Copeland ordered Murillo to move ahead five meters. He constantly checked their azimuth to insure the villager did not deviate. They progressed well, he thought. According to the captain there was sufficient time and the sun was still high. He glanced at his watch. It showed 1740 hours. When he looked up Copeland saw that Murillo had stopped on the trail.

Murillo was not sure of what it was; he did know that it was not a part of the natural setting. He leaned forward, straining to see into the thickets. *Should I say something?* he thought. Would the mechanism prove helpful or hindering? Deciding one less man was worth the risk, Murillo chose to take what he knew was a calculated chance. As Copeland approached from behind, Murillo pondered for an acceptable reason to halt.

"Why'd you stop?" Copeland asked. "Something ahead?"

"No," Murillo replied. "I—I have to piss. You go on ahead. I'll catch up."

Copeland nodded then proceeded ahead, while Murillo stepped to the side. The villager positioned himself before a tree. He untied his drawstring. Copeland continued forward and confronted the threat Murillo eluded.

When he felt the toe of his boot trigger the tension cord Copeland realized it was already too late. The mechanism actuated in the time it took for him to glance down then up. He watched as the eight wooden spikes suddenly emerged from under the leaves. He blinked once before feeling the ten inch, pin-sharpened stakes bury deeply into his chest and midsection. It happened so quickly, the spikes protruded out his back before the concept of pain registered. Copeland used his last few seconds to comprehend what took place.

He eyed himself. He silently analyzed the butchery that had befallen him. He used his last bit of strength to turn his head. The impaled man gazed upon the villager who had duped him. Murillo turned from the tree while retying his drawstring. He stepped to the soldier who simply waited to die.

His head slightly wobbled. More like a twitch of nerves, Murillo thought. The man let his head go forward, taking in the full impact of what had happened to him. Murillo casually stepped up to Copeland and saw the dying man's eyes glaring into his. He heard the soldier attempt to speak. He lowered his ear next to the dying man's lips. It sounded as if the man tried to say his name. He decided it was time the intruder got it right.

"That's Major Murillo," he whispered.

Murillo unsnapped the canteen cover and lifted the flask from Copeland's LBE. The officer unscrewed the cap and took a refreshing drink from Copeland's canteen, while quietly watching the man pass. Copeland died within seconds. The major took one more drink before Richter stepped into view.

As he approached, Richter scolded himself for being so naive. He recalled how Murillo told them he was good—able to get them through the jungle swiftly and without incident, or, in the villager's own word, "safe." He saw how Murillo held the canteen to Copeland's lips. After stepping around them and looking upon the fallen comrade, Richter began his personal siege.

"I know what!" he began. "I want to know why."

"We didn't see it," Murillo said. "I don't know—what—what else to say."

The balance of Team Bravo moved up. The men quickly converged on Copeland, all witnessing the results of Murillo's silence. As the men looked upon their fallen teammate, Richter gazed at the canteen still in Murillo's right hand. The major noticed the captain's focus and believed a simple explanation might reduce Richter's animosity.

"I tried to ease his pain. I thought maybe a—a drink of water..."

Ramsy moved up.

"What's the hold...Damn!" he said.

The sergeant major circled Copeland. He observed the wooden spikes sticking out of dead man's bloodied fatigue shirt. There were eight of them, he saw. All eight sticking through Copeland as if he were some kind of pin cushion. The sergeant major resumed his inspection as the team leader demanded answers.

"You were in the lead," Richter said. "Why didn't this happen to you?"

An unnerving silence filled the air. As the major shrugged his shoulders Ramsy felt obliged to remark.

"Yeah, I admit. The captain's wanted you dead from the beginning. So, why don't you tell us how you got by this one?"

"And make it good, Gomez," Gable cut.

"I—I had to piss. That's all."

Richter eyed the angry men surrounding the villager. He sensed the direction in which the swift interrogation would lead. Innocent or not it was too convenient. Murillo had evaded death a second time while the people around him had savagely succumbed to it. Richter glanced toward the villager a final time. He then casually turned away from the group and quietly stepped to the side. He lit a cigarette and nonchalantly permitted the villager's destiny to run its course. A few of the men wondered over the team leader's disassociation.

"Hey. What's with the captain?" Levits asked.

"He's taking a break," Ramsy answered. "He knows sergeant's business when he sees it."

"Yeah? You trained him pretty good, Sergeant Major."

"I did," Ramsy said.

"In all the years I've been doing this shit," Marcoli said, "you're the first I've seen saved by a piss."

Ramsy looked upon Copeland.

"What the hell's something like this doing in the middle of nowhere, anyway?" he asked the men.

"We were probably led into it," Sanford said.

"We didn't veer from the azimuth," Ramsy said. He turned to Murillo. "Is there a settlement nearby?"

Murillo shook his head no.

"Ain't no point in asking you, anyway," Marcoli said.

"Why don't you just show us where you took that piss, boy?" James said. "Couldn't be far."

Some of the men began to smirk over James' demand. Not that it was unacceptable evidence for what the villager claimed. More like something that none of them had to ask of anyone before; they felt a little ridiculous over the need to look at a man's patchwork. James held his ground, cutting through the subtle laughter.

"No! I'm serious," he went on. "If you say you had to piss then you show us where you pissed. Now!"

"It happened just before. I couldn't," Murillo replied.

At that point James' query was no longer considered absurd. The men looked at one another. Their expressions revealed their agreement in the fellow soldier's demands.

"So that means you still gotta go. Don't it?" James pressed.

Murillo looked from one face to the next and saw no sympathy. Even if he had to go now he couldn't, the major thought. He was about to speak but was cut off by another soldier.

"Whoop it out, boy," Marcoli commanded. "And you better piss long and hard."

Murillo eyed the captain and saw the team leader's back to him. Richter continued to stand aside, able to hear everything said but refusing to prevent what he believed was the inevitable. Again, the major studied the hard face of each man standing around him. He turned away from the hostile group and stepped a few feet down the trail. He untied his drawstring while concentrating to provide a realistic quantity. *This is ludicrous*, he thought. *They're unreasonable.* As he stood with his organ in hand providence showed Murillo a way.

He was about to give up when he heard the huge explosion in the distance. The tremendous blast bellowed through the valley. It caused him to jump. He believed one of the impatient soldiers grew tedious over his lack of results. A split second later Murillo realized he was not shot. The major wheeled about. He saw that every man looked down the path they had just blazed. He knew it was his one and only opportunity. Murillo scurried into the brush.

It was Gable who turned first and caught a glimpse of the villager. He raised his rifle but stopped before squeezing off a round.

"No!" Richter said. The captain turned to James and simulated a throat cutting by motioning his fist across his neck. "James...silently."

James pulled his bayonet.

"Roger," he said.

Within an instant he was gone, chasing after the villager. The team remained in place and waited for James' return. Gable commented after denied the sure kill.

"You should have sent me, Captain," he said, holding up his LAW. "I would have jacked his ass with this."

"No way," Richter replied. He pointed to the radio on Gable's back. "As of now, you're our only link to the outside."

"Judging by the direction and size of that blast," Ramsy added, "looks like we might be thumbing a ride home."

"That's two aircraft in one day, Captain," Masterson said.

"Yeah, well. I guess I outdid myself, Lieutenant." He looked upon the fallen soldier. "Let's get Ray off this thing."

Eighteen

Treadwell stepped into the tent unexpectedly. He told his radioman an hour before that he did not intend to return to operations for two hours. Tommy thought it peculiar for the commander to be away from the nerve center, especially when an interdiction team was in the bush. And, in particular, since Team Bravo took a substantial beating at the Gulf of Urabá just a few hours earlier.

And now they were missing, Tommy thought. Somewhere in the jungle or mountains, landed or crashed or who knew what. When it had to do with Captain Richter there was no telling what the erupting Team Bravo would get itself into. That was the rumor he heard, anyway. Treadwell was the colonel, the radioman conceded. The operator knew the man could do just about anything he chose to. Reiner did not appear concerned by the commander's absence.

Reiner, as chief area DEA, oversaw the deployment, intrusion, and extraction of all the paramilitary teams. Their missions came directly from him, as his agents and he cultivated the informants to be in the know.

He permitted the team leaders latitude in developing their operation orders. He knew that most of what took place beyond cantonment was more like a small unit offensive than a police action. He realized that the jungle conditions called for unorthodox techniques. The variables rendered most of his agents and their Hessian counterparts to either spies or mountain guerrilla fighters. The situation dictated that he exploit his team leaders at every opportunity when applying their headhunting craft. His intermediate goal was to squeeze every sound tactical advantage from the paid-for-hire officers. The neutralization of Zorrilla was, of course, Reiner's primary goal. He did not like referring to the men as mercenaries.

Paid for hire, hirelings, freelance, Hessians, soldiers of fortune—all names depicting troubled men with disturbed histories, men looked upon as having little worth irrespective of the contribution they made in the outback. True, Reiner sometimes thought, they were paid well for their skills—four times the going rate of a comparable soldier in the regular forces. The lucrative compensation was necessary, however, to entice such men to dump themselves into the midst of imminent danger. It also made up for the lacking accommodations they settled into when not in the field. Reiner liked to think of his teams as paramilitary forces. It took what he thought was a sharp edge off their degrading alternate titles.

At first he was not enthusiastic over the Justice Department's plan. Reiner wanted only enough to do with the project to let his higher-ups know he was on the job and making a contribution. He did not trust the money-oriented professionals. He believed many would sell out to the highest bidder, that being Zorrilla. But, he had to reluctantly admit, some of his own hand-picked DEA men had already stupidly compromised themselves. Initially, it was a smoke screen. A bureaucratic ploy to meet the simplest needs of his seniors while holding himself at a distance. Upon familiarizing himself with these estranged men the agent gradually came over to them. Reiner developed at least a mutual regard for most and even a high degree of respect for a chosen few, Ramsy and Richter being two he held in high esteem.

He was not excited by Treadwell's absence. If the colonel was not on station he was sure it was due to a matter of equal importance. If not mission-associated, Reiner thought, no reason for leaving could take priority over the men in the field. Epecially when not knowing the redeployment of a team subsequent to its calamitous encounter at the Gulf of Urabá. But he could only speculate while Richter and his team remained in the bush, attempting to drop the net.

Tommy could not tell him of Treadwell's whereabouts. The only thing he could tell Reiner was that the colonel stated he would return within an hour and a half. The agent graciously thanked the regular army specialist. He told the soldier of his intent to take a short nap on one of the shift worker's cots, and that if anything mission-worthy came up Tommy should wake him.

Reiner stretched his lengthy six-foot-five frame upon the cot. He pulled the bill of his red St. Louis Cardinals cap over his eyes. Upon a second notion he raised his head. He looked along his outstretched body, to the two size twelve and a half, E-wide skids, he called them. They dangled off the edge of the aluminum cross brace. He smiled over his critical self-analysis before returning his head to the mat. He closed his eyes with the idea of catching up on the sleep he lost in the last twenty-four hours. Reiner did not know for how long he dozed but knew it was not long. Instead of announcing himself he quietly lay and monitored the conversation between Treadwell and the operator.

As the colonel stepped in Tommy looked up from his station. He noticed Treadwell's face was bright red, looking, he thought, as if the old man was about to burst a vein. The colonel was thirty-eight years old and Tommy, who had just turned nineteen a few weeks earlier, debated over telling the older commander to sit down and catch his breath, because the elderly have to rest more often than younger men like himself. He considered it, but the idea became short-circuited when Treadwell began his probe.

"Tommy, you heard anything from Richter?"

"No, sir," the operator said. "Not since they hit the objective…or it hit them."

The colonel's uneasiness grew more apparent as the minutes elapsed. Treadwell rolled his perspiring hands over one another. He glanced at his watch after a third unconscious wringing of his fingers. This was totally out of the norm, he thought. Completely unacceptable. What the hell was that spiteful bastard up to? He looked at his watch once more. It showed 1730 hours.

"That's about four, four and a half hours ago," he said.

"Yes sir," Tommy replied. "Bout that."

"Anything on radar?"

"Canal Zone reports two aircraft in the area. One's Warrant Officer Taylor's scout plane. The other's commercial."

"How long ago was that?"

Tommy purposely glanced at his radiolog. He made the procedure as obvious to Treadwell as he could. He searched for the time entry of their last communication with the higher headquarters. The colonel expected the radiomen to log in every communication and later be able to accurately refer to it by time, subject, and with whom communicated. Tommy wanted to make sure that Treadwell knew he had complied with his demands.

"I logged it in twelve minutes ago, sir."

"Anything on the alternate frequency?"

"Not so far, sir," Tommy said. "I'm monitoring the primary and alternate simultaneously."

"Transponder?"

"Negative, sir."

Again, the colonel looked at his watch. He removed the beads of perspiration that smudged onto the crystal when he folded his arms. It showed 1734. He pondered the possibilities a moment more. He envisioned how an oblique measure could degrade their aims. He faced east, to the Serranía del Darién peaks rising like an impregnable fortress wall in the distance.

"Well, hell! They either landed or crashed," he said. "They don't have enough fuel for this much flight time."

"Roger that, sir," Tommy added.

Treadwell turned upon hearing the radioman's reply. He looked over Tommy's shoulder to the speaker screen. Like a child hoping for an outrageous wish from the supernatural, Treadwell eyed the speaker mesh and hoped to hear the phantom captain's voice. A quarter-minute later the colonel regressed to reality.

"Keep monitoring the primary and alternate," he said. "Check the secondary alternate frequency every fifteen minutes. If they're trying to communicate they'll be up on one of those three."

"Roger, sir," Tommy replied. "You want me to get back with Canal Zone?"

"Give it another twenty minutes then see what they have."

"We could…"

"You lose my team, Colonel?" A voice sounded from the back of the tent.

Treadwell looked to the far end of the tent. He spotted what looked like two bear paws drooping from the end of a cot. He could not see who it was because the screen, a sheet stolen from the supply tent, blocked the image above the knees. Already put out by the renegade captain's deviation from the operation order, Treadwell did not want the complication of uninvited guests sharing his acceptance of mission failure. He also did not need a witness to the potential for a complete communication breakdown.

He dashed for the rear of the tent. The colonel intended to seize the moment before it seized him. When he rounded the screen and saw Agent Reiner lying lazily on the cot, Treadwell attempted to put the DEA man on the defensive.

"Where the hell have you been hiding?" he began. "I've

been trying to reach you since 1400 hours."

Reiner quietly lay back. He was fully aware of the psychological edge the regular tried to gain over him. *He still thinks it's his command,* the agent thought.

"Is there a problem, Colonel?"

"Probably," Treadwell answered. "Richter's almost five hours overdue. He was suppose to return with the medevac. They said he took off in-country. We've had no radio contact, and they reported he had radio trouble. That's one of the oldest bullshit excuses in the inventory."

Reiner gave the tense man a few more nervous seconds. It was too easy. He said only five words to Treadwell, and the colonel provided him a complete brief of the situation. *He's really uptight over this*, Reiner thought.

The agent rose and sat on the edge of the cot. He raised the brim of his cap. He took an added moment to adjust it, in order to position the bill just above his eyebrows. Reiner liked the squared off edges low. It displayed a straightforward look about him. He liked the snug fit about his head as well. He looked up at Treadwell from over his left shoulder.

"Don't worry yourself, Brad," he said. "The Captain knows exactly what he's doing."

"And how do you know that?" Treadwell asked.

"'Cause I told 'im to do it."

The answer could not have cut Treadwell more severely than a slashing razor. In one simple reply it became clear to the colonel that he had lost control of his equipment and people. The big picture closed in. It left his command worthiness in question, he knew. Not even to be informed suggested doubt in his mission usefulness, loyalty, or both. Like a surrounded animal preparing for the final defending pounce, Treadwell verbally assaulted the agent.

"What the hell are you doing with my people!" he blared.

Reiner was in no mood to be made a victim of Treadwell's mouth.

"Your people, Brad?" he said, while jumping up from the cot. Reiner stepped up to the man. He coldly faced off with the officer. "Richter and his team are contract. Contracted by us. Not you."

"He's under my command!" Treadwell countered. "My equipment! My crews! My pilots!"

"No!" Reiner retaliated. "He's under my command, as are you, Colonel."

Their stonelike faces broke from one another. Treadwell relinquished first. He knew Reiner was right, that from an authoritative standpoint Richter was under Reiner in the operational chain of command. He was also within that chain, Treadwell realized, as everything was OPCON to Reiner. Like it or not, it was a Justice Department venture utilizing the military as a support vehicle for a freelance offensive. Like most of his fellow regulars, Treadwell found the idea loathsome. He bit hard onto the inside of his lower lip while listening to the agent.

"Brad," he resumed, "you have to understand. You do provide the operational support, but Richter is under my operational control. I will dictate what is required missionwise, and the captain will move by that direction. That we keep you informed, Colonel, may be looked upon purely as an intercommand courtesy."

"Well, what are my—your people doing out there?" Treadwell submitted.

"Can't say. It's classified."

"Classified!"

"Sure, Brad," Reiner counter. A broad smile covered his face. "And you know the rules. If I told ya, I'd..."

Keenly focused on the conversation, Tommy could not contain himself. He smirked. It was loud enough for both men to hear. The agent didn't care, but Treadwell was not pleased by the idea of being this E-4's object of amusement.

He sharply glanced to the specialist and delivered a glare that told the enlisted man everything he needed to know. It was a foregone conclusion for Tommy. If he did not redirect his attention upon the radio latrine detail was in his immediate future. He returned his focus onto the transceiver. He fiddled with the frequency selector knob to show he got the colonel's silent message loud and clear. Treadwell faced Reiner.

"I don't have to take this shit from you, Reiner," he resumed. "You may be some god-almighty GS-16, but this is still my command post, and I don't have to allow you in it."

Reiner took another half step into the colonel. His face was only inches from Treadwell's. It was apparent to Treadwell that his words had little impact on the man.

"Oh, you got that right, Colonel," Reiner bitterly said. "God almighty. Tell me, Brad. Are you undergoing a little outside pressure? Business constraints?"

Upon hearing the agent's question Treadwell realized there was more behind Reiner's purpose for being there. The agent had a decided ulterior motive behind his pretext of monitoring team progress. It was an ambiguous question. Dangerous.

"What's that suppose to mean?"

Reiner saw he unnerved the soldier. The agent knew that his message about who the colonel worked for, and how Treadwell fit into the overall picture, chipped away at his ego. Even more, Reiner liked the way his subtle question put the regular in a defensive static state. *If he only knew what we did*, Reiner amusingly thought. For the present it was sufficient for the colonel to understand that he had no control. Reiner knew it all along. Treadwell only began to realize it.

"Can't tell ya," the agent replied. "You know the rules."

Nineteen

James incessantly prosecuted the villager. He maintained a deliberate and even pace, reserving his energy for the stand off. His oxygen intakes corresponded in rhythm to his tiger-like foot pounces. He knew that steadfast rhythmic breathing would overcome the short malnourishing breaths that most others ran by.

Undeviating in his methodology he rigidly pursued in the adrenaline-pumping hunt. He became aware of a building excitement within him the further he advanced along the killing path. At one point he maliciously reduced his speed. He held back, only slightly, to draw out the stimulating process. He centered his vision on broken twigs, compressed grass, and other distortions at ground level.

The jungle did not have an imposing effect on James. He

accepted the dense greenery, thinking of it as a friend. In some ways the blinding brush invigorated the soldier. The idea of not being able to see his frightened quarry made for an exceptionally interesting stalk. When he reached the shallow stream James took a full minute to analyze the banks.

His eyes darted left and right, skimming over the pliable surfaces. He searched about his feet for sandal prints. He gazed across the stream to the far bank. He peered upon the soft mud for the man's exit trail. It was not there.

He looked into the rushing water, glaring downstream first. He eyed upstream and searched for a revealing sediment flow washing down. There was none. Downstream, he was sure. The poor creature headed downstream. He analyzed the far bank once more.

The eroded bank rose to ten feet above the water line. He noticed how hundreds of plant roots, from the vegetation at the bank's crest, coiled out of the earthen wall like emerging snakes. As James eyed downstream once more, Murillo resumed his evasion effort.

The major sideslipped on the submerged stones of the uneven stream bottom. He made too much noise, he told himself, while stepping over the alge-laden rocks. The coarse soles of his hemp sandals were little help. The fibrous material became saturated and denied him any substantial traction. He clumsily moved through the knee-deep water. He felt the heat building under his tunic.

The heavy tropical air took its toll. Murillo smelled his malodorous flesh burning under the thick fabric. The tunic came from the Segovia hamlet after the Americans tore his shirt from him. He felt his collected body temperature escape through the narrow neckline. It licked at the underside of his chin before filling his nostrils with the repugnant odor of unbathed body crevices.

Murillo untied the sash about his waste, discarding the constricting cord. He threw it into the water, letting the stream take it. His tunic hung open. It allowed for a free flow of air between the garment and his superheated flesh. He felt his rib cage rapidly expand with every breath. A feverish heat rose off his forehead. His brain cap felt as if it were about to blow from the fiery temperature inside his skull. He sensed he was on the verge of collapse.

He stood in the middle of the fluxing stream. The only sounds were of his dramatic exhalations and the driftage moving by his legs. He looked to his left, to the bank from where he approached. He knew that somewhere along it were the invaders stalking him. He eyed to his right, up the embankment on the far side. He prudently glanced behind him while reaching into the water.

He cupped his palms, cradling the water as he raised it to his face. Murillo doused his forehead and eyes. The water streamed over his chin and along his neck. In an instant the water's tempering effect permitted him clearer vision and thought. The yellow and red spots before his eyes began to vanish.

He reached for another palmful. He looked back to the summit of the far bank while again dousing himself. The major thought it peculiar that he did not see, or even hear, the soldiers who pursued him. His mind refreshed by the stimulating deluge, Murillo took a moment to reason out a direction for evasion.

He decided to cross the stream and climb the steep embankment. Murillo then realized he had already made up his mind to do so a full minute before. As he closed on the far side he felt the stream bottom give under him.

The chiseled wall of earth was his clue. He felt the bottom suddenly drop out from under him. The water rose up to his chest. He sensed the pliable mud replace the sturdier rock base only seven or eight decimeters behind him. He felt the vacuumlike mud grasp tightly about his settling feet. He tried to pull his left foot free. He strained the muscles in his leg while slowly lifting the extension from the sucking sediment. He simultaneously felt his right foot lower further into the silt. He eyed ahead and saw his goal was only a few meters from him.

He leaned forward, letting his upper body drop face down. He felt his redistributed body weight pull on the back of his legs. It shifted his heels moderately higher than his toes. The measure created enough space between his heels and the mud pockets to break the suction. The water seeped into the small gaps, eliminating the adhering affect of the gripping sediment. He used his hands and legs to dog paddled to the shore.

The water-soaked earth at the far bank enveloped about his hands. Hand over hand, he reached out and clawed at the resilient base. The denying ground tease him with the notion of progress. He felt and saw the water-laden soil ooze between his fingers on every grasp. He gripped at the beguiling bank at least ten times before reaching solid earth.

When he pulled himself from the mud Murillo saw himself covered in it. He wanted to wash himself but knew time was against him. The major whipped both his arms, flinging the loose sediment from his limbs. He began to tackle the almost vertical earthen wall.

He reached from one coiling tubercle to another. His open-toed sandals were of little use. He dug his exposed feet into the loose earth between them. He felt his fingers and arms cramp from his over gripping. The closer he neared the summit the more desperate the major grew. He felt the loose soil dislodge under his feet; he hectically scratched at the embankment with his toes. He clung to fragile stems that he was not sure could support him. As he stretched his quivering right hand high above him, reaching up to overlap the summit, Murillo began to grin. He almost laughed.

He clamped upon a clump of high grass at the apex. He used the collected stalks to draw himself up and over the edge. Murillo pulled at the reed clumps until he felt his painful knees resting on the solid crest. The climb exhausted him.

He rolled onto his back. He took in replenishing oxygen while giving himself a moment of peace. Through the jungle canopy a spot of sunlight. Its warming beams engulfed him from neck to thigh. Though exhausted from the difficult climb, he felt relieved by the sun, which was pleasing on his overheated body. *As if a sign*, he thought. It was like an exploding manifestation of renewed life surging within him. He permitted himself the luxury of another silent moment to regain his strength.

The major rolled onto his stomach. After rising to a stance he turned and faced into the sunlight. He let the warm rays splash upon his face. When he opened his eyes Murillo looked to his left and right, searching for a new course. He turned to look behind him.

James jabbed the seven-inch blade into Murillo. He watched how the villager's eyes bulged. He buried the steel piece up to its muzzle jacket. It penetrated the slender man just below the bottom left rib. Murillo did not move. He simply stood stiff. Like a mannequin, the major gazed into his killer's eyes. James took a quarter of a minute to study Murillo's pupils, while securing the paralyzed man on his feet with the immersed blade. He could not help himself.

"They always go for high ground," James whispered.

James yanked the blade from Murillo's chest. He felt the compressing meat's resistance on the steel as he withdrew it. He clung to the man's tunic with his left hand, supporting the almost lifeless frame. He reared once more. Again, he swiftly lunged his bayonet forward, in an upward arc, and connected with the man's midsection. He followed through with a surge upward, using all the strength that his right arm could muster. The corpse dropped to the ground, sounding a dense thud. He studied Murillo and wondered who the man actually was.

A bitter villager? he pondered. *A government soldier or plain backwoods informant? Perhaps one of Zorrilla's men? No one at all?* Regardless, Ray Copeland was dead because of what the man did or failed to do. That was enough. If he was just another victimized peasant it was no great loss. If Murillo was more than he claimed he may have known everything. It was peculiar that Richter would select him. All in all, the day went pretty well. He was alive, his secret still intact, and that was enough for the present.

James stooped over the body and wiped the blood-covered

blade upon the dead man's tunic. He replaced the bayonet into its scabbard before rising. He stared at the body a moment more. Again, he tried to pinpoint the man's true purpose for being where he was when they found him. Giving into his loss for an answer he turned away and stepped into the foliage. As James negotiated the stream, Lieutenant Santos escorted Alicia to Mendez.

The colonel sat at a small folding table in his tent. He thought over all of the additional safeguards he had put into place. He was sure his dozen heavily armed soldiers were sufficient to repulse anyone who might attempt to steal the cargo. He felt comfortably secure. The older survivors from the village, he was sure, had already spread the lethal word. Major Murillo would help to insure the word spread throughout the region. Mendez poured himself another drink while considering how in only three months he rose from a mere soldier to a highly regarded member of the network.

This particular shipment was worth almost thirty million American dollars. It was flattering of Zorrilla to entrust him with such an enormous transaction. For the cartel to give him such freedom proved their belief in him. Mendez also realized that his association with the army played a significant role in his worth.

Without his military connections, his access to classified military and police information, Zorrilla would treat him no better than one of the peasants. Regardless of his current importance, Mendez realized that what he did on this night had to take place flawlessly. He knew that if everything went according to plan, by 2200 hours he would become one of the richest and most powerful officers in the armed forces.

Upon reconsideration the colonel decided to let his lieutenant escort the children to Ecuador. He and a driver would return to Bogotá in the off-loaded truck. Santos would pay off the men and return with the balance. By the time the lieutenant returned from the border his power thrust would already be in motion. With Zorrilla's help he would return Colombia to a rightful military rule, himself as a general of the armed forces.

He would gain the power and regard equal to that of Torrijos in neighboring Panama.

His destiny, living or dead, hinged on this one critical transaction. If it went right he would be a brigadier within a week and perhaps the leader of Colombia within a year. If he somehow failed on this night Mendez knew he would not outlive the week. As he considered the consequences of failure, as opposed to the rewards for success, Mendez sipped on a glass of Canadian Club.

It was a gift from a U.S. military associate in Panama. Someone who also wished to enhance his military retirement with help from the outside. He raised the glass to his lips, consuming the entire three shots in two swift gulps. The colonel belched once. He covered his mouth with his hand before releasing the stomach gas. He began to pour himself another drink when Lieutenant Santos pulled the tent flaps aside.

The lieutenant herded the lovely woman into the tent. He stayed close behind Alicia while shoving her toward the colonel's table. When he tried to take hold of Alicia's arm the woman cocked the limb and snapped it from his hand. A mild show of spirit, Mendez judged. Nothing more. She simply attempted to retain her self-regard before Santos and himself. But not so much that it would result in her death. That was a peculiar thing about most people, the colonel came to realize over the years.

It was little people who frequently advanced their self-proclaimed nobility. They based it on some kind of common denominator usually predicated on an archaic ancestral or theological linkage. They claimed how their origins shaped their current behaviors and helped them to center their lives for tomorrow. They believed that their rich cultures commanded that they be looked upon with high regard. They demanded more stateliness for their own ethnic, religious, or cultural orientations than those of a village, neighborhood, or border away. They rattled their bamboo sticks or bottles because they have no swords. Semipowerful in small aggressive packs but seldom in mass, knowing, if they strayed too far from the security of their borough or culture crib, the government could swiftly eradicate them.

This woman was nothing more than another spiteful peasant who lost her origins earlier that day. She would comply with whatever he told her. Like all human species, Mendez knew, this beautiful creature would most likely opt for human degradation in life than dignity in death. Like the 99.99% of the people on this planet, Alicia was not special. She was just here.

"Leave us," he order.

Santos immediately backed away and lowered the tent flaps as he left. Alicia snapped her head to the side. She looked over her right shoulder at the lieutenant as he departed. Instead of looking to Mendez, the young woman chose to maintain her focus rightward. She slightly lowered her chin while relaxing the muscles in her neck and face.

Mendez leaned in his chair. He balanced the folding piece onto its back legs. He paused to take in the splendor of the voluptuous woman.

He saw that Alicia had secured the back of her torn dress. She fastened the material at the neckline while still revealing a bare right shoulder. He saw how her long neck disappeared into her exposed collar bones. The flesh tightly pressed against them. Alicia's peasant garb complemented her. It gave the beauty an earthy rawness. He looked down to her bare feet, taking them in. His eyes followed along her calves. Like her sun-kissed face, neck, and shoulder, the flesh was almond colored and tight, yet supple.

He rose from his chair and stepped around the table. Mendez became anxious by the idea that Alicia wore no underclothing. The notion toyed with him. He knew that this delicate body was only a garment's thickness away from his taste buds.

He slowly stepped around Alicia while eyeing every part of her. He moved in close behind her and pressed himself against her buttocks. When he touched her, Mendez felt the bat of a reflex. Alicia tightened the muscles in her legs but almost as quickly allowed them to go limp.

"As I told you before," he whispered over her shoulder, "you are a very lucky woman."

"Am I?"

Mendez lifted the woman's shining hair off the back of her neck. He cradled the silky, blue-black stands in his gently caressing hands. He spotted the safety pin someone gave to Alicia to clasp her torn dress. It was most likely one of his men, he considered. He unfastened the pin and discarded it onto the dirt floor. He watched the material slip from her left shoulder.

Alicia caught the falling garment with her arms. She tightly clutched the material to her. The slender limbs compressed her large bosom. The pliable breasts spread wide over her ribs. He watched as she briefly looked down at herself then up to him.

"Let it fall," he whispered.

She slowly withdrew her arms and allowed the material to fall away. The garment collected around her ankles. When the dress fell, Alicia cradled her breasts in her arms, not thinking to conceal the rest of her bareness. He took hold of her upper arms and held to the fragile extensions with a tender grasp.

Mendez gazed along the woman's elongated spine. He detailed every vertebra from Alicia's soft neck to her firm narrow buttocks. He took Alicia by the wrists and gently tugged on them. She let her arms ease downward. He circled before her.

He softly cupped her breasts, delicately caressing them. Alicia felt a shiver surge through her. The shudder raced up her spine. She felt a tingling sensation in her breasts. He released her bosom and slid his warm moist palms out from under them. He took one step back.

"You are an incredible thing."

"You will keep your promise?" Alicia asked softly. "About the children?"

"As I told you," Mendez said. "They will be treated well."

Mendez reached out with his hands. He waited for Alicia

to rest her hands in his. She slowly lowered her soft limbs into the officer's. He guided her to the edge of his cot and eased Alicia onto the canvas. She watched as the colonel settled her arms to her side.

The colonel's face became a shadowed outline. Alicia imagined she was in a place far away. In this way, she abandoned her body and escaped the colonel's presence.

Twenty

James returned to the awaiting team within forty minutes. He kept an eye out when he was in close proximity to Bravo. He knew that if he did not make his presence known in advance his teammates would likely mistake him for a pointman of an encroaching patrol. Men died for less out here, he knew. He called out the preestablished sign and stayed low until the team recognized him. Team Bravo acknowledged James by responding with the predesignated countersign. After he confirmed to Richter that the villager was nothing more than a food supplement for forest organisms, Team Bravo resumed its heading.

The last leg of their trek consisted of the same redundancies as of most patrols—many minutes of cautious stepping interrupted by an occasional geyser of fear—fear that erupted from the sudden race of a snake or the fluttering of a bird dashing from the brush.

Marcoli reassumed the point. He moved about twenty meters farther beyond his normal distance. Richter occasionally lost sight of him when the forest grew too thick. Levits moved up behind Gable. James brought up the rear. Masterson and the copilot stayed where the captain had placed them—the patrol's middle. Ramsy took eighth in the column. It was two and a half hours since James disposed of Murillo. The sun was decidedly lower.

Richter saw that twilight was upon them. He knew it was to the team's advantage to set up their strangling encirclement before full darkness. They would not interfere until the exchange was in progress. He wanted to optimize their effort by taking both the supplier and the buyer simultaneously.

As the transfer was not scheduled until 2100 hours the rendezvous took place well into darkness. Night offered the traffickers the same tactical advantage afforded the team. *They might not be able to see us*, Richter thought, *but if the traffickers are permitted to disperse, we will lose them.* The team slowed its advance. The men shortened their survival intervals in preparation for the night movement. Levits closed within easy speaking distance of Gable.

"Hey, Art. Didn't you tell me you were a medic in Vietnam?"

"Yeah."

"I thought you had to have a combat background to be on one of these teams."

"You do," Gable said.

"Well then, what are you doing here?"

"I was the only medic in my unit that carried one of these." Gable patted the M-72A2 LAW dangling from his shoulder. "I call it preventive medicine."

"Wasn't that against the Geneva Convention?"

"Sure was." A big smile covered Gable's face. "But nobody fucked with me."

As the team moved up Marcoli pulled back a low-lying

branch. The alternate objective came into view. The pointman surveyed the area from his much higher vantage point.

The remote location was at a road junction. Frequent vehicle use etched out the dusty paths. They were new routes, probably made within the last two or three months, he speculated. The trails and crossing were not depicted on his grid map. Marcoli looked beyond the dirt throughway. He used his pocket-sized binoculars to study the small encampment.

Two fires blazed within the camp. One was of bonfire proportions and accommodated the enlisted men sitting around it. He counted eight men. Some of the idle soldiers roasted bits of meat on sticks while others drank. They passed a bottle of liquor along the circle for each to take his share. If they had only one bottle, Marcoli determined, it was not enough to get eight men drunk. The other fire, much smaller, burned just outside a gable tent.

The shelter was approximately sixty feet from where the enlisted men gathered. Marcoli knew it was the officers' tent. *Keeping their distance—like our own*, he thought.

He searched beyond the tent, farther back, and spotted the old U.S. Army three-quarter ton truck the villager had mentioned. It sat in the brush, partially camouflaged. One armed guard posted next to it. Marcoli eyed the officer sitting in front of the small tent. He tried to get a better look at the man who jabbed at the burning coals with a stick. He lowered his binoculars when the team approached from behind.

Richter signaled his team to disperse. He moved up and assumed a prone position next to Marcoli. The captain surveyed the site using his own binoculars. He skimmed the area three times before lowering the glass. He looked at his watch.

"We're early. It's 1950."

"I count ten," Marcoli said.

"Yeah, and all of 'em uniformed Colombian *federales*," Richter added. "How does it feel to be in competition with your ally's military?"

"It'll never make the ten o'clock news."

"That's for sure," Richter said. "The administration could

never explain this and keep the backdoor funding coming."

"Ten isn't much, Captain."

"Murillo told us six."

"Yeah, but he doesn't count anymore. Shouldn't be too difficult."

"Hm. Plus what we don't see," Richter said. "Given the market value they should have at least three or four guards beyond the perimeter...an observer at the road junction, anyway. I don't see one. If this commander is worth his salt, he should at least put out a couple of listening posts. He's got the manpower. Why don't he use 'em?"

"Couple of grenades in there, we'd have total chaos," Marcoli suggested.

"Yeah, well. Don't forget Murphy's Law of combat operations."

"What's that?" Marcoli asked.

"If it looks like the attack is going well, it's an ambush."

"Roger."

The two men glanced back upon hearing a sudden rustle of brush. It was the sergeant major. Ramsy moved up and lay between Richter and Marcoli.

"Spot 'em, Captain?"

"Down there."

Ramsy gave the site a thorough twice over. The camp's deficient state of combat readiness surprised him. It would be dark soon, he knew. Their fires stood out like neon lights, visible for meters even through the thick underbrush.

"They're confident," Ramsy said. "Big fires. No fear."

"Looks that way," Richter said. He turned to Marcoli. "You think you could get a look in that truck without being seen? If it's what I think it is, the payoff hasn't taken place yet. If it has, then they're just bivouacked for the night."

"It's starting to get dark enough," Marcoli said. "I'll move down to the road and wait another ten minutes. See you guys in about thirty."

Marcoli began to rise. He felt Ramsy's large hand grip his shoulder. The grasp was tight. Marcoli knew he would not go anywhere until the sergeant major permitted it. He looked at the hand then into Ramsy's eyes. He saw the concern the sergeant major showed for all of his men.

"Don't John Wayne-it, lad," Ramsy cautioned.

"Safe and silent, Sergeant Major."

Before Marcoli could face forward he felt the sergeant major plant an encouraging slap on his back. Ramsy's gentle nudge almost drove the NCO to the ground. Marcoli glanced to Richter. He saw the captain smiling. He made a muffled cough before rising to his feet. Ramsy heard the sergeant facetiously clear his throat as he moved off and wondered if something was wrong.

"What's with Marcoli?"

"Anybody's guess," Richter said.

"Mind if I have a look?"

Ramsy gestured for Richter's binoculars.

He scanned the encampment twice more. He detailed personnel placement and their armaments. As he guided the lens back to where Richter and he lay, Ramsy saw Marcoli dart across the open roadway. He watched as Marcoli disappeared into the foliage at the opposite side.

"Looks like Stan made it across without being seen."

"Already?" Richter asked. "You spotted 'im?"

"Hm."

"If we can see 'im, they can," Richter said. "It'll be dark pretty soon. He can move more freely then."

Richter rolled onto his back. He pulled a piece of paper from his upper left pocket. As he snatched the scribble sheet a photograph inadvertently snagged within his fingers. The picture fell onto the ground next to him. Ramsy caught the falling photo in his peripheral vision. He saw that Alex did not notice its misplacement. He picked up the picture while Alex jotted down a message for Gable to radio to Reiner. The sergeant major admired the petite girl that he knew meant the world to the captain.

"Pretty girl, Alex," he said. "You're a lucky man."

"Huh?" Richter said, jolted from his message. He watched

Cliff reach out to him with the photograph. "Oh, thanks! I don't want to lose that."

"You should be more careful," Ramsy cautioned. "That's a special little girl you got there."

"Yeah," he replied.

Richter held up the photo. Ramsy readily saw the admiration and affection in Alex's eyes. He was sure that he knew exactly how the captain felt.

"Courtney's my baby," he went on. "She's about fourteen or fifteen, now. You know, it's true what they say?"

"What's that?"

"Doesn't matter how old they get, they'll always be your baby. Especially the girls."

Richter paused a moment more. He took in the beauty of his lovely daughter. It then occurred to him how peculiar it was that he could not recall his child's precise age. Besides the monthly checks, he sent money on every birthday, at Christmas, or whenever Courtney wrote or called. It was obviously not the same as being there.

It struck him that his inability to recall the age of his only daughter might be the first stage in losing Courtney altogether. The idea of it frightened him. He realized he had been gone too long. Time did not make the heart grow fonder, he knew. It impaired the memory. He looked up from the photo and motioned for Gable to move forward.

The radioman advanced to where Richter and Ramsy lay. He knelt in the dirt just behind them.

"Get this off to Reiner, ASAP," he said. "Tell the men to start their combat checks. We'll move to the attack position as soon as Stan gets back."

"Roger," Gable said.

Gable took the paper and moved to where Levits positioned himself behind a tree.

Richter returned his attention onto the photograph. He used the last few minutes of twilight to gaze upon the richest gift he could give to the world. The photo was not current. It had been a little more than a year since he received it. *Could she have changed so much in a year?* he wondered. He gazed upon his daughter's image for a concentrated half-minute more. Something then occurred to Richter.

"You know, Cliff," he began, "in all the years we've soldiered together I don't ever recall you talking about a family."

"That's because there isn't none."

"Not one?" he asked. "Not an ex-wife—child?"

"Ah hell, Alex," he flippantly began. "I guess a man can't barnstorm around the world for almost forty years without leaving some residue."

Ramsy's off-the-cuff statement surprised Richter. He heard irate parents call their children many things. A few not so pleasant ones from his own father and one disturbed uncle. It was the first time that he heard of a child referred to as residue. The more Richter thought about it the more he grew bewildered.

It was funny for dry humor, he guessed. Sometimes the morbidity—the absurdity—of an event or a phrase caught him when he was on the edge. He realized, or hoped, what Cliff said was in jest. He looked upon Courtney's photo and used the final seconds of light to his advantage. The concept of residue seemed out of place when applied to any child. He turned to the sergeant major.

"Residue?"

Richter replaced the photo into his pocket. He made sure the two buttons securely held the flap in place. By the time he unconsciously smoothed the pocket flap twice, the sun descended low enough for Marcoli to begin the perimeter breach.

The sun was well below the horizon. The jungle surrounding him took on an eerie effect. The silhouette of every tree, vine, and bush assumed a sinister display. Dusk was the worst time, Marcoli knew. It was when the eyes played tricks on the mind. There was just enough light to make him think he knew what he was looking at but not enough to confirm it. It would be another five minutes before his pupils adequately dilated.

The fires from the camp boldly contrasted against the forest. He saw the same eight enlisted men still hunched about the flames. They passed the rapidly depleting bottle between them. At the smaller fire two men sat on folding stools.

The body count rose by one. *Richter was right*, he thought. *"Plus what we don't see..."* Their docile manner, coupled with their purposeful distance, identified them as the leaders. Reasonably sure of the manpower placement Marcoli began his breaching maneuver.

He crouched low as he made his way to the perimeter's edge. He circled eastward and moved parallel to the margin, about five meters out. Again, he eyed the three-quarter ton truck about twenty meters from the tent.

An inviting, soldier-friendly shadow swallowed the vehicle opposite the fires. He followed the dark pathway and entered the bogus encirclement. One additional guard posted at the front of the truck. *The body count grows*, Marcoli remarked to himself.

He reached the tailgate and untied the rope tiedown at the vehicle's right rear quarter panel. He pulled the rear canvas cover aside and quietly lifted himself onto the truck bed. Once firmly planted in the bay Marcoli lowered the canvas to its original position. He left everything as he found it, except for the one loose tiedown. He faced forward and searched the narrow interior.

Using a penlight held between his teeth, Marcoli focused on a large rectangular stack beginning a quarter way up the vehicle bed. The pile covered the floor's entire five-foot width and rose to about four feet. It extended to the canvas separation at the forward cab and lay under a heavy tarpaulin.

Marcoli scooted forward. He lifted the canvas edge and saw 772 kilograms of cocaine packed, sealed, and layered in two-kilo plastic bags—all 386. He gazed upon the fortune he knew could last him ten life times. He took a moment to envision what such wealth could do for him. The fantasy fell aside quickly. As he lowered the tarp Marcoli felt better in knowing their effort was not wasted on a bogus alternate objective theory.

"That's it," he whispered.

He turned on his heels and mistakenly twisted his right foot into a small wooden crate.

One guard was sure that he heard a knock come from the truck. The other, forward the vehicle, was not sure of what he heard. They cautiously moved to the rear of the vehicle. Marcoli followed their progress by the sound of crushed twigs and leaves under the senties' boots. He eyed the box he collided with. Using his penlight he saw an inscription on the container. The markings revealed that the crate contained M-33 fragmentation grenades from the U.S. Naval Depot at Guantanamo Bay. He switched off the tiny beam while deciding what to do next.

One soldier remained back, three meters, and covered the other who pulled on the untied canvas edge. The guard standing rearward shined his flashlight into the cargo bay. Nothing appeared out of place. Curious, Mendez questioned what they did. The sentry stated that he believed he had heard something, but that it turned out to be nothing. As the guard retied the loose tiedown, Mendez congratulated the two on their positive sense of security. The two men returned to their posts while Marcoli lowered himself from the bay ceiling.

As he slowly lowered himself Marcoli probed in the dark for the metal floor, using the toes of his jungle boots. When he again felt secure on his feet he released the cross rib above him.

On his hands and knees, he reached over the tailgate and out the back of the truck. He tried to work the knotted rope lose with his left hand. He couldn't. Marcoli pulled his bayonet and sliced the tiedown. After severing the cord he slipped under the canvas and lowered himself without detection. He was about to return to the team when Marcoli saw the young officer rise.

The officer stepped to a group of silhouetted images huddled together. They sat about thirty feet forward the vehicle's front end. Marcoli also saw the additional guard posted next to them. *Another*, he thought. *Body count's still growing*. He lowered himself below the vehicle's undercarriage and low-crawled under the truck. He observed the movement of the sentries and the officer by watching their feet.

The man stooped before the captured children and one woman, who tightly clung to one another. Some glanced up at the lieutenant, but most did not acknowledge him. Marcoli saw how the officer rested his elbows on his knees, as Santos casually evaluated the worth of each captive. Mendez watched his junior officer from the fire, amused that Santos also found Alicia striking. He decided the young man had to be kept in his place.

"Santos!" he said. "She is mine. Pick something else."

Marcoli watched as the lieutenant select a small boy. He gripped the ten-year-old by his wrists and guided him toward the tent. The boy tried to fight him off, but the child was no match against the officer's strength. While Santos escorted his little prisoner tentward Marcoli heard the enlisted men at the fire laugh and jeer. They yelled catcalls and made obscene gestures with their hands. As their words were in Spanish Marcoli could not understand what they said, but could easily venture a guess.

Mendez looked up from the fire and peered at his men. The colonel listened to their teasing while watching the grotesque motions they made with their hands. Santos ignored the abrasive enlisted men. By the time the lieutenant reached to where Mendez sat, the men had already settled themselves. Santos pulled the boy into the tent. The colonel eyed the glowing embers while wondering where and when his junior officer got such outrageous ideas.

"Oh, you are a peculiar one, Santos," he said. "Ah, do what you want."

Mendez picked up another dry branch near where he sat. He poked at the yellow-white coals while hearing Santos tie down the tent flaps.

Marcoli looked on in awe. He saw the sudden spark of

match light penetrate the canvas. The radiance briefly filled the blackened space inside the tent. The abrupt white flash quickly subsided, replaced by the soft glow of lantern light seeping through the material. Marcoli also saw where the light could not penetrate.

From under the truck he watched as the larger silhouette seized the smaller. The slighter image was unable to prevent the greater shadow from having its way. Through their mutual angry words in Spanish, Marcoli saw and heard two consecutive slaps crack out. After the second blow the petite shadow went silent. He saw how the larger black image drove the tiny figure floorward. *That's enough*, Marcoli decided.

He backed out from under the truck and headed for the rear of the tent. Marcoli wanted to run to the boy's aid. He knew, however, that to do so could mean himself ending up as a casualty. He crept to the back of the tent. He heard the officer make subtle, affectionate demands of the child. He heard the boy murmur and whimper.

He pulled his bayonet and used the double-edged tip to pull aside the material between two tiedowns. With one eye, Marcoli peered through the quarter-inch gap and witnessed the atrocity Santos submitted the boy to. He cringed while briefly looking away. He sliced two of the three ties. Marcoli took a slow deep breath and held it momentarily before making his rush.

He clamped over the lieutenant's mouth with his left hand while ramming the seven-inch blade into Santos' abdomen. The boy was so frightened and humiliated he could not speak. The child pushed himself away while spitting. Marcoli tightly held about the man's face, trying to quell the high pitched "Hmmmmmmmmm!" coming from Santos. He slowly, purposefully, lingered on the upward pull of the blade. Mendez caught the sound of a suppressed whine of ecstasy, mingled with the boy clearing his throat.

"Santos," he said. "Don't play so rough. The boy has worth."

The enlisted men at the fire began to laugh. In the time it took for Mendez to caution his lieutenant, Marcoli lowered the body to the dirt floor. He used the dead lieutenant's bare ass to wipe his blade clean. He replaced the bayonet into its scabbard then readjusted his rifle. Marcoli slowly, reluctantly, placed his hands onto the boy's shoulders. He feared he might frighten the boy further, but he had no choice. For their own safety, he muffled the child's mouth with one hand while grasping the frail bundle about his waist with the other. He slipped between the rear tent flaps and quietly made his way beyond the perimeter. Marcoli entered the hasty defense line with the human bundle draped over his shoulder.

"What have you got, there?" Ramsy asked.

Marcoli set the child down and watched as the frightened boy quietly move aside. The boy lowered himself next to a tree. He leaned into the wide trunk for security. The men saw how he curled his legs and rested his forehead on his pulled-in knees. His arms tightly wrapped about his legs while he pressed his right shoulder into the bark. Marcoli looked to Richter and began his reconnaissance summary.

"It's as you said, Captain."

"What?"

Richter faced away from the terrified child. He recalled that when Courtney was his age he still had a family—a life.

"I counted thirteen men," he resumed. "Four on guard. No listening posts."

"Locations?" Richer asked.

"One officer at the tent and eight men at the fire. Four on guard duty—one on the other road going north, two at the truck and one with the villagers. He's about twenty meters forward the truck."

"You didn't by any chance get a look inside that three-quarter?" Ramsy asked.

"Sergeant Major," Marcoli countered. "You underestimate me. It's there. No exchange, yet."

"So they're waiting," Richter said, "and they're confident. Minimum security."

Ramsy looked to the boy. He saw that the child did not alter his position against the tree.

"He's one of the villagers?"

"Yeah," Marcoli answered, a subtle tone of regret. "Uh…he's also the reason we can't wait for the link-up."

"Why?" Richter snapped.

"There were fourteen of 'em…I killed one of the officers."

"Why did you do that?" Ramsy excitedly asked. "Oh, we got to move now, Captain."

Marcoli shrugged his shoulders while motioning to the boy. He realized he had put the mission in jeopardy. He threatened the entire operation when altering the human condition within the camp. Marcoli knew that he had erred from a militarily perspective, but he was a man as well, he rationalized. A human—with some feeling.

"You wouldn't believe what he made that kid do," he said.

James crouched nearby. He stayed low in the grass while listening to every word traded between the three men. As he concentrated on their voices he began to finger his weapon. He flicked the selector switch from the safety to the auto mode. He tightly wrapped his fingers about the pistol grip and nervously ran his trigger finger back and forth over the firing mechanism. He felt the slippery sweat on his hand and how his trigger finger slid over the smooth metal. He just stayed low and watched, listening.

"All right," Richter said. "We move to attack position in one minute. Get that kid to stay here, so we know where to find 'im when it's over."

"Roger," Marcoli said.

"If we hit 'em before the link-up," Ramsy cautioned, "the buyers'll know where we are. They could be at our backdoor and we'd never know it."

"I'm counting on it," Richter replied. "Since the exchange wasn't made they'll still have their money. There's no love loss between 'em…They'll back off, negotiate for a new buy, later."

"Well then," Ramsy said. "Let's get to it."

Twenty-one

Mendez gulped down the last ounce of Canadian Club. He turned the glass over and watched a remaining drop cling to the rim. With one eye he peered through the liquid crystal and observed the soft light of the coals refract through the fluid prism. When it broke free he saw how the liquid ball drove into the ash. He considered the whiskey much the same as Alicia— a delight to the palate, but when finished with the desensitizing affects of his overindulgence had to be eradicated.

She was practically everything in a woman a man could want. But to bring Alicia to Bogotá was a ludicrous notion. Within her own setting, a small outback village, Alicia was a woman of confidence and wit. In Bogotá, he knew, Alicia was nothing more than a backwoods peasant and would bring him down with her. Deciding he had no recourse, Mendez concluded it best for Santos to take her on to Ecuador. Santos' journey in mind, the colonel wondered for the lack of activity at his back.

"Santos?" he said, while glancing over his shoulder. "Are you resting?" Mendez turned on his stool. He stared at the tent flaps for a moment more. "Santos?" As the colonel patiently waited, Team Bravo began its deployment.

The team descended the embankment to the trail. Gable lost his footing while hauling the excess equipment he refused to discard. The men held their breaths while waiting to see if his rubber legs disclosed their presence. After a tense quarter-minute it became apparent that luck stayed with them. No one from within the camp or the four sentry posts sounded an alert. The team resumed its descent and held at the southeast leg of the intersection.

The sergeant major took a moment to confront Gable. He gave the soldier a silent but decidedly disciplinary squeeze on his left arm. In his own silent way he made it clear to the radioman just how close Team Bravo came to discovery.

The men darted across the open trail in groups of threes; that is, after Bard eliminated the sentry at the crossroad's northwest leg. On the opposite side the team began to fan. James was in the last increment. He held back while wondering how to protect his investment.

He slowed his pace while crossing with Levits and Sanford. He purposely held back to be the least exposed to the fire that would ensue. As Levits and Sanford were ahead, James realized he drew no attention from the two. Farther forward, inside the camp, he saw the unprepared men. The soldiers sat about their fire. The one remaining officer eyed the tent behind him.

James knew that it was not suppose to happen like this. The idea was for Team Bravo to return after losing the chopper at the Gulf of Urabá. If Richter had followed his orders they'd be back at the staging area instead of hot-shotting through the jungle. It was Richter's fault, he decided. Whatever happened to these men would be the result of Richter not staying within the parameters of his own OPORD. Treadwell would acknowledge that as well. While applying another ounce of pressure with his trigger finger, James began to search for a place off to the side. He knelt near the trail's edge and watched as Mendez rose from his chair.

The colonel slowly ascended while turning tentward. This was suspicious, he thought. No matter how engrossed Santos may have been, he would never have ignored him. Mendez unsnapped the flap on his holster. He withdrew his pistol, holding the weapon out from his waist. Sergeant Gorgas noticed his colonel poise the pistol and told the others to be on their guard. The entire camp went silent.

"Santos!" the colonel demanded. Mendez waited five seconds more. He stepped forward and pulled the right tent flap aside. "Santos! Get your a…"

Looking in, Mendez saw by the lantern's radiance how Santos had violently died. *But there was no sound*, he thought. He flashed through his mind all that he had heard from the time Santos and the boy entered the tent. When he turned to yell for his men to take their positions a rifle shot cracked out.

Briefly numbed by the unexpected round, the *federales* paused a full two seconds before darting for their firing positions. The colonel frantically yelled his orders. Mendez's men rapidly deployed along the overextended perimeter. Richter felt that he had no choice but to follow through.

Most of the men were already on line and waited for Richter's signal. When the rifle shot snapped out, the entire team whirled about and aimed their weapons rearward. Richter faced into the camp and saw the soldiers diving for their positions. He knew that anything short of a full attack or a total withdrawal was suicide. Already having his fill of mission failure, the latter was not a realistic option for him.

"Fire!" the captain yelled.

The team immediately open fired and filled the jungle and the encampment with rounds. Their volume was not concentrated, however, as the men did not know which way to aim their weapons.

Richter emptied a banana magazine in an attempt to suppress the dug-in soldiers. As he turned the empty clip over to insert the full one taped to it, the captain eyed along the line. He saw his men firing in both directions.

"No!" Richter yelled. "That way! Fire into 'em!"

Those who concentrated their fire rearward pivoted about, but confusion and chaos remained the standard. Richter lobbed a fragmentation grenade between two positions. Upon hearing the device ignite, the other men followed through with their own arsenals. Someone complicated the episode by throwing two red smoke canisters into the small encirclement.

It blinded not only the men within the perimeter but those attempting to breach it. The sergeant major glanced skyward and wondered if there was any further room for misguided human creativity. As Ramsy considered the probability for a total breakdown in effort, Captain Velázquez paused in the darkness.

The rhythmic snapping of gunfire echoed through the black forest. Velázquez halted his men and stood silent in the dark. He listened to the distant sound of automatic weapons laced with periodic explosions. He judged the gunplay to be within two grid squares of their location.

He was not aware of any other units in the area but realized that meant little. Higher frequently dispatched small force elements while neglecting to inform those units already within sector. It sometimes made for a deadly confrontation between two aggressive commanders of the same side. In the end, each blaming the other for their inability to check troop hostility.

He motioned for his men to follow closely. They intensified their pace. A mounting desperation rushed though the captain the farther he progressed. His need to make a difference began to engulf him. While Velázquez drew closer to the noise the buyers stopped on the trail.

The two International Scout land rovers stopped on the narrow road. The men inside them paused, their weapons poised, while listening to the horrendous gunfire coming from a short distance away. They shut down the engines, turning off the lights, and sat in the darkness. They heard the explosions intermingled with small weapons fire. Cabello, leader of the group, exited the cab.

He moved to the front of the lead vehicle and leaned against its grill. He listened to the firefight only two or three hundred meters down the road. The cautious man decided not to jeopardize the eighteen million dollars packed in the three duffel bags. Although Zorrilla agreed to a twenty-three-million-dollar exchange, Ling provided for only eighteen. The pacific rim overlord intended to demonstrate a decided power wedge.

As it was not his money, Cabello knew that to place Ling's wealth in jeopardy meant having every Chinese enforcer on the island of Oahu gunning after him. As the local middleman for Ling, Cabello was the focal point between Zorrilla and the Chinese link—the former supplying the Ling pacific empire with high-grade cocaine, the latter supplementing his lucrative opium trade within the five islands of Hawaii. Cabello waited against the vehicle while sending a lookout forward. As the man cautiously advanced to within fifty meters of the besieged camp, Team Bravo continued its decimation.

Richter watched two of his men advance using fire and maneuver techniques. He spotted Levits only a few meters from a machine gun emplacement. He saw how Levits low-crawled to the pit and lobbed a fragmentation grenade into it. The captain watched as the machine gunner and his weapon piecemealed in the night air. Knowing that Levits could not move any farther without supplemental support, Richter decided the softening period had elapsed. He also realized that their logistics became a factor. If they did not bring this to an end soon there would be no ammunition left to threaten anyone.

"Let's go!" the captain yelled.

Richter dashed toward the tent. He believed the commander was somewhere among his men or dead, but without knowing more it seemed the most practical place for him to begin his search. He was three-quarters of the way to the tent when Richter felt a powerful smack on the right side of his head.

Everything went black. He felt himself lifted off the ground. Whatever it was, he hadn't see it coming. He raised his upper body from the dirt. He looked ahead while trying to support himself and saw everything blurred. He saw the fuzzy, double outline of the tent. The image was so distorted, however, that he would not have known it was a tent were he not headed for it.

Richter looked over his shoulder to the hazy bonfire. Through his double vision he observed the large flames and shimmering sparks rising. He touched the right side of his head and felt the crease in his skull. He felt the comingling of grit and blood in the wound. Swelling emerged at the margins of the elongated dent. The blood ran down the right side of his face, blinding him in that eye.

He probed at the ground, searching for his rifle. His fingers raked at the dirt. He heard profound laughter coming from only a short distance.

Richter reached down and pulled open the flap on his holster, drawing the .45 pistol. He looked up at the fuzzy, laughing image and saw a man raising something to his shoulder. He knew it was a weapon. Richter pulled on the slide, chambering a round. As he awkwardly aimed onto the blurred image the captain felt someone take hold of him at the left ankle.

The man dragged him in the opposite direction of the laughing figure. As he felt himself yanked across the clearing Richter let go with four rounds, pulling the trigger in rapid succession. He saw how the hazy human outline fell to the ground. He rolled onto his back and eyed the dark image dragging him. He felt safer in knowing it was one of his camouflage-clad men. Which one, he was not certain.

Upon settling the captain against a tree Ramsy decided some words of caution warranted mention.

"Alex!" he shouted. He looked into the man's glazed-over eyes. "You know, I ain't always gonna be here for you."

Richter squinted, trying to focus upon the face looking at him. He leaned forward for a better view. He recognized the voice as Ramsy's but tried to see Cliff anyway.

"Yeah!" he replied. "I know that."

"Sit tight, son."

Ramsy returned the fight.

Incapacitated for the present, Richter could do nothing but remain at the tree. The captain observed the hazed images running back and forth. He heard the screams of dying men and of horrified children through the snapping of weapons. James fought furiously.

He did his share of the killing while making his way to the truck. Upon reaching the vehicle he slashed the rope tiedowns and climbed into the back. He used his cigarette lighter to locate the edge of the tarp. He threw back the material and grabbed one of the two-kilo bags.

James tucked his hip-length jacket into his trousers before stashing the package inside it. He connected the zipper on his flak vest and pulled the body armor partially closed to conceal the bulk. By the time he finished storing his profits the gunfire began to settle. He hopped from the tailgate and saw the camp neutralize.

By the time Ramsy returned to Richter's side, Gable and Marcoli had already administered first aid. Ramsy watched Gable press a wet compress against Richter's head. The captain wiped the blood from the right side of his face. Knowing that Alex was well taken care of, Ramsy chose not to inquire.

"We got three dead, Captain," he began. Ramsy stepped to the group. "Colfield, Sanford, and Bard...it went bad." He faced the men and showed anger over the outcome. "Who the hell popped off that round?"

There was no response.

"Well, whoever it was three of our boys are dead because of it," he said. "Marcoli! You've been known to be trigger happy."

"Hey, Sergeant Major!" Marcoli jumped defensively. "I

was right in front of you. If it had been me, you would've known it."

"That's true," Ramsy conceded. "Sorry lad. Well, if it was Bard, Colfield, or Sanford we'll nev—"

Ramsy stopped midword, torn from his comment upon spotting Masterson and the copilot escorting two prisoners. When they reached the group the copilot shoved the colonel onto the ground. Masterson, not wanting to be outdone, did the same with the enlisted soldier.

"We found 'em hiding under the truck," Masterson explained.

"The rest are dead, Captain," Ramsy added.

"You are a captain?" Mendez asked. He looked up from his hands. "You have no insignia."

Richter lowered the bloodsoaked compress from his head. He glance at the wet cloth while deciding whether to answer the man. He laid the compress back onto the gougedout portion of his skull. He viewed the officer through his blurred vision.

"Some of us cling to our memories."

From his hands and knees, Mendez looked about the group. He saw that none of the men wore military grade, nor had service or nameplates sewn above their breast pockets, except for the pilots. That Masterson and his assistant were pilots was evident. Both men still donned their flight suits and had aviation nameplates adhered to their coveralls above their left breast pockets. But they were the only two.

"You're not American army," he said. "Professional? Contract?"

"We'll ask the questions," Richter said.

The captain leaned against the tree.

"In ten minutes this place will be surrounded by my soldiers," Mendez threatened. "Then, I'll ask the questions."

Richter looked to his men, a partial smile showing. His vision began to clear. *A hopeful sign*, he thought.

"Well then," he resumed. "We better kill you two right now and be on our way. Art?"

Gable instantly raised his weapon waist high. He leveled the rifle point-blank onto the colonel. He was about to pull the trigger when Mendez yelled out.

"Stop!" Mendez raised his hands defensively. He reared onto his knees. A subtle smile followed. "Maybe—maybe I exaggerated."

"Maybe," Richter said. "All right, Colonel. Let's get back to business at hand. You're going to tell us two things—who your buyers are and how your people knew of our initial objective this morning."

"Can I stand, Captain?" Mendez asked.

Richter took a second to consider the request. He gave his permission with a subtle nod. Mendez rose slowly. He concluded that except for the pilots his captors were not soldiers but killers like himself—men without a sense of loyalty, renegades with ambition. One, he knew for sure. Once onto his feet Mendez brushed the dust from his uniform. He straightened his blouse.

"If I told you this," he said, "I would be a traitor to my people."

"If you don't tell us," Richter replied, "you'll be history to your people."

"I understand. Maybe we can make an, ah—arrangement."

"For instance?" Richter said.

"Why don't you take half the cocaine. You'll all be millionaires overnight. Who's going to know?"

Richter smiled while looking to the truck. He saw how the firelight reflected off the tarpaulin cover. He glanced up to Ramsy, who quietly stood off to the side. He looked to Mendez.

"Colonel, you have no appreciation for the big picture. If we were after the cocaine, we would simply take it and leave your bodies. As I see it, you have no choice. Tell us what we want to know and we'll bring you with us… You can't go back, Colonel. They'll never let you live after losing all that. They'll make you an example—like San Delbaro."

"Who?" Mendez innocently asked.

The team heard Levits approach from behind Masterson and the copilot. Richter watched as the sergeant escorted the village woman to them. Even by the fire's subtle glow the men recognized Alicia's beauty. The woman approached them with her chiseled jaw jutting proudly. Her exposed neck, shoulder, and partial cleavage seized their eyes. Upon closing with them, they witnessed the subdued woman transform into an enraged wildcat.

When within grasping distance of Mendez, Alicia abruptly whirled about with her right hand. Her fist connected with the colonel just above his nose. When he hit the ground Alicia began to kick him. She ruthlessly swung her right leg three times, battering his kidney. She followed through with short and choppy jabs to his face. Richter permitted the woman a free quarter-minute. The men watched as the colonel became overwhelmed by the woman's foot jabs.

The captain motioned for his NCO to contain her. Levits grabbed the woman by her arms. She spit on Mendez while being pulled away. As Levits dragged her off the defenseless man the safety pin securing Alicia's dress popped.

"Oh, my god!" Richter said.

Alicia yanked her arms free of Levits. She quickly collected the material at her hips. Not in sufficient time, however. Every man gazed upon her taut robustness. Her large and wildly undulating breasts stunned them.

Richter could not help but notice, as well, but maintained his businesslike demeanor—with difficulty.

"You're one of the villagers?" he asked, for the lack of something better.

Alicia clung to her front, pressing the garment tightly to her bulging bosom. She took a few seconds to regain her breath.

"Yes! And that pig raped me!" she blared. "I want him dead!"

Richter said nothing. He quietly studied the woman while Mendez rose from the dirt. Again, the officer brushed himself off. He took an added second to check the bridge of his nose.

As he lowered his hand Mendez could not help but comment. "Did I?"

Alicia instantly charged for Mendez while swinging one wild roundhouse with her left arm. She pressed the dress tightly against her with the right.

"I'll kill you myself. You son of a bitch."

Levits stepped forward and grabbed the woman once more. Richter saw how Alicia fought to keep herself covered while trying to get at the colonel. It was an admirable effort, he thought. Again, he motioned to Levits.

"Give her a hand with that dress."

"Gee, Captain," Levits began jokingly. "It looked awful nice. I'd—"

"I said secure it!" Richter countered coldly.

All became silent. Alicia recognized that the man resting against the tree commanded with absolute authority. The men looked at one another before returning their stares to Levits. As the NCO fuddled with the safety pin Mendez chose to speak in his defense.

"You know how these women are, Captain," he began calmly. "They always have something to complain about."

Richter glared into the officer's eyes. He sensed that Mendez had no regard for anything—perhaps not even for himself. He looked at the woman and took in the sternness emanating from Alicia's pupils. He recognized the burning hate in them. He also witnessed her sense of self-respect. He found himself captured by the woman's harden features but quickly broke his gaze.

He watched as the captured children stepped forward. They cautiously moved toward Team Bravo from across the encampment. All of them headed for the only adult they recognized and felt safe with. The men said nothing as they approached. Richter eyed the colonel.

"We were told that children were taken. We can see that," he said. "How many?"

"Fourteen," Alicia said.

Without warning, the boy Team Bravo left across the trail

ran from the brush. He dashed straight to Alicia. Every team member immediately leveled his weapon upon the child. Some came so close to pulling their triggers they had to take a moment to calm themselves. Richter saw how the boy clung tightly about Alicia's waist and how the woman reciprocated with nurturing warmth and affection. It reminded him of Courtney and himself some years back. He looked away.

"This is what you get, Colonel," he said. "You come with us voluntarily. When we get back you tell us what we want to know. You'll become an operational advisor, so to speak. You do that, we'll keep you alive. You betray us, we'll give you back to your people. But before that, we'll make damned sure your leaders know just how grateful we are for the help you gave us."

"You don't leave a man much choice," Mendez replied.

"It's a better one than those people in that village got."

"Village?"

The colonel took a moment to evaluate his options. He knew Richter was correct. Zorrilla would never let him live after losing the cocaine. His only chance for survival, even if as a traitor, meant clinging to these men. *For now, anyway*, he thought.

"You're right, Captain," Mendez said. "I can make my life worth your while." The colonel glanced in James' direction. Mendez recalled it was this soldier who leaped from the back of the truck. "There are some things I can tell you about."

James stared back at the man. He felt as if a sign hung from around his neck. The other men were not aware that the colonel selected James as his focus. His paranoia gnawed at him. He was about to make a spontaneous remark when cut off by the woman.

"No!" Alicia roared. "He must die! He destroyed our village. He killed everyone. He wanted to sell our children, keep me for himself, then kill me when finished. I want him dead!"

"Alive, he can make a difference," Richter countered. "Dead, he's no good to anyone."

"Captain?" Mendez said.

"What!" Richten blared back.

"About the cargo? I mean, it's a lot of money. It, ah—ought to do someone—some good?"

"It could help our bank statements," Richter said. "Anybody feel like being an overnight millionaire?" He glanced to his men. He looked upon the face of each before eyeing Mendez. "My people don't come cheap, Colonel. I guess it's just not enough." Richter turned to Gable, gesturing to the LAW slung on his shoulder. "Art, do what you do best with that thing."

"Oh, yes sir."

"Art gets to play, again," Marcoli broke in. "They let you have all the fun."

Gable unslung the shoulder rocket. He extended the tube after dropping the sling and end caps.

"That's because I'm the radioman and the medic," he explained, while mounting the tube upon his right shoulder. "You got to keep me alive and happy...And don't forget," he resumed, while pulling forward on the arming device. "This is Gable's LAW."

Some of the men began to chuckle over the soldier's claim. Mendez felt nothing but remorse.

"Oh, Captain. No."

No sooner had Mendez made his sorrowful remark did Gable press onto the trigger boot. The HEAT round hurled straight for the truck. When the vehicle ignited, a large fireball shot upward. It rose through the overhanging foliage and filled the night sky with a tremendous luminescence. Much to everyone's surprise a multitude of smaller ignitions began to crack off. It then occurred to Marcoli that he forgot to tell them about the frags stored in the truck. As he dove for cover Marcoli yelled to the others about the grenades. Velázquez watched the penetrating light from less than a grid square away.

Velázquez froze upon hearing the immense explosion. He stared in the direction of the sound. He could not see the rolling flames rise through the trees, but observed as the dynamic yellow-white radiance cut through the foliage.

His pointman easily trailed the insurgents from the destroyed helicopter to San Delbaro. The human tragedy that befell the village solidified in him a vengeful tenacity. He tried to question the surviving elder village women, but they were too afraid. Like with Team Bravo, the women ran from the sight of the uniform-clad men. They did not care about the national origin the military represented. All they knew was that soldiers did the murdering. That was enough. Unable to gain a rebuff to the idea that who he looked for were the perpetrators of the settlement's execution, Velázques pursued his nation's invaders. He said nothing while watching the light subside. He used the last bit of luminescence to signal his men.

Marcoli rose to a stance and saw the shock on the faces of his comrades.

"I forgot," he innocently said. "There was a box M-33s in the back."

While Levits threw a handful of dirt at Marcoli the other people started to pull themselves together. Richter watched as Alicia guided the confused and frightened children back into the camp.

They huddled about her. Three clung to her waist while she spread her arms. She tried to cradle as many as her extended limbs could reach. Mysterious to everyone was Gable's inability to check himself.

Like the delay-action of a time fuse, Gable rose from behind a clump of tall grass. He stared at the flaming truck. He quietly watched as the fire began to diminish. Suddenly, Gable burst into loud laughter. For a half-minute the soldier hysterically carried on. Ramsy was the only one who understood the purpose behind the man's irrational display. Richter recognized it, as he watched the sergeant major stand near Art and silently observe the man release his uncapping fear. Marcoli was not so kind.

"That is one peculiar medic," he said.

Richter ignored the sergeant's remark.

Mendez rose to his feet. When the colonel was again on solid footing Richter resumed.

"I doubt that your buyers will try to help you," he said, "but if there's other troops in the area they'll be sending a patrol shortly...I think it's time we move out, Colonel. Art, get Reiner on the horn. Tell him—mission partial success. That we're en route to PZ. Two hours ETA."

"Roger."

Richter looked at the woman and the children of varying ages.

"Fourteen?"

"Yes," Alicia said.

"Your brother's dead," he went on.

"I don't have a brother."

"You know a man named Murillo?" Richter asked.

"I know Murillo," she said. "He came to our village a month ago. He lived with us—with my people."

"He said you're his sister."

"He lies..."

"Major Murillo is one of my men, Captain," Mendez cut in. "An officer of the highest caliber. She has nothing to do with him."

"Major Murillo?" Richter replied. "Well, thank you for clarifying that. You're already earning your keep. For a while it occurred to me we may have killed an innocent man."

"Murillo is dead? You're sure?"

"Very," James answered.

"Your men are no different than mine," Mendez claimed.

"My men have their moments, Colonel," Richter countered, "but there is one decided difference."

"And?"

"Mine are alive...Sergeant Major!"

"Sir!"

"What the hell are we going to do with fourteen kids?"

"Got me, Captain," Ramsy jokingly replied. "I've always stayed away from 'em as much as possible."

Richter wiped the oozing blood from his wound. Ramsy's

claim caused him to think back on the sergeant major's earlier comment.

"Yeah, I imagine you do," Richter said. He paused a moment to consider Cliff's descriptiveness. "Residue."

"I can lead them back to the village," Alicia offered.

"Since you're here," Richter explained, "I was hoping you'd lead us to our PZ. It's tough enough moving through this in daylight. Will you help us?"

Alicia motioned to one of the older children. The boy stepped forward and moved close to the woman. She rested her arm on his shoulder.

"Pedro can take them," she said. "He knows the forest as well as his father did."

"Then you'll help us, even if it means the colonel lives?"

"You don't have him there, yet."

Richter gazed into the woman's eyes and saw the determination, the resolve, in them. Mendez saw it as well. He looked to the captain for a response on his behalf. Richter was indifferent.

"Well, I guess that's the best deal we can get, right now. If I were you, Colonel, I'd watch my back."

Twenty-two

Darkness imposed a greater hindrance for Alicia than she had initially judged. The captain was only moderately pleased with their progress but still thankful he asked for the woman's help. He momentarily dismissed his concerns for the team's advance while thinking on the men they left behind.

The sergeant major collected their personal effects. He stashed Bard, Colfield, and Sanford's dog tags in his top left pocket and stored their personal documents in his rucksack. Beyond that, there was little done for the bodies. Time constraints prevented any significant measure of respect. At least they had time to bury Ray Copeland, he thought. The burial had some dignity about it. Although they marked fair time it became increasingly apparent that the jungle won over them.

He gave the element what he thought was adequate time. Richter believed that from one to one and a half hours was sufficient to reach the pickup zone. The coordinates placed the PZ within two and a half grid squares of the interdiction site. The further along their azimuth the more the forest seemed to close in. The less prominent elevations shown on his grid map failed to coincide with what they traversed. They were on a north heading, paralleling the skirt of a Sierra de Jungurudó spur. He wanted his team in Panama as quickly as possible. For some reason he felt the men had a greater chance of survival there. Believing it might enhance their progress the captain positioned his best pointman forward with the woman.

Marcoli remained just rear of Alicia, as the underbrush confined the two's trailblazing effort to a single path negotiation. He also kept a vigil eye on his compass to insure the villager did not veer from Richter's intended course. Behind Marcoli, Richter maintained a five-pace interval. Their stinting advance continued for another four hundred meters when Richter abruptly walked into Marcoli's back.

"What is it?"

"River, Captain," he said.

Richter glared forward. He saw the break in the jungle by the subdued glow of the quarter moon. The captain eyed the dark forest across the lighter, moon reflecting sheet of water. It was big. He judged the distance to be no less than forty meters. *Delays*, he angrily considered. He looked at his watch. It showed 2207 hours.

Richter stooped onto one knee. He pulled his map from inside his shirt. He studied the typographical features of the region using his penlight. He knew the coordinates of the last battle site and the azimuth he put the team on. It was a small matter of following the penciled line that he had marked for easy reference. Following the designated heading, the captain's finger stopped at the only probable water barrier. He observed the unnamed, broken blue line intersecting with the azimuth mark.

"This shows an intermittent stream," he said. "Damned

thing looks like the Amazon. It's got to be the Rio Balsas or a tributary."

The rest of Team Bravo bunched forward. Ramsy quickly moved to his disciple's side. He also recognized the misrepresentation on the map.

"What do you expect from our typographers, Captain? Accuracy?"

"It's wide but not deep," Alicia said. "We can cross it."

"She's right, Captain," Mendez broke in. He spoke from off to the side. "My men forded near here many times."

"Into Panama?"

"It's not Panama yet, Captain," Mendez resumed. "But what difference would that make? Look around you. Out here there are no borders. Just—jungle. This is not a bad place to cross. We're on the high bank. Deepest is about two meters. The far bank is forty, fifty meters. The bottom'll start to rise almost immediately."

Richter turned to Alicia and searched the woman's face for a confirming sign. He saw her validating nod.

"All right. We ford here."

No sooner did Richter give the order did Ramsy take hold of Gable's arm. He pulled the radioman close to him and gave the man some soldierly food for thought.

"I don't care if you drown," the sergeant major said. "If we find your body and that radio's not dry and operational, I'll kill you again. Got it?"

"Got it, Sergeant Major."

Ramsy released the man's arm while showing a smile. As he gave an encouraging pat on Gable's back-mounted radio, the sergeant major noticed a dark streak running down Richter's right cheek and jawline. He stepped to the captain and inspected the source of the peculiar manifestation.

"Captain, you're starting to bleed again." Ramsy looked at Alicia. "They don't have piranha this far north, do they?"

Both Ramsy and Alicia watched as Richter's eyes widened. Alicia, judging by the sergeant major's inflection, sensed Ramsy's words were in jest. The woman showed a partially repressed smile as she looked first at the horrified captain then at Ramsy. She saw the smirk on the sergeant major's face, coupled with a spirituous gleam in his eyes. A man farther back, no one knew who, overheard the sergeant major's comment. He laughed through his nose while trying to hold back the reflex. Richter heard the subdued laughter and was not impressed. When she heard the fathom snort Alicia began to lose control. She covered her mouth with her right hand while looking away. Richter saw her turn from him and knew the woman attempted to mask her amusement. *This isn't funny*, he thought.

"Well! Are there?" Richter asked, a tone of desperation evident.

As her smile broadened Alicia replied in the negative. The others looked on and began to grin as well. He did not know whether to believe the woman or not. She told him no, but her smile suggested he was about to be made a fool of. *This is no time for jokes*, he thought. As Ramsy organized his people for the crossing, Treadwell contemplated his status.

"Rare, blended Scotch Whisky," it said on the label. "By appointment to their late majesties King George III, King George IV, King William IV...," *and all that shit*, Treadwell thought. He squinted while raising the spectacles higher on his nose. The colonel took a closer look at the small print. "And to H.R.H. Prince Bernhard of the Netherlands." Evidently Bernhard did not fit in well with the rest of the clan, he speculated. Small print, like himself. He looked over the front and back labels three times. He searched for the number of years the scotch had aged prior to bottling. The age was not shown. Treadwell determined that he had underwear older than what he just drank.

He tossed the empty bottle onto the plank floor. He leaned forward and folded his arms on the fieldtable. He rested his chin upon his right forearm. He looked about the dull lantern-lit tent and wondered how it was that after nineteen years of service his existence encompassed the narrow confines of a GP small tent. He looked forward to when he gained access to the thousands stashed away. But it all seemed so distant to him for the moment. He sensed the faceless bureaucracy reaching out for him.

Something dramatic took place that day, he knew. Something by men who prevented him from being a part of it. His alienation suggested the Justice Department's opinion of him. The drug enforcement agent placed his integrity, his word as an officer, in question in the face of higher. He pondered the consequences until Reiner unexpectedly stepped into the tent.

Reiner pulled back the flap and stepped up to the colonel. He dropped a piece of paper onto the field desk. Treadwell reared back, pushing his chair from the table. He looked at the paper then at Reiner. Without a word the colonel picked up the document and saw the ten-digit grid coordinate inscribed. Before he could ask what it meant Reiner started in.

"Richter's on his way in," he began. "Here are the coordinates. He'll be there..." Reiner looked at his watch, "in about forty minutes."

"Why didn't my radioman bring this to me?" Treadwell asked.

"Because your TOC didn't receive it."

"You did? Richter's talking to you? You only?" The colonel jumped from his chair and angrily faced off with the agent. "It's a military operation, Reiner. Not some backwoods, homespun, good-old-boy field day."

"Now you're catching on, Brad," Reiner caustically countered. "Like it or not, it's my mission. Your assets, but my field day. As I said before, if you want to take it to SOUTHCOM, make your call. I'll get around to making mine to the Justice Department."

Treadwell eyed the paper once more. He pretended to study the numerical location. He used the time to think of a way to rebut the agent. The Pentagon would never buck the Justice Department, and Reiner was not bluffing about his contacts in the attorney general's office. Seeing no way to depose the agent, the colonel decided humility was his only means—for the present.

"Ted, what's going on out there?" he asked. "Look, I realize I'm operational support, but I care about those men. What are you doing out there?"

Reiner leaned forward and rested his hands onto the fieldtable. He jutted his face close to Treadwell's. He briefly stared at the colonel and studied the man's eyes. He caught a faltering look of doubt in them and sensed the guilt behind them.

"You do?" he said. "It's a whole new ball game out there, Brad. I got men all over that jungle. And you know what?" Reiner motioned to the paper in Treadwell's hand. "Until I gave you this I was the only one who knew where they were. Now, you're a smart, perceptive man. Why do you suppose I'd do something like that?"

"Damn!" Treadwell blasted. He threw the paper onto the desk. "I'm not going to play your kid shit games. If there's something you want to say, say it."

"Sit down, Bradford!"

Treadwell held his glare but for only a few seconds. He tried the schoolboy macho approach, knowing its effectiveness within a military setting. Reiner was not military, however. Because of his civilian status, coupled with his strong arm in the Justice Department, Treadwell realized he could not coerce the man. He slowly took his seat while not knowing what to expect. He waited.

"I wasn't going to do this now," Reiner went on. "But since you still want to play kid shit games, we'll just settle it right here. Right now."

"What?"

"I want your resignation, Colonel," Reiner demanded. "I want it sent to Headquarters SOUTHCOM within the hour…and I want authentication of receipt."

Treadwell leaped from his chair. Again, he desperately tried for a stand-off.

"Never!" he roared. "For what?"

"For aiding and abetting the enemy," Reiner said.

"I'll see you dead first."

"Or die trying," Reiner said.

At Reiner's counterclaim the tent flaps drew back. Two DEA agents swiftly stepped before the opening and stood with their machine pistols poised. Treadwell looked beyond Reiner, seeing the agents, and realized he had spoken rashly. He wanted to apologize for his impetuous remark, but Reiner canceled him out.

"Your record shows you won the Silver Star in Vietnam for gallantry. Resign and go, Colonel. Before it's all a matter of record."

"Ted?" Treadwell pleaded. "I got eleven months to retirement."

Reiner spun around and stepped toward his men. He made three strides before stopping to consider what Treadwell said. He turned and faced the colonel.

"Within the hour, Colonel...Oh! And just in case you thought your early release would be a breeze, the Justice Department had your Venezuela accounts seized. The ones you didn't think we knew about. You're broke, Bradford. You got no pension, you got no savings...and you got no place to be."

Treadwell watch as Reiner stepped between his men. The two agents followed at his heels, letting the tent flaps fall closed. The colonel stared at the canvas while wondering what to do next. His Venezuela accounts eliminated meant that nothing remained. Nineteen years and one month of service ending in a void of uselessness and waste. His wife and children, whom he had estranged, left him with only a remnant photograph of their past lives—lives that no longer had a place for him.

He lowered onto the stool. He took a quiet moment to consider his worth as a husband, a father, and as a soldier. He caught sight of the empty scotch bottle on the floor. He picked up the container and rested it on the stretched fabric of his cot. While doing so, Treadwell noticed his .45 pistol resting on top of his rolled-up sleeping gear.

It was his personal weapon, with him since 1966. He

recalled purchasing it at the post Rod & Gun Club at Fort Benning. That was just before he departed overseas for his first tour in Vietnam. Two more combat tours later, and some intermittent boredom at a couple of training facilities, his prized pistol was all that remained—the only thing, it seemed to him, that lasted through the years.

It protected him in combat. It helped him to perform under stress, its companionship culminated into his being awarded the Silver Star. It gave him a sense of purpose and direction when nothing or no one else cared enough to. It had flawless reliability. It remained loyally at his side, and it had never betrayed him. It was peculiar, he thought, how after a lifetime of dedication one character flaw could leave a man with nothing but a piece of iron for a companion.

Although powerful in its capacity the weapon was lifeless. It had no compassion, no dignity or self-respect. It was cold, hard, and senseless. It was impotent. Treadwell ran his finger tips over the weapon's nickel-plated slide while wondering where to go from there. Reiner cared less.

The agent stepped to his jeep. His two associates followed after him. Upon reaching the vehicle the younger of the three revealed his novice standing.

"You think he'll do it?"

"He'll do it if he wants to save what little he's got," Reiner said. "Whatever that is." The agent turned to the older associate. "Get down to Treadwell's TOC. Make sure Richter's got a chopper waiting for 'im." Reiner wrote the coordinates on a piece of scrap paper. He used the hood of his jeep to write on. "Here. That ship has got to be there in…," he looked at his watch, "thirty-one minutes. Make it happen."

"It will."

The loyal agent headed for the tactical operations center at the opposite end of the staging area.

Reiner stepped around his jeep and hopped into the shotgun side. The younger assistant knew that one of his new-guy duties was to drive when with Reiner. He automatically jumped behind the steering wheel. He stepped onto the clutch pedal and prepared to switch on the ignition while Reiner spoke.

"Let's get back to—"

BANG!

A heavy caliber shot thundered from the colonel's tent. The two men looked in the direction of the blast. They searched for something out of place. Both saw, by the glow of the lantern inside Treadwell's tent, a black shadow oozing along the interior ceiling and wall. Overwhelmed by the unexpected shot, the driver could not contain himself.

"Jesus! You thinking what I'm thinking?"

Reiner sat stiff in his seat. He faced the colonel's tent. For a short time he said nothing. He simply stared at the lantern light filtering through the fabric and watched how the dark, streaking blood ran down the canted circular ceiling. His driver looked at him. The novice thought he saw a look of aversion on the chief agent's face. He could not be sure, the driver thought, but it seemed that way. A few seconds later his chief confirmed his suspicions.

"Fuck 'im," Reiner coldly said. "Let his own men find 'im...Let's go."

As they drove off Reiner focused on more important matters, while Team Bravo began fording.

Marcoli led off. The village woman entered close behind him. Ramsy stood off to the side. Richter was third. He waited at the bank for Alicia to gain distance before entering the water. While waiting at the bank, standing next to his mentor, Richter dwelled on the sergeant major's poor taste in humor.

"Piranha," he softly repeated.

Richter checked the compress a final time. He wanted to be sure that no blood oozed out from under it.

Ramsy looked to Richter then grabbed him with both hands. He held to the captain's shoulders. A large grin slowly materialized. The gleam in his eyes showed in the subtle quarter-moon light.

"Just a joke, Captain."

The sergeant major delivered another one of his affectionate blows. This time the captain prepared for it. He saw his friend's enthusiastic nudge coming. After recovering from the gorilla love tap Richter stared at the stream.

He convinced himself that he detained his entry to allow the village woman an adequate tactical interval. As he paused the officer envisioned the water laden with flesh-eating piranha. He pictured them nibbling at his feet, his calves, his thighs—whatever.

He took a deep breath while stepping into the water. He slowly exhaled, trying to relax himself. While feeling the river spill into his boots he checked for blood a final time. When the surface reached his knees, Richter's mind kept flashing images of shredded and gobbled flesh. He imagined pristine white skeletal remains on the river bottom.

Ramsy watched as his tough little offspring stepped off the bank. He saw that his joke had far more impact on Alex than he intended. *But he went in the water, anyway*, the sergeant major thought. Alex confronted his fear and that was good. Behind Richter stepped Mendez.

The colonel stepped up to the sergeant major and raised his bound hands. Without a word Ramsy pulled his bayonet and inserted the blade between the man's arms, severing the cord. Mendez looked up to the big man and gave the sergeant major a nod of appreciation. Ramsy nodded back as the *federal* turned toward the water. Behind Mendez the enlisted prisoner stepped up and also lifted his hands to be freed. Ramsy complied with the man's gesture as well.

Gable followed the *federal*. He moved past the sergeant major with his rifle and radio held noticeably high. James trailed Gable, also holding his weapon above him. When he reach the bank James paused to give Gable time to move ahead. Ramsy noticed the zipped-up body armor. James was about to enter the water when Ramsy placed his hand on soldier's shoulder.

"Will?"

"Yeah."

"A bit stifling zipped up like that, ain't it?" He motioned

to the flak vest. "What if you have to get out of that heavy thing in the water?"

"Just call me bullet conscious, Sergeant Major," he said.

James showed a grin while patting the front of his vest. Ramsy returned the gesture, also showing a slight smile. He motioned for the soldier to follow after Gable. Behind James approached Levits, who also stopped at the water's edge. As the two paused adjacent to one another, Ramsy decided to exchange what he believed was rudimentary information.

"Greg—you wear body armor. You don't zip it up, I see. Why not?"

"Never, Sergeant Major," he replied. "You know as well as I do the stuff only stops shrapnel. A straight-on round'll go right in you. If you close it up, it'll just slow the round down enough to keep it from going out the back. What about the water? What if I have to get out of this thing? Why do you ask?"

"Uh huh. And who'd know that?"

"Anybody that's been in combat and used 'em. What's up?"

The sergeant major looked to the river. He watched James vanish into the darkness. He pondered a second more.

"Nothing," Ramsy replied. "But I agree with that. Move on, lad."

Ramsy stepped into the stream last. He waited in knee-deep water until Levits gained enough distance. By the time the sergeant major began his crossing, Marcoli stepped onto the sandbar at the opposite bank.

Marcoli made two steps up the bar and lowered onto one knee. He surveyed the concealing border of trees. When Alicia was again behind him Marcoli and the woman moved to the treeline. His eyes darted from one blackened image to another. He never kept his focus on one thing for more than three seconds. The soldier knew that the trick to a good night vision technique was not to concentrate for too long on any one subject and to keep the object focused slightly off center. When Alicia lay down next to him, however, Marcoli's eyes locked.

The woman's water-soaked dress clung to her like a diver's wet suit. Marcoli could not actually see much by the moonlight. Alicia's protruding buttocks and breasts, however, enabled his creative mind to complete the details.

The woman rolled onto her left side. She brushed her hair back with the fingers of her right hand. Marcoli uncontrollably stared as her breast seemed to spiral against the dress on every stroke of her fingers. On the fifth run of her arm Alicia noticed the soldier's eyes fixed on her.

"Put your eyes back in your head, Sergeant," she said, "or I'll cut them out."

"Oh, yes, ma'am," he replied.

Marcoli faced away. He refocused his searching eyes treeward while waiting for the remainder of Team Bravo to cross.

The team cautiously progressed through the swirling water. The surface current was mild, no undercurrent noticeable. Noise discipline was priority, as no one knew what was just beyond the opposite bank. When Richter reached the shore he lowered onto one knee as well. He searched the silhouetted treeline before advancing to where Alicia and Marcoli had positioned themselves. Behind the captain, Mendez carefully negotiated the water. The colonel realized that he could also be cut down in a Panamanian or Colombian crossfire. The other prisoner had a greater motive.

He began to shorten his stride and caused Gable to close on him. Gable saw he was too close for tactical safety and purposely slowed his pace. He expected the distance between himself and the prisoner to extend. Gable also knew that the team began to bunch up behind him. He moderately lengthened his stride and tried to find an acceptable interval between the captive ahead and James behind. With the prisoner only three feet from him, Gable grew edgy.

"Move up, Gomezzzzzz," he said. "Keep your distance."

Upon second thought Gable wondered why he gave the order. He did not understand Spanish and the prisoner most likely did not know English. When the *federal* stopped in the stream Gable almost walked into him.

"I said move, Gomez…"

Had it been daylight, Gable flashed through his mind, the *federal* would not have had a chance. But in the dull glow of the overhead moon, the prisoner's jab into his face happened so quickly there was little he could do.

He fell back upon feeling the man's fist on his nose. The shooting pain in his face felt as if someone shoved a hot cinder up his nostril. His eyes instantly teared, further distorting his vision. He reared and jammed his toe into the mud to prevent himself from falling over. The prisoner struck him once more while grabbing for Gable's weapon.

Disarmed and unable to see through his tears, Gable blindly tried to back away. Hearing the bolt on his weapon slam forward, Gable rushed to what he believed was his left. In the confusion he became turned around and stepped into the prisoner.

He felt the hot projectiles penetrate his midsection. It felt as if someone ran a branding iron through his stomach. He dropped the radio and pressed his hands against his solar plexus. The wild spray of brass lasted for only a second, mortally wounding one and grazing another.

The firing came from everywhere, James thought. He felt a renegade round tear through his flak vest and shirt, piercing the plastic underneath. He checked himself for wounds and for the safety of his stash. In his haste to protect his wealth James forgot about his friend dying ahead. Ramsy reminded him of his purpose.

"James! Get up there."

James lunged his left hand under the flak vest. His fingers sank into the costly bundle up to their first joint. He hastily withdrew his hand, mistakenly tearing the plastic wrap further. A large portion of the drug spilled from the elongated hole, falling into the river. He pressed on the package, palming the tear. He held his weapon in his right hand, but could not move the selector switch to auto without the use of his left. He popped off two useless rounds into the dark.

Hearing the gunplay behind them, Richter and Mendez dropped prone onto the river bank. They searched the darkness for the source of the gunfire. Richter turned to the colonel.

"There wasn't going to be any trouble," the captain said, "or did your man forget?"

"He is no longer one of mine, Captain," Mendez countered. "My agreement with you is still good. But he is a soldier. Like your own, it's his duty to escape."

The two officers waited on the far bank while listening to Ramsy's voice slice through the night.

The sergeant major rushed to behind James and grabbed the soldier by his left arm. James yanked the limb away and shoved his hand under the zipped flak vest.

"Are you hit?" Ramsy asked.

He noticed James pressing onto his side.

"No. It's not bad," James lied.

Again, Ramsy grabbed at James' left hand, startling the soldier. James fought against the sergeant major's tug. Ramsy ignored the soldier's lack of personal concern and pulled the limb from what he believed was a bullet wound. Upon yanking James' hand from his side, Ramsy watched the crumbled substance spill from the gaping hole in the shirt. Ramsy gazed in disbelief, frozen by the realization of what James had. He looked up at James, his pupils eating into the soldier's.

"It was just a little," James said. "It wouldn't hurt anything. For myself—that's all, Sergeant Major."

Ramsy grabbed James by the left sleeve. He raised the soldier's arm and pulled that side of James' flak vest from his shoulder. He tore at the soldier's uniform. The large rip allowed for the remaining cocaine to spill into the water. Ramsy took hold of the man by the back of his collar and lunged him forward.

"Move!"

Although the men scattered along the sandbar Ramsy quickly consolidate his people. As Levits carried Gable from the water, laying the dying soldier onto the sand, Velázquez rushed his team in the direction of the shooting.

They saw the bodies of fellow soldiers strewn throughout the position. They found three dead gringos as well. Upon finding Santos, his stomach ripped open like a gutted deer, the captain concluded that the only officer on site fell during the fight. A few of his men inspected the destroyed vehicle. They spotted the damaged, some intact, packages next to the truck. After bringing one of the bundles to Velázquez' attention the captain understood what had truly taken place.

He held a large two-kilo wrap in his right hand. He looked at the package while asking himself where the honor went in what they did as soldiers. This was not what he was about, Velázquez angrily told himself. He was a soldier, not a profiteer. As quickly as he believed the slain possessed worth for their gallantry in battle, his admiration for the dead evaporated. Drug runners in uniform. They were dirt. He was about to order his men to search the dead when he heard the spray of an automatic weapon sound in distance.

He immediately put the priority of identifying the dead aside and ordered his pointman forward. Drug runners or not, he thought, they were still his people and Colombia's problem. He would not allow any outside invader, interdiction team or otherwise, to kill his people without retaliation.

Velázquez stayed close to his pointman. His will to kill the presumed American intruders was further nurtured by the blood of more Colombians soaking into the earth. They had to be shown that Colombia was a nation, a people in their own right. That change, if any, would evolve from within and not from outside interference.

Twenty-three

Levits stepped onto the bank. He cradled Gable in his arms as he made seven steps up the slope. He dropped to the sand and crossed his legs. He supported Gable's limp body in them. Gable's head rested against his chest while Levits folded his arms about the man. Ramsy knelt next to Gable and felt the open wounds in the radioman's stomach. James held back a few meters. Richter also stood off to the side.

He eyed into the dark forest while the enlisted men consoled their dying combatant. Gable concerned Richter. He cared about all of his men but purposely showed no reaction. He looked beyond the bank and searched the jungle that his men and he still had to negotiate. The radio was gone, their only link with the outside world severed. He looked at his watch. It showed 2244. Although he regretted Gable dying in the sand he had to insure the survival of the remaining men and one woman.

The soldier coughed up his stomach contents. Richter turned away from the gagging sound and tried to fill his mind with mission essentials. He used the excuse to avoid the minute details of death. He listened as Gable's gasping voice sliced through the thin layer of river mist.

"Sergeant Major—I lost the radio."

"That's all right, lad," Ramsy replied. He pulled his hand from Gable's abdomen and felt the tackiness of the warm blood covering his palm. "Lad. Your wound is bad…"

"That's—okay," Gable cut. He gagged once more. The blood spurt over his lower lip. It dribbled down his chin and along the neck. "I'll see you guys—later."

"Later?" Ramsy asked.

"You know—we don't die," he explained. "Just go to hell—regroup."

The gurgling of passing air and blood sounded from the soldier's throat. The last bit of strength drained from Gable. Levits felt the body go limp. Ramsy watched the man pass and took a quiet moment before looking at his watch. He glanced up at the captain and saw that Alex deliberately looked away.

"How much further we got?"

"Grid square," Richter replied, his voice choked. "Maybe less."

"Ah, we don't have time," Ramsy said. "Pull his personal effects. Give 'em to me."

The sergeant major rose from the body. He searched the dark faces about him while Levits sanitized the remains. Ramsy spotted James' smaller frame off to the side. Richter watched the sergeant major bear down on the soldier. He did not understand the motivation behind Ramsy's assault, but realized it was a sergeant-to-sergeant issue, for the present. Richter listened while peering across the river.

"If we didn't have to keep moving," Ramsy began, "you and I would have a little talk. When we get back it's going to be conference time. You got that?"

"Got it, Sergeant Major," James said.

Ramsy pivoted and looked upon the other shadowed faces. He was angry, wanting to kill something—anything to release the built up animosity that swelled inside of him.

"Cover the body," he said. "Then we'll move out."

James and Levits dragged the body to the forest's edge. They used their entrenching tools in the loose sand to dig a hasty grave. Once they interred Gable, Levits cut large river ferns to camouflage the grave site. As Team Bravo moved out, double-timing through the underbrush, Velázquez broke out of the jungle and onto the opposite bank.

The patrol quickly forded the river. Their familiarization with the region proved a considerable edge over the less knowledgeable interdiction team. Upon reaching the opposite bank Velázquez sent one man in each direction along the shore. The tracker he directed eastward quickly located the renegade team's exit point. It was luck, he thought, or providence that allowed his man to find the invader's trail within a matter of minutes.

His men fanned out and surveyed the shore. They searched for the point at which the running men reentered the jungle. After a five-minute lapse one of his soldiers yelled from the trees. The captain was about to direct his element to follow the pathfinder but suddenly changed his mind. He ordered everyone to remain silent. The men stood like statues on the open beach. They looked at one another's silhouettes and saw their dark figures motionless and mute. Velázquez locked his joints and stood like a piece of stone. His concentration narrowed. He stared upriver, directing his right ear across the stream. He strained to recapture the trickle of sound that he believed he had heard earlier. As his men silently waited, Velázquez listened.

He was not sure at first. It was merely a hunch. Gradually, the percussioning rotor built in intensity. He heard its distant whisper transform into a hacking roar, slashing at the night. It came on fast and low. It was the rhythmic popping of a ghostly UH-1 racing just above the jungle like a giant insect on a nocturnal prowl.

Velázquez ordered his radioman to call in. He wanted their headquarters to confirm any friendly aircraft in the area. He listened to the aircraft's chopping volume build while his technician spoke their call-sign into the microphone. The info exchange took less than sixty seconds. As the radioman glanced up from his equipment, informing Velázquez there were no friendlies in flight, the helicopter broke from just above the treetops on the far bank. It raced over the patrol, some seventy feet above them.

Velázquez watched as the bird raced over them and disappeared above the trees. It flew in the direction his tracker said the intruders headed. He yelled for his men to pursue in that direction. While Velázquez's men deserted the shore Team Bravo stayed their course.

Alicia advanced three strides ahead of Marcoli. She increased the team's pace to an almost dead run. Noise discipline was no longer a matter. Everyone tripped and stumbled over fallen branches and logs. The saplings under the higher growth slapped at their faces, cutting their hands and arms as well. The stifling temperature and humidity caused their lungs to heave. Marcoli unknowingly began to fall back, unable to maintain the exhaustive pace the woman imposed on them. He felt the captain's boots graze on the back of his.

"Hey, Captain," he called out. "No grab ass."

"Just move, Marcoli."

"Damned good thing you brought her along," he went on. "How much farther we got?"

"Can't tell," Richter said. "We're moving too fast." The captain glanced at his watch. "However far it is, we got thirteen minutes to get there."

"Thirteen, huh?"

Team Bravo collided with every branch, log, and rock in its path. Marcoli ran straight into a downed tree. He claimed that no one could have seen it, even though the woman leading them easily ran under the rotund trunk. Richter almost struck the beam as well.

He ran into Marcoli when the pointman bounced off the

dead wood. When Marcoli could continue on, a half-minute later, Richter ordered the team to move out. But suddenly the captain froze and listened for the shallow popping originating from behind.

The entire team went placid. They looked to the blanketing foliage above. They searched through the small gaps in the overhead vegetation. The sound of its rhythmic hacking increased as the aircraft drew near. They gazed at what little sky was visible and hoped to spot the ship as it flew by. As the bird thundered over them Ramsy broke the silence first.

"We're close, Captain, but we got no way to confirm our mark."

"Keep 'em moving, Sergeant Major," Richter said. "We'll wing it."

Alicia resumed her long stride through the bush. She felt the serrated edges of the ground foliage lacerate her ankles and legs. She no longer concerned herself with Richter's prescribed heading. Instead, she simply ran in the direction the helicopter flew. As Team Bravo closed on the PZ, the awaiting pilot tried to establish contact.

The helicopter hovered at ninety feet above the zone. The crewchief and copilot searched below. They squinted into almost absolute darkness. There was nothing, the crewchief and copilot agreed. Nothing but blackness and the threat of being spotted and downed by a Colombian patrol. With no reference point the pilot felt that she had little alternative but to break radio silence. She discarded SOP, initiating contact.

"Leopard. This is Falcon. Over," she said into her mike. "Leopard. Come in. Over."

The pilot waited a quarter minute. She listened through the static noise of her helmet. There was nothing. She hovered another fifteen seconds and hoped for a reply.

"Leopard. This is Falcon," she began again. "Arrived PZ. Need your marker. Over."

"You think they're down there?" the copilot asked, after switching their communications to the internal mode.

"Who knows," she said. "We're at the coordinates. Let's

hang on a few more minutes. Use your goggles. See what we got down there."

"Let's not stay too long, ma'am," the crewchief remarked. "It only takes one round."

"Roger, Sergeant," she replied. "Couple of minutes. Then we'll move off." The pilot switched her radio to the external mode. "Leopard. This is Falcon. Over."

The copilot lowered his night vision goggles and positioned the sighting instrument even with his eyes. Upon activating them he peered through the ports and adjusted for focus using the focus ring on each lens. He looked upon the fuzzy apparition of terrain. It was devoid of color. Only shades of gray differentiated the contour features using the intensification of the star and moonlight. He visually swept the area four times.

"Nothing—nothing. If they're down there, ma'am, no one could tell it."

"Yeah."

Team Bravo broke from the thickets. Alicia ran into the clearing. She did not think of her vulnerability on the open ground. Marcoli, staying with PZ procedure, held back until he could verify to those in the aircraft who was on the ground. But within seconds all sense of the rules drained from Marcoli. He watched the helicopter make a ninety-degree turn and lunge forward, disappearing into the night.

The idea of being left behind when so close consumed the soldier. It caused him to briefly lose control. Marcoli picked up a fallen tree branch and threw it at the departing aircraft. He ran to the center of the clearing.

"Shit! Shit! Shit-shit-shit!"

Richter watched as Marcoli chased after the bird. He looked up at the helicopter and observed as the olive drab fuselage disappeared. He looked down at Marcoli and saw the shadowed image wildly swing his arm, apparently throwing something. As the captain eyed to where he last saw the chopper, seeing only empty sky, he decided Marcoli's venting had merit.

"Shit," he said softly. Richter paused to consider their options. He decided there was only one plausible recourse. "Sergeant Major! I want a triangle PZ marked with three flares. As wide as this clearing'll permit. Now!"

Marcoli swung around. He stared upon the silhouette of Richter. It was futile, he thought. There was nothing left.

"But they're gone, Captain!"

"Do it!" Richter countered. "It's all we got."

"Yeah," Marcoli said. "That's for sure. Sure—shit! Greg! Move down about thirty meters. Pop a green one."

"Roger."

Levits quick-stepped toward the end of the clearing while counting off his extended strides. He ignited a green flare at a thirty-pace count. He dropped the blinding torch onto the ground, marking the apex. Marcoli observed Levits' placement of the first marker. He rushed twenty paces in the opposite direction and set the base. The pointman dropped the second thermal canister forty paces from the first. The PZ established, Alicia and the two men moved to the edge of the trees.

Team Bravo watched as the flares' eye-irritating intensity illuminated the zone. A shimmering phosphorescence seemed to originate from within the surrounding trees. They saw how the radiance reflected off the massive trunks, overhanging branches, and varied-sized leaves. The team waited while realizing that all that could be done was done. The luminescence spilled through the forest. It alerted those in the near distance.

Spotting the green radiance sift through the forest caused Velázquez to grow more determined. He pushed and goaded his men on. Two soldiers became casualties. One broke his arm upon stumbling over ground vines. The other twisted his ankle when he stepped into a depression. Velázquez left the injured behind. He was unwilling to give up a chance to make a bloody point for his people.

The fluttering luminescence was no farther than two or three hundred meters, he judged. Although the helicopter came and went, the captain felt there was a chance, though slight, that someone did not make the rendezvous. The glow's gradual intensity grasped his eyes, drawing him in. Team Bravo had no alternative. It quietly waited.

Richter's people remained at the PZ's edge. The hissing of the phosphorus canisters was the only sound leaking into the still night. It sounded like a persistent belch of gas from a ruptured line. Aware of the team's vulnerability Richter tried to initiate some kind of positive action, even if only minute in worth.

"Take cover farther back," he ordered. "We're exposed this close..."

As if punctuating the final word of Richter's command a rifle shot snapped out. It came from some distance, Ramsy judged. Their deeply entrenched tactical reflex caused the men to immediately dive farther into the brush. Alicia remained where she was and searched for the source of the shot. Marcoli rushed out and yanked her into the trees. Only Ramsy saw the round penetrate.

At the instant he heard the rifle crack, the sergeant major happened to look in Levits' direction. He watched the man's face reveal a neutral expression as the bullet drove through him. Ramsy heard the "tick" sound when the bullet pierced Greg's chest. Before gravity grasped him the missile exited at the back. The body armor between his shoulder blades appeared to ignite. Levits dropped quietly, his face still barren of expression when he fell to the earth.

Ramsy stooped to beside Levits. He gently lifted the man's upper body from the ground. He cradled Greg's head in his left palm while hearing Richter bellow out the command.

"Cover! Now!"

By the time Richter shouted his directive only Ramsy had failed to comply. The others already caressed the ground with loving enthusiasm. The sergeant major did not hear the officer's command, or he ignored it. He stayed at Levits' side. Ramsy studied the dead man's calm features. He saw, by the fluctuating light of the nearby flares, the tranquil appearance of sleep emanating from Greg's face.

Two more rounds blasted from out of the darkness. They cut into the earth near where Ramsy cradled the soldier. The bullets threw up debris. Ramsy appeared not to notice the barrage hitting around him.

"Sergeant Major!" Richter yelled out. "Take cover. Now!"

"I guess you were right, lad," Ramsy said softly.

He delicately lowered Greg's head upon the ground. Another round struck a few inches from his right foot. The scattering dirt flew up and into his face. It tore the NCO from his brief mental drift.

He sprang upward and pivoted toward the jungle on the rise. Ramsy leaped into the foliage. Looking up from the ground, the sergeant major saw the multiple firing of weapons. He spotted the dissipated flames escaping through the flash suppressers. Above the team, the pilot redesigned her mission parameters.

If no radio contact or PZ markings manifested it was the pilot's responsibility to return to the staging area. If Team Bravo did not make the link-up, she found out during the flight briefing, the men were to be discarded, labeled as a self-contained contingent of freelancers on an anarchical rampage through the countryside. The team's survival becoming her priority, the pilot broke from criteria.

She began a wide rectangular flight pattern over a twelve-grid-square block. She banked her aircraft and made another steep course change. As the ship leveled off for another down leg run, the copilot spotted a distant soft illumination rising from out of the ocean of black.

"Major, look!" the copilot yelled, while pointing to the radiance. "Over there."

"It's not standard PZ markings," she said, "but it's them—I hope. Try and get Richter on the horn."

"Leopard," the copilot began. "This is Falcon. Over."

The aircraft made another steep bank. Major Arlington aligned her aircraft toward the subtle glow rising from the forest. As the pilot maneuvered her ship toward the luminescence her copilot tried and establish radio contact. The copilot repeated the call-sign seven times while their bird closed in. As he listened to the atmospheric static coming through his helmet, Velázquez maneuvered the rest of his men on line.

He organized his team left of Bravo, near the triangle's fired base. Velázquez's men fired over the bright light. Their shots were wild, as the blinding flares ate at their eyes. As he ordered his men to concentrate their fire on a specified sector the helicopter shot out from over the treetops.

Its whirling rotor shoved a blast of blinding air and debris into the Colombian patrol's face. Marcoli, ecstatic over the aircraft's return, yelled from where he lay.

"All right, Captain! Lucky hunch."

Marcoli rose onto one knee. He focused his flashlight on the chopper's forward section and signaled the pilot. Richter looked to the aircraft, and watched the ship slowly descend after the pilot recognized Marcoli's light pattern.

"Lucky," he said under his breath.

Richter shook his head over what he knew was an unlikely probability.

The ship began to take rounds. Velázquez redirected the fire of three men onto the helicopter. The pilot and crew heard the projectiles ricochet through the cockpit and cabin. All three knew it only took one well-placed round in the hydraulics or engine to down the aircraft. The copilot's nerves began to fray when a bullet fragment shot by his face.

"Damn, ma'am! There must be a battalion out there."

"We're committed," Arlington said. "Hang on, Lieutenant."

The pilot hastily descended. She was unable to pull back sufficiently to prevent a hard contact. The helicopter lobbed upon the clearing. The ship bounced twice before settling. The crewchief picked himself off the cabin floor and quickly reaimed his machine gun rearward.

The gunner manipulated the trigger. He delivered four second bursts to prevent the barrel from overheating. He checked his alignment to target by the glistening red arc of the intervallic tracer rounds. The heavy concentration of 7.62mm displaced most of Velázquez's men. It forced the element to move back and take cover from the voluminous delivery. Seeing their pursuers momentarily suppressed Richter ordered his people forward.

Marcoli dashed forward first. He rushed to the aircraft while firing his weapon on automatic. Alicia and the remaining team stayed close behind him. Richter expected Marcoli to jump into the cabin, but the soldier chose to remain outside the bird. He moved to the rear of the helicopter and lowered onto one knee. He assisted the door gunner from under the aircraft tail. As the people threw themselves into the bird the copilot observed aftward. He watched as the bodies rushed past the excited door gunner.

Ramsy boarded prior to James. He pulled the soldier's weapon from him when James climbed in. James briefly glared at the man upon being disarmed but said and did nothing. Instead, he submissively headed forward the ship. Richter noticed the sergeant major take the weapon but had little time to consider it. The copilot watched the chaotic human display.

He leaned to the left and turned in his chair. He watched from over his shoulder as the remnants of Team Bravo lunged through the door. The woman entered strangely enough. Apparently, someone or two threw her in headfirst. Behind the woman followed two men in flight suits. Behind the presumed pilots boarded a Colombian officer, followed by three more airborne bodies. After what he believed was everyone, the copilot decided it was time to get them the hell out of there.

"Ma'am, they're loaded...Ma'am?" He turned to the pilot and saw the bullet hole in Major Arlington's helmet. Blood oozed from under her headgear, down the right side of her face. "Oh, shit!"

The copilot grasped the controls. He pulled the stick free of the hunched-over body. Upon hearing the revolutions build, Ramsy stood in the doorway and announced their departure.

"Sergeant Marcoli!" he yelled. "It is time to go!"

Marcoli realized the helicopter was about to liftoff. He rose to his feet and pivoted toward the port door. Suddenly, a round caught him in the right leg, shattering his knee cap.

Ramsy saw Marcoli go down but just as quickly pick himself up. The man hobbled to the door while dragging his useless limb. The aircraft left the ground a second before he reached the door. Marcoli clasped upon the skid as the helicopter began its rapid ascent.

Ramsy lowered onto the cabin floor, laying belly down, and stretched his arms. He reached over the runner and grabbed hold of Marcoli's wrists.

He reacted so spontaneously that Ramsy forgot about his own safety. He felt the weight of his upper body begin to draw him out of the aircraft. Richter saw Ramsy begin to slide forward and threw himself over the sergeant major's legs. He clung to Ramsy's thighs while anchoring them both with his left foot braced against a doorframe bulkhead.

Ramsy saw how the ground beneath Marcoli fell away. His narrow field of vision broadened the higher the aircraft ascended. All three flares came into view simultaneously. They appeared like fluttering phantasma luminescence framing Marcoli's image.

The sergeant major maintained a viselike clamp upon the man's wrists. Ramsy looked down at Stan and saw the wounded and frightened soldier looking up at him. He felt the muscles and tendons in Marcoli's wrists flex and pull. He saw Marcoli glance earthward, the man only then realizing his boots were roughly a hundred feet off the ground. Marcoli frantically eyed up to the sergeant major.

"Don't let go, mother fucker!"

"Got you, lad! Hold tight!" Ramsy said.

He gripped Marcoli's limbs tighter.

Velázquez watched as the helicopter rose. An emptiness within him began to swell. He order his men to stop firing. Instead, he called upon his best marksman, the team sniper, to take an aim on the soldier dangling from under the aircraft. He instructed the man to relax, to take his time and insure accuracy. By the time the helicopter climbed to 150 feet, the capable marksman impressed his captain with a tight three-round-shot group.

Marcoli felt the hot rounds pierce his abdomen. One bullet followed another in rapid succession. His entire body went numb from the multiple high-velocity impacts. He knew something was wrong but could not pinpoint the cause.

Ramsy saw how the projectiles tore at Stan's uniform and watched the spray of fabric, blood, and flesh. He felt the jolt in Marcoli's wrists. He watched Marcoli look groundward.

"Don't look down, lad!" Ramsy yelled.

The soldier searched for the cause of his lack of sensation. When he spotted the open wound and the draining blood running down his legs, Marcoli saw no reason to fear any further.

He glanced up at the sergeant major. Stan's calm eyes revealed a contentment, an acceptance of his destiny. He applied more strength to his grip but for only a second. He let his body go limp and allowed his fingers to slip from around the aircraft runner. Ramsy felt the body go heavy and realized Marcoli no longer tried to live. Marcoli maintained his gaze on the sergeant major. A subtle smile emerged.

"Oh man!" he yelled, as blood spurted from between his lips. "This is something!"

Ramsy clamped harder onto the soldier's wrists. He strained to hold on to the man and the weighted gear strapped to him. The load was not overwhelming for Ramsy, but Marcoli's sweating arms did not permit him an adequate grip. Stan's limbs began to creep through the sergeant major's fingers. Ramsy helplessly felt and watched him slip away. As Marcoli's fingers squeezed through Ramsy's grasp, the soldier's eyes went wide.

"Yeah!"

Ramsy watched as the pointman fell away. He saw the body strike the clearing before feeling the tug on his legs. Richter and Alicia pulled him into the cabin.

The exhausted team sat quietly. Everyone took a minute to

regain composure. Each, in his or her own way, silently thanked fortune for allowing them another night of life. Heavy, nervous breathing characterized most of the occupants. While the silent minutes passed, James considered his options.

He sat forward on the port side, next to Masterson's copilot. He eyed the *federal* colonel sitting next to Richter at the aft firewall. He looked to Ramsy and recalled how the sergeant major had ignored him since the river crossing. Treating him, James believed, as if he possessed no worth—like at Fort Jackson. James knew what he did was not uncommon among the freelancers, but it was something seldom talked about.

Getting away with an occasional stash made sound economic sense. It permitted a man to put aside a lucrative nest egg while also drawing a salary for risking his life. To be caught at such a thing, however, was officially inexcusable. Do it quietly, the enlisted men of the camp unofficially whispered. Don't talk about it, and don't get caught. He was caught, and the *federal* colonel had the potential to implicate him in something far greater.

"Hey, Captain!" Will yelled over the rotor noise. "How much truth you really think we'll get out of this guy?"

Richter looked up from the cabin floor. He gazed upon James while wondering the motivation behind his question. James never asked about the prisoners in the past. That he questioned the worth of someone of such high rank, who already helped the team, suggested that James had underwent a striking attitude change.

Richter looked at Ramsy and saw his top NCO turn away from James. The sergeant major stared at Richter with dead eyes, suggesting doubt in something or someone. *Something took place out there*, Richter thought. Whatever it was, Cliff would tell him about it later. Richter looked at the officer sitting next to him.

"I will keep my word, Captain," Mendez said. "I promise to tell you everything. But you must keep me alive."

Although he could not hear Mendez's words James did

recognize Richter's acknowledging nod. It suggested to him that whatever the *federal* told Richter it was enough to secure the worth of his word. His mind began to race. James conjured image after image of how the Colombian colonel would victimize him, and how the lieutenant colonel at the basecamp sat comfortably on his ass. Not knowing what Mendez knew was the worst of it.

As if by reflex, James reached for the .32 Ruger he secured in the small of his back. He popped off three of the small-caliber rounds into the *federal*'s chest and abdomen.

Ramsy lunged for him as the soldier fired into Mendez. He easily reached James but could not disarm him before the third shot. As he yanked the pistol from James' hand Ramsy's disappointment peaked.

"Are you asking to die?" he yelled. "Try it again! I'll give you what you want."

Disarmed and subdued, Will settled against the cabin wall. He watched as Masterson tore open Mendez's uniform and inspected the wounds, two in the stomach and one in the chest. Masterson looked to Richter and revealed a decided expression of futility. He glanced at the wounds a final time before looking at the others.

"Good old sucking chest wound," he said. "Anyone got some cellophane or plastic wrap?"

"Let the piece of shit die," Alicia said.

"Can't do that, lady," the pilot countered. "Like the captain said, he's worth a hell of a lot more alive."

Richter maintained his weapon on James until sure that everyone settled to an acceptable state of pandemonium. He silently watched Will for a half-minute more, then diverted his attention out the aircraft door. He observed the black treetops swiftly pass under the ship's belly.

Twenty-four

Reiner stood at the margin of the iron helipad. His fledgling agent remained at his side. He looked at his watch and saw that it was 0111 hours. Team Bravo had been deployed since 0530 the morning before. In that space of time the devastation grew far reaching.

All three nations had suffered dramatic combat losses. The Panamanian, Colombian, and American elements piecemealed to almost nonexistent. The cocaine destroyed was not enough to stop Zorrilla. The buyers never connected, which meant the money was still active. The basecamp lost its commander—first by disgrace, then by suicide. The Team Bravo leader was on the casualty list and had to be told of his daughter. Reiner scanned beyond the helipad and saw the lesser residual affects of the haphazard mission.

Down from the pad, about twenty meters, a military ambulance was parked. A driver and two medics waited for the wounded while smoking and joking. Adjacent to the truck parked a jeep containing three of the four military policemen assigned to the staging area. Their principal duty was as a convoy security contingent for equipment trucked overland. Their purpose on this night was to escort Mendez to the dispensary and to remain with him. He assigned one MP to guard Will James, holding the soldier in a semiconfinement status. There was no hard constructed lockup on the installation. He began to have second thoughts about the soldier's detainment. The one chaplain provided the encampment, a Catholic, was also on site. The gentleman waited nearby to administer the last rites to Major Arlington.

Father Ankor provided multidenominational services for the men. He helped to alleviate the guilt felt by those who still believed, and to afford confidential counseling to those who felt comfortable enough to vent their anger in a controlled setting. *I guess he has a purpose*, Reiner thought.

He fingered the crucifix attached to a gold chain around his neck. The idea of theology, of any kind, seemed foreign at best in the savage encampment. Even his men, the agents from Virginia, tended to lose themselves after a time in the bush. Some returned to the staging area no better off than the freelancers they contracted. Sometimes it baffled the agent how Ankor spent most of his waking hours in solitude.

The majority of the installation avoided him. They did so either out of their lack of belief or because they grew numb and soulless from their enervating escapades. What religious inklings the men still possessed, if any, were repressed deeply within their subconscious. *Out here a shaman could reach them as easily as any priest, reverend, kahin, or rabbi*, he thought. Beside Reiner's novice stood the new staging area commander.

As Treadwell was dead his executive officer automatically, eagerly, assumed command of the encampment. Ringwald, a fourteen-year regular, became abreast of Team

Bravo's classified mission solely out of intercommand courtesy. Reiner saw no point in leaving the new facility head uninformed the first day in his new post. When briefed of the second objective, Ringwald appeared mildly shocked, momentarily taken aback by their freelancer's extremely bold and aggressive act. Reiner believed he spotted fear in the major's eyes.

It was a simple assumption that although agreeable on this night, Ringwald would eventually attempt to exercise his pseudoinstallation authority. As his predecessor, the major would sooner or later utilize his facility, the logistical support and technician manpower, as a bargaining chip for control. And like Treadwell, Reiner assured himself, Ringwald would fall into line. Stubbornly, even bitterly perhaps, but in the end the major would coexist with them or exist with someone else somewhere else. As Treadwell, Ringwald was a small man, an easy man to anticipate. Reiner was about to asked the new commander a question. Something light, unimportant, to suggest at least a trace of mutual regard—that is, until he heard the distant sound of a rotor softly rise from out of the darkness.

The ship approached from the south-southeast and pivoted 180 degrees above the pad before delicately resting its runners onto the iron. As it descended most of the men on the ground turned away from the bird. They tried to prevent the rotor downwash from throwing debris into their faces. Reiner did not look away. Instead, he faced straight on while squinting his eyes and holding on to the bill of his cap. The cap was a gift from his son. His proud boy had mailed it to him after watching the Cardinals win a doubleheader. No sooner did the aircraft touch iron than did the occupants began to off-load.

As the medics rushed forward Masterson and his copilot left the helicopter. They ignored Reiner while stepping by him. The pilots did not forget to recognize the still presumed executive officer. Masterson informed the major that they intended to return to flight operations for debriefing prior to turning in. Ringwald acknowledged Masterson's remark with a nod and returned the lieutenant's salute. The major decided the time was not appropriate to make Treadwell's fate known to them.

James jumped from the port doorway. Ramsy stayed close behind him. He stopped James when the solder reached the end of the helipad.

"You!"

As if walking into a concrete wall James froze midstride. He paused before turning. Ringwald heard the thirty-five-year-plus veteran yelled after the man and wondered the reason for Ramsy's boldness. Reiner said nothing. He was already aware of James' indiscretion by radio with Ramsy during the return flight. The agent conveniently discarded that vital piece of information when he updated the major. As far as Ringwald knew the MPs were in site on behalf of Mendez only.

As James stood at the helipad skirt an MP began to approach him. As the buck sergeant passed by Reiner, the agent decided on a quick change of plans. He grabbed the arm of the duty-conscious sergeant and motioned for him to back away. The sergeant studied Reiner's features for an inquisitive moment and realized that the chief agent's request was for more than to simply let the man go. It was for him to forget about Will James altogether. James did not notice the approaching MP. He was too preoccupied with the encroaching sergeant major.

"Don't say anything!" Ramsy blasted. "Go to your quarters. Stay there. Got it?"

"Got it, Sergeant Major!"

James spun around and stepped to his tent. He felt as if his entire world came down around him. He tried to keep up a guarded front. He angrily lashed out at those who appeared to close on him. It was his only defense mechanism. Ramsy watched as the man walked across the narrow airstrip.

Richter and Alicia approached from behind and stopped at Ramsy's side. Alicia fixed her eyes on Mendez as the medics carted him to the ambulance. She watched them slide the stretcher-bound colonel into the bay. Reiner moved up to the three. He extended his hand to the captain first then to the sergeant major.

"Good job, Captain," the agent said. "We at least nailed part of their asses." Reiner looked to Alicia. "What have you got here?"

"Agent Reiner," Richter began. "I would like to introduce you to Alicia, ah…"

"Rojas," the woman said, while pointing to the ambulance. "And I want that son of a bitch dead!"

Ramsy pulled the woman's arm down while frowning over Alicia's hasty demand. Reiner looked in the direction the woman pointed.

"He the one I should know?"

"One each, Colonel Mendez," Richter said. "Our new operational advisor."

"Really?" Reiner replied. "Will he live?"

Richter glanced at the ambulance and watched as the vehicle drove off. It headed for the installation dispensary.

"Long enough to give us what we want," he said. "He's a butcher, Ted. Those photos you showed me the other morning…"

"Yeah."

"One of the villages no longer exist."

The four went silent upon seeing Major Arlington laid upon the helipad. Father Ankor knelt next to the fallen pilot, administering the gallant woman the last rites. Richter caught sight of her face just before the plastic zipped over her. He gave the major a subtle salute. He looked away first.

"Do your debrief in the infirmary," he said to Reiner. "Just in case Mendez doesn't last." Richter looked about the helipad and spotted Ringwald. He nodded to the major. Ringwald acted as if he did not see. Richter couldn't care less. He turned to Reiner. "Where's Treadwell?"

"He's no longer with us," Reiner's assistant said.

"We were right?"

"We were," Reiner said. He noticed Richter's head beginning to bleed. "You sprung a leak, Captain. Well, it's debrief time. Let me get my hands on that colonel before he dies. Why don't you get yourself over to the infirmary? Get that hole plugged up."

Reiner turned from the three and started for his jeep. He made five steps before abruptly stopping. He realized something extremely important had slipped his mind. All of the mission activity caused him to put aside the captain's personal dilemma.

Of course, there were two destroyed helicopters to think about, as well as the Panamanian regulars killed at the initial objective. Treadwell had already notified the Panamanian military attaché and provided their office with a casualty list. The Colombian attaché's office had not yet acknowledged the incident. SOUTHCOM wanted to know what happened to the two aircraft and the regular army pilots and crewchiefs that manned them. Fortunately, they eliminated the crewchiefs from the initial assault. *There's a lot of accountability to be done*, Reiner thought, *but fuck 'em.*

Richter watched as the agent slowly approached him. Reiner eyed the ground ahead of him. He appeared to be in deep thoughtfulness.

"Ah, Alex…I'm not going to be in there long with Mendez," he said. "My people will handle him. As soon as medical is done with you I'll be at my jeep. It's, ah…very important. We need to talk."

Richter stared into Reiner's eyes and searched for a clue. Between the look of sympathy and the compassionate tone in Reiner's voice, it was obvious to him that whatever the agent wanted to discuss was not in his best interest. After what had taken place over the last twenty hours, Richter envisioned anything from a long stay at Fort Leavenworth to a quiet escort into the forest, never to be heard from again. He studied the agent's features a moment more.

"All right," he said softly, suspiciously.

Again, Reiner turned from the three. His assistant and he headed for the jeep.

Alicia grabbed the officer and forced him to face her. Her

glare showed a cutting hardness.

"I want him dead, Richter," she said. "I helped your people…"

"You helped my men because they saved what was left of your village and killed the men that did it," Richter cut in. "Alicia, go back to your village—or what's left of it. I promise you, after we have every conceivable piece of worth out of this man—it's a ruthless business. Anything can happen."

Alicia gazed into the captain's eyes, looking for the truth. She believed she saw it. She looked to the officer's right and watched the sergeant major reinforce Richter's remark with an affirming nod.

"You have our word on that, lass."

Ramsy's confirming remark helped to put the woman at ease, but the idea of not being there, unable to see Mendez die, left an empty feeling within her.

Revenge from a distance had a certain shallowness to it. She wanted to see, hear, and almost feel the anguish the man would succumb to. Vengeance had a certain style about it—in its firmness, in its result, and in the message it delivered.

While the village woman and Ramsy escorted the captain across the tiny airstrip, James attempted to gain an informational edge.

James ignored the sergeant major's directive. Will left his tent and walked about the staging area. He considered his options, if any. Word of Gable's death spread within the first fifteen minutes of Team Bravo's return. Most of his fellow soldiers avoided him after receiving it. He crept to the infirmary tent. Will saw the light from inside seep through the nylon screening where the window flaps tied back.

He stood about four feet from the opening and listened to the agents interrogate the wounded colonel. He spotted two agents and the accompanying MPs standing over Mendez. The demanding men prevented the surgeon and her one nurse from anesthetizing him. As the agents spoke in Spanish, Will could not understand the questions. More importantly, he could not understand Mendez's answers. As he stepped from the dispensary, further discouraged by his inability to know what had transpired, Will's disparity began to peak. Again, the uncertain climate reduced him to a level of irrational desperation.

Twenty-five

Rumor control spread the news faster than any formal declaration before a company formation. By the time Team Bravo returned, better than half of the men on the installation knew of the untimely demise. By 0700 hours the next morning a few men had already made their condolences. Before 1200 hours intermittent groups had begun to drop by to express their sympathies. Reiner and his men apologized the night before. Ringwald said nothing. He sent his aid to express his sympathies along with the camp's. Richter lifted the wallet-sized photograph from the fieldtable. He held it close to him.

In his mind's eye he saw Julia, Courtney, and himself five years before. His daughter swung from an inexpensive, assemble-yourself swing set. Julia took the picture he then held in his hand. Richter recalled his little girl's sputtering giggles, and the way Courtney demanded he push harder. It was a warm afternoon. April or May, he believed. He could not be precise. Richter recalled what it was like when he was forced to leave. He glanced about his tent while wondering where his life had led him.

He looked over his shoulder, to the eight-by-ten-inch photo of Courtney. It rested on the orange crate he used as a bunkside table. He glared at the foam matting and sleeping bag positioned at the head of his cot. The kerosene lantern above him was no more impressive. The table he sat at and the wooden folding chair he sat in had a drab lifeless air about them. The duffel bag and its contents leaning against the bed were his only testimony of tangible worth. Above him the canted circular ceiling angled downward to the encircling walls of olive drab canvas. It surrounded him, it seemed, like a pallor-padded cell. It looked so dull, like a fuzzy black and white photograph.

Everything about his life had a hueless shallowness to it. He stared ahead, out of the tent to the encampment and the hills beyond. He saw only pallid, lackluster highlands and the vulnerable staging area below. His mentality, his point of view on everything, had taken a bleak direction when Julia and he separated. Julia gave him something he never felt prior to her, and somehow he unwittingly lost upon their division. Passion, Alex guessed—Julia gave him passion; but it was Courtney who gave him susceptibility. He gazed upon the photograph once more. He reacquainted himself with every line of his daughter's face. Ramsy stepped to the tent, jarring Alex from his thoughts.

"Alex?"

Richter's flashback instantly went dead. The mental picture disconnected as if the film in a projector broke. He looked up and saw his old friend at the tent flaps.

"Oh, Cliff. Come on in."

The sergeant major stepped in. He took a seat on the edge of Alex's cot. He leaned forward, resting his elbows on his knees. He glanced at the dirt floor before sorrowfully looking up at his scion.

"Alex?" he said, not truly knowing where to begin. "You doing all right?"

"Yeah—I'm doing."

"Alex, I'm awful sorry to hear about Courtney. I know how much you loved her. If I can do anything at all…"

"I'm fine, Cliff," Alex replied. He rested his hand on Cliff's shoulder. "I'll do fine. Thank you."

"When you leaving?"

"This afternoon." He laid Courtney's photo onto the fieldtable. "Danny's going to fly me to Tocumen. I'll get a commercial out of there. Make a connection in Houston. Should be in New Orleans by…this time tomorrow."

"Well," Cliff interjected carefully, "it's Mardi Gras time. You get all the necessities out of the way, maybe you can lose yourself for a couple of days."

"Maybe," Alex said, only half-conscious of his response.

Ramsy paused, not sure what to say next. The seconds of dead space tormented the sergeant major.

"You know about Treadwell?"

"Reiner told me last night," Alex said. "Just after you told me about James, and before he told me of…No way to end a career."

"He picked it, son."

"Yeah, he did. Still regretful. All in all, I guess it's still more of a choice than some of us had."

"True enough," Cliff replied. He pondered for a way to gracefully change the subject. The sergeant major knew that the team needed to put its house in order. In staying with his customary method of problem solving, Ramsy could not repress his hard-driving, up-front approach. "Alex…that leaves only one nut to crack."

"James?"

"Roger. I had a couple of men on him last night," Cliff resumed. "He didn't stay confined to quarters, but then nobody figured he would. He changed out of uniform then took a trip to the vill. Got laid then hopped a bus for Puerto Obaldía."

"Puerto Obaldía?" Alex said, surprised by the soldier's selection. "Through the mountains? It would take him all night by bus, at least. And that's only if the roads aren't out. That's not far from where we were yesterday. Just across the gulf. Who'd want to escape to there?"

"It's a way out of here," Ramsy answered. "When they pulled him off the bus he had eighteen thousand dollars American on 'im."

"Where's he now?"

"Waiting outside. Still keeping up a front," Cliff said. "You feel up to it?"

"Bring 'im in," Richter said, "but give me a minute."

The sergeant major stepped outside. He pulled the flaps down behind him to give Alex the solitude he asked for. Ramsy waited a full four minutes before directing Will to enter. He motioned for the MP to wait outside. Will pulled back the tent flap and stuck his head inside.

"Captain?" he began. "Sergeant major said you wanted to see me?"

Richter looked up from the table. He stared into James' innocent-looking eyes. Will's naive display briefly baffled him. *A good front*, he thought.

"Yeah, Will," he cordially began. "Come in." The captain motioned to the vacant chair he placed before his table. "Have a seat. We need to talk."

James stepped inside. He moved to the chair while wringing the jungle hat clenched within his fists. He started in slowly, as if expecting something to pounce on him. Although Will's eyes had an unaware, guiltless aura about them, his body language betrayed him. As he pulled the chair from the table Will extended his sympathies.

"I'm sorry to hear about your daughter," he said. "I heard about it at chow this morning. Got one of my own. I know how I'd feel."

"I guess it's all over the camp by now," Richter said. "Can't keep something like that quiet for long."

"Not really, Captain."

The tent flaps suddenly drew back. Ramsy charged in, swiftly taking a seat on the cot next to James. The suddenness of the man's entrance startled Will. James tightened. He turned in his seat and studied Ramsy's stern expression from over his shoulder. He was about to speak but was cut off before his first word.

"Let's get on with it, Captain!" Ramsy blared.

"Hey!" James countered. "What's going on?"

"Will," Richter began again. His voice remained calm. "We need to talk about the operation. About you shooting Mendez—about yesterday."

"Oh, I can explain that."

"You can?" Ramsy yelled. "Well, don't let us stop you, soldier."

"Will," Richter went on, "it doesn't take a genius to know you shot Mendez to keep him quiet. It wasn't smart."

"No!" James countered. "I thought he was going for a weapon."

Richter paused. He looked down while wondering just how narrow the cornered soldier truly believed Ramsy and he were. But cornered was the key, he decided. James was at an impasse. He had nothing to lose by insisting his denial. Richter decided to let the Mendez incident go unanswered for the present.

"What was waiting for you in Puerto Obaldía?" he resumed. "Is that where you're paid off?"

"No!" James said. The harshness in his voice began to frail. "After what happened to Art I just wanted to run. Be away from everything. I would've come back."

Ramsy leaned into the man. His face was only inches from Will's right shoulder. James felt his personal territory invaded. His already trembling hands shook even more from the sergeant major's nonverbal intrusion. Ramsy saw that he had the right affect.

"Tell us, lad!" Ramsy blared. "Tell us everything. We'd still like to think you're one of us."

"Tell you what?" James said. "Look—I took the cocaine, and I'm responsible for Gable. I know that. I'm everything you think, but now I got to hold on to my ass. Ain't I suppose to have a lawyer here or something?"

Richter and Ramsy's eyes locked onto one another's. Both men knew what the other thought. It was evident that Will did not fully comprehend the magnitude of his dilemma. When Richter faced the soldier again he could not help but feel some pity.

"You're on a military installation, Will," Richter explained, "but you're not military. You're contract. There's no Uniform Code of Military Justice here. Not for you." Richter leaned over the table. His eyes locked onto James'. "And you're about twelve hundred miles from the nearest Miranda right. We handle our internal problems in our own way...you know that."

"Oh, god," Will said, wincing.

His mouth hung open. He tried to speak, but his taut vocal cords would not cooperate. His lower lip began to quiver. It oscillated from his desire to speak while his numb mind refused to provide him adequate words. A tear began to roll down his left cheek. Richter watched as the man tried to fight back the drops. There was one tear, Richter saw. Then another.

"After the firefight," Richter continued, "you took the cocaine..."

"Yeah, but that's no big deal," Will said. "Hell! A lot of guys are doing it."

"The men who died yesterday didn't!" Ramsy countered. "Only you. And I don't care about the conduct of the other teams. Just this one."

"I—needed the money," James yielded. "My god. There was over twenty-five million dollars of cocaine in that truck. Who the hell would miss two kilos?"

"How did you know that?" Richter asked. "I didn't state that in the OPORD. I didn't mention it during either briefing. How did you know the second objective's worth?"

James went mute. His mind raced for an answer while he stared into the dead eyes of the soft-speaking officer. He knew that behind the empty glare was an uncompromising character. He also knew that he had implicated himself in something greater by assigning a value to the second objective. It was a guess, he thought. He saw the stack in the truck and estimated. He didn't know about a second objective.

"I was in the back of the truck," he said. "Lucky guess."

"It's because of that stuff that Gable's dead!"

"I told you, I know that!" Will countered. "I think about it more than you know, Sergeant Major."

"The round you popped off," Richter continued, "just prior to the attack on the encampment. It was a signal?"

"No!"

"Colonel Mendez said otherwise!" Ramsy shouted. "Mendez says that you—"

"All right!" James shouted. His tears intensified. "Mendez says—fucking spic colonel. I didn't know about the second objective. All I knew was that if stuff didn't get through, Treadwell and me got nothing. I had to do something. Treadwell. He said with him in control at this end there was no way we'd be found out...and that stupid fuck blows his brains out." James wiped his face with his left hand. He began to laugh. "He's the only one who really got away. Why not, he said! For every kilo we destroy, five hundred get through. It seemed a cinch with him back here."

"But you went on the mission, too," Ramsy said. "How'd you know which chopper they'd blow away? You were in as much danger as the rest of us."

"That was easy enough," Will explained. "Just before the operations brief yesterday morning, I put a strip of tape on the aircraft's belly. No one could see it when the ship was on the pad, and those who did see it when in flight wouldn't think anything of it. I knew they'd see it as just another aircraft marking. The army's got 'em all over their equipment."

"But our aircraft aren't marked," Ramsy said.

"Who cared!" Will shouted. "That was it. We got regular army aircraft coming in and out of here all the time. Danny's Skymaster—it's got U.S. Air Force all over it. Who was going to question a line?"

"How did you know which ship we'd take?" Ramsy

asked.

"Oh, you two are creatures of habit," Will said. "You never fly in anything except Echo-1115. That's going to get you two killed one of these days."

Again, Richter and Ramsy looked at one another. Both were astonished by their inability to recognize the lethal flaw in their routine. They considered the helicopter a lucky piece because of its many hours of flawless flight. James' explanation made potent military sense. If anyone wanted them dead, all they'd have to do is fire on Echo-1115. Ramsy broke their cautious silence.

"He's right, Captain. Echo-1115. The only one we use when not in maintenance."

Richter did not respond. Instead, he turned and faced James. He wanted absolute clarification.

"They were only suppose to shoot down one of us? The one you marked?"

"There are regular army pilots and crews in those ships, Captain," Will said. "They wanted to slow us down. They didn't want a war. Besides, the Colombians hate the Panamanians in their territory more than they hate us. They only wanted one ship downed. The one with the *federales* on it. I guess they didn't figure it would crash into their faces, or that you had another mission planned. That was good, Captain. Nobody knew what was up on that one."

"Then you knew when Mike got in that chopper he was going to die?" Richter asked.

"Pretty much. Yeah."

"Jesus," Ramsy said under his breath. He glared at James momentarily. "How did you know we wouldn't put you in the other ship?"

"I don't speak Spanish," Will said. "So...what now, Captain?"

He believed he already knew the answer.

Richter sat back and quietly considered his options. Not that there were many.

"First off, you're going to give that eighteen thousand to

the sergeant major."

"What? I—"

"He's going to break it down!" Richter coldly said. "Give every enlisted man on this installation an equal share. Is that a problem, Sergeant?"

James faced the floor, shaking his head. Richter paused and waited to hear if Will had anything further to add. The soldier remained silent.

"A military tribunal is out of the question," Richter went on. "I don't know, Will…we're desperately short of manpower."

The sergeant major abruptly turned to Richter. He showed a bewildering glare. True enough, he thought, they were short of men. Some of the teams were at only sixty-percent strength. But the idea of returning a traitor to the ranks on the premise that one more body might make a difference seemed absurd. James saw the look on Ramsy's face and knew the captain caught his sergeant major off guard. He looked to Richter. The captain saw a spark of hope in Will's eyes.

"I'll have to think on this," Richter resumed. "Right now, you'll be confined to your quarters. Under guard. You walk out this time, even go to the latrine without authorization, the guard'll gun you down. Is that clear?"

"Yes sir."

Again, Will wiped the tears from his face.

"That's all, lad," Ramsy gently added. "Go straight to your tent. Don't leave it. Don't even step outside it. The guard's outside."

"Yeah," James softly replied.

Will rose from his chair and stood at attention. He held a salute until the ex-officer returned the formal gesture. Richter was somewhat taken by the maneuver. He never expected a salute from those within the contract circle and knew there was none to be had by the regulars. Upon returning the courtesy Richter asked the soldier to leave the tent flaps open.

Ramsy remained silent after James' departure. He tried to comprehend the motive behind Alex's leniency. He waited patiently. The pressure within him began to build. Richter waited until James was halfway across the compound. He took a moment to think over what had to be done.

"How's his wife and kid doing?"

"Doesn't talk about 'em much," Cliff said. "I wonder how he'd feel if he knew Mendez couldn't tell us anything?"

"Sends 'em money?"

"Pretty regular," Cliff said.

"Insurance?"

"Personnel record shows fifty thousand, VGLI. Same as most of us vets."

"Check it again," Alex said. "Verify the policy is still good. Between that and the eighteen thousand—it should give her and the kid a solid start. I'll write the letter when I get back."

"You know, Alex, for a second there, I thought you were going to let him slide."

"Always give your men hope, Sergeant Major. You taught me that."

"I did," Ramsy said. "I surely did."

"Make it look like an accident. There might be a double indemnity…something like that."

Twenty-six

Richter stood before his tent. He looked at his watch. The time piece showed 1408 hours. The stifling, early afternoon sun blanketed the staging area. He saw the undulating heat waves rising off the oil- and dirt-packed runway. The high humidity persisted as it had the day before. He felt an irritating trickle of perspiration glide down the inside of his right arm, the one holding to the duffel bag. He looked at himself and saw a wardrobe too heavy for the climate.

He knew that his worn blue jeans did not look good at all. The black, string-laced, army low-quarters only complemented his already dressed down fashion statement. What truly brought out his lack of style were the white boot socks creeping out from under his too-short pant legs. While at the basecamp he misplaced his only pair of dress socks. He decided against borrowing or buying a pair. *Why the added expense if most of your time is spent in uniform, anyway*? he thought. Until he got a good look at himself it made sense.

He found his only white shirt while searching through the duffel. He hoped the nine-year-old tweed jacket would sufficiently conceal its wrinkles. The jacket was plaid. He was not conscious of its style or design. Just knowing it had little squares differentiated by thin black borders seemed enough. As he started across the encampment, heading for the airstrip, Richter felt another rush of sweat from under his left arm. Ramsy unexpectedly approached him from behind.

"Alex!"

Richter stopped and pivoted. He watched as Cliff advanced on him. He lowered his duffel and briefcase to the ground. As Ramsy approached he saw the way Alex dressed himself.

"Ah, Alex!"

The sergeant major spread his hands wide apart, gesturing to the absurd match.

"Don't say it, Cliff. I know."

"I forgot we came here looking like that," Ramsy said.

"Does it look that bad?"

"You know us professionals. We always look sharp in uniform but damned if we know what to do with civilian clothes."

"Then, it looks that bad?" Richter asked.

"Well, son—you won't make GQ."

Ramsy took hold of Alex by his arms. The captain looked in both directions, at the large hands clamping onto him. He looked up into the concerned eyes of the man who favored him as family. Ramsy gazed upon Alex. He wanted to give the younger man some words of comfort, fatherly advice. His mind raced for the right thing to say. In the end, he settled for the first thing that came to mind.

"You got everything you need?"

Richter reached down and latched onto his duffel bag and the silver metallic briefcase. Besides the photographs, the case was the only family memento that he had. As he straightened Richter replied forthrightly.

"I got everything I own...I thought you were with Sutton."

"That's been coordinated," Ramsy replied. "Now, you go on. Put us out of your mind for a week or so."

As Richter turned he felt another one of Ramsy's dramatic blows upon his back. It landed like a sledgehammer. He felt himself heeling forward, but regained his balance by quickly stepping out with his left foot. Ramsy watched as Alex moved off. From the back the tough little bastard looked like a lost orphan with all his worldly goods in two small rag-bags. Richter almost reached the awaiting aircraft when stopped by the woman who helped to save their lives.

"Wait!" Alicia yelled.

She ran up to the captain. Richter did not hear Alicia over the roar of the plane's twin engines. She grabbed him by the arm. When he turned to see who held to him it surprised Richter to see her.

"I thought you'd be gone by now!"

"I heard about your daughter!" she yelled over the engines. "I'm sorry!"

"Thank you!" Richter yelled back.

He turned from the woman and stepped toward the plane. Richter made only three steps before he, again, felt Alicia's grip on his sleeve.

"You'll keep your promise!" she shouted.

Richter gazed into the beautiful woman's eyes. He recognized a desire for Mendez's death like none he had witnessed for any man's. He did not speak. Instead, he nodded, confirming to the woman that Ramsy and he would not forgive or forget. Alicia saw the sincerity in the officer's face. As Richter turned away Alicia felt sure that she and San Delbaro would be avenged. Not today, she thought. Not this week, perhaps. But she knew the officer would keep his word. He was too rigid to do otherwise.

Alicia waited for the aircraft to take off. She watched the tiny plane run the full length of the short airstrip. By the time the landing gear lifted from the dirt Ramsy's coordinated effort was in place.

James sat on the edge of his cot. He felt the perspiration from his brow collect on his fingers. He raised his buried face from his palms and looked to his left. He saw the armed MP standing at the entrance. Occasionally, one of his fellow freelancers would pass by the tent but continue on without a word. James wiped his brow with his forearm, clearing most of the annoying droplets. He rubbed his wet arm upon his camouflaged trousers. He suddenly found himself torn from his hopeful visions of redemption.

"Get your gear, lad!" Ramsy said.

James looked up and saw Ramsy standing over him. The sergeant major's energy overwhelmed him. He reared from the man's great bulk.

"What's up?"

"Lucky for you we're short of personnel," Ramsy explained. "The teams are stripped. You'll be moving out with Team Delta in forty-five minutes. Be on deck in thirty-five."

James snapped to a stance. He looked at the sergeant major, a gleam of hope emanating from his eyes.

"You mean, the captain's giving me another chance?"

"Didn't say that, lad," Ramsy resumed. "I do know that if you help us now, it's going to go a lot easier on you later. What's it going to be?"

James saw no reason to refuse. He knew that the alternative was far less promising. A broad smile slowly crept over his face.

"Yeah!" he said excitedly. "Yeah, why the hell not? What have I got to lose? Just my life."

James faced away from the top NCO. He hastily collected his gear. Ramsy watched as the soldier began to fill his rucksack, glad that he could provide Will some momentary optimism.

"That's right, lad," Ramsy replied. "And for people like us it's not that much."

"Got it, Sergeant Major!"

Ramsy turned from the preoccupied soldier. He stepped out of the ovenlike heat in the tent. He informed the MP to move off. The soldier complied with the sergeant major's directive without question. Like Ramsy, Richter focused on more important things.

The aircraft leveled off at two thousand eight hundred feet. Richter cracked his window to allow for a cool, controlled blast of air in the cabin.

It was a short hop to Tocumen Airfield, perhaps forty miles. It took no more than thirty minutes of flight time once at altitude. Danny refrained from his usual talkative self. He did not want to bother Alex under the circumstances. Richter said nothing as well. He simply looked out of the aircraft, upon the jungle-covered terrain.

The first twenty minutes flashed by for Richter. It surprised him how quickly the aircraft entered Tocumen air space. Danny established contact with the tower and received their approach heading and altitude. For Danny, the trip felt much longer than when made under other conditions.

"Hey, Alex!" he yelled over the engine noise. "You got a cigarette?"

Richter checked his shirt pocket and found an empty pack. He reached over the seat and pulled his attaché case from behind the chair. He laid it across his lap. As inconspicuously as possible he angled the case so as to block Danny's view when it opened. He fingered between the two lead-sheeted file separators. He kept glancing up to see if Danny spotted the .45 pistol and silencer, the two fragmentation grenades, and the one brick of C-4 neatly packed within. As Richter closed the lid Danny reconfirmed their close proximity to Tocumen.

"Oh, thanks," the pilot said. "We'll have you on the ground in about eleven minutes. What time does your flight leave?"

Richter looked at his watch. It showed 1517 hours.

"I got about fourteen minutes to take off," he said. "We'll make it?"

"We'll make it," Danny assured.

Danny put the aircraft into a steep descent. He did so without authorization from the Tocumen tower. Richter knew that the man violated FAA regulations by making the unsanctioned maneuver. But it was Danny's plane, he decided. The pilot would have to deal with the tower personnel in his own way once on the ground.

Richter pressed his right hand against the control board as the aircraft maintained its nose-down position. He watched the end of the main runway come at them a little faster than what he had planned on. As the plane's landing gear touched down, James completed his premission preparations.

Will strapped on his rucksack after donning his LBE. He ran to the supply tent to be issued his weapon. As he double-timed to the helipad he heard the aircraft engine induced. When he cleared the tents he saw Team Delta waiting at the pad. The men stood near the open port door, as the main and tail rotors began to increase velocity. He raised his weapon while yelling for the team to wait. He saw a few of the men raise their arms and motion for him to move faster. He picked up his stride as Richter put down his duffel bag.

Richter released the three-quarter-filled duffel next to the ticket agent. He dropped the limp and raggedy olive drab sack onto the scale. He recalled that as he made his way through the airport the patrons gazed at him. They gawked at his late 1950s, half-country, half-city boy style of dress. The looks on their faces said everything. The ticket agent noticed the primitive condition of his luggage. She masked her amusement while recovering from her state of awe over the Spartan cloth sack. His peculiar wardrobe was equally as stunning for her.

Richter watched the woman give him a condescending eye-over before asking him if he wished to check in his satchel. He declined, telling her he had some important paper work to catch up on. That or sleep. After the mortifying analysis, he promised himself he would purchase some up-to-date garb upon arrival in New Orleans. As the jet was about to depart, Richter immediately stepped to the boarding ramp.

He found his seat in the coach section easily enough. The

flight attendant asked him if he wanted the briefcase stored above. Again, he refused to relinquish his lethal tools. At first, Richter wondered if the attaché case could breach the airport security system. He realized the satchel revealed precisely what it was redesigned to show when allowed to continue on. Either that, he thought, or an air marshal would nail him in flight. He rested the case on his lap after buckling in. He looked out of the window as the ship began to back away from the terminal, and as James caught up with his new assignment.

Will reached the helipad skirt and linked up with Master Sergeant Sutton, the team NCOIC. Sutton shook hands with the new man while the others greeted him with pats on the back. All warmly welcomed their new associate while guiding him across the pad. James allowed himself to be guided rearward of the aircraft. Suddenly, he found himself shoved to the right and pushed off balance. As he heeled head-on, his combat load too much weight to counter, Will helplessly looked upon the other men. He saw their neutral gazes as he fell headfirst into the whirling tail rotor. He tried to scream, but there was not enough time.

The clanking of the engine and tail rotor could be heard across the airstrip. Reiner looked up from his fieldtable, pulled from the team's mission report that he had to forward to El Paso within two days. He looked out of the tent and across the strip. He listened as the turbine lost revolutions. The sporadic clank of broken metal intermingled with the engine's declining whine.

"Let me see your annex to this report," he said to his aide.

Reiner put the entire Will James matter out of mind upon taking hold of the report insert—something the men of Team Delta could not easily do.

They scrambled to avoid the ship's tail section. James' rifle, ammunition, LBE, rucksack, clothing, and body fragmented. A portion of the tail rotor cracked off. The eighteen-inch, knifelike projectile spun wildly as it shot across the airstrip. It landed a one hundred yards from the damaged helicopter. The remaining intact rotor sprayed James' minced cadaver beyond the helipad's margin. Some of the men were unable to avoid the bloody shower. When signaled, the pilot cut the engine.

Ramsy casually stepped to the helipad after hearing what happened. He took sixteen minutes to get there. A few junior officers were at the scene, but it made little difference to the sergeant major. As if in charge, the top NCO moved through the cluster of Team Delta personnel. He stepped to the helicopter's tail section and looked at the broken rotor. He observed the torn blade and saw how the blood on it had already begun to coagulate in the afternoon heat. He eyed the thickening puddle beneath the tail section. He scraped the toe of his left jungle boot through the tacky substance that was once Will James. He turned and faced the men.

"Anybody see it?"

No one spoke. The entire Team Delta contingent silently stood before him. The men eyed Ramsy as he eyed them. He searched each face and looked for signs of weakness. There wasn't any, he judged.

"You mean, not one of you is a witness to the loss of this man's life?" he persisted.

Again, there was only silence.

"Master Sergeant Sutton!"

"Yeah, Sergeant Major!"

Sutton stepped out of the group and took his rightful place at the head of Team Delta.

Ramsy pulled two cigars from his top left pocket. He handed one to the fellow senior NCO. Sutton bit the stogie. He sank his teeth deep into the tobacco prong, almost biting it in two. Ramsy was more subtle. He removed his cigar from the cellophane wrapper and rolled the tip over his tongue before gripping it between his teeth. As he moved off, back through the group, the sergeant major gave his final instruction.

"Make out your accident report, Sergeant."

Ramsy stepped from the helipad. He decided to return to his quarters for a late afternoon nap. As the sergeant major made his way to the tent he wondered how his son held up.

They were twelve minutes into the flight. Richter believed the aircraft was at approximately ten thousand feet altitude. He leaned back in his seat and began to relax. He concluded that if an air marshal did not corner him by then it would most likely not happen. But then, he considered, there was always customs at the other end.

He reached into the right pocket of his tweed jacket. From it he lifted the wallet-sized photograph of Courtney. He still found it hard to comprehend that his little girl was gone. Again, he envisioned those special episodes, when Julia, Courtney, and he had nothing more on their minds than the three of them—occasions when all outside variables had no impact on their three-way bond of love.

Alex looked up from the photo and stared out the window at the mountainous cumulus clouds the aircraft ascended to. Their great billowings appeared to take on assorted manifestations. He concentrated on the magnificent natural display. His eyes moved back and forth, searching to recapture the unmistakable image. He was sure he saw Courtney's face in them.

ACRONYMS AND ABBREVIATIONS

aeromedevac	a nine-line message fromat used in calling for a medical evacuation by helicopter
AIT	advanced individual training
BDU	battle dress uniform
CEOI	communications electronics operating Instructions
COMSEC	communications security
CP	command post
DEA	Drug Enforcment Agency
Dustoff	the act of calling for a medical evacuation by helicopter, e.g., "Call for dustoff!"
DZ	drop zone
EOD	expolsive ordnance detachment
ETA	estimated time of arrival
FNG	fucking new guy
HEAT	high explosive antitank (the charge itself)
LBE	load-bearing equipment
LZ	landing zone
medevac	medical evacuation

medic	medical personnel (one medical corpsman)
MP	military police
MRE	meal ready to eat (like old-time C-ration, but now in plastic instead of tin container)
NCO	noncommissioned officer
NCOIC	noncommissioned officer in charge
OCS	officer candidate school
OP	observation post
OPCON	operational control
OPORD	operation order
PZ	pick-up zone
R&R	rest and relaxation
SOP	standard operating procedure
SOUTHCOM	Southern Command
TOC	tactical operations center
UCMJ	Uniformed Code of Military Justice
VGLI	Veterans Group Life Insurance